John Muckle was born in the village of Cobham, Surrey, but lived most of his adult life in Essex and London. Amongst other things he has been a copywriter, an editor, a lecturer, a careworker, a bookshop assistant, a library assistant, a freelance writer and a motorcycle courier. In the 1980s he initiated the Paladin Poetry Series and was General Editor of its flagship anthology, *The New British Poetry* (Paladin, 1988). His previous books include *The Cresta Run* (short stories), *Cyclomotors* (a novella with photographic illustrations), and *Firewriting and Other Poems* (Shearsman Books, 2005).

Also by John Muckle

Poetry
It Is Now As It Was Then (with Ian Davidson)
Firewriting and Other Poems

Prose
The Cresta Run
Bikers (with Bill Griffiths)
Cyclomotors

As General Editor:
The New British Poetry (eds., Allnutt, D'Aguiar, Edwards, Mottram)

John Muckle

London Brakes

a novel

Shearsman Books
Exeter

Published in the United Kingdom in 2010 by
Shearsman Books
58 Velwell Road
Exeter
EX4 4LD

ISBN 978-1-84861-101-6
First Edition

Acknowledgements
Excerpts from this novel were originally published in
Bazzin' (Tony Baker), *Infolio* (Tom Raworth)
and in *Bikers* (with poems by Bill Griffiths,
Amra Imprint, 1990).

With thanks to Dave Cook, Tony Frazer, Chris Noble,
Martin Stott — and for Robert.

I wish to gratefully acknowledge a Hawthornden Fellowship
that was helpful in the early stages of writing this novel.

London Brakes

Make me a mandrake, so I may growe here,
Or a stone fountain weeping out my yeare.

John Donne, *Twick'nam Garden*

One

I used to notice Gladys on my way out in the mornings. Gladys was a notable woman. I noted her. After the men had all left for work she'd hesitate for a moment in her doorway in a quilted housecoat, then generally started her day by unnecessarily polishing the liver-coloured landing tiles and obsessively rearranging a row of green wellington boots beside a doormat that said OH NO NOT YOU AGAIN. Typically I'd be late for work myself. If it was cold I'd put my helmet and gloves on indoors and move my head up and down like an astronaut signalling in weightlessness; the principal difference between me and an astronaut being that my gear was subject to the force of gravity; also a distinct lack of TV coverage of my more routine missions. What was so great about astronauts, anyway? You didn't hear much of Yuri Gagarin, John Glenn, or Neil Armstrong anymore—not in 1986.

Gladys and myself never spoke beyond this muffled hello. I spoke to her because she was the next-door neighbour and because she reminded me slightly of my mother. It's even possible I reminded her of one of her own sons, but I won't bore you with a lot of crap about how people are often reminded of things by other things which even they know are completely dissimilar to the things of which they're being reminded. After all, what would it really prove except that some people's frames of reference are limited, or that they can't stop themselves trying to tease a bit of interest out of nothing?

When the weather turned bad I wouldn't go out except for a few days at the start of the month, not till the worst of it started to ease off towards the end of March; then I'd put in a couple of heroic weeks on circuit to pay the previous quarter's bills, well after the cut-off date but shortly before the actual cut-off. Otherwise I'd sit around on the sixth floor on my own listening to various sounds floating up from outside: kids calling; somebody kicking a can or the wind blowing it; snatches of music high in the tower—reggae, dance-music, salsa, heavy metal—any of which I'd much rather have been smooching to in somebody else's kitchen than agitating a teabag of sorrow in my own. Stray seagulls flapped across the big fuzzy double-glazing of the flat.

I turned the yellowing pages of a book somebody else had left behind.

All the stuff in the flat belonged to a guy called Willie, who was subletting to me. He also left a Humphrey Bogart mirror behind, like one of those Snoopy mirrors that young girl tourists buy. It was silk-screened and it seemed Bogart was wearing black lipstick. I took it down immediately and hung it in the bathroom. After a time I didn't notice the picture anymore, but I still saw my own face in the mirror when I was shaving and in the large murky fish tank as I crumbled tubifex worms for Willie's catfish and his tinfoil barb. Toothpaste got spattered over Bogart, obliterating his no longer operative charms. I kept meaning to do something about it, out of loyalty no doubt to my teenage years, but I never got around to properly cleaning it.

Willie had told me that Gladys was agoraphobic. That they were a particularly lumpen crowd over there. Frontish, bad news. The next-door neighbours were Scottish, like Willie himself, and so escaped this casually contemptuous description no matter how drunk they got in the long afternoons of their late antiquity. I was what we called a despatch rider myself, a motorbike courier. You didn't get any more lumpen than that in Willie's eyes. Gladys probably even thought I was a student; that was the received wisdom about me in the tower, or so the fat lady who cornered me in the lift once muttered, but that was way back before she started singing.

So. I had plenty of time on my hands and nothing to do with it. Even so, Gladys wasn't very high on my list of priorities. Meeting other tenants outside the flat was a bit like noticing graffiti by the lift that said SO NICE I WILL SUCK NICELY. You wondered if the message was for you (no way, José) and then it dropped from your mind. Or else I'd be thinking about some news from the old days—more dead star stuff—about Bob and me hanging around in the Country & Western cafe on Shaftesbury Avenue with the rest of the blokes and breathing in steam and the smell of frying while somebody else's radio crackled in anger at a nearby table or turned out to be your own machine; or else we'd be outside, pulled up in front of *Les Misérables* on Cambridge Circus, lounging back on our top boxes as we munched through a Wendy burger and watched the tourists milling past like great drifting herds of kindly bison.

It was like—but it's easy to compare things when what you really mean is simply that they're out there, pushing in on you like the small smells and sheddings of someone you're sharing a flat with, the rasp of your own neck against a new collar. I keep on trying, you see, to get going on the Gladys business, but somehow she eludes me. I'll end up playing music or watching a film, something like *Desert Mice* with Sid James and Alfred Marks. That's quite a funny film, by the way, about ENSA in the North African campaign.

I was trickling along in traffic—fresh cool spring water finding its immutable way through igneous rock. In my top box I had a book going from a publisher in Soho to a publisher in Mayfair, artwork from Covent Garden to a Kensington ad agency. I could practically taste volcanic ash on the roof of my mouth, my spine felt it was like under compression in a vertical G-clamp and a lava of molten anger was about to blow off the top of my helmet. My arse was itching like crazy in a permanent sweat bath. I wanted to get home, wanted to scratch it, really make the dog cry, bathe it in hot water and pamper it with talc and exotic unguents—say hello to whoever preceded Buffy, and let my mind open its wrists in a pointless dream before the first documentary—before the big turn-off.

Anyway, I was standing outside the ad agency trying to loosen off my shoulders when the radio started up again. It was a sound like the noise of the sea withdrawing over gravel, slowly, forever, and every slave of the signals that bounced off the Telecom Tower (the maypole we all danced around) waited to hear their call-sign between shushing breakers, crackling like some call to further distress. Mine was Alpha 2-7. A long time ago it had been my age. Now when I heard it I knew Nick the fat controller had another job lined up, and at that moment I didn't feel even remotely like doing it.

"Got one you- -an do on -o-r -ay home." His voice came over between clicks on a slipping tape: "A-igh-?"

On your way home could mean anything at all, just about: usually a run out to Heathrow Airport. Nick's grasp of London geography was pathetic at the best of times. It would've disgraced a novice, in fact, especially in the late afternoons.

"What is it, Nick?"

"Cash job," he rapped. "Pick up round the corner."

"Okay," I said, "but it better not be the airport again, is it?" That's exactly the sort of thing you don't say to a controller, not if you want to carry on working.

"Do -our way- it or -to?" he shouted. "I -a-nt -ot all bloody -igh."

I wanted it. "Roger-dodge," I said. "Sorry, mate."

Nick handed me the job out. Surprise, surprise: it really was just round the corner and the drop was in Acton. You couldn't say fairer. At least the bastard was giving me something I could do on my way home. I turned right into Queen's Mall without further complaint and did a swift left-hander into a nondescript residential row in Kensington where it wasn't until you got up close to the houses you noticed how well the brickwork was kept and caught a glimpse of dark, heavy furniture through parted curtains—and realised you were dealing with the serious, old rich: people who had it all from way back; who bought and sold—and ate—your grandfather and mine ten times before breakfast, then deciding they'd better stick to the Fruit 'n' Fibre.

I lifted a black glossy latch on a gate in the railings and walked down a flight of sandblasted steps to the basement flat. It was a cash customer. He waited for me inside the door, but it was shadowy in there. I couldn't see him too well, but he looked like some sort of sky pilot or crafty, a man of the cloth, or something, anyway, in those regions: a bit disappointing, really.

"Six pounds?" His voice hesitated, queried; his fingers were scrabbling through a worn purse. Typical—and, of course, he was fully expecting to be ripped off.

"Yep," I said.

He pushed a package into my hand with a fiver on top. "I'm afraid the rest will have to be in change."

I felt my left hand weighed down by an assortment of metal. "Thanks, chief," I said.

Back on the pavement I glanced at the address before dropping the packet into my top box. I stood there not knowing what to do, nor whither which way to go; I wanted to go back straight away and explain there must be some mistake: it was a small rectangular old-fashioned brown parcel, tied up with string—and it was addressed to Gladys. My neighbour. Gladys. I rode away with it and for some reason I found myself trembling. I rehearsed a few lines I'd never dream of saying, and on my way into the tower read a notice pinned to the caretaker's notice board:

PLEASE DO NOT PUT RUBBISH DOWN THE SHOOT AS IT IS BLOCKED—THE MORE YOU FORCE IT DOWN THE HARDER IT WILL BE TO UNBLOCK

Some bright spark had already crossed out SHOOT and put in SHUTE. I fished a biro out of my pocket, deleted the S and put in a C. I didn't want to have to bang on their door and get her to sign a docket, for some strange reason (who did she think she was?) but there wasn't much else I could do, so I did. Harry Chambers came to the door wearing the bottom of a tracksuit and three day's growth of beard on his still-handsome boat-race.

"Delivery for you," I said.

I passed him the packet, along with my clipboard and a biro, trying to make out this happened every day. Harry seemed to feel that some discussion of the matter was in order. I was determined to frustrate him. I looked off at a random point on the doorframe while he signed his name with a jagged flourish across the gap on the docket.

"We was thinking of getting away for the weekend," he said noncommittally. "But there don't seem much point."

"What's up, not warm enough for you?"

"Roads'll be chock a block, won't they?"

Harry was exactly the sort of miserable bastard who avoided travelling down to the seaside on a Bank Holiday so he could watch the news and gloat over the idiots stuck in traffic all the way down to Brighton and Southend. All had been revealed, or at least set in motion. I went indoors and made myself a cup of coffee. I surveyed the washing up and three bin liners which had begun to disgorge their contents over the floor, left the coffee to cool and ran some hot water. I scrubbed at the congealed food, and, stopping to unblock the sink, thought about the delivery—trying to work out some sort of wild thriller plot including a Kensington packet going to Acton.

My first ideas were things like Gladys having a bastard son who'd made it big and sometimes sent her presents. Maybe even his laundry. But that was ridiculous. Not enough edge on it. Anyway, the packet was too heavy (too heavy for what?) and maybe she herself was the daughter of a wealthy family (who married beneath her) and on, and on, and on—exactly the sort of thing that reveals the limits of your imagination and drives you right on to the very end of the night, till false-dawn. Exactly the sort of thing I'd stopped doing some time ago.

Ideas of this sort are two a penny, and mine were neither spectacularly original, nor, in the final analysis, remotely plausible, although I suppose they might just have done in some old melodrama; as far as my morale was concerned, they had a similar result to my correction of the notice downstairs. Because if earthly power and the city were conceived as a great vaulted arch of light in which beings of various stations buzzed around forever, the lowest scarcely able to conceive of the ways of the highest in the inscrutable eminence of their motivations and activities, then a person like me was doomed to be one of those moth-like creatures who are attracted upwards by hot lights that could only scorch and blind him.

Before I really knew it I'd scoured several weeks worth of filth from the drainer, the sink was clean and the steeliness of its metal had startled the whole sordid question from my mind. I picked up three bulging bin bags and wrestled them onto the landing; but it wasn't till I'd reached the chute I remembered the notice I'd altered. I felt ashamed of myself for some reason. I couldn't pin it down. And as I swung the bin bags down the first flight of stairs, baked bean juice started to trickle out between my legs.

I'd started on the courier game many years ago, not long after moving in with Bob, Stig and Rudy over at the flat in Twickenham. They were quite well into it, cleaning up three hundred a week sometimes, no tax, although you had to take off quite a bit of off that for wear and tear on the bike. Rudy and Bob went for new RDs, a brand new one every eighteen months, 400 and 250 Yamahas; both were on what was called the gold circuit. Probably it's the platinum circuit now. Even the uranium circuit. But it seemed like a good life, the good life: cruising around the North Circular waiting for jobs to come in, sheering into the centre and out again, and doing what you liked doing best—what could be more perfect?

I was riding an XS750 myself, which even then they considered to be a bit of a dinosaur—not a Tyrannosaurus, just sluggish and unhandlable in traffic. A Diplodocus. It looked fierce, but its brains were in its arse. They had a point, I suppose, especially at the sort of speeds they were employed to do. The XS was a shaft-driven bike (only the BMWs, the old Sunbeam S7, and the water-cooled Honda CX500 V-Twin—a despatcher's bike par excellence—were shaft-driven at that time) billed as a Super-Shaft (with a unit rumoured to be designed by Porsche) and advertised with semi-naked women draped over it, as always. Anyway, that shaft unit was bulletproof: it might well have been an ideal courier's bike, except (as I say) for the poor handling, and the moped brakes. These were the same as those on the RD400—but fitted on a bike twice the weight (half a ton) you'd sometimes find yourself with no brakes in the wet. You just had to knock her down through the gears until the back wheel locked up solid—and hang on. Still, the XS was economical (60mpg) and most importantly she was what I had. I liked the bike a lot and managed on her for years and years and years.

In fact, they only let me move in because I happened to know Rudy's brother, because they needed somebody straight away. They weren't prepared to advertise: it would've meant emptying the roaches out of the ashtrays, cleaning the place up, and that was just too much trouble. Rudy tried to hang that name on me at first, of Super Shaft, and it nearly stuck for a while (he was trying to say I was uncool, I think) but mercifully it didn't stick for too long and after that I was happy to be plain Tony. The flat was a great place to live. Rudy was dealing at the time. There was always a joint or three on the go. We'd bring in a few cans of Holsten in the evenings and listen to a few Floyd albums. Nobody said very much, which could get you down after the first ten; but Rudy had worked out his very own little private dope-language, just to make sure that anyone who came round to score didn't Bogart any of them.

When someone held up a joint and said 'Quiz' you were supposed to say 'Ago' and the first to say it got the next toke. I found out what it meant, eventually. It was 'Ego' not 'Ago'. Benefits of a classical education. But at the time outsiders certainly did look pretty stupid sitting there with their fingers out and their mouths open, although you could get pretty stoned by taking a few deep breaths.

At the beginning of that time I was still working at the garden centre over on Richmond bypass, second job I got after dropping out of college. It was quite a nice place to work, relaxing. The money was liveable but lousy. I didn't learn much about plants and shrubs—like Rudy and the rest, I was more interested in the prospect of turning over a spare greenhouse to combustible greenery production. So in the end the lure of despatching was irresistible. You could make up your own hours, within reason, as the others said (that's how they got you in) and this particular aspect of my new job suited me fine.

I took to Bob more than to the others. Immediately, as you often do. His most notable characteristic was an intense, undiscriminating kind of enthusiasm, and as well he had a peculiar vocabulary he invented for describing his mental processes. He wanted people to listen to him, I suppose. Don't we all. Rudy liked the idea of it—like the way he'd describe a whole space station on the side of his hamburger when they were tripping—but didn't have much real patience the way he rambled on day to day, and anyway, he had quite enough of a gob on him for the rest of us put together. I'd plenty of patience myself, I'm a patient person; but eventually it ran out, or I realised it was something a bit different.

Bob was sitting in front of the gas fire. Talking about the peculiar world he seemed to live in half the time, of the amazing James Railio and the ominous Mr O, with digressions on the way someone had once looked at him as he was getting into a sleeping bag some years before, in the back seat of someone else's car, travelling nowhere at a leisurely pace. I took out a cigarette, dropped the packet on the couch. It fell on its side and the cancer warning was level with my eyes. I flipped it over and moved the lighter diagonally towards my mouth. A long blue flame jetted across. I sucked it in. And I looked at him across the littered floor, nodding at him, staring, and mentally enacting a scene in which I just leaned towards him, putting my hand out, or maybe shifting my weight a little.

"This is how James Railio disappeared on the beach, right?" he said. "He was sitting over his chessboard with Morgana, right? Next to them was a sandcastle of a mansion with seven floors and seven rooms on each floor."

"Why seven?"

"I don't know, there just were seven. Anyway, James Railio turns to look down the beach. Mr O is walking slowly towards him. So he looks back and the chessboard is gone. Morgana is slowly walking into the sea. Railio walks towards Mr O at the same slow pace. Then, when they're about ten feet apart, they pause and -" Bob brought his hands together so that they appeared to walk through one another "—like this, you see they just disappear into nothing, they just keep walking, just leaving this echo on the empty beach—and then a wave washes through the rooms of the mansion."

"Wow, that's amazing."

"Fancy another tea?" Bob sprang up, and then squatted again, bouncing his arse on his heels.

"Okay."

"Another bubble I had," he went on, dangling the mugs from his fingers now, "was that I'd write the book of this—" he gestured vaguely beyond the room "—bury it in a time capsule, dig it up in about ten thousand years and see if it was still true."

"But it's not true now," I said.

Bob got up and stalked out into the kitchen; I heard the valve whining on the cold tap as he blasted out the cups and filled the kettle. I stood up to stretch my legs and ran my eye along Rudy's bookshelf. They were carefully arranged by him in an order of author and colour, with the SF at the top and the Fantasy at the bottom. I'd already been through the first two, from Asimov to Zelazny, now I was coming down to the greens and the mauves, to the weird stuff like William Morris and Lord Dunsany.

"Looking at the models?" Bob was standing behind me carrying two mugs of tea awkwardly in one hand.

"No, just for something to read."

"Look at this." The so-called game box was wedged into the bottom shelf, a group of tiny hand-painted models in positions on top of it.

"Hmm." I was the only one who didn't play the game. It was quite a complex, absorbing one, but it didn't involve any glass beads—and their absorption in it made my life quite a lonely one sometimes. Though I'd tried hard, I hadn't been able to get into my assigned role as a dwarf. And the other blokes, Stig in particular, had become so irritated with me I decided to bow out of it gracefully.

"This is me." Bob picked up a tiny figure in a starry cloak. "I'm a level three wizard, but at the moment I'm operating with level two spells."

"So, if Railio's dead, I suppose you'll be spending more time on this game?"

"Railio's not dead," he said impatiently. "I thought I'd explained. He's walking away along the beach—and I still have the bank accounts."

"So how much are they worth?"

"Mr O's got twenty quid and Railio has a fiver."

"I wonder if Rudy's left any blow behind?" I wondered absent-mindedly. "He wouldn't miss it if we twisted one up."

"No way," Bob shook his head, "no way can we nick his blow."

"He wouldn't miss it."

"That's not the point. What sort of mate are you?"

I looked away at small bits and pieces on the carpet, some of which could possibly be dope.

"Oh well, I suppose we could always just take enough for a toke." Bob was on his feet again searching through the pockets of the leather Rudy had left hanging on the back of the door. He struck lucky in the little key pouch sewn into the left sleeve.

"Where is he now, round Rosie's?"

"Yeah." Bob was chewing a chunk off the lump with his thumbnail. "He's probably getting a sore prick right this minute."

"You get used to it," I said, which I supposed you probably did.

We passed the joint back and forth between us, taking little gasping tokes. I got up and put *Highway 61 Revisited* on at low volume—it was the only half-decent record in the place and it belonged to my friend Bob.

No dope, no hope. What a useful time-waster, loosener of stiffened joints, and creative spur to sporadic splurges of nonsense. It came down around each of us like a soft bird cage you didn't want to break out of as we listened intently to an album so familiar it barely needed to be turned up or on. I was looking at Bob in that knocked sideways sort of way. His brown hair was a mess of tangled curls. There was a couple of day's beard on his face, which made him look darker than he really was. On his cheesecloth shirt some buttons were undone—and underneath it his deep chest swelled and sloped away, as chests do.

I wouldn't say Gladys had started to obsess me, but when you're on your own the strangest little things catch at your interest. Usually I tend to turn into a vegetable when no-one's about; but the packet had triggered off a curiosity I find it hard to account for or even remember with much accuracy. I refactored even the smallest glances in a thousand ways, taking it seriously; and before I knew what was happening my pathetic excuse of a life had been taken over by people and things I didn't really care about and a series of thoughts meant as no more than allowed playful fantasies took on the fishy smell of truths revealed by people who always seem to think they know exactly what truth is. And don't.

Sometime during the next couple of weeks they bought a dog—a hideous dog, designed by a marketing committee specialising in creatures to be cherished by people who liked defective beings: the same firm who'd designed my mother's cats. I was made fully aware of the existence of this one morning when the lift door opened and it scuttled at my ankles, yapping furiously as its little paws skated away over the tiles.

Gladys's miserable bastard of a husband was on the other end of the lead.

"Whoa, boy," he said, and smiled at me, strangely.

Harry. Harry Chambers. He was a bit friendlier after that, although the dog never settled down. When he was with it he'd chuckle quietly as he jerked at the lead—and if I made a noise on the landing (like pushing my key too briskly into the lock) there'd be a heavy thud opposite as Gladys's dog hurled itself against their door. I'm not even sure why I thought it was hers. Probably it was smallish and a bit yappy. Her husband would have needed some reason for the pleasure he got out of this animal. Here, I bought you a dog, I imagined him saying, as he pulled out the small furry bundle from under his coat. Personally, I'd have taken it straight to the cleaners to be de-haired—or better still just thrown it in the bin and bought another one. Another coat, I mean.

I seemed to see her whenever I left the flat. She was always herding the dog back down their hall with a slippered foot and simpering—but I also spotted her outside the tower, huddled into the main entrance, in the draughtiest spot, peering out across the walkway at the grass beyond as though the way out there consisted of big chunks of broken ice on a thawing pond. She was holding one of those extending leads on a reel in her hand and the little dog was careening on the end of it like a particularly noisy fish.

One of these occasions another tenant was passing by into the tower. "When's she due now?" this friendly woman asked. "It seems like ages."

"September, end of September."

"Still with you, is she?"

"Nowhere else for her to go, mate."

Many people went in and out of their place. I wondered where they slept at night. I imagined three generations of them overflowing from a three-piece suite, trying to see the screen over one another's heads, Gladys bringing in their dinners on juggled trays, and after a while an argument developed about the boxing or the snooker or the nags. The ugly little dog was jumping about over everyone, continually yapping to go out, and they cuffed its nose away from their plates. The family seemed to bring out a bit of the snob in me: they were one of those bad families you'd heard about, if you grew up in the suburbs, like me.

I started to have a suspicion that Gladys wanted me out of my flat in order to install her daughter in my place; this idea seemed to make as much sense as anything else I'd been able to come up with, so why not run away with it? I stood there in the lift one day with members of her family; a young father cradled his baby daughter in his arms, his pregnant wife was next to him and a girl of sixteen was crammed into the back—her mouth continually twitching as another possible sarcastic comment occurred to her developing young mind.

My finger was hovering over the buttons.

"Six," one of the women said.

The bloke looked down at the child in his arms—she'd been crying hard and was thinking of doing so again. He pinched her gently on the cheek. "You didn't like the black man, did you?"

"Blak man. Blak man."

The two women shuffled, the lift jerked upwards with a whine of effort. It was the usual coffin of scarred aluminium with a puddle of piss on a thoughtfully rubberised floor.

"What's he called?" he looked into her eyes and bounced her. "He's a coon," he said, pronouncing the word carefully.

"Coo-coo-coo-n."

The three grown-ups laughed.

"You mustn't say that!" said the younger woman, pretending to smack the child although she too thought it was a good thing to teach her.

"Coon. Coon. Coon." Her brother smiled into baby's eyes, folding her close to him in his big forearms.

I really hated those stupid bastards. But it was like that, or I thought it was—everybody I ran into seemed to be in the grip of some sort of grudge that consumed everything else about them. This small, neat woman who lived upstairs looked at me with a loathing she couldn't easily disguise, and soon I realised it was because she thought I was responsible for every single soggy sheet of newspaper, every whiff of piss or disinfectant in the lift—the Kentucky Chicken box under my arm was just more of this future litter, more high octane fuel for her raging, desiring but never to be satisfied disgust: this universal feeling that can fix itself on anywhere, and so often does. But why me?

"There used to be nice people living here," she said, "now we've got allsorts. licorice allsorts."

How long had this been going on? Forever, I supposed. Anyway, it was my main reason for continuing to keep myself to myself.

In the West End roads were treacherously slippery; dark grease-patches loosened by now and again rain—and at night I listened to the madding weather batter at the double-glazing like a battery of angry ghosts out to scare the living daylights out of anyone living in bad faith or fudging their debts to the dead. It was the screaming abdabs all right, the kind that settle in for good and stab at your heart and your hopes with the strafing fire of a continual argument you've started and already lost with a friend who turns out not to be one, some antagoniser who turns out to be—fuck, I don't know, how should I?—rain, rain, go way—and sometimes I'd remember how I used to get a nice feeling of safety and well-being from that, long ago when I was doing my first forty blinks in my blue carrycot by the old caravan window.

I didn't even think about Gladys anymore; that mystery had settled down to a dull nothing-feeling, but I knew there were goings on around me I didn't want to know about. I didn't care much but I seemed to know inside that I was being carefully watched and reported on—and late one Friday something happened to push me further in that well known direction. I was coming up in the lift again, drenched at the end of a rainy afternoon, when the doors slid open on the sixth floor and another messenger faced me, a gloved finger jabbing the call button. I thought it was a small man at first, but it wasn't. It pulled its helmet off to reveal one of them. The woman-thing. The thing from planet porky. This one was only slightly drier than me: a pinched face under her visor, a Swallows bib (grey with the little stencilled bird flitting away in one corner) and full wets. We nodded and stepped round each other, like crabs.

The lift door closed behind her. I glanced at the tracks leading towards Gladys's door. She'd be out there in a minute, mopping them up. Their hall light was on, a friendly patch of pale pink against the blue council paintwork. That little dog sounded like it was tearing its throat out—what a pity it wasn't capable of it, I thought—and as my lock crashed open with a dry report of nothing doing in moo-moo land, I stepped through into the hallway and scuffed another day's brochures in front of me.

Bob always made himself a large mug of coffee after work. He would sprawl with his head on the edge of the couch and pick up whatever he happened to be reading. In those days he seemed to go through about ten books a week, most weeks, half of them SF and Fantasy, the rest drawn freely from the curriculum of the previous decade. I'd read quite a bit of this stuff. Bob handled Rudy's books with extreme care, but always cracked the spines of his own purchases as a first gesture of possession. He'd paid for them out of his own hard-earned money and now he was going to gobble down the meat.

He consumed print by holding an open page against his cheek, opposite his right eye, and greedily blotting the words off that page before moving on to the next. On some occasions he would reach out impatiently and snatch handfuls of meaning-laden dust motes from the air.

The rest of us just chewed our way through a kebab and side two of *Dark Side of The Moon*. Bob crossed and recrossed his legs as he turned pages, lifting up his arse, jerking it from side to side (as a concentration aid); then he'd slap the splayed open book down, spring to his feet, and unwind; dancing around the shared room in a half-circle as words spilled from his mouth in fed-out spasms and his trembling kung-fu hands chopped at the joint-thick air. He would explain and explain and we were utterly astonished by the flashing light of his mind; but at the end of it, when he slumped back down onto the dusty old couch, I couldn't help noticing that he hadn't properly understood the stories he was telling. Not so any of us could really understand what they were about.

He often seemed to be quoting, but the source was usually himself. "James Railio said something interesting to me the other night," he would start off, "which incidentally has turned out to be one of his top five favourite sayings ..." What followed wasn't generally a saying, just another of what he called his bubbles, which he wrote down in blue notebooks where he kept: banks of quickly put down quotations in his weird handwriting: a broken, slightly wobbling line a bit like Morse Code, mixed up with the wavering calculations he made when casting horoscopes, with the unbroken and moving lines of mysterious, soon to be understood hexagrams from the *I-Ching*, the Book of Changes. Biting Through was one of these. The lean meat is caught between your teeth and all you have to do is chew through it.

"Your energies are fitful, like mine," Bob pronounced. "You and me will never command the instant respect of strangers." This was while looking at a star-chart in the back of the 1958 ephemeris. "You will fail to achieve any of your ambitions, but you will die with honour."

But I didn't really have any strong ambitions. He was staring hard into my eyes. I stared back, believing in him as long as his quiet, nervous speech was right there under my attention. "What about you?" I said. "What did yours say?"

I looked away at the books lined two deep around the skirting boards. Bob scrabbled around on the floor, pulled another ephemeris from under his bed, quickly pawed it open and began to examine its map of his own birth date. He didn't say anything. I closed my eyes, opened them. The record player's lid (its bass cabinet) was up and the defective auto-turntable was continuing to spin a finished album; a ray of late afternoon sunlight hit the record, bounced off the slope of the ceiling and threw up a wobbly spiral of light behind his wide head.

"I could go one of two ways," he said. "No, make that one of three. I see myself living to a great age, and assuming the powers of the gods. On the other hand, those same powers could destroy me."

"What's the third way?" I looked down and saw the splayed lime-green cover of Colin Wilson's *The Occult* between my feet, a book I'd read too, poking out from under the bed.

Bob didn't seem to hear me. "Do you want to know what dying is like?" he asked. "Well, I'll tell you, Tony. It's like diving into a swimming pool. It's there on your nerve and the angle of attack—you either slide into another dimension and keep on moving, or you break up immediately on impact."

I woke up on the couch at 1.30am. The closing tone was shrieking in my ears. I crawled across to the TV and turned it off, trying to concentrate against fragments of dream, to bring back a memory of exactly what film I'd been watching. *Blind Terror*. Mia Farrow staggering around in deep mud with her arms flailing, then banging on the rusty body of a wrecked car with a rusty silencer she picked up. A poor little blind girl in a panic, flailing away in the middle of a deserted breakers' yard—crying out for help where there was no help to be had. The camera pulled back to reveal there was nobody and nothing around for miles and miles. Why was that so frightening? Why was that more terrible than so many of the more terrible things that are often shown?

Because it was much truer than most of them, or that's what I thought to myself. I threw myself back on the couch and let my eyes close. The tangled-up dream started again immediately: they bundled the girl into a Landrover, drove her to Kensington. Gladys opened the door of the basement flat. They carried her in. I was standing there like a complete plonker with a parcel under my arm, trying to get a docket signed. Nobody had any time for me. Nobody gave two shits. In the dream I woke up again, and there was a moment's relief before I looked outside. The city was an empty place. Cars moved—driven by what? Rooms were lit up—lived in by what? The sky was empty, empty. Somebody or something picked up an identity bracelet from the carpet. My call-sign was written on it in indelible ink.

I stood up and stumbled around the fading in room. I rubbed at my eyes and I found the door to the kitchen and I fought my way in there by touch, through fog. I plugged in the kettle and my hands shook as I quickly spooned coffee into a mug. I cooled the coffee down a bit with a splash of milk that went everywhere, gulped it down and my brain started to clear. Jesus Jesus. I'd read somewhere that you should always wash and eat before remembering your dreams; but there was no food in the kitchen, no soap, no nothing, and anyway, I felt as if the touch of water would damage the surface of my skin.

What a film, I thought, to push it away. The reason it was so frightening was because of all the things she didn't know. Because she was forced to trust what she already knew couldn't be trusted—and worse, she didn't know that there was no help, no solution of any kind to her main problem. In *Blind Terror* Mia Farrow was totally alone.

It hadn't taken me long to work out that these packets to Gladys were happening regularly. They were if I allowed myself to generalise from the two incidents. The day before I'd seen Harry Chambers carrying out his granddaughter from the flat, followed by a teenage schoolboy on crutches. Who was he? A grandchild? I tried to count up the inhabitants of their flat on my fingers. They mounted quickly. I couldn't get them all in. I knew they were humans but I had some need to know. Then I forgot which ones I'd counted before and I started counting again, until I was just staring down at my empty hands.

I had to do something, something. You know that feeling? But what the fuck did any of it have to do with me? A question that popped up and was swept aside, it reappeared and teased me, but somehow I couldn't make it depart, like an irritating sort of person of poor character you've had the misfortune to fall in love with, like an *I-Ching* hexagram meant for some other poor fucker, one that you keep persistently throwing, or I did before I stopped that game. I felt in myself that I had to go back to the basement flat in Kensington to find out what was happening. I just had to, that's all. There was no reason, no excuse for it, and at moments such as these I expected anyone could see just what sort of person, sadly, I really am.

The streets were deserted and the big old Yamaha was clattering a little at her bottom end, echoing around the dark shop fronts that faced into Shepherd's Bush Green, like the stands of an end of the meeting racetrack still blowing with dropped programmes and ticket stubs after a day's cruel sport. I thought there'd be more police around Hammersmith. I carried on up to the roundabout, did a sharp right, idling up to each junction and accelerating away from them in a game where speeding made me invisible—to myself, to them, to the others, and to God Almighty.

I parked around the corner and walked back to the house. I pretended the streetlights were lasers. I must've been somewhere similar thousands of times. They had a similar layout. If you walked out this story in the day with a guidebook in your hand you wouldn't understand it. There were no lights left on in any parts of the building. No cars were parked in the street. I slowly walked back to where I'd left the bike.

In my top box there was a small tool-kit, which I kept wrapped up in soft rag to keep it from rattling and damaging the packets. I selected a pair of tasty Mole Grips and strolled back to the house. My head was pounding. I tried to think, work out what I might be looking for. What if I was caught, found out? Well, well. I dismissed this thought. The best I could do was to think it would bring everything out into the open. But what exactly? I turned the handle, taking up slack in both directions. The flat was locked. Of course, of course. What was I expecting? I wanted to go home suddenly, curl round the spring in my mattress and fall asleep. I tested the wide sash and it slid up easily. I looked in stupid astonishment at the velvet curtains beginning to move a little in the night air.

I put one leg over the windowsill. My foot touched the deep carpet of the room. There was a row of brass bells arranged in descending order of size along the sill. I picked up each one, muffling the clapper with my gauntlets, and lowering them down behind the curtain. I pulled my left leg after me, crawled into the room, waiting for my eyes to adjust to the darkness, keeping low. I was behind a large overstuffed armchair with a flowery old-style cover. On the far side of the room a carved wooden table loaded down with knick-knacks. Beside the fireplace was another armchair. I sniffed it. Somehow it smelt like an old person's room, as I already knew it was. Sitting room of a retired couple, perhaps. A newspaper was draped over an arm of a chair, rustling when I placed my hand on it. In front of the fire stood a tray bearing what was left of a cold meal.

At once the room possessed a reality that chased way the idea I could find out anything useful here, anything I needed to know—and that meant I was really scared. I couldn't remember what I was supposed to be doing here, even. Doors presented themselves, and, as so often, I took the one that was slightly ajar. To the kitchen. Soft light bled in through a barred window, catching at taps and a sink. The fridge turned itself off, ran down, unwound. I thought it must have decided it had got cold enough. Icy spam temperature.

There was a stripped wooden table beside it and a cork board on the wall, and the cards of two messenger firms were pinned up in the bottom corner—one of them was us, the other was Swallows—and on the table was a small cardboard box. I tried to get hold of the lid and look inside, but my gauntlets were getting badly in my way. A black finger was there in my mouth; I was pulling, when I heard a sudden noise from next door of somebody coming through from the bedroom.

"What the..." Whoever it was shivered and padded across to the open sash and pulled it down. "Stupid woman..." his voice trailed away. "Who is it? What's going on?"

I flattened myself along the edge of the open kitchen door. I closed my fist around the Mole Grips and raised them above my head. Silence. A scrape, maybe. I looked down at the back door. There was a key in the lock and my hand looked so stupid reaching for it.

"Dennis, are you all right?"

A light came on in the living room and feet in slippers were scuffled quickly across the carpet. When he came round the door with the poker I tried to bring the Grips hard down, but I was severely unbalanced. Before I could recover he let me have it across the ribs and kicked me right in the balls—and I fell back against the edge of the table and rolled off onto the tiled floor. A wave of nausea broke through me. I felt like a baby who's been dropped, who hurts and only wants to be picked up again—between my legs there was a black hole of pain that was sucking the world up into it.

This pair had my helmet off and the bloke's wife was trying to revive me with a dishcloth. Evidently she'd succeeded. The pain was still there, but more in one place. I had my hands pressed into my balls, my left side throbbing. I wanted to pass out again, but they kept gabbling at me. The woman was still dribbling her water on my face and I turned my head from side to side to make her stop it.

"Call the police, woman," he said. "I'll make sure he doesn't get up."

"Dear oh dear, dear oh dear," she was saying. She started to wring out the cloth in the sink.

"Don't hurt me," I managed to say. "I didn't come here to steal, I was just..." I was choked up with tears; they oozed out of me. Everything was clenched, straining to push them out of my eyes in a series of violent spasms, each of which stabbed deeper into my left side. As I cried I felt deeply aggrieved. I was the innocent party in this. I'd been conspired against, abused, driven from pillar to post, put upon, and what's more ... my spasms slowly slowed. I was lying on the floor of someone else's kitchen in the terrible brightness of their strip-lighting. I was guilty.

"Make him a cup of tea," the old man said, "or perhaps a cup of cold water would be more appropriate." He looked at me, smiling faintly. "Child, you are deep in sin. Will you join together in prayer with us?"

Somehow I struggled onto my knees. We said the Lord's Prayer, followed it with Psalm 23; then the old man said another prayer, one of his own, a prayer I hadn't heard before.

Two

All weekend I thrashed the streets to grey ribbons; a twisted out-of-kilter monkey toy that couldn't stop trying to bang its cymbals together, couldn't stop trying to do its one pathetic trick. I thought again of the way I'd wallowed around on their kitchen floor. I wasn't sure what I was more ashamed of, the stupid break-in or that exhibition. They'd let me sit on a tubular kitchen chair while I drank Earl Grey tea. I felt I'd never taken a more powerful drug. It zonked me completely, but I decided not to tell them my life story. By the time I'd put down the cup it seemed they were going to let me walk out of there. I wasn't sure if this demonstrated the power of faith or what.

Why were they so fucking generous? My gear had saved me from serious injury, but a big purple stripe had swollen up between my ribs. I fingered it gingerly and it triggered a boiling rage inside me. I had to struggle to remind myself that he had, in fact, been acting in self-defence. But to tell the truth I didn't struggle too hard. I didn't believe them, anyway. I knew the police were going to knock on my door any minute, and when they did I'd fall sobbing into the arms of the hated man in blue.

I woke up early on Monday, called in from the car park.

"You're brave," Nick said, "fancy a nice little out of towner? Chelmsford. Collect and return. You'll be coming back into Camden."

"Twenty-five quid?"

"Twenty, mate."

Within a couple of minutes I was out on the North Circular, fighting my way through the rush hour snarl. A crisp, sunny morning—and, although I was tired, an amazing stillness and clarity came down over me. I passed Gants Hill and opened up the XS750 on the inside lane of a stretch of dual carriageway where flat, empty fields dropped away on either side. I was as happy as I'd ever been. I was on someone else's errand again with nothing to worry about except doing it, doing what I did best. It was a totally cool feeling that came out of nowhere and I rode along on it for as long as it lasted.

The Chelmsford pick-up was at the Girls' Grammar School—a tight-lipped little receptionist directed me to the staff room where a young woman teacher was hastily taping sheets of brown paper around a large African mask. She scrawled the address on it with a bright green board marker and when I reached Camden a plumpish, scruffy man dressed in a way that spelled a r t i s t opened his door, ripped away the wrappings and started to caper around with this mask held over his face. This bloke must've been on something. He reached into his pocket, but I held up my hands, managing to resist temptation to get paid twice. Basically there are some stupid bastards out there and it helps if you're prepared to play along with them.

I called in clear outside TV-AM around 11.30. The channel was so quiet, so I took the opportunity to get a cup of coffee and gave myself a ten-minute breather before plunging back into the city to work.

I called in one more time.

"Rogerrogerroger." Nick's voice came over faintly, breaking up in static. "Where've you been 3–5?"

"Chelmsford."

"Oh yeah. Right. Listen, we've got a slight problem here. Come back in. Come back into the office, 3–5. Someone wants to talk to you."

"Who?" I felt sick to my stomach. "Who?"

"Quick as you can, Okay?"

I rode back down Euston Road under the Westway, signs for Kilburn and Notting Hill flashing up, so many trick exits leading back onto the merry-go-round that I lived my days in. Before I'd been thinking I could ride away from it all. Down to Cornwall, maybe. Up to Scotland. But who did I really know up there who'd hide me? Nobody, nobody, that's who. There was also my parents' place in Aldershot. It wasn't Rio de Janeiro, but the truth was that the police were reeling me in, like a little Gladys' dog on a retractable leash. I saw them looking up as I walked in through the door, and tried to stop myself from mouthing off at them, like what I really was—a loser, an absolute loser. My shadow appeared. You're a loser, Tony, he said, an absolute, total fucking loser.

Anyway, they led us into a large, strip-lit meeting room divided in half by fraying screens of various pastel shades. A wasp's nest of saved drawing pins clustered in the corner of one of them. I stared at it until it started buzzing. We were all kitted out in full winter gear, crash hats under our right arms, like footballers, Stanley Matthews and the like, old ones, pictured with winning balls on the fifties cigarette cards. We were meant to look as though we'd stepped in off the street. They lined us up against a pale green wall and told us exactly how to stand. I stood the way they'd instructed us to, suspecting the others were all police plants.

The old boy's head was heavily bandaged and he was leaning on a walking stick. I got my first good look at him. In his kitchen, it was his large, sandy-coloured head I'd noticed first, as well as a certain bulk about him. In the clear light of day he was revealed as being one of these tall, fat people with permanently soft skin, the look of an overgrown child. There was something repellent and attractive about him in just about equal measure—with perhaps a tip on the reptilian side: the scales showed through his skin.

I felt a twinge in my groin and tried to make my mind go blank. The old man walked along the line—so arrogant, you could tell—and his cheeks were wobbling slightly as he tried to look in-charge and fix everyone with a beady, alert, revealing stare. I blinked as he passed me and he pointed at the bloke on my left. I glanced across at this bloke's face, or up at it—he was a full head taller than the rest of us: a dead man's beard pushed out through the skin of a mummy. I thought he looked seriously ill.

D.S. Wheeler opened a drawer, pulled out a pair of imitation Mole Grips and clunked them down on the wide desk between us.

"Have you seen these before, Tony?"

"Definitely not," I gabbled. "I would never use a tool like that. What do you think I am? They came off a stall on the market. Probably made in Taiwan—out of butter."

Well, they were. My own were the real thing, they belonged to my brother. I wondered how I was going to tell him that I'd tossed his prize Mole Grips over Hammersmith Bridge on my way home. The old man had obviously told them what he'd been hit by. But why? Why didn't he shop me at the time when he'd had the chance? Why hadn't he picked me now? I sat it out, like you're supposed to, playing though all the pathetic little loops of fact my story allowed. I tried not to think too hard—that seemed favourite—but I couldn't help myself from worrying about those bandages. Maybe the old boy slipped over on something, on the stone steps outside his flat for instance, ahhh. Amnesia, perhaps, a result of this mishap. Why not? I couldn't remember fuck-all about it, and after a time I managed to shut down altogether.

Wheeler had one of those horrible whiny, insistent little voices, like a Ken Livingstone clone doggedly investigating the whereabouts of some misplaced fifty quid allocated to the basket-weaving committee. "Now, are we going to sit here all night, or are you going to tell me how it happened?"

"Look, there must be—I don't know —thousands of courier firms in London."

"Do try to act sensibly, Tony. I'm not an idiot. You're not telling the truth, I know you're not, I'm a trained public servant."

There was a knock on the door and a nasty-looking little she-cop leaned into the room. "Sorry to interrupt, Jim. Telephone call for you." The bitch stone-faced me. "Your wife. Shall I ask her to call back?"

He breathed out heavily in irritation, sat back in his chair, and pinched the bridge of his nose between two fingers. I recognised that gesture. He was quoting it from somewhere—from human beings he'd observed as a training exercise. It meant he was tired and that I should feel sorry for him. If I pushed my luck any further I should feel more afraid. Not that I wasn't taking it seriously, I was; but I knew by now there were some right big lies going on—and that gave me a chance. My survival depended on making myself be here and away, and as a result what should have been real to me showed up as a series of tics and knee jumps. But if I made too many more wrong moves I was going to get the shit kicked out of me, and in a way I deserved this, but I'd managed to avoid it so far and hoped to carry on doing so.

"Tell her I'll be with her in a moment." Wheeler stood up, leaned over the recorder. "D.S. James Wheeler interrupting this interview in Room 5c with Mr Tony Guest for ten minutes." He looked at his policeman watch. "Time is now 4.15pm."

I let my eye lingeringly inspect the tape machine, which looked a bit like a standard double cassette deck but more heavy duty—something like an industrial vacuum cleaner or one of those items of wood-encased electrical equipment they use in schools. I was about to ask Wheeler where they got them when he pressed pause.

"Don't go away, Tony," he said. "We'll continue this shortly. But in the meantime, perhaps this -" I didn't feel it coming. "- cuff round the head will make me feel better."

I felt an explosion detonate against the left side of my head, the room tilted and I was thrown onto the floor. I did feel plenty of pain too, though I can't recall exactly what it was like; just that my ear was feeding back, the sound building up and up and up, like a rosined finger insanely running around a wine glass on maximum revs, until it was at the very point of shattering. I thought my eardrum would burst, or already had. I tried hard to shake the noise out of my head. I couldn't though, I couldn't—I managed to pick myself up and saw the door closing behind him. One thing was certain; he didn't like the look of me much.

"Sit down!" the constable shouted. "Just sit there. Can you do that for me?"

He retreated and I sat rigid. I'd been staring at a single picture, of myself on the old man's kitchen floor. Another one slid into its place. Two small courier cards pinned to a corkboard.

"My wife and myself are hoping you'll remember this act of kindness," the vicar was saying, "and perhaps try to exercise a little more forbearance—and foresight—in your own future dealings."

Wheeler, I thought, wasn't on the phone to his wife; he was in another interview room, another cell, trying to coax a confession out of the rider that the old man had identified. Why hadn't Poore picked me out? I kept asking myself that question. I felt cheated. Why wasn't I allowed to be guilty? When I obviously was? Why the palaver, why the silly games? They were ridiculous, really. I'd broken into his flat—fair and square—and I'd tried to hit him. But for what, for what? I laughed to myself at the complete absurdity of it.

"Is something funny?" The constable angled his pointed chin in my direction. "Perhaps you'd like to share it with us? Give us all a laugh?"

All who? These bastards automatically multiplied themselves, as if they were members of the royal family. "Sorry," I said, "just thinking."

"Just thinking what?"

"Nothing."

"You're up shit's creek, Tony. I'd think about that if I was you."

D.S. Wheeler came back and we carried on talking, covering much of the ground as before. I tried to bear in mind that he didn't have anything on me. Nothing. I hoped. Sooner or later they'd have to give up, just drop it and write the whole thing off—stick it on the long list of several thousand unsolved cheque card frauds and acts of random violence that slipped through their capable fingers in a single day. The side of my head kept moving in and out, in and out, in and out: the way they used to show throbbing in cartoons. They'd got it exactly right in the cartoons. The Toons. I had a heavenly vision of being at home, making myself a nice hot cup of tea, eating a big bar of chocolate and watching some really old ones.

"Look, Tony. We know you're mixed up in this. Your pal's told us you were involved."

"What pal?"

"Not got many friends, have we? Oh dear."

"A few," I lied.

"So where's the money? Give it to someone to look after, did you?"

"What money?"

Wheeler looked at the tape—which was recording silence. Bit of a waste, I thought.

"You mean the one he picked?"

"Yeah."

"I-never-saw-him-before-in-my-life." That much was true. Surely I could convince him of that?

"Are you sure about that? Absolutely?"

"Search my flat."

"We already did, Tony. Ever thought of getting a home help in?"

The constable dipped his head, concealing his stupid laughter. Wheeler ground on for a bit longer, but achieved no further bursts of outrageous wit. I was waiting for him to hit me again. He didn't. Should've done, most probably. It might have worked wonders; instead they put me in an empty holding cell and left me alone.

There was a wooden shelf in it with a lip at the edge to stop you rolling off; a vinyl mattress had been thrown on the floor. I chose the mattress. I could lie on my right side, facing under the shelf, or on my back, looking up at the nowhere to hang yourself from ceiling. A patch of light came in from the corridor. I stared at that and put up with the incessant whining in my ear. I was going to have him, promise to God, he was a prime example of that orifice of which every police horse has one in the middle of its back.

I was going to fuck him. Ace him. Stamp on his ugly little head a lot of many times and savour the memory of it—bore my grandchildren, if any, with how it felt. Right. A tyre lever would be favourite for a job like that. No, no. A common or garden house brick, or half a paving stone. Splat, a fucking insect. But sadly it was going to have to be legal. That'd fix him. Yeah, yeah. I'd go to the doc the minute they let me out, get a statement, a sworn statement, get myself a real sworn statement. A doctor would help me—a proper quack would have to help, wouldn't he?

I saw the so-called expert witnesses they'd line up, the truth-tellers, all of them: the self-doubling constables, every liar in the directory of liars (the Met phone book) and every last little prick of a policeman anywhere—reading out of black notebooks, each with that little word truth stamped on the cover in gold-block letters, stuffed full of filth-lies from a shit-house wall. I remembered how I'd winced when they patted me down. I felt sick to my stomach. So what were they going to do? They could do anything they liked. They could put me between a couple of mattresses and beat the shit out of me. Why not? That sort of thing was routine if they decided they didn't like you. I squeezed my eyes slowly shut and a fat tear rolled back, cooling down that hot bruise above my cheekbone, making it itch. No peace. Not even a moment's respite. More tears came—I cried them for as long as they lasted and dredged up more. Self-pity, that was better.

In the middle of the night I was woken by the sound of the cell door opening. A drunk pissed in the aluminium pan in the corner while another wall-eyed WPC looked on. Surely there must be another toilet? I thought of this sleepily, resentfully: they were doing it deliberately—but I didn't like to say, in case they really were. Every stupid idea I'd ever had offered itself up for further consideration. I cocked an ear to the bustle of the charge room, where it sounded like a party was going on. Why hadn't the bastards invited me? If I pushed my face into the hollow and shouted, would one of them give me a cigarette?

My ideas fell away—they weren't even ideas, as such. Nothing except the flickering light tube in the corridor and the fact that, for some reason, the old man (maybe he was all right in some way I hadn't understood) was lying. At crack of dawn they gave me back my gear and my keys and they turned me out in the cold, telling me on the way out that my bike was locked up in the police pound under Park Lane. I'd have to come back for it later, get a none-about black cab, or walk home.

The Secret History of Twickenham. That's the one where Queen Anne, Horace Walpole, Alfred Tennyson, Alexander Pope and John Donne don't get much of a look in, not really; and Rugby Union, nobody gives a toss about that either. That secret history is what this is trying to pass itself off as—and Stig, I'll have you believe, Stig is really important. Stig plays a major, major role. Stig was the owner of a 1957 Meteor Minor, the 350 model, and a scar that ran down from the top of his forehead and stopped above his upper lip, denting his flesh as though a thread had been looped through his head, and deliberately tightened up with a twisted stick. An injury sustained by riding the old Royal Enfield into the back of an unlit skip one dark and stormy night. He was rebuilding the bike in his bedroom.

Stig didn't speak to me at all for the first three months I lived there—when he did it was in a leaning forward, confidence-sharing kind of a way that I soon learned was his only mode of communication. Me, I was taking a dusty old dustpan and a stiff brush to the sitting room carpet—making a decent job of it too, and banging the bent bristles hard into the weave and pulling out the hair of previous tenants in great big brittle looms; so much of it, so dead. I tried to piece together a bit of a poem I'd read—and that spurred me onwards:

> Love in these labyrinths his slaves detains,
> And mighty hearts are held in slender chains.
> With hairy springes we the birds betray,
> Slight lines of hair surprize the finny prey,
> Fair tresses man's imperial race insnare,
> And beauty draws us with a single hair.

I put the kettle on and gave Stig a shout. Stig was a strange one: a total tea-hound. Even the most infinitesimal chink of crockery, let alone that hot delicious pouring sound of a cup of tea immediately brought him sniffing out from his stinking room and he'd push his stained enamel mug onto the draining board with a noise, a small throat-noise with a whimpering yes-please inflection attached to it: a sure sign someone was later going to steal his name.

"Thirsty?" I asked.

He didn't reply. He didn't really need to.

"See, I just cleaned the floor?" I spoke out loudly—I wanted a good witness but only Stig was available. "There's all this hair compacted down underneath it. I had to, er, really bang it down hard."

"You want to know what really bothers me?" He picked up the mug, held the circle of hot liquid close to his face and inhaled the rising tea-vapour with narrowing eager eyes.

"What's that?"

"I don't seem to be dreaming anymore."

"Everyone dreams," I said, "whether they know it or not."

"Not me," he said. "When I lie down it's like I'm a machine that's been turned off for the night."

I looked away. I couldn't give a shit.

"What I should really do is I should drop some acid," he went on, "—if that doesn't give me dreams nothing will."

"Acid doesn't give you dreams," I spoke out pompously—trying to remember if it did or not. Anyway, there hadn't been a decent drop of acid around for many years now, and, anyway, anyway, I somehow couldn't think that Stig would manage the finding of any of it.

But when he repeated all this later Rudy remembered he had three blotters left, tucked into the back of his copy of *Stranger in a Strange Land*. I suppose we should have suspected, really, since the book itself was always kept in the fridge: the lysergic may have been preserved, but the crisping, yellowing process seemed to have been accelerated (one reason I'd never read the thing) and for some reason Rudy didn't fancy any of this primo acid himself. In a flash of generosity, he suggested that Stig, Bob and me do one blotter each. We looked at them dubiously—each one was hallmarked with a faint purple print of Saturn—and we gobbled them down.

Bob was reporting for duty at the Stargate in record time, a plethora of things to describe seemed to press in on his head straight away. Stig wandered into his room as soon as he started talking. When I boiled the kettle and took him in a nice hot cup of tea, I found him cleaning up a couple of spark plugs with a wire brush, scrubbing and holding them up in a pool of concentrated light from his bedside lamp, scrutinising each magnified pock and blemish with amazed, amazing fascination, before dunking them again in the bedside petrol bath.

"You all right?" I turned the handle of the hot mug towards him, my fingers pressed around its rim, till eventually, eventually it dawned on him he was meant to take this steaming object.

The street was a blowing desert of pizza boxes; greasy papers bucked up on the pavement, ready to fly, fix themselves across our faces, suck the breath out of us. I floated into the air. Blackened chicken bones on the roof of a bus shelter foretold doom and some giant milkshake cups rolled around in eternal circles. Bob strode off left on a circling, lit-up route that would take us over the rainbow bridge. We were ambling down a lit up causeway, hugging the King Street shop fronts, past the Reels arcade and its gallery of lit-up slots. Pac-man munching his way through everything in his path, the first un-super Mario failing to tempt us with his twinkling eye and his twitching moustache: running and jumping, running and jumping, slicing somebody's unwary head off down the long mazes of days that would eventually lead to a future obsession with the secret sequence of commands that snatched off Lara Croft's little black panties.

We tried to look natural past the cop shop and The Cabbage Patch, crossed the road towards a trellis-grille pulled across to stop the late trains escaping from Twickenham railway station and turned into an avenue lined with swanky 1920s timbered houses: a row of laughing teapots with mock thatch cosies, if the stuff we'd swallowed had been as good as the packaging. I wondered instead what you had to do to get one, a laughing teapot, that is. I already knew. I also knew inside that I didn't have whatever it takes in a thousand light years.

Neither of us had said anything since we descended to the realms of mortals. The wind had dropped away to nothing and our footsteps echoed across a freshly resurfaced road scattered with uncut diamonds, there for the picking up, the taking, if only the council hadn't embedded them in so much tar. I remembered walking around the nearby private Estates at night and speculating about the damage a Russian tank might inflict on the big houses of the rich. Happy, unhappy days. I wanted to tell him about them, but something stopped my tongue, it always did, and if I opened my big mouth all this stuff—I searched for words—would get in? come out? stay put down there? I owned nothing, never would, not even ... even that had rolled up, had been rolled up, and this world and its reference-points was about to disappear—a slapping roller blind in a cartoon about running from ghosts.

We turned into an alley, crossed a footbridge over a ditch which someone had once told me was the River Crane, arrived in a deserted playground on the edge of St Margaret's Rec and climbed up onto an old warped roundabout painted long ago in dark green gloss, picked down to grey wood by fingernails and scored by seven-blade penknives sent away for with a dozen waxy bubblegum wrappers from pink-faced Bazooka Joe. We lay down in the centre of it and watched bright stars turning around our empty heads.

I remembered it all, it seemed, how I'd done this at the end of another trip, and then another—on a whole backward series of similar occasions stretching off through my gone teenage years. So I got up and jumped off. I felt dizzy and sick. I wanted to go home straight away, and did; and when we got there I fell into an inescapable tinkling nightmare about the bear, the jealous dwarf and the princess who lived around *The Singing Ringing Tree*.

"Not a light." Stig looked gloomily away from the TV screen. "Not even any colours, man."

"I said they were old." Rudy's crossed feet were draped over the arm of his chair as though he was having a rest from wearing them. "Anyway, anyway, quite a lot of this modern blotter is just a bit of speed and a bit of strychnine."

A sharp pain knifed across my chest. Bob came in. He'd a stack of groceries clamped between his hands. Bread, sausages, eggs, beans, margarine.

"So, what did you see?" he asked eagerly.

Nobody said anything. There was nothing to say—and that was the trouble with us. That's what we were. Real fucking mongs. We just couldn't compete. Not with anyone or anything. Me especially, I have to say. If we'd been capable of finding any surprising situations, life might well have taken us by surprise. Except we didn't, and it didn't. It seemed to me that we were set up to be amongst the lost ones in a land of pre-factored, costed-in redundancies—a real bunch of losers, the sort of people who thought Value Spaghetti was just as good as the real thing.

When I'd first started at ABC it was comprised of two controllers and a dozen motley riders operating out of a tiny office above a kebab shop in Harlesden high street, right on the corner there by the red and gold Jubilee clock. They'd done all right, all right enough so that my bosses, Don and Brian Nello, could afford to cruise around town in near identical candy-coloured Granada Ghias, those candy-coloured clowns they called the cunt-twins keeping tabs on their branch managers by means of their brand new toys: a pair of giant walkie-talkies, courtesy of Cellnet.

Don and Brian built up the business by renting the cheapest premises they could find in any new area, installing a couple of experienced controllers and taking on anyone who walked through the door with a bike licence. If they'd a gob on them they were even more impressed; it indicated potential for future advancement. They paid you rock bottom rates, fed in a certain amount of work from the surrounding branches and pretty soon the new one would start to pick up its own regulars. If it didn't they sacked the managers one by one from the top down, promoting another nervous candidate for the chop every couple of months. If that failed to motivate the rest of the workforce, they sacked everyone and started again from scratch.

Dulwich would be a useful case study of the Nello management technique in action. The whole staff reported for work one Monday morning to find themselves surplus to requirements. The figures weren't working, apparently. Don and Brian were in a state of panic, terrified that their particular bubble was about to burst. Ominous talk about fax machines came to dominate conversations all over town. I should've been worried, I suppose, scared that I might be next. But I didn't give a shit. I tried really hard to look upset about each item of bad news; but inside I was enjoying that secret warm glow of satisfaction I always got when my bosses fucked up. I had nowhere else to go and no secret ambitions left. Tough shit. I put in a couple of days a week and was happy if my beloved workmates left me alone to get on with the job.

Nobody said anything, but it was obvious I'd seriously blotted my copybook. I hadn't been charged, of course, but that didn't seem to come into it. I'd managed to get the fabulous Nello brothers taken off the air (sharp intake of diesel fumes) and every rider in the branch lost money over it (so they said) by having to park up somewhere or other and wait for me to reappear from Chelmsford. Why didn't they just call me there? I wondered. And they knew there was something to it—or thought they did. I thought taking them off the air must have been pure malice on the part of the cops; but I didn't want to think about it any longer.

What I wanted was to forget about the whole sorry business. Gladys was only a tired middle-aged woman who worried about her family a bit too much, the old man ... that phony bandaged cleric who had let me go, was innocent of doing anything wrong. There was nothing I could do about it. My tools were made of butter. Nay, margarine. The cops had left a heap of junk in the hall. I concentrated on that instead, spent most of Tuesday night replacing it in the end cupboard. I put in a solid three days for ABC at the end of the week, I was so absolutely determined that Don and Brian weren't going to have an excuse for sacking me.

On Friday afternoon I picked up a ticket turning left into Oxford Street. I'd been in too much of a hurry to get down to the bottom of Mayfair and pick me up a collect and return from the surgical appliance emporium in Wigmore Street. I'd hoped it was going to be a box of glass eyes—all the better to see you with, my dear—but I'd lost that job to some other lucky bastard. There I was, standing under a row of mechanical can-can girls as they lifted their stocking-clad right legs in unison, and I stomped around in a rage on the pavement—pointing out other riders turning left in a steady stream.

"Look at him," I said to one of the cops, "and him—and him."

"We're not supermen, unfortunately." The affable one walked over to the kerb and looked vaguely at the Yamaha—this wanker didn't really know what he was doing—"How much do you make on this game?" he says. "I stop blokes who say they're on £500 a week."

"I don't make that sort of money. I don't know how they do it."

"They ride like maniacs."

I didn't answer. He was right. His partner was taking forever with my documents but I decided it wasn't worth bothering to argue with either of them. Especially as that's what they expected and what they got all day long. The one standing next to me blinked and tried to think of something else to say. So we stood there. Duhhh. A couple of Americans walked up to him and asked where they could find the nearest fish and chip shop.

Suddenly I really loved them. I wanted to take them there myself, as my personal way of welcoming them to our magnificent country. Seriously. There were so many important subjects they knew nothing about at all, things of which I knew totally, off by heart.

Synthetic brass, a single mouth breaking up into many smaller mouths, each one open, each of them grassing somebody up. I was sitting on a replica of my XS. Somebody on the pillion was pointing a big Handycam over my shoulder. I stopped outside a chalky building and they followed me down the steps through an open sash window. I held a plumber's wrench in my right hand. Time, place and date glided effortlessly across the lower half of the screen. There was a shoebox on the table. The lid was half off and fat bundles of ten pound notes were stacked inside it. An actor rounded the door and I clubbed him mercilessly to the ground.

"The thief escaped with five thousand pounds, which had been collected by a team of charity volunteers."
I recognised Shaw Taylor's voice, hoarser than my memory of it.
"If you know anything about this, or any other crime mentioned, those *Crime Search* desks at Metropolitan Police Headquarters are waiting to hear from you right now. You needn't give your name—and you could earn a Community Action Trust reward."
How did they know where to send the money if you didn't give your name?
A yellow box appeared containing the *Crime Search* number.
I switched off.
I tried to go over it again in my head. Another can rolled around in the car park. Two opposing teams of players I'd fucked up in previous lifetimes were playing five-a-side with this one. I couldn't concentrate. The *Crime Search* pictures had replaced my own memories of the incident. I wondered if they didn't have it right. What had I been running from—and where was I running? I was slowing down. It felt like death, or judgement. I felt the weight of the spanner in my right hand. It was the weight that had done most of the damage: all I'd done was let it fall.

I parked up in Howland Street against the grey base of Telecom Tower, sitting there on the bike with my helmet off and slurping at the day's first cappuccino. I put the lid back on between lip-scorching sips and cast half-an-eye over three other bikers who were waiting next to me in the self same spot. We nodded but didn't speak, treasuring a few of those moments of peace and solitude before the day, the week, and the whole stupid month ground away into another rapid September—and once again I hadn't managed to do anything worthwhile with my holidays.

How long would I be able to keep this up before relapsing into my old ways as a part-timer? Two or three weeks at most. If Don and Brian hadn't forgiven me by then, I'd just have to start looking for something else. It was about time I got sorted out, anyway. I saw myself in front of a series of back protections of places I thought I'd like to see and could've done easily if I'd taken the trouble: the Arc de Triomphe, the Taj Mahal, the flat-topped mountains of Nevada. Oh well, well. I'd have to give it some more serious thought some other time, some other lifetime.

The first of the other three took off about ten minutes later. I wasn't in too much of a hurry myself, not unless Nick had another spare out-of-towner: as one of my uncles said, if you see a bus coming don't run for it, you might slip over and break your neck, and after all another one'll be along five minutes later. Ancestral wisdom of the terminal, I was sick of it—I felt like getting out on the motorway and blowing some of the shit out of my head. Not that there was much chance of that. Those jobs tend to be given to starters: it's the only way a controller can put something in your wage packet if you don't know your way around.

The radio muttered away on my shoulder—a parrot rehearsing perjury. I turned it up and listened. Nick was signing someone else off. I called in a reminder. "Alpha 3-5. Still parked up."

"Roger 3-5. I'll bear you in mind."

I drained the rest of the cappuccino, dropped the cup on the ground—oops—and the nearest rider shot me a hostile glance. Typical, he was thinking, typical of the scum I have to share my life with. Scum, arseholes giving us knights of the city such a bad name. That was me. I felt sorry for him. He was right. But I turned my back to watch a group of student nurses chatting as they hurried towards the Middlesex Hospital, as he started up, blipped angrily and bumped his bike off the stand.

The nurses had clipboards crushed against their breasts. I didn't have to be a despatch rider, I thought. I could always do something useful with my life, I don't know ... hospital orderly? morgue attendant? surgical instrument cleaner? Or maybe an ambulance driver. People got out of your way then. I watched their twitching behinds disappear. That was something I tried not to think about too much, apart from occasionally stroking the hamster and putting it back on its wheel. No justice for hamsters: dog eat dog in the world of the cockroach.

The last waiting rider spread a cloth out on the saddle of his 900 BMW and started to eat a dainty picnic out of a Tupperware box and to drink the coffee he'd thoughtfully prepared and metered for himself at home from the lid of a small neat thermos. This bloke thought he was seriously cool. He was a round-faced man in his early forties, classic clever bastard look in black racing leathers and a walrus moustache. When he'd finished his breakfast he folded up the cloth and packed everything away in one of his £250 each panniers, flipped open a clipboard of Teutonic design, consulted a neatly folded map and called in ready to work.

I really admired people like him: this bloke was dead serious. He wasn't waiting for any controller, his controller was waiting for him—until he was good and ready to go; only then did he call in clear and issue his instructions for the day. The 900 BM—a few years old but in immaculate nick—started with a soft creak and he glided away on a hydraulic cushion of German efficiency. I should get myself as organised as that feller, I thought. Okay, he was a tosser, but so what? He was probably a lot happier than I was. And if he wasn't any happier, he certainly handled it considerably better.

I glanced at my watch and caught the final zero as it changed to a one. It was 10.31. Soon it would be 10.32. Nick hadn't given me a job. Wanker. There was no doubt the bastard was starving me, deliberately starving me to death.

"Alpha 3-5," I called in, "am I working today or what?"

"Roger 3-5. Are you working any fucking day, that's what I want to know."

"Nick?"

"Yeah, Nick here. I've got a big multi wants knocking out. You're not going to take all day on it, are you?"

I couldn't believe this shit.

"It's account 359. You want 7 West Ones, 3 SW3s and a West Eight. Got that 3-5?"

"Account ..." I fumbled for the account book, turned a few pages "...what was it again, mate?"

"Don't tell me you don't know the book, Tony. How long have you been doing this? That's three-five-nine. Got it? Got it?"

"Sorry, Nick. That's, um, 6 West Ones, 4 SE2s..."

"Come on, don't waste my time." Nick rattled out the job again, faster than I could write it down. "Basically, it's the same as last time, the same as every fucking time."

"Got it control," I lied. "You know how it is; sometimes you don't..."

"People do think, Tony," he said. "It's just you that don't."

"What's up? What's up?" I was trying to control the shake in my leg. "I mean, just because I..."

"You shithead, Tony. What are you? You're a fucking shithead."

Nick was enjoying himself. A hush had fallen over the channel. I knew they were holding off to listen, Don and Brian chuckling in their brand new cars, and he loved every minute of it.

"Beta 1-9. Where are you mate? Got a multi for you if you can handle it. Over."

"Is that my job you're dishing out? To a fucking van?"

"Fuck you, Tony." Nick coughed, a dry chuckle. "You're off."

"What do you mean, I'm off? What about the multi?"

"No way, prick. You're off. Now clear the fucking channel."

Three

It was like throwing your bike up the road only to remember tarmac doesn't have a lot of give in it: there's that long, sickening glass moment when you're into a tankslapper, your front wheel's skated away and you know you've really lost it; there's a millisecond before impact, and when, after free flight, the big crunch finally comes, it's a relief. Only that, only a graze, only a twisted ankle, only a—uh-oh. But bent forks can always be straightened, can't they, and bent arms put in a sling, and for the time being you don't give a shit what the damage is, what it's going to cost, or even whether the fucking bike will ever run again.

Best thing is to climb straight back on, if you can; I was breathing hard, suffocating, struggling for a last breath. I tried hard to get a grip on myself. So Nick had unplugged me. Fucking wanker. But so what? It wasn't as if I didn't know that's all he was. There was that special way he always had, of pushing his sleeves up to show off his crummy tattoos. But I had to be philosophical about it. I had no choice in the matter. I had to think of this as yet another stage in the long slow painful downfall of Don and Brian Nello. I hoped so, I really did.

On Thursday morning I went straight out and bought myself the first edition of The Standard. Yes, yes ... of course there were plenty of ads for couriers, loads more jobs where that one came from; one-liners, two-liners, two-column display ads that promised company bikes and guaranteed minimums to your fast, experienced riders. Swallows had one of them. Swallows. Staffed by Amazons. Tent supplied. Heading south for the winter. Huddling under a single hurricane lamp. No time wasters, it said, which I immediately took to refer to me. Yeah, fuck Swallows. I tracked further down the column of microprint:

FORWARDING AGENTS. "Tomorrow's news today." Riders wanted. Own machine. Beginners welcome. Call now for immediate start.

Name was slightly familiar, but I couldn't place it. Let's face it, there are only so many possible names for courier firms.

Once you've run through Greek mythology, the kingdom of the animals and the Wild West you have to start using what people like to call their imaginations—even if RIDING HIGH WITH TRIPS turns out to be your best, your most confidence-inspiring stab at nomenclature. I counted the rings, going over and over what I wanted to say until simple words broke down into particles, articles, fragments of out-and-out nonsense—and a croaky female voice answered me right away on the seventh bird warble.

"I called about the job. You're looking for riders?"

"If you're good we need you. If you've got a bike and an A-Z we need you. Can you come in this afternoon?"

"I can come in now, if you like."

"Make it lunchtime. Bring your documents and ask for Barbara."

"Okay Barbara."

The office was above a burnt out butcher's shop on Kentish Town Road. I rang the top bell—still faintly marked with the name of another—gone, defunct—courier firm, fought my way up scorched stairs through a smell of charred flesh to where a mound of air freshener cans had been abandoned, empty, by the top step. There was some difficult to pin down but indissolubly forged link between courier offices and burnt meat.

It was a little outfit run by a bloke named Bill Nicholls, a rider himself at one time, although he hadn't sat on a bike for years. Bill still had the old scraggy biker beard and his hair fitted on his skull as though he'd just taken off a sweaty helmet; and he drove a filthy old Volvo Estate between the Camden branch and the Croydon one, humming little bird snatches of classical music, looking worried. The tattoos on his arms and hands had turned into illegible graffiti a long time ago—you couldn't tell his axe from his anchor. I suspected his moorings had parted with them years ago.

My new controller was a young Arab, a sharpish dresser who proudly admitted that he only knew London from maps. His name was Araf. Naturally everyone called him Alf—or so I thought till I learned different and started to discern the gobbled middle syllable, and by that time it was too late to change what I called him. Alf possessed quiet authority. Whatever that is. Authority: quiet or noisy, shy or loquacious. Where does it come from? Who hands it out? Who says? Having none myself, I'd often wondered, but came up with no decent answers. Intelligence? What's that? I used to think I had it; but I was obviously wrong. Knowledge? Of what? And who'll be the judge of it? Wondering what new piece of smart-arsery I could pass off as pith, that was me. Authority of position, coerced. Or famous so-called natural authority: devious power-tripping of false-wise second-guessers, discerned by the credulous in the cut of their cloth or the turn of a phrase, generally someone else's. Universal jockeying for position, in families, in every group—for Power, or perceived Power—and, once attained, it was always consented to. Refuse to pay the bearer and invariably he tries to kill you, if you don't heed the first warning shot or two, if you don't have the common good sense to back down.

Alf transmitted this quiet authority to all and sundry through the mouthpiece of an old black telephone taped to the neck of a broken anglepoise lamp, inspiring the boy racers to take suicidal risks for monkey nuts.

"You was winding me up like a rubber band last week," one of them said to him. "Still, I was twenty at the weekend, so I thought, fuck it, if you die you die."

Alf sipped at his bottle of non-alcoholic Kaliber.

But he stood for a lot on my score. Truth is, I wasn't as good as I'd said I was. Not that I'd lied of course. You can ride around this city for years and think you know it, but really you're just running on a complicated track between familiar accounts.

They were familiar, whatever Nick had pretended to think. Even in West One I missed the old drops and pick ups. I spent a lot of my time parked up in Berkeley Square, hoping that someone I knew would pull in; outside Ed's Easy Diner on Old Compton Street, remembering when it used to be a real Wimpy: streets empty of associations, full of a confusing strangeness, deprived of any order I'd learnt with Bob and Rudy. Alf handed me out jobs one by one—I did them and called in for more; streets I half-knew turned out to be not where I thought. Memory deceived me or went dead, and I banged around on a ghost train whose switches and scares no longer shrieked and lit up for me.

I'd found myself back down the bottom with the improvers: an improver who hadn't improved, scuffling for multis and taking all afternoon to get round them; from that angle I cast a fresh eye over my fellow riders, the loners in worn racing leathers and the green and white squadrons who came to rest on Holborn Viaduct—the pensioners who rode the underground with their half-price travelcards and ancient A–Zs from where whole big streets and areas seemed to be missing when they came up to you and asked you for directions—and for a brief, lit up moment, you too could be an authority—and that must be why so many people always handed out such bad advice.

Learners were buzzing across three lanes, doomed insects, buccaneers of buzz—one grinning as he danced out in front of a white Mercedes on Marble Arch and £500 worth of pressed steel wing crumped behind him; and a kid on a 250 trials bike in a torn anorak had FAST AS FUCK scrawled on his bag in black marker and BLOOD GROUP O POSITIVE dyno-typed across the back of his helmet. This one stood upright in the saddle, as if he was about to climb over someone's bonnet, and as the cars parted for him like the Red Sea twelve tribes couriers came trickling after him through gaps he'd made in the waves of heated up bright metal.

Rain was coming down steady most of the time; you couldn't even see through a visor, had to put up with constant needle massage to avoid the tracks of spilt diesel that wove under your front wheel, slopping from overfilled cabs and buses, glistening like slug trails. Clouds of steam poured up over your tank. Time for a pit stop. Time for a Picnic. Time to turn in those intermediates for full wets; and you kept every part of yourself that wasn't in direct use battened down, tipping brown liquid through the crash hat slot between your drops—shaking, shivering and congratulating yourself on surviving another lap on hell's endurance circuit; on the Bol d'Enfer.

I'd lost confidence in a big way. I'd started to hesitate when pulling out onto Park Lane, where none of the basic rules apply and affable van drivers will try to wipe you along the side of the

Transit (one less bastard clogging up the roads) and three lanes of jockeying maniacs simultaneously putting their boot hard down at the sight of an empty carriageway; on Parliament Square some joker nudged my back wheel to force me out onto the roundabout. I twisted in the saddle to give him a mouthful and saw it was an African with diplomatic plates—pulled away sharply but he came up on the inside, gleefully trying to run me down, to squeeze a bit of fun out of his immunity—if I so much as marked his motor he'd jump out, pour petrol over me, strike a match; and there I'd be, one more human torch staggering between the giant statues of Gladstone and Churchill, one more human sacrifice.

I'm sitting at the lights in Wigmore Street with half London running down my face (which half?) when a spindly, careworn man in white raincoat, cord flares steps out of the pavement ruck and pushes a leaflet under my glove. He stood there for a minute but when I looked back at him he ran off. I stared down at what he'd given me and the rest of the whole world took off on amber, ground past my warm ears.

There was a blue tombstone printed on a red background. Black daffodils were growing around an untended grave:

TOO LATE

said the heavy capitals across the top; carved on the stone:

I EXPECTED THIS—BUT NOT YET.

I tore it open and read the page:

Why doesn't the man of the world give a place in his thoughts to the GREATEST THING in the world? In boyhood he is TOO MERRY. In youth he is TOO BUSY. When manhood arrives he is TOO PREOCCUPIED and in his declining years he feels TOO OLD. On his deathbed he is TOO ILL. In death he is TOO LATE.

I skipped to the end hoping to find out what the Greatest Thing In The World was all about. St Paul on the nature of love. But it was where I fitted into the story that occupied my wavering attention as rivers of cars flowed past me: I was in the prime of manhood; and in the long evenings I tried to go through the day sheets and remember where I'd been and what I was doing, floods of half-made-up and true scenes acting themselves out in front of me, one after one, again and again, until I was reworking the whole day on my own time.

An ad agency in Clerkenwell; the lift was out-of-order and you picked your way across discarded planks and plastering tools, climbed four flights of stairs, arrived in a deep pile office where barefooted secretaries padded around desks littered by glasses of flat champagne. I picked up every night at six. "Comtech?" I'd say—and they'd pass me on down the great chain of command, and a junior junior enough to suffer an interrupted call unwrinkled her nose and stuffed the contents of an out tray into a brown envelope. I battled on my unsweet way down to a tower off Marylebone Lane, arriving thirty seconds before lights out.

Its top floor was populated by middle-aged men in pushed up shirtsleeves sweating from nicotine withdrawal, gasping for a gasper; they burst out into a partitioned reception area and thrust a jiffy into your hand and you waited for the lift to clank up from the pit and then they rushed out after you to add another item to the packet. They sent typesetting out to a small printer's in Hackney, Silesia Buildings. Their workshop seemed to be the only inhabited building in a square of warehouses, gutted tenement blocks. I cruised towards it over broken glass, eyeing three young dogs that fought in the road as a sort of gypsy in a thin suit and muffler appeared from nowhere and whistled them off. Somebody else's territory—a group of vans behind a wire fence on a lot strewn with half-bricks, rusty tyres and burning rocks; children played in near-rags: giant boys in knee-length shorts; girls in cotton frocks rolling up balls of play-wool from their own unravelling cardigans, playing hopscotch with real pebbles, their treasures, chanting riddles in a made-up tongue. A German Shepherd hurled itself against the wire, went berserk, and slunk back into an upended gearbox crate to which it was chained; a dog that really ought to be set on me.

But it wasn't till later I thought of these three places as linked—of myself moving between them, going down through even shabbier and more defective worlds and right adjacent to it, right to the bottom of the tip, where malign warriors melted out the walls and the trapdoors were poorly marked, like one-way streets in the A-Z. I plumbed depths below which further, furthest depths still opened up: places I'd guessed existed but didn't want to know about—of myriad creatures in the peopled grass, of the river slime; and when I woke up on the couch the day sheets were fallen from my hands. I'd been dreaming. Dreaming hard. In my dream I'd been trying hard to kill myself by throwing knives into the air and running underneath them.

Could I sleep? Could I fuck. Thinking, of all things, about the way Rudy didn't seem to care for anyone or anything except himself, and yet how that wasn't really true. I folded my pillow in half, propped my head, reached for the cigarettes, and sparked one up. I wondered what had really been going on the first night Bob brought back a girl he'd just met: a receptionist on *Girl About Town*, doing research for an article that was to be called 'Courierism': dictating his memoirs to her as they came in the door, telling her about the time he'd once flashed, in a conversation with James Railio, that this crazy world was nothing but the dream of some vast intelligent life-form floating endlessly through time and space.

This young woman was holding a pristine junior reporters notebook, but I noticed that she was only pretending to write in it. We looked up from the fish and chips on our laps, Rudy walked over to the TV, silenced Mork, then offered her his chips—and she darted forward, bird-like, to take a hold of one.

"Rosie." She offered a greasy hand, unsmiling, regarding him intently as if she was expecting some card-like behaviour to ensue—but she was good-humoured, a good sort just the same.

"Don't worry about Bob," Rudy drawled. "He's a very very good friend of mine."

I was supposed to be a better friend, but I thought she must've been crazy to come back home with him. What did I know? I'd never picked up a woman in my life, and as the charm bled into Rudy's mouth, Bob and me stood and stared at him:

a pair of moronic apprentices at the arts of seduction, which seemed amazingly to work.

"How about if we go round the corner for a drink?" Rudy rubbed his hands together. "Maybe a pint or two'll get this lot talking."

Rosie nodded, keen.

"Not me." Bob was flicking the pages of a closed book with his thumb. "I've got a few things to get on with."

That was that—the Rudy touch. They didn't come back that night nor did they the night after, but the day after Rudy and Rosie reappeared together, and then they spent lot of time around the flat. We'd watch TV together until about nine, then, by a pared down signal, Rudy and Rosie would disappear into the master bedroom.

Remembering, I ground out my fag in a bedside ashtray and lit up another. It took a lot to budge the tolerance I generally felt for anybody who was passing me a lot of joints; I was still apologising for him, but that's what happened. I didn't like Rudy much, not anymore. Although the stupid thing was Bob didn't seem bothered in the slightest. So what did Rudy care about? He cared about Rosie, maybe. He definitely cared about Stig.

They couldn't stand the sight of each other. She was a nice girl, all right; she tried, but every time she smiled at him Stig ran away and hid his face from her in his room. I started to feel sorry for her. Mostly she kept quiet. The rest of us had skating conversations about nothing, and the fragile easiness that can make a flat fun to live in fell apart around us. Rudy could really piss you off sometimes, but at others he might come up with what passed for a masterstroke, like producing a pack of playing cards. Am I boring you? Sorry. We played rummy and whist and some version of sevens I could never get the hang of, then we switched over to poker for pennies and so began a new era: The Age of Games.

Stig turned out to be a reasonable poker player—his dead face was impossible to read. In the beginning he'd keep his head down, mumbling his bids; but as his new confidence started to grow, he lifted his eyes and began to scan us coolly. Really, it took off from there. All what? All it. Rudy just walked into the flat one evening with a shiny cardboard box under his arm. I thought it was going to be another jigsaw, but I was wrong. He tore off the brown paper and showed us the lid: it portrayed a helmeted warrior with mighty thighs; and a double-edged sword, which he waved in the face of a dwarfish creature with pointed ears. Printed across this was the power-word of the game: RUNERUNNERS.

*　　　*　　　*

White exhaust was pumping onto High Holborn from the arsehole of a bus. Outside the red terracotta Prudential Building a phone rang in an empty box—a succession of wide-shouldered women glanced at it and hurried on to work; a cycle courier clicked by in a matt black tin helmet stencilled ARP—and I, I bought a nice fresh bacon and egg bap from the Wimpy and ate it at a pavement table. It tasted good. My radio was reeling out lengths of noisy silence: someone was holding a button down somewhere but didn't know what to say. Croydon control had started handing out the first multi; I turned him down and looked at my watch, called in to Alf and told him where I was—sated, almost, and ready to work.

"Roger, 2-7. Park up. We've got a slow start this morning."

I forced myself to idle, to dismiss the fear of being starved. You want the parish hall, the parish hall, the parish hall, said the Croydon controller. I turned him down and tuned into the three Moves riders sitting at the next table, talking about different brands of crash hat while two doors down a glazier's van pulled up and a bloke hopped lightly out of the passenger seat wearing a nail pouch and a T-shirt that read MENTAL BLOCK. This van had a sheet of glass strapped to its side, doubling the width of the pavement, creating an arcade that a young black girl immediately trotted down, checking out herself, deciding she still looked eminently shaggable, as DON'T MISS IT, TDK IT slid out from the far edge of her mirror world on the side of a passing cab.

"Mega-offensive," one of the Moves riders said. "I must be getting old." He tilted his small, bloated head back and laughed—enthusiastically slapping his leather gut in self-congratulation as a street cleaner knelt at my feet, to free a drift of stuck Wimpy wrappers from the green plastic base of the table. I retracted my legs, swept my wrappers into his bin, spilt my coffee on his arm, took gauntlets out of my helmet, stood up and moved off in the opposite direction to the first slight embarrassment of the day.

I'd tucked the bike away in the square at the bottom of Brooke Street. I crossed the road, glanced up at the Prudential Building—an intricate piece of unfired pottery, the sun flashing above it between wispy cirrus. A young rider was sitting on his helmet against the wall, lifting his face to the warmth; his eyes sprang open like a wary doll's as he tilted his head toward the flame of his Zippo. I looked back towards the Moves riders, helmeted up and lumbering off towards their gleaming company bikes; to where an assortment of vehicles were crawling around Holborn Circus, an animated flow-diagram of traffic; stock footage—and I walked slowly away from it.

Outside the Church of St Alban the Martyr birdsong was drifting from trees shading a phone box and a bench. I turned my radio down, listened to the rustle of the leaves that could be heard so amazingly close to that hammering racket, my own eyes resting for a moment on the torso of a young black guy who was putting up scaffold next to the church. He kicked forward his yellow hat, pouted, and I flicked on the ignition and tried the lights. I remembered that the bulb had blown on Friday afternoon.

"Alpha 2-7. Still with us?"

I fumbled the volume up, lifted the front of the radio to my mouth. The black guy was still staring at me, maybe because I was looking at him like something in a film—he looked as though he was actually about to come over. Tell me to piss off? Ask me for a date?

"Roger, Tony. I've got a 13-drop multi for you. It's 3 in the Temple, 6 West Ones and 4 south of the river. Reckon you can knock 'em out by lunchtime?"

So I looped across High Holborn, gave her a good handful down Grays Inn Road, turning into a backed up snarl-queue trying to get over Farringdon river into Clerkenwell: a thickset van driver had picked up a young barrister by his black silk lapels and was dragging him into the road, while his companion—a man in a similar coat—looked on, wondering whether or not to intervene, deciding against. I rolled on past like a kid with a shopping list, eager to pick up every last item and take them speedily home to mum.

But when I'd picked up for the Temple I stopped at the bike garage in Old Street. The mechanic had a battered CX500 on the ramp, frowning in concentration as he tried to remember the order he'd taken it apart in and I broke in on him to ask if he knew what bulb I needed, couldn't remember it offhand. I tend to expect every mechanics to know everything. He peered up through a curtain of corkscrew hair, saying:

"The very brightest one you can possibly get."

As if by a miracle they actually had one, I fitted it successfully and got off on full beam—and against the odds it turned out to be a dream job, the routes clicking out like teletext on my synapses; some great signalman in the sky moving levers as I dished out packets like a mechanical packet-dispenser, diving back into the protective traffic, like a silver fish running between rocks: my connections piled up; but there I was—totally on top of them; I could do anything, go anywhere. I thought once again about zigzagging back and forth across the eight bridges (one over, always) and—with a sharp needle and a bowden thread—stitching up a five mile gash from Battersea to Blackfriars.

It was good to feel good for a change, but then I had to go home and remember what my real life was like: I didn't really have one. The neighbours' dog still yapped when it heard me on the landing. That packet I'd delivered over there could've been full of used fivers for all I knew—and that was the end of the road for the lost boy of whom so much had been expected back at moon base. Even the police had given up on me. Perhaps they thought I was too much of a loser even to be a bad thief. Like everyone, I wanted to think of myself as a survivor, looking back on this from a fireside chair somewhere. Wanted to actually be one. I wanted to work on that, but I couldn't let go of Bob and Rudy. All that stuff kept on swimming up out of the murk; because I was feeding it, probably, and for the lack of any better ideas I cruised over to Twickenham one night, and looked up to see if any lights were still burning on the third floor, which they were, and brighter than I remembered.

I rang the bell. A slim young woman in a wool dress came clacking downstairs and opened the door. She was wearing thick glasses; behind them her tiny little eyes blinked under a lot of mascara.

"Yes?" she said, arching her eyebrows. "Can I help you?" She tipped her head on one side.

The light from the stairs was haloing her body. I couldn't remember what the point of ringing had been. "Er ... maybe." I pulled at the popper on my chinstrap and took off my helmet, standing with it over my arm. "There were a couple of friends of mine used to live here," I said. "I wondered if they left any forwarding address?"

She tapped her teeth with a forefinger. Still sound for the time being. "Well, we've been here about eighteen months now ... before that it was, er, let me think, Eileen and ... oh, they weren't bikers by any chance were they?"

"That's right," I said, and gave their names, which sounded falsely in my mouth, like the names of book-characters I was making up on the spot.

"Yes," she said, "or rather ... no. They didn't leave an address as far as I know, but some letters came for them." She looked me over, frowned, decided I was relatively-speaking harmless. "Come in for a minute. I'll look them out for you."

I followed her upstairs. I liked her dress. "If you ever find them," she said over her shoulder, "tell them it's about time they grew up. The state this place was in—it was disgusting when we moved in."

"They were never too domesticated."

"You're not kidding. Their bloody mothers want shooting."

I laughed. "I used to live here too," I said, "oh, years and years ago."

She showed me into the sitting room, told me where to sit myself down while she tried to find a box of stuff she'd seen in the hall cupboard. I perched on the edge of a chair and remembered how the room used to be. The walls had been freshened up, of course, and the furniture exchanged for stuff about the same age, but which somehow managed to look good. The room's centre of gravity had risen from the floor to about knee height. A wooden lamp with a glass bowl cast soft light from one corner of the room—a paper and a couple of magazines were lying on a glass-topped coffee table.

I picked up a folded copy of the *Mailed Fist* and tried to tease a teasel of cheese from a page of waffle written by a columnist I used to like. No joy. She'd become a strident advocate of home ownership. I was reaching for *Harpers and Queen* when Fiona reappeared and thrust a bundle of scuffed envelopes at me. "Here," she said, "you might as well take these."

"I'm not sure I should," I told her. "I haven't seen any of them for years. I probably never will again—"

"It's entirely up to you." She exhaled in mild annoyance. "They'll only get thrown out if you don't."

I nodded. She thrust them into my hand. Most looked like circulars, and there was a large fat manila envelope, but the rest were bank statements addressed to a Mr Omega and to Dr James Railio.

"Have you come a long way?" she asked. "I was just putting the kettle on; stay for coffee, if you like."

"Just up the road," I said. "Thanks, but I should really—" I stumbled into an explanation "—we used to be quite good friends, you see, but we lost touch years ago and I thought..."

"Fine," she said, "why don't you leave a number or an address, in case they do pop by?"

"Right." I stood up while she went to find a pen and paper. When she got back I wrote down my name and number carefully and thanked her for her trouble.

"That's okay," she said, "no trouble. By the way, my name's Fiona."

"Tony," I said, edging my way downstairs to the front door.

I hadn't wanted to take it really. After all, I had no idea how to reach any of the old crowd. I wondered how you went about tracking somebody down; and alone again in the light from the carpet shop I riffled through the envelopes like a wad of notes, stuffing them deep into the pocket of my Bellstaff and buttoning it down, as if they were alive and might try to escape. I rode home with special care in case death should try and cheat me of their contents.

Indoors I took my coat and gloves off and made myself comfortable, lighting a cigarette, squirming, putting it down—getting up to switch the overhead light off, I looked through each in turn in a white pool from an old desk lamp the cops had found for me in the hall cupboard.

There was some junk mail for Mark Stigwood. I opened that first. Reader's Digest and American Express. Both missed Stig by a mile. Next I pulled out the bank statements.

Mr O had £5.57. The figure repeated itself down the page at monthly intervals for a six month period two years ago. I opened the other envelope. Railio's was a recent statement for an account in which the cash deposits settled in small, erratic bird-flurries; a varied larger sum blipped in at longer gaps, a low persistent heartbeat gobbled up by life's three standing orders: rent, a loan, and another loan: it looked like the account of a despatch rider.

Then there was the fat brown envelope addressed to Bob. I felt it. I couldn't bring myself to tear it open. I rode home slowly in case death should try to cheat me out of its contents.

Four

Cycle-couriers took off that year. They were everywhere, vibrating with health and good-looks, slipping in and out of the traffic on Piccadilly, labouring up Albemarle Street and sitting in the gutters of the City with their Ray-Bans pushed up and flipping through brand new Nicholson's Streetfinders. The Lost Boys, someone christened them, and it spread around fast among the couriers before ending up in the vox pop graveyard of an *About Town* column and a straw-poll of cafe pundits revealed that motorcycle despatch riders were still the cream of the crop and would continue to exist on a higher plane—for the time being.

Turnover was high, it always was high. Hardly a week went by at ABC without a few broken limbs across the branches— some foolish virgin leaving half his face on the road or writing off a brand new pride-and-joy iron. Another Perfect Opportunity for the death stories to be told again: a rider who approached the Westway flyover too fast to be blasted over the edge by side-wind; a bloke who slid neatly under the front wheels of a Range Rover; a black rider who ran up the back of someone at ten miles an hour. Poor old smoky sailed over the front forks, caught his head at an awkward angle, and snapped his neck like a twig on a Porsche's rear bumper.

The Lost Boys weren't any safer, but they hadn't yet found that out. They pumped around on those bikes as if they were immortal; just as the city runners had passed their jobs on down from father to son, so it was told, and the gone armies of copy clerks had just been common or garden plagiarists—and those systems of pneumatic tubes they used to have in department stores for noiselessly sliding around glass capsules containing money and orders, managing to resemble the vehicles in the glass city at the beginning of Space Patrol … whatever happened to them? It was all history, history; whether you brought it back to the present or left it where it was in the mud of your spent days, where it probably belonged anyway.

I seem to recall that Moorcock's Eternal Champion changed sides at the last moment—he laid waste to warlike Humanity as well as to the beautiful Eldren. But our champions, though often recalled from Valhalla by those whose era they defined, were actually only the stars of a few short seasons: Giacomo Agostini faded out in the mid-seventies, passing the MV Agusta baton on to Phil Read and to Barry Sheene's Suzuki; to "Rocket" Ron Haslam, the British people's champion who had never really won anything, not even a Grand Prix—and for a while the Italians Marco Luccinelli and Franco Uncini had held sway, gradually supplanted by epic battles between Wayne Gardner— first motorcycle champion to employ a professional sports psychologist—and the shining magnificence of Wayne Rainey.

Kenny Roberts won the world championship three times. Well-groomed, ginger-haired and born again Fast Freddie Spencer took it off him: quickly declining into Fat Freddie, whereupon he lost to steady Eddie—Eddie Lawson—but not before he'd won the 250 and 500cc championships in the same season, whatever year that was, and Wayne Rainey paid a heavy price for those knee-scraping dust ups with his childhood antagonist, Kevin Schwantz; battles for supremacy which took over their lives, propelled them to the top.

"You see God and you back off," the Texas Rodeo dirt-tracker Schwantz said after out-braking him and he was soon paralysed for life in a high-speed smash while leading the world.

It fell apart for me after that. I could barely call back the names of the great Superbike champions—Fred Merkel, Virginio Ferrari, Doug Polen. Freddie Spencer Jr had ditched his father's legacy, switched to the Suzuki and won the laurels on his own. Remembering them, it was only Foggy who hung on—his laser-stare, his small wired-up body crackling with aggression as he crawled over the bike; Foggy was only one rider though and sunlight gleamed equally on all the paladins of Necranal and Mernadin—their strange mask-like helmets resembling the faces of beasts, standards bearing the names of chain lubricants, dark gauntlets of dream-light.

I dropped off a film at a preview screen in Dean Street where a Brummie in a ginger toupee and a tonic suit signed the docket. I looked down at his chunky wristwatch: time for a break, time for a Kit-Kat. I had a pick up in Grafton Street before lunch, so I headed over to Mayfair and parked on the blind chicane corner of Berkeley Square. I'd been buzzing non-stop since eight and I was totally knackered. I closed my eyes, letting the beat lull me as it raced up to the bend and changed down, heels of too many secretaries scratching across the zebra crossing, bright snatches of their talk jumping out of the roar, the muddy megamix, the day being overcast and mugginess its order: the growl of tired tigers after non-enticing prey.

Pointless. Jointless. I flopped back and started to slide into another warm drifting gusset fantasy when, awoken by a gloved hand tapping on my horn, I swung myself upright and saw a small rider in a Swallows bib. In a blink I was standing over him with the standard greeting: "What's your fucking problem, mate?"

"I know who you are," said a surprising voice. "I know exactly, so don't give me any of that shit."

"Look—"

"I was delivering at one of those tower blocks over in Acton and you came out of the lift—remember? " I remembered. It was that crab-girl. She pulled her helmet off and shook out a longish, mousy-brown grow-wig of hair-stuff.

"I remember that." I tried to look her in the eye, bent down to flick a dead leaf off the toe of my boot, glanced up at her. "I thought you were a man." I didn't know what else to say. Stupid.

"Thanks," she said.

"I live there, in that tower."

"You did have a key in your hand."

Her face was pinched, raw-looking. "It was the XS750 I remembered. I heard there's not many of them still running."

"I've been around the clock on this one." I took a deep breath. "Busy at Swallows, are you?"

"So-so." She shrugged her narrow shoulders. "I wanted to ask you about something. okay?"

"What?"

"The police lifted one of our riders, a friend of mine, for a break-in a few weeks back. We heard they pulled someone from ABC. I thought it might've been you, for some reason." She smiled, knowing she could get away with anything, the way they do.

"I don't work for ABC."

"But you did—did you not?"

I gave a quick nod.

"So, did they pull you in?"

"Yeah, they did. But I don't see what—"

"Marie." She pulled off her glove and stuck out her hand. Her hand was thin, clammy. The contact hit me with a sudden jolt. "How's tricks," she asked. "Would you have robbed any pensioners lately?"

"Oh, fuck off. Just fuck off." I swung my leg across the Yamaha and reached for the ignition. "All right, where's my -"

She tossed the bunch of keys into the air and caught them. I swiped and missed. She tossed them back, laughed. "Sorry, I shouldn't have said that."

"You want to be careful," I said, trying to jam the key into the slot, "Not everyone's as—"

"Go, if you want," she said, "if you don't want to know what's going on."

I hesitated.

"Come over the road where we can talk properly."

I followed her over the zebra crossing; into the green shade where everything was suddenly less urgent, less serious. She walked for some way down the middle path and sat on an empty bench. I could see her inhaling, ready to start up again.

"Reverend Poore's an account customer of ours. He pulled a friend of mine out of a police line up. You were there, were you not?"

"I was," I said.

"I did a cash job for this old man; the same drop you did. That's all I knew about it."

Her face tightened again; she squinted. "I hope you're not lying. Don's got other friends, you know."

"What?" I said. "What did you say?"

"Wise up," she snorted. "They're not bothered, now they've got Don. And Don's..."

Her voice trailed away. I was staring at a statue of a naked water-nymph, couldn't see if she was trying to cover herself or just drying her legs. On the grass a couple of large men walking another man's dog, pretending to be interested in what one another were saying. Office workers began filtering into the square, sitting on benches, pulling out sandwiches and apples.

"Anyway," she said, "he wouldn't do anything like that."

"Neither would I."

She sat next to me. I waited to hear threats, accusations. When they didn't start coming, I breathed a little deeper, and slower, happy to let her think she'd screwed up.

"What about the others," I said, "couldn't one of them?"

"No way, no way."

"I've got a pick up before one," I said, and then, I couldn't help it; "But I'll meet you later, if you think—if you want."

"Okay," she said, "that would be best. Do you know Mama Rosa's?"

"Old Compton Street?"

"Yeah. Six? Half past?"

"Make it half past." I smiled, but she'd stood up already and pulled on her helmet. I dawdled after her to the gate, watched her flat-foot it out of the square, jump on a Superdream with a rusty dent in the tank and shoot out ahead of a black cab. She lay the bike over and twisted up Bruton Street. I waited for a few seconds, let it sink in, and nosed out in the direction of my next pick up.

Rudy and the other two were after big money, gold circuit money. Through keeping an eye on them I'd learned that an easy way to keep the pace up was to surf around on a wave of mounting anger that led you to shout abuse at dithering office workers on their lunch hour, kick out at the doors of any cars taking liberties, and at all times to go for the gaps; and by the time they got back home they were wound up tight—there'd be half an hour's commentary from Rudy on the BASTARD who cut him up on the Westway, the FUCKING SLAG who kept him waiting in reception. We'd all had more or less the same sort of day, and after the first couple of joints ... blonggg ... vacancy, the forgetfulness of TV or familiar music; that was how it was before the game started up and a whole other world of fun opened up.

Rudy was the Runemaster, calculating probabilities, working out new scenarios in a series of thin red notebooks (one for each character) that took on the authority of sacred texts—The Books of Runeworld, as they were known. He carried them around with him all day, refusing to trust the others not to peek, and worked out the next evening's play between jobs with a special thinking biro he'd chewed down to half its original length, blackening the rule book with his big thumbprints. I watched their backs as they hunched over the table, speaking in low whispers and passing joints back and forth. Now and again one of them would look up and pass me a roach. At first I tried to watch TV, but that disturbed them, they said. I tried to read books but couldn't concentrate, listened to music on headphones until an earpiece shorted out. After that I'd come in and go straight to my room with a few cans of Holsten.

Bob and me soon got into a routine of meeting up in the C&W cafe at lunchtimes if we were both free. It wasn't exactly an arrangement, but I always looked out for him: we tended to run into one another a couple of times a week. One summer afternoon we saw a fight in the road outside, which, looking back on it, was the first link in a chain of events that made me realise I was going to have to move out of there. The It, the Whasname, the How's Your Father—our words for traffic failed to match those of the Inuit for their snowy habitat, either in reputed beauty or quantity—slipped down Shaftesbury Ave like lard sliding across the surface of a burnt pan. Bob and me weren't saying much, not even looking at each other. We glanced back and forth between the street and the food on our plates. I watched as Mercury trickled down the white line on a 500 Kawasaki, dipped a crisp chip into the runny yolk of an egg; Bob stared away over my shoulder at the clouds of steam rising from a chrome coffee machine, whose operator, Plug, would far rather have been an engine driver.

There was a sudden crumpling bang outside and we both looked up to see the Mercury sliding along greasy Shaftesbury Avenue behind his bike. A faint cheer went up as he leapt instantly to his feet, pulled the bike upright and kicked out the stand. The Escort's driver just sat there: people behind him leant on their horns, and this Escort cheekily flashed his lights, as if to say—you're all right, now get out of my fucking way.

The Mercury walked back and tapped on the Escort's offside window with his finger. Beckoned him to get out of his motor. We couldn't hear what he was shouting. But it was all too easy to fill in the blanks as pedestrians slowed down on both pavements and a bunch of riders who'd collected on the doorway of the C&W began to stir and wisely shake their heads. The Mercury hammered on the Escort driver's wound up window with his gloved fist. The bloke just would not get out, wouldn't wind his window down. I didn't blame him. Mercury was kicking in the driver's door panel by now, in between staggering around like a demented puppet and screaming abuse at the top of his lungs.

"Jesus Christ." Bob screwed up his eyes and looked away. The driver got out—a stringy little bantam-weight black guy in a dark suit—immediately put his fists up and started springing on the balls of his feet, sparring. This took The Mercury aback. The Escort's driver went straight for his head, took aim through his helmet slot and connected with three swift right-handed jabs.

They broke and the spectators closed in, egging them on, shouting the odds. "Come on," I said, "let's fuck off out of here."

Bob felt exactly the same way. He was out of the door before I'd picked up my helmet and I followed him down through the stalled traffic and he just kept going, heading south; Knightsbridge, Chelsea, Fulham, up Putney Hill, out onto the A3. It only seemed to take a few minutes then we really opened up, chasing one another through the suburbs as the empty brown fields fell away on either side. Bob dipped off down a familiar exit and we were twisting along the lanes of Surrey. He stopped by a stile over a bridge, and when we killed our motors the silence was absolute for a moment. I pulled off my sweaty helmet, the birdsong came in, and a low overhead jet slowing down for Gatwick. It was a hot day in the country; everything was as calm and as still as in the aftermath of a murder.

We left the bikes parked at the end of a lay-by, crossed the stile, sweltering in boots and leathers. Bob led the way down a ferny path beside a small, fast-flowing river and I followed. He'd been here in a before and we were far away from the road and nothing in sight except a scattering of honey-coloured houses at the edge of a housing estate screened off by narrow-slat fence and poplar trees. The weed-strewn river and a high overgrown brick wall on the far bank screened an estate of a different sort.

"Let's swim." Bob sat on the riverbank, pulled off his boots and pushed his jeans and leggings down in a swift movement. He pulled his leather over his head and it was so startling somehow to see his smooth body appear out of that lumpy gear as he eased himself into the water over the muddy bank and launched himself out into centre-stream—and stood up suddenly as the water-foam broke like sort of natural soap around his bare chest.

I waited for him to start swimming, then followed him, sneaking off my clothes like a shy kid, and we splashed around for a bit, swam a few strokes, dived for each other, our bodies brushing as we swerved from contact, like cavorting dolphins.

"Over there!" Bob shouted and pointed out to the far bank. I plunged after him, the current sucked me downstream a yard or two—and when I stroked at the mud-bottom I stayed on course by slimy tiptoes till Bob spied the root of a fallen tree upstream. We made for that and scrabbled up the sheer clay of the opposite bank. He was strong, but I was weak with a nagging womanish worry that he might get hurt—almost a hope, as the usually cocky bastard self of him he pulled up over twisted spikes, tugged a fat tap root, trusted his weight on it. He found a foothold and was swiftly up and over, pushed himself onto a far grassy bank with splayed frog legs he drew up after him: only then did he become fully human again.

"Come on, Tony."

"You must be joking!" I toppled into a splashy backstroke, kicking spray high in his direction.

"Come on!" Bob pointed to an old wooden door in the wall.

I waded over and he moved downstream towards me, knelt down and put out a hand, I grabbed his forearm and he pulled me up over the slimy mud. We were both caked in streaky clay. We grinned at each other like wolves and approached the door of powdery scabs of white paint overgrown with purple flowerings of dead and grown over again ivy. Bob squeezed the rusty latch;

its hinges squealed as we pushed our way in and onto a rolling coverless lawn.

A great house rose up at the far end of it. There were a couple of tennis courts on one side of it and we lay flat on the grass, listening to the faint popping of the returns from afar, watching the distant white smudges of two women players stretched up to serve, darting from side to side, stooped, hands on irritated hips, to retrieve their missed balls. The sun was baking mud onto my back: I could feel it stretching my skin over me drum-tight.

"Let's get closer," said Bob.

But I didn't want to, really. We were stark bollock naked for a start and they made our naked bodies so childishly ... I wished they weren't there. I uninvented women. I wished we were alone, just the two of us. Anyone looks good from a hundred yards in a tennis skirt; but they were just the usual mother and daughter. I knew the sort. They weren't about to provide any refreshing glasses of Fanta. If they so much as caught sight of us they'd run off inside and call the law—rightly, quite rightly—and, anyway we weren't about to do anything too bad, too dramatic.

Bob was squirming over the lawn in a flat crawl. My stomach tightened. By now he was halfway between them and me. He dropped down onto the grass. The two women had stopped play, flicked towels back across their shoulders. High peals of their laughter reached back to us intermittently—a thin, fragile signal from another time, a good time. For their sort it still was, always would be, always. They left the court by a door in the fence and ambled towards the house. I scuttled over the lawn and dropped beside him. He was looking at me with a blank excited expression like a dog rubbing itself off against your leg. I pressed my forehead into the lawn—sweat streaming into my swollen eyes—my throat was parched ...

... I gasped, "So what are they like?"

"Both about seventeen," he said quietly. "One of them's got a really juicy little pair of tits on her."

"Come on, we're not going to do anything."

"They were both talking about it," Bob continued, "yours went and said uhhh ..."

Words had failed him. One of his eyes was wandering up bosky. He rolled onto his side and his cock sprang back against his body, like an arched bow. I gasped, reached out for it, then he was moving fast away, moving away over the scratchy grass-stalk lawn to the door leading back onto the sure safety of the riverbank. My skin was bumpy, inflamed. My cock scraped painfully on the ground, a blunted prong, a not-plough shrivelling back into me. I stood up and scuttled away, away to cross the last twenty yards to the river gap in the hairy wall and squeeze in through the straitest gate that led back into starry heaven.

Bob was already climbing out of the water. I lowered myself into the icy sluice, calmly breaststroked towards him and sneaked a look as he was drying himself on a pullover as I washed off the clay clinging to my bone-white body. As he got dressed I scrabbled through my clothes, waving my arms in front of me like antennae, my legs buckling underneath me. He stood straight up in his gear, made to go off without me, then he thought better of it and sat down to watch me get dressed with an idly appraising eye.

On the way back into town we stopped for a pint, partly because we had to cook up a story for Brian Nello—still a controller in those days—and we sat in a sullen silence over our almost empty second drinks as a man some years younger than us, sporting a beer gut and sweatshirt bearing the name of the forgotten pub, started to set up disco equipment around us.

"Look, this doesn't matter, really," I said. "It's just that I ..."

"Excuse me mate, can I run this behind you?"

"Oh sure ... sure." We stood up, our heads bowed. He quickly pushed our chairs aside and gaffer-taped a cable to the floor.

"Just a thought," I said when we'd sat down. "I thought ... why not?"

"Well, it seriously gets in the way of the bubble, that's why." Bob looked across at me openly, honestly. "I'm just definitely not into it, that's all."

He hadn't left me anything to say, anything except fair enough. "It's your loss," I said quietly—but I knew it was my loss really. I nodded slowly with him. Fuck it.

I parked up in Wardour Street and picked my way past the dossers who hung around outside the park in front of St Anne's

Church: a pair of rangy Scots stripped to the waist, sharing a bottle of cider with a black guy who wore a faun duffle coat and a plastic bag on his foot. The weather had turned close as the afternoon wore on and the smell stopped my breath like bleach in a steamy bathroom. I headed on into Old Compton Street and found myself on the tail of a six foot blonde in a microskirt, her bouncing long hair in a big fat ponytail. I tried to keep pace with her, to catch a glimpse of her face, but she turned left into a newsagents ten yards ahead, then a man wearing a dark blue suit brushed past her on his way out and the tall girl was instantly back on the street.

She took a running stride after the bloke and kicked him hard up the arse with the pointed toe of her thigh-length boot. "That's for you, twat."

The bloke spun around, white-knuckled at the wheel of a tan briefcase he swung up to protect himself. "But I didn't do anything!" He was appealing to a non-existent jury, to me. I looked into his eyes, into the eyes of the damned, and he tried in his turn to recognise me as a version of himself who hadn't yet been caught.

"Keep your hands to yourself next time." The woman glanced at me. "He touched me up. I don't have to put up with that, do I?" She turned away and went back into the international newspaper shop.

I followed him down towards Mama Rosa's. He was walking fast. He turned to see if anyone was behind as he fled from the scene. I looked back into his eyes, tried again to decide whether he was innocent or guilty, as he looked right back, accepting me as his judge. But I couldn't tell. What if he'd brushed against her accidentally? What if I had? Or what if she'd just been having a bad day? Nah. The little bastard thought he'd cop a free feel off what he thought was a peepshow girl; but even she thought she was better than the likes of him, and she was, and perhaps he'd even pestered her in the past.

"I didn't do anything." He squared off his innocent shoulders and shook his head as he pronounced the words, explaining it to mummy, then hurried on his way: a dead creature made of he knew not what substance, unable to bear the inner horror of his own face, and then I knew from that moment I'd never be able to tell what the truth was from looking into someone's eyes, only my own right-or-wrong prejudices or feeble innocent purchases in the trocadero of human reason.

Mama Rosa's was a nondescript sandwich bar during the hours of day, but by half six the last office workers and students were on the tube and now the only customers were those same girls between peep show shifts, a funny little loud-mouthed guy on crutches they seemed to have taken a shine to—and Mama Rosa herself, dressed in widow black and looking out into the busy street without a flicker of interest or pleasure in anything that was moving out there.

Marie turned up and joined me in a booth. She looked different somehow. Her face had settled down into a particular shape, a shape I liked.

"Coffee?"

"I'll get my own." She put her helmet on the bench and started to struggle out of her gear.

"I left mine in the top box," I said this for want of anything better to say.

"That's how you get it ripped off."

Smug, I thought. But right. The sort of thing Barbara would probably say. I didn't answer. I wanted to tell her about the man who'd been kicked up the arse, but I didn't know her well enough. She would automatically believe the woman, I suppose. But did I? I knew it would lead us automatically straight into deep water, instead I asked, "So—how long you been on this old game?"

"Eighteen months," she said. "It's okay. But I reckon I'll head off soon, when it gets a bit colder."

"Where to?"

"Oh, I don't know," she said. "Around and about." She looked away at a slice of varnished tree on which Mama Rosa or one of her sons had poker-worked THICK JUICY STEAKS. Another, in the next booth, had *cool it! with a salad* written in shaky gold modelling paint. "Have you eaten anything?"

"I've been eating all day."

Mama shuffled over with a couple of cappuccinos and scribbled the extra damage on my bill without asking.

"I'll give it to you outside." Marie picked up her cup.

She was about ten years younger than me. There was a nasty spot coming up on her chin and I tried hard not to look at it, not to imagine rooting around in it with a needle and a dab of cotton-wool. "Listen," I said, "about your friend. I'd like to help, if I can."

"What's it to you?"

"It could've been me, in a way, so easily."

"Could've been but wasn't." She stared hard at me, patted around her breasts with the palms of her hands, looking for cigarettes. I flicked my own across the table. She took one out and placed it beside her saucer. "Don's not a bad being, you know. Not as bad as he looks. But he's not the best at helping himself." She spooned some froth into her mouth. "I gave him a perfectly good alibi and he couldn't even get that straight."

I guessed what it was.

"To be honest, you were my last hope." She looked at me, lit the cigarette, made a sour face at the taste of the match. "I haven't a clue what to do next." She looked again. "But I expect I'll think of something."

"What about the old man? What's he up to exactly?"

"Up to?" She was surprised. "Running a charity, so far as I know. He probably even does a bit of good—a lot of good, so everyone says."

"Oh?"

"Right. Tools for Change. It's a charity. They collect up tools and send them out to the third world. Money too, but they use it to buy tools." She spoke fast and fluently, showing her open hands over the table's edge. "They sometimes use us for various things."

"What things?"

"Oh," she said. "I don't know. For example, he used us to send around a load of presentation bibles last Easter."

"Who to?"

"Volunteers, I suppose." She seemed to lose interest. "Oh well, I'm hungry. I think I'll head off round the corner to MacDonald's."

I stood up and waited while she gathered her stuff, then I paid and we were outside again. She seemed to want to get away from me, but I tagged along. "I'm doing a bit of detective work of my own," I called over her shoulder, "trying to trace some friends of mine."

She didn't reply; maybe she hadn't heard me. I tried to draw level, but that was nearly impossible in the slipstream of loiterers, and she kept her back to me. I caught up in the queue at Macdonald's, scanned the menu as we edged closer to an oriental girl with four gold stars, working like a small automaton for her fifth. Downstairs we perched on giant green baby furniture and put little bunches of salty fries into our mouths. She wasn't saying much. I read the sheets of nutritional information in the bottom of the tray, once, twice; wondered if I should make a quick exit back to the flat and try again to forget about the most stupid night of my life. I'd have to tell her everything. I knew I'd have to, sometime, someday. I pushed the words of confession down my throat with mouthfuls of Filet o' Fish.

I could always go back and knock myself out with a few cans of Holsten. I filed that as a contingency plan.

"Fancy a drink?" I asked as soon as she'd put away the last of her Big Mac.

She wiped her fingers on the napkin. "Tell you what I fancy, now."

"What's that?"

"A fillum," she said.

"Any film?"

"High Hopes."

Sitting next to her in the Lumiere I looked up at the big screen for the first time in a few years and watched scenes of my life flash by, a life I would've had if I'd had one, containing everything that might have defined me for someone who didn't know me. Most people. But I could see why she'd wanted to see it. I stole little glances at her, her feet up next to me on her helmet, fascinated, gone out of herself, lit up by the moving screen-light.

Film over, we headed back to Soho, parked up, and walked back around the corner into the Admiral Duncan. I hadn't been in there for ages, but they were still longer playing a tape of hits from the mid-seventies. The booths were awash. Towards the back, where I'd always liked it better, a floating population of drunks fought over a few odd-looking milking stools. We grabbed a couple. Sat on them.

"What did you think? Good?"

"Goodish."

"What about the man?"

"What man?"

"The despatch rider."

"Miserable pompous bastard."

"Do you think his girlfriend would've stayed with him in real life?"

"Yeah," she said, "she was even more stupid than him."

"Patronising, wasn't it."

"Pretentious, I'd call it."

"Patronising and pretentious."

"Both I'd say."

I drank the rest of my pint and put the glass down and felt the panic that had begun to grip me slip away. Marie was completely different in here; softer, more malleable. Or so I kidded myself. Finally she went up to the bar and forked out for a couple more drinks.

"What he should've done, right, was make the yuppies more sympathetic. The other two, as well. His sister, or whatever she was. That's what spoiled it for me."

"Then you would've believed in them." I hadn't seen it that way. I found them perfectly believable. Saw people like that every other day. I thought he should've shown them dying.

"Then you could've had the yuppies being kind to his mother," she went on, "and not really knowing they were driving her out of her home—or whatever."

"But they would have, they just wouldn't give a shit."

I didn't know if that would work. I hated yuppies.

"Yeah, but -"

"You think it would've worked better."

"I don't know. Maybe not. The whole thing was up the spout. The characters just didn't have any dimension."

"What about his sister? She was revolting."

"Misogynist crap so it was." Marie drained half her pint. "Her husband!"

"Unfair to men."

"Quite good."

"So where are you living?"

76

"With some friends," she hesitated, "in Brixton."

"Sounds okay."

"Oh, you know." Her gaze drifted down to the interlocking Olympic rings she was making on the table with the bottom of her glass.

I looked up at the rows of matchboxes from all over the world stuck in neat rows along the black-stained beams on the ceiling. "So where are you from, originally?"

"Ireland," she said. "Jesus, what a stupid question."

"What part?"

"Derry." She looked up suddenly, angrily. "County Derry."

I'd thought she was about to tell me something else, but seemed to have thought better of it. She swirled half an inch of beer in the bottom of her glass, puffed her cheeks and trumpeted a tune to herself, keeping the notes inside. I could tell she wanted to be away.

"Anyway," I said. "Better get back; I'm knackered for some reason." The trouble was, I thought, that I couldn't think of anything to say; anything I did think of came out of my mouth flat, dull, as if it hadn't really happened. If it had happened ... so what. "I'll give you my phone number, in case anything comes up."

"That would be handy," she said, "if anything does."

I scribbled it on a mat and passed it over. While she was looking at it I placed my hand over hers. But she took it away.

"Tony, can I be honest with you?"

"Of course you can."

"I don't really like you that much."

"Why's that?" I might have expected it.

"I don't know." She sighed. "There's something dodgy about you. You're not what you seem."

"I'm not that bad. I'm okay."

She smiled, oh yeah. So that was the end of that. We walked together back to our bikes. The lights were on now and the street was full of lurching European kids, out of town drunks with wet hair and sweat pouring off them; each one of them looking for an open door, for Heels Of A Hell Cat. I threaded after her through kid-crowds slipping past my shoulders, solitary drunk drivers half-asleep at the wheels of their indestructible bodies.

She was still one of them, she thought. Compact, self-possessed. I found it difficult to keep her small darting form steady in my viewfinder; I let her go.

Five

After that I often saw her idling, sidling past the ends of one-way streets, collapsing to a mathematical point as she twisted away in the dog rain; flat on her tank in the death lane of the North Circular, blipping at lights in Great Portland Street. One time I drew alongside her and watched as a wind tear coursed down her cheek; I beeped and waved, beeped. Her face got tenser for a moment but failed to turn my way. I daydreamed finding her bike parked up on the edge of Hampstead Heath, Parliament Hill Fields, or even Blackheath, and how we'd roll around together on the grass. Give a woman in inch and she'll park on it. Right in the centre of your brain, where the interesting thoughts used to live—and if the ground happened to be damp we'd probably shelter for a while in a handy cricket pavilion.

When I sighted her in a row of bikes on Hanover Square I did a circuit past Vogue House and the Bank of Tokyo to check her out. She perched sidesaddle on the Super dream, a dusty boot in the saddle of a nearby Honda Revere, its bulbous tank giving it the look of a misshapen toy. A whole summer of big Swallows were gathered round them, creased up with their usual idiotic laughter.

At weekends I tramped around streets of Acton, thinking of nothing much. I'd been doing the same thing for years. I didn't have a dope connection any longer and my preferred solution was to pick up roaches. The south Acton estate was favourite for this. People actually threw half-smoked joints out of their windows, and there was I ...

... ready to refurbish, ready to recycle. Saturday morning was the best time for this activity. Everybody still comatose from the night's cavortings, and beacon-like poundings of a sound system somewhere high in a tower told you that somebody was dancing in a kitchen whose sink overflowed with Red Stripe cans. Either that or the DJ was unable to get up and turn it off—so I inspected the party debris under the windows: roaches, spliffs somebody sparked up and decided they didn't want, daisies of screwed up foil and chunks of dope that had fallen out with their rightful owners. All for the taking into my eager, battered lungs.

The George was best: a black pub on the edge of the South Acton estate whose backyard usually yielded quite a yield of bent disposable works, easily identifiable wet roaches swilling in lager, sometimes even a half-rolled joint forgotten on the window shelf by the back door. And an hour or three folded up in newspaper in the drying cupboard soon cleansed them of any lingering impurities. I'd got to know the estate by wandering round it, noting little connections between people I'd never get to know. Mechanics running a business out of adjoining lock-ups. Two men waiting early in a black Golf with green-tinted windows and tick-ticking sound system, for a woman they took to work; who got in silently, no greeting. Wheel-less wheels arrested on thoughtfully supplied breeze blocks, caved in sidelights and ripped out stereos; a derelict fifties ice cream van showing tell-tale signs of activity. Someday, somehow the old dog was going to get up and bark again, and another generation of kids would soon be trotting out to say hello to Mr Whippy.

I kept my eyes peeled along Bollo Bridge Lane and Gunnersbury Avenue. Both there and in the long High Street peculiar marks were carved into the kerbstones: triangles, spirals, crosses, broken arrows, tail-eating snakes, the odd domino. And I'd wonder (idly) who had carved them, how they'd come to be. No answers. I watched my shoes. If it hadn't been for Marie I might have forgotten; that woman had pushed my big nose right in it, right in the dog shit—where it and I belonged, no doubt— with nothing to make me feel alive, and routine dangers, big hopes gone up in borrowed smoke from someone else's party. Another failed human from Nonsville. No point in another retread. Nothing you could reasonably pop rivet a panel over and disguise with grey filler.

Too young. Too merry. Too busy. Too pre-occupied. Too old. Too ill. Too late. (Too dead). But they weren't going to catch me out that way. So I pulled out the largest envelope, the one I'd left sealed. Addressed to Bob in funny writing. Sheaves of a yellowed narrow feint foolscap tumbled out, covered (one side only) in unmistakable handwriting. I spread them out on the coffee table, tried to read a few words: a column of numbers, and sometimes a whole sentence hopped out for inspection; but as to its import, its relation to what had followed or preceded it, to the development of any connected sense of what was being said: that was much slower in coming, slower indeed. The first page was headed T I N A C R E A, and underneath a series of schemes were written; story-lines, scenes and fragments of scenes, word-clusters, lists, isolated squiggles:

I sat down on the couch and cast my mind back to when I'd given up on my old college books, because they'd started bothering me on things I no longer wanted to care about. I'd once read Freud and Pascal together, one in each hand, noticing how similarly unanswerable they both were as I burned lines of print off the pages with my X-ray eyes. *Civilisation and its Discontents*. That man to man is a wolf. The Absolute Truth. Who can look into history or into his own heart and deny it? How the fuck can I be expected to love my neighbour when I really haven't got enough love for my nearest and dearest (or myself)? How Jesus' injunctions to love thine enemy seem even more absurd, till you realise they amount to the same thing: My Neighbour Is My Enemy.

Turning to Pascal I'd seen his account of human nature was about the same: lust, vanity and seeking distraction from your own wretchedness. Freud was a Christian really, I thought, and his wretched book smouldered under my gaze. He was just in denial—or something—sort of a pseudo-Christian with a piss-poor idea of the Good. Who'd somehow managed to place himself in pole position. Friedrich Nietzsche never wore an umpire's suit. Like his poxy reading of St. Luke. Who humbleth himself shall be exalted. Which according to Nietzsche meant that He who humbleth himself wants to be exalted. But what sort of negation was that? I mean, what was so wrong in wanting exaltation? Really, it said the same thing as Luke, didn't it, because in order for these wishes to come true you had to humble yourself, really humble yourself in front of what had previously been thought and done. Didn't you? Didn't you? For the poor were humbled by their circumstance, not really by themselves.

I remembered when it had come crystal clear, or so I'd thought. Blaise Pascal had his God and the God-given mind that apprehendeth its own wretchedness. Freud had sublimation, which was only dispersion of everything. Ultimate alchemy: transmutation of shit into sugar. And if one thing's certain in this life, it's that shit definitely drives out sugar. Because pure sugar. With a bit of shit in it. Is still sugary shit. Freud's revelation of universal sex motives led to retooling on a big scale. Soon they were turning out Terraplanes in kit form. Say what you like about Pascal, he had a sense of human frailty—and horror, plenty of. When Christ reveals himself to you in a night of fire, better write it down and sew it into your clothes or you're very likely to forget it happened. Horror, of human forgetfulness. I threw the books across the room and kicked out the flames, realising I'd better forget about it. Realising I was too stupid except for these lowly truths of the heart. Ends of thought. As Blaise Pascal said (sort of, anyway).

So why not get yourself a nice little job in a garden centre? Do some despatch riding? Best forget it, sunshine, and let the unhappy round of lusts, betrayals and distractions continue, as they do, obviously. So you think, you notice. That your main options are taking pleasure in evil or shutting down. Therefore you see it in yourself, you try to frustrate it. Not to want anything you're not going to get. Trying hard only to want what others want, or failing that, to keep yourself separate, apart. Which is the easiest thing in the world for some people—the lost ones like us—the black sheep that runners of these ultimate dice games won't let play—Bob—Jesus—Me. What was this crap? Why was I looking through it? Why had he sent it to himself? Why hadn't he picked it up from the flat? It seemed to have something to do with spiders . . . *Spiders?*

The travisphere rolled to a slow standstill in front of the largest dome at the very farthest edge of the Western desert—where the Eastern desert began, the empty planet's two suns close to the horizon, about to change places, apparently. The moment of the crossing. It really did look like they were dancing together in some sort of trepidation of the spheres. Railio wondered whether the fear they aroused in him was merely due to his being an off-worlder, or if Tinacrea's inhabitants had once felt the same, before they ceased to teem—some time ago, in fact. Anyway, they were why this strange planet never got dark. Why it was a desert. And why had the fecund caves of Arttrth given rise to the Tinacreans: the only known life-form hardy enough to survive in this wretched corner of ( ) ( ).

Railio consulted his ( ) stepped through the 'sphere's thin walls and out onto the gleaming ramp. He wondered what sort of reception he would get from the ( ) of ( ). Tinacrea's network of ( ) ( ) of multicoloured ( ) glowed for a few seconds and ( )ed to wafer thinness, revealing the dome's light interior. The ( ) ( ) parted and he stepped briskly inside.

The Tinacrean Ambassador moved to greet him in a graceful disrupted rhythm of furry legs. Was that a hand? Was he supposed to shake it? He'd been fully briefed on the protocols, of course, but faced with an actual social situation ... he took her foreleg's forked ( ) and found it surprisingly light and pleasant to the touch, but with no real grip, unlike the bone-crushing Nebulons...

Eventually she came to rest and crossed her rear legs, which twitched idly, scratching one another as if to indicate her ease in the presence of an honoured inferior. A soft voice sounded in his head, almost caressing but with a ( ) of steely ( ) underneath. A synth-voice, but not altogether unpleasant. "I trust you had an agreeable journey Mr, er, Railio ...?"

"Fascinating, Ambassador."

"Strange, is it not," the voice buzzed, "that you should address me as Ambassador when it is yourself who is the visitor to our humble ( ). Strange as it may appear, given the long alliance of our ( ) ( ), I have never before encountered one of your species. Most ( ). Perhaps it would be better were you to address me as ( )?"

"Very well, ( )."

"You will be in need of ( ) ( ) after your journey. A container, no that is the ... how you say ... incorrect word, a ( ) of our ( ) sometimes revives the spirits of travellers in these dusty climes. May I?"

"Most welcome." Railio allowed himself to take in the dome's featureless interior: a shimmering, unfocused quality. Areas of shadow engulfed ( ) ( ) ( ) except for the lit up area where he and ( ) faced one another. Such furnishings as he could make out were low, hard, sparkling, made of a material very like (   ) (   ) or marble. Icy ... warm, somehow. But without what he would have called a personal touch.

A panel slid back beside his hostess, revealing two coconut-like cups of a brownish liquid of unappetising appearance. "Ah!" (   ) exclaimed, "Just what the Ambassador ordered!" One of them had a straw in it. She picked up the other and greedily dipped two black tube-like protuberances into the liquid, quickly draining the substance from its fibrous goblet.

His stomach did a somersault as she appeared to vomit the liquid—which had taken on a foaming, slimy consistency—back into the receptacle, only to suck it up again more eagerly, or so it seemed to him. She cleaned both her tubes with deft, graceful movements of her front mandibles while a spare (   ) removed the cup, dropped it into the still open hatch. There was, yes, most definitely, a tremulous glow on what might have been her face, if she'd had one; a slightly intensified attentiveness towards his person.

"Come, Mr Railio," the synth-voice purred. "Please accept what little we have to offer in the way of hospitality. Otherwise we will think you a poor guest."

Railio grimaced, lifted the cup and manfully sucked on the crystal straw. Several weeks in hyper-drive on dried M-rations and Vita-sludge for the duration of the long trip out to this godforsaken corner of (   ) (   ) had prepared him for anything, or so he told himself. Somehow he ingested the liquid, as fast as possible. Even worse than he expected: lukewarm, not at all refreshing, the cloying texture and taste (he supposed) of artificially sweetened baby shit. He gagged involuntarily, and stopped himself. He felt a wave of hopeful, empathic appreciation emanate from the Tinacrean, followed by disappointment; a sense of having cast pearls before alien swine. He passed the empty receptacle back to (   ).

The Ambassador swiftly disposed of it, withdrew from his mind, appeared to consider him from a greater distance.

"But as I was ..."

"I meant to ask ..."

Something that might have been laughter—a warm breath stirring wind-chimes—floated through his mind. "Please, Mr Railio, I am at your disposal. I'm sure you must by now have absorbed all there is to know about our, er, civilisation. I am authorised to co-operate in every way possible in whatever way you wish."

"Understanding," he said. "I wish only to further understanding."

"But what, exaacctly?" She drawled the last word carelessly, inserted an impatient mechanical click in the middle of it. Laughter. "Are you certain it is not you who wishes to be understood? That is quite common amongst our visitors."

Railio ignored this, groped for a beginning. "How, for example, did you come to be an Ambassador? What was involved? That might tell me something of ..."

"Curious title, is it not, for one who never leaves the thin atmosphere of Tinacrea. But, you see, there are really very few of us left. Care must be taken in the impression we give visitors. And, you will think me ungracious, but we must insist on protecting ourselves from ..." She appeared to falter. "But surely, you know enough of what you would call our history. Suffice it to say that it was over thousands of (   ) ago and that we, er ... we wove a tangled web." Laughter again. "Spiders, I believe you call us. I understand you have several amusing proverbs relating to our kind, a number of phobias and superstitions ..."

"Indeed, Ambassador. Spiders, to whom you are, I suppose, distantly related, are the most respected of our smaller creatures. But to return to Tinacrean history—its tribal conflicts and alliances—the, er, rapidity of your social development, the elusive beauty of your art, the (to us) unknowable complexity of your technology—and its apparent lack of a material basis. What exactly was at stake in the wars of succession when (if you'll forgive me) on a planet as ill-appointed in natural resources as Tinacrea, the spoils of victory cannot have been that significant ..."

"What was at stake was the succession," she replied impatiently. "Come, this is schoolbook material, even in your ..."

"Forgive (   ) (   )."

"(   ) you (   ) slightly amiss.

"(   )."

"(   ) (   )."

Now he knew why they drank the revolting liquid, and why (   ) (   ) so freely to honoured visitors. The effects began with a sparkling at the edge of his peripheral vision, something like the onset of an attack of (   ) but soon (   ) the curious thing was that (   ) remained

a stable element (   ) and most beautiful (   ) he had ever (   )
(   ) (   ) he tried to remember the (   ) of his (   ).

It petered out into a series of worm-like jottings; something resembling words and paragraphs resumed on the next page, but the work of transcribing them into my own handwriting was too much for now. I straightened out the wedge of papers and crammed them into their envelope. I went through into the bedroom and plunged straight into a bottomless sleep. No dreams. No nothing. And in the morning, I started again.

(   ) cradled (   ) (   ) (   ); (   ) (   ) edge of (   ) (   ) pulpy, between the sharp edges of her (   ). Very slowly she (   ) (   ) (   ) cleft of (   ) (   ) moist ( ) smooth leathery carapace of (   ) (   ) (   ) imprisoned him (   ); (   ) gently (   ) (   ) (   ) (   ) (   ). ( ) crab (   ) (   ) (   ) tenderness (   ) (   ) spent (   ) (   ) (   ) (   ) ingeniously (   ) had lost.

"(   )! (   ) (   ) are you (   )?"

"(   )."

(XXXXXXX) (XXXXXXXXX) *dipped it towards him in affectionate salute* (XXXXX) (XXXXXXXX) *caress and* (XXXX) (XXXXXXXXXXX) *chitinous* (XXXX) *her* (XXXXXX) (XXXXXX) (XXXXXXXXX) *!!!!* (XXXXX) (XXXXXX) *searing pain* (XXXXX) (XXXXX) (XXXXX) (XXXXXXX) (XXXXXXXXXXXXX) *snaking into his* (XXXXXXXX) *between* (XXXXXXXX) *fire eyes* (XXXXXX) XXXX) *opened* (XXXXX) *probing* (XXXXXX) *trembling impossibly* (XXXX) (XXXXXXXXX) (XXXXXXXX) *drawing it from him, somehow* (XXXXX) (XXXXXXX). (THIS IS SHIT!) (XXXXXX) *held fragile* (XXXXX) *underneath* (XXXXX) *how infinitely more complex the perceptual world appeared, and* (XXXXX) (XXXXX) (XX) (XXXXXXX) *like moist hair* (XXXXXX) *her head was aglow, warm* (XXXXX) *a thousand objections* (XXXXX) *arguments strafing him like fire from a nearby ship.*

Railio (XXXXX) (XXXXX) (XXXXXX). *Useless now, irrelevant* (XXXXX) (XXXXXX) (XXXXXX) *and how he wished with all his heart he was one of them.*

"(XXXXX)?"

"(XXX) (XXXXXXX)??"

"(XXX) (XXXXX)   (XXXXXXX) (XX) (XXXXXXX) (XXX) (XXXXXXX), (XXXXX?)"

"(XXXXXXX)."

"(XXXXX)?"

"Deep (XXXXXXXX), in the cave of the (XXX) (XXXXX)."

"(XXX) (XXX)?"

"Thirty of your millennia, (XX) (XX) (XX) it is said."

"(X) (XXXX) (XXX)!"

"(X) (XXXX) (XXX) (XXX), Railio."

"(XXXX) (XX) (XXXXX)." There was something so pleasantly reassuring about the lightness of her limbs, their multiplicity. (XXXX) (XXX) (XXXX) wept, and (XX) (XXXXX) (XXXXXX). (XXX) (XXX) (XXXXXXXXX) (XX) musky (XXXXX). (XXXXXX) (XXX) (XXXXXXXXXXXX), (XXXX)!!!

(cut to previous?)

His crossings out were done with a different pen, at a later date, some with a furious intensity, obliterating words and then modifying or keeping the essentials for a later rewrite (or so it seemed)—and so this first section of Bob's manuscript came to a close. I flipped onwards. There was plenty more of it, but for the time being I decided to put Tinacrea aside. I wondered if I'd ever known the person who'd written it. There was something about it that was almost too exciting, too strange.

Six

I'd stopped in for a swift pint in the Cat and Bauble on the Bayswater Road. I'd always liked the look of that place. It was a real nowhere pub but on warmer nights a heady mix of Eurobrats, Middle Eastern businessmen and teenage whores spilled out onto wide pavements that were thronged with their light suits, wispy silk miniskirts, and bright-coloured sweaters with crocodiles on. How appropriate. You wouldn't smile at one of them in a hurry. I just wanted to push in amongst them, to forget myself for an hour. Maybe some of their happiness and easy pleasure would rub off on me ...

... fat chance. I crammed into a back corner by the cigarette machine and inched my pint up to my mouth. Sweat fell off my face, I kept on trying to put my full glass down on top of a machine whose slope had been designed to prevent just that, whilst other customers tried to elbow me out of the way to get their coins into the slot. Most smokers punched the three Silk Cut buttons in turn, and, finding those columns were empty, switched to JPS or Dunhill in a ratio of 6:4. I noticed these things. Hah! They should be paying me to do this kind of research. But they weren't. It soon became obvious I would've been better off staying at home.

Marie elbowed her way in through the crowd, shaking her charity box like a marimba. I shrank back into my corner. Her right arm was in a plaster cast and a grubby sling, but before she got too close a couple of young blokes in double-breasted suits started taking the piss out of her.

"I'll sign that for you, love." Said by one with weeping acne in the stubble on his neck, glowing in a bright red heat flush.

"Tools for Change. Helping the third world to help themselves."

"Never heard of it," said the other one. "Helping yourself, I expect."

The corners of her mouth lifted on strings.

He dug into his pockets, fed change into her slot. "Don't spend it all at once, love."

I watched her do a circuit, perform her short unvarying speech and escalate through the same gesticulations, explanations, ending with a wan smile. Often she didn't get beyond a quick rattle before they turned their backs. Only some of them asked for ID. Tourists offered a look of mock bafflement. Men in groups proved the most generous: roughly one in sixteen coughed up, which wasn't too bad as a straw poll for the league of decency. I wondered what had happened to her arm. But this was obvious: she'd come off her bike. Now, I indulged in a bit of ready cynicism, she was collecting her own sick pay: a cast-iron necessity in the courier game.

Maybe she was a genuine volunteer. Everything I wanted to think about her made that the best explanation. I had her down as a child saint. Laid off from gainful employment, she still sacrificed her free time to help the world's poor. Or maybe the cast was a fake. I watched her shoulder her way out of the pub and struggled in her wake through ankle taps and elbows as the yapping mob took revenge on me. Outside she was disappearing around the corner onto Bayswater Road on the pillion of the ugly Revere; I trotted quickly down to Craven Hill Gardens where I'd tucked the XS away. I unlocked the chain, stowed it in the box, but by then I knew that I'd lost her.

Still, they were probably only going home, either that or into the West End. It was beginning to look (to me) as though all of them worked for Poore. Don too. Why not? That might explain why he'd picked him out of the line up, somehow. Don-boy had crossed him in some way. What if. I sat on the bike in the stillness beside the locked garden, and tried and failed to suck a little bit of its rustling quiet calm into my brain.

Because it had been me, me who tiptoed in through his shrouded birdcage of a room, into his narrow kitchen. I couldn't pretend it hadn't happened. Don hadn't broken in there: I had. I was the bad man. The Blackheart Man in Bunny Wailer's song. For the stone at the head of the corner is the same one that the builders refuse. Maybe, maybe. But not until they manage to scratch your name off it.

I had to get hold of something and follow it. A clue, a true. That's what I was short of. You followed a clue to another clue. Finally the whole tangled knot fell apart under your busy fingers.

I rode up to the junction, headed back into Soho and there they were outside a disco pub in Old Compton Street. Jack Daniels promotions and special offers on day-glo stars in its wide bay windows. Used to be The Swiss Tavern, so I remembered, a skinny black woman called Diane had sung I Will Always Love You in there years before Whitney Houston got hold of it. Bob had even danced with her friend one night when we ended up in there and now Marie's boyfriend sat patiently outside in the saddle of his Revere, drumming idly on its swollen, pregnant-looking tank. Behind its polished bow windows, Marie was doing her wounded sparrow charity act.

I right-handed into Dean Street, passed the soundtrack album shop, turned onto Shaftesbury Avenue.

A blue light was stroking the window. It chased its long shadows across the room; I levered myself upright and peered out, rubbing at sore eyes. Underneath the tower three fire engines were parked, yellow hoses snaking around the car park. I looked up. Smoke pouring from a window on the ninth floor. A pair of big firemen with stretcher passed behind the streaky frosted glass of the stairwell. I padded out there in my socks. A policewoman ran up the stairs, one hand clamping down her checkered flag hat. A young boy and his mother shrank back to let them pass. I went inside and looked out of the window. Hardly a light was on in the whole tower. Sensible people had rolled over and gone back to sleep. Three or four thrill-seeking insomniacs peering into the night. Whoever they were. Whatever their motives. People, like me, who happened to be awake. I joined the going-back-to-sleep party. The party of never hearing about it again. If you didn't, it was good. It meant nobody had died.

In the morning there was Wally. I AM A WALLY inscribed on the front of his red baseball cap, scrawled across the notice board: FUCK OFF WALLY YOU FAT DOLLOP. You Wally, Wally. Oh you stupid giant ambulant basketball in dungarees gone baggy all over, you silver-haired, brass-tongued ... and now he was at the end of his last days as caretaker, he was old and he knew it. After seven years he'd finally got used to me, and that meant I had to listen to him. I was cornered in the open lift. I kept jabbing six and fourteen, but his finger was stuck firmly to the call button.

"I had them screwed up last night," he moaned. "Now the animals have smashed them open."

I nodded my usual pretended interest in his non-problems.

"Of course, there was a time when I used to know what people had in them." He eyed me (and a woman sharing the lift) and tried to frame what he wanted to say about this vanished golden age. "Then I'd know what was stolen," he said. "I don't know, I don't know. What sort of bloody animals are they?"

Before he could provide a predictable answer to his own question the lift clunked into action and he disappeared in a slow wipe. He must've let the button go. That meant he no longer had any answers, any ideas.

"There's nothing much in ours," the woman confided to me. "Still, we have got a latch on it."

"Hmm." The door opened at six. I stepped out of the lift, exhaled in relief.

I'd grown to quite like Wally, much preferred him to the new caretaker, even if he was training up his boy to join the South African Army. Better the devil you know, which wasn't saying much: the new one was an outpatient dressed in loose denim, always half-shaven, always dragging a stiff broom around on its back. He had a Jack Nicholson gleam in his eyes, or was it just a harried look. That morning I'd seen him slamming doors, wilfully abusing a locked storeroom with the sole of his boot. The tenants' association was trying to get rid of him, Wally said, and Wally knew. He'd been in the same position. Had to live with it. Had to keep swabbing out the lifts, on call. Had to keep on hanging onto the tied flat and the anger.

Forwarding Agents. Sorry for myself, for a change, I'd put in a five day week, but I was unable to pump up the enthusiasm to get out there and go for it day after day. I'd even thought of asking if I could go part-time. But what if Alf and Barbara didn't like it? What if they refused? If they did I'd never be allowed to forget I'd had the cheek to ask. I pulled my gear off and started to feed the fish. The tank needed topping up, so I filled up a few buckets and left them to let the chlorine evaporate. The big barb's tail was out of the water. He motored up and down, a silver flash in a grey murk of fish shit which was meant to be hoovered up by the catfish—and, of course, by the clogged filtration system.

I watched a silhouette rushing across a pebbledash wall next to the Texaco station on Horn Lane. Male or female? Human or Eldren? Headlights riffled a roof of leaves; a deck of cards; indicators indicated left and right, explaining dim shapes as objects in a familiar world. I'd been riding around this town too long. My eyes crossed a page without reading. Zebra crossing. Mule in pyjamas ... half-familiar streets unfolding in a hilly town I sometimes dreamed of whose lower levels were underwater arcades where gangs of dockers unloaded bones from black barges driven by dead Egyptians, whose buildings were encrusted with gaudy paste-jewels, sherbet sold on every second corner by cackling tray-crones laden with pastel sherbet flying saucers.

The coffee houses were all boarded up; I struggled across heaps of worn out tyres from abandoned dodgems; dumps of the gutted cars themselves, electric sticks waving in a rust forest on a grey lake of dead sparks; to a quiet estate of houses with loop railings where I was trying to find an address behind a churchyard. A pair of laughing ghosts appeared and raced down a curving avenue of terraces and one of them handed me a packet for an address I didn't know or recognise any longer. It was where Bob used to live—in some sort of hall of residence place where a rainbow stew of students were milling around with trays and scraped their full plates into a waste bin.

I asked after him, like Phillip Marlowe. They shook their heads. I scanned the notice board for clues and was immediately approached by a small dark woman in glasses. Fiona, the woman who'd given me the letters, who said in a pleading voice:

"I've done my best with him, I've tried I really have. Oh well, I suppose you'd better see for yourself."

Bob was laying there in a cell, rolling around on a bare mattress surrounded by empty pill bottles. His body was translucent, skin orange with the off-sheen of a sweating yoghurt. Skin, and bone. Tranks and downers crackled underfoot. He pushed himself up painfully onto an elbow. A pile of books next to the bed caught his interest; I watched him flipping vaguely though the pages of some ancient tome, his cracked lips mumbling a half-remembered quotation. I shook him. I tried to get him to wake up, to come awake and recognise me.

"What are you doing?" I shouted at him. "What are you trying to do?"

Fiona stood by the door. I knelt on a carpet of multicoloured capsules, which I tried to shovel into an empty carrier bag as they scuttled off like armoured Colorado beetles.

"Good idea." Fiona wrung her hands, crying, trembling in fright.

Something made me join a queue to a waste bin where students were scraping piles of uneaten food off their plates. I shuffled towards it, and when my turn came I emptied the whole bag of pills down a waste chute. The smell of burnt carpet underlay, absolutely disgusting. I wondered why I'd come here, tried to remember. Maybe should I have brought him some cigarettes, or fruit? Fiona's eyes were rested on me from an open door by the spiral staircase. I had to go back up, climb up those stairs and tell Bob that his friend, James Railio, was no longer with us. A miserable mission indeed. I didn't want to have to take it on. I woke up sweating.

Iron steps curled down to a corral where a group of giant galvanised bins were gloomily meditating on various truths consequent upon the last bin round-up. I hammered down them, trying to produce my thunderous clanging bells of doom effect, succeeding a bit. A bin-liner excitedly threw up its contents across my path at the bottom of the steps and a rag-bundle turned out to be a woman. She was lying face-down by a grating clogged up with a twisted streamer of pink toilet paper. Her face was mashed into the ground, her nose punched out of joint, her arms turned in opposite directions at the elbows. I looked up for an open window, knelt down, hesitated to feel for a pulse, but did. Her skin was spongy, warm to the touch. I thought of trying to lift her. Couldn't touch her though. I decided it would be better not to.

"The inspectors, the inspectors are coming." Gladys's eyes opened, shifted in malice. "They'll be coming in another minute."

Gladys. Gladys.

"It's me, Tony! From next door! What inspectors? What inspectors?"

But I knew very well which inspectors she was referring to. There were always inspectors in your head. Her tears welled up as she blushed, sitting up and brushing at her clothes. "I am sorry," she said. I put my hand on her shoulder and she offered her arm. I took it, helping her to her feet, steering her around to the front entrance where a gentle slope led us straight into a lift. A light smudging of dirt was on her cheek and stuck to her clothes, her capacious shell suit made of that odd shiny material whose main characteristic is to look highly inflammable. I remembered that people can only blush with their uncovered parts.

"Thanks dear," she rasped unsteadily, fumbled her keys. "Jelly legs, that's what I am. Old Jelly legs."

Bulging objects, uncontained by scale, filled up their sitting room. Her carpet was brighter than mine, its mustard-coloured ice floes breaking up over a depthless black contingency. Gladys lowered herself onto a bright tan sofa. I shut myself into the kitchen and made a cup of tea while the little laughing dog scrabbled at the door.

"Pack it in," she called, feebly. I heard a struck match, a cough.

Her kitchen was identical to mine but much cleaner. I hoped she didn't mind having a stranger in it. I watched myself at a distance, dropping tea-bags into mugs, agitating them for a few moments, and squeezing them out. I re-entered the sitting room and her dog attacked, a mobile mop-head animated by some killer virus. I tried slyly slopping hot tea onto its head without getting any on the carpet. Ho ho.

"Gina! She won't bite you, dear. Pick her up, dear. Shut her in the bedroom for me."

I scooped the animal into my arms, carried it through and tossed it onto the bed. I noticed on the way out that its previous claw marks had deeply scored the bedroom door

"I should've taken her with me, I know," said Gladys. "She really helps me. Gives me something lively to look at. The doctor said we should get her."

I gulped at my tea.

"Thanks, Tony," she said. "You must think I'm a silly old woman who can't even go out on her own."

I nodded. I was so eager to be gone.

"The sky comes down," she explained, "it's sort of like there's no gap left between the ground and the sky. Or something." She laughed a little laugh. "You don't know what I'm talking about, do you?"

"Yes I do."

"This'll be the death of me."

"Just a bit sick of the place, I expect."

"Not so much the place as the people in it," she flicked vaguely at the four corners of the earth. "Mum do this, gran do that. They're after you till your legs go."

A key went into the lock and yapping broke out in the bedroom, a frenzied wordless scrabble to be out where the humans were. Harry rounded the door, followed by the blond beast I'd seen in the lift; a young woman pushing a baby buggy; a fourteen year old boy in school uniform who swung nimbly in after her on a wooden crutches, a sports bag slung between his shoulders.

Gina overtook him to wheel and jump and yap.

I stepped back. The girl casually unstrapped her baby; the boy propped his crutches against the sofa, and vaulted over the back, miraculously cured. He slid down next to Gladys and swung his plastered leg across the coffee table.

Harry milled aimlessly.

"I took a bit of a tumble outside," Gladys said. "Tony here helped me up the stairs."

Harry wasn't listening.

"Tumble?" the blond guy said anxiously, angrily.

"I slipped. I couldn't get up."

"Ttt, I don't know, mum."

Harry went through to the kitchen, banged around the familiar cupboards. Poked his head out. "Cup of tea?"

"No, thanks." I handed him my cup. "I'll leave you to it."

"I'd better start getting the dinner on, I suppose." Gladys pushed herself up onto her knuckles. "Will mince do?"

She remembered all of a sudden what she'd gone out for, came over funny and sat back in confusion.

"Okay." The boy picked up a dud remote, zapped at the TV, inert. No joy.

"Sit back there, can't you?" Harry shouted. "Just sit yourself down there for once in your life!"

The phone started ringing, triggered off by my approach. On the seventh ring, the last ring, the one with a fractional delay on it to let you know your last chance has come too late, I answered.

"Am I speaking to Mr Mackenzie?"

"No."

"May I speak to your mother?"

"Pardon?"

"Your mother, Mrs Mackenzie."

"There is no Mrs Mackenzie."

"Am I speaking to the head of the household?"

"Yes."

"Well, Mr Mackenzie, may I take up a few minutes of your time?

"I'm not Mr Mackenzie."

"Who are you then?"

"I'm somebody else. Is this is a promotion?"

"Do you live there?"

"Yes, I do."

"Fine."

"And?"

"Well, Mr, er -"

"Guest."

"You're a guest? A paying guest?"

"Tony Guest."

"Good. I'm calling on behalf of the charity, Respond, Mr, er, Guest. We wondered if you'd like to help us—and the needy—out by volunteering a couple of hours of your time to do an envelope collection in your area."

"What does it involve?"

"Delivering envelopes in your, um, tower, collecting them a week later, counting the money for us, then paying it into a nearby branch of Barclays Bank. Between late in October and mid-November?"

"Sorry, I'm not interested."

"We do let you keep half the money."

"Half the money?"

"It used to be a third."

"Seems like a lot to me."

"That's why we're called Respond—we get results. Good results—for everyone."

"Sounds like it."

"So, Mr Guest—are you interested in our work for the needy?"

"Not really, I've got a job."

"That's perfectly all right. Goodbye."

"Goodbye. Sorry I couldn't help."

I put the phone down and walked back down the hall. Shit! I could so easily have found out everything right there: everything I wanted to know about charities—and I'd let a perfect opportunity to do just that slip through my fingers. Why did I do that? Because I was a lot stupider than I had ever let myself admit, that's why. Odd buzzing details stuck to the flypaper of my short-term memory. Counting the money. Taking it to the bank. Yes, please. They were big on that, it seemed. Totally brazen. But there was nothing to stop you ripping off the whole lot. Very trusting people these charities; they had to be. Unless they were relying on your innate sense of right and wrong. Unless it was random mass cold-calling in hopes of turning up a few saints. Possibly, possibly. Perhaps they could tell, somehow, if you were going to be all right.

They were planning for some sort of rake-off, I realised. They actually expected you to steal. If they sent out envelopes and I stole all the money, what did they lose but stationery? If I ripped off half they'd still have the rest—or whatever I thought I could get away with. They wanted you to steal. From your neighbours, from anyone. They were counting on it. They issued licences to do just that. I tried to bring back the conversation I'd just had, to run it through again; but the version I had kept on changing, modifying—he couldn't have said that about keeping half, could he? How many calls did he make a day? Forty? Fifty? Why hadn't it worked on me? Maybe I wasn't that greedy—but I knew I was, really. I just hadn't had the chance. I'd never been shown the cities of the pain, the plain, on the pane, where the rain was mainly disdain, which fell mainly on the lame. If I had I didn't remember. I walked over to the drying cupboard, took a pinch of recycled roach tobacco from last year's paper, twisted it into a single skin joint.

Not bad; it'd do. The Chambers family lurched out of the mists—returning Zombies from half-an-hour ago. They wanted something. I hoped it wasn't revenge. For what? For what? I wondered if the blond couple I had seen were brother and sister, husband and wife. Did it matter? That boy: late son or early grandchild? After a few tokes I realised I didn't need to ask myself these questions. I already knew the answers. The only new element was really of my own making.

Of course! Of course! They were just like Del-boy and Rodney! Oh well. I'd managed to turn my neighbours into a stray sit-com. Brilliant. Poore's outfit was called Tools for Change. So what did Harry sell on the market? Tools, naturally. Power saws, Black & Decker workmates. Socket sets. Etcetera. Unwanted Christmas gifts donated by well-heeled well-wishers of everybody, quickly and very well recycled into cash by the obliging Chambers family. The junk, the absolute dross, could be set to one side for Africa: Whitworth spanners, horseshoe unbenders, restrainers for stoats, rat saddles, rivet guns for which rivets were no longer available— pinhole cameras, keyhole cameras. They used a lot of that sort of thing in developing countries.

Gladys, I speculated, would most likely be on the envelope game. On the door to door. But how the hell could an agoraphobic woman possibly be a charity collector? I imagined she must take that revolting dog with her. Gina would yap yap yap until they cough coughed up to get rid of her. Hahahahahaha. Yikes. Nothing to be scared of, Scooby. It was all turning into a big joke, this game where I made things up. Quite a long tail on a cat I was chasing. I buzzed with it for a long time before I calmed down enough to watch TV again. *The Hit Man and Her*. I wanted to hit him. And as for her ... agh, she was too annoying to watch.

Harry Chambers started to corner me on the ramp or in the lift after that, and in every one of our conversations he'd oh so casually unpack more of his family relationships, attempting to orient me somehow in his world, to reveal its hidden orders. I knew that Acton wasn't a single place, more of a series of overlapping zones, I knew that, I already knew. Everybody knew, didn't they?

But what I hadn't realised was that they were all populated by members of the Chambers family. One of his grandsons was a professional cricketer. That was the proudest thing in his life. Bound to be, wasn't it. He'd seen him play at Lords—and therefore he was one. Their eldest daughter had been a nurse before she married. She would be again. His son-in-laws and daughters, nieces and nephews multiplied uncountably on my sticky fingers: barmen, security guards, shop assistants, secretaries, telephone engineers, decorators, car mechanics: an army of extras.

That was why he could slouch around in his vest, play with the dog and not be too bothered about anything. Because he'd made it happen. He could afford to be casually, lightly proud of the unexpectedly prolific fruit of his loins; he was empowered to speak on their behalf, and on mine if I let him. I found myself edging away from these revelations of his. I didn't have the patience to try and remember them. He always referred to 'my son', 'my daughter-in-law', without specifying which one exactly, implying that he couldn't remember them either, or you were supposed to know already—giving an impression of a handful of people leading multiple lives: a whole sprawling labour force he'd sired and forgotten.

For another thing he started pumping me for information. I wasn't having any of it. I was happy to go through the motions of helpfulness, but the idea of talking about myself in the way seemed to expect brought me out in a cold sweat. I wasn't going to play that game. Not so stupid, so wised up. Not really a person at all, not by Harry's exalted standards of personhood. I let him think what he liked. I was keeping something in reserve, something for a rainy day. Something that I knew and nobody else did. What was it? A higher level of knowledge, of something or other (bullshit) I seemed to have at my fingertips, my disposal, connecting me to the chain-gang of dead armies just as fully as he was connected to his living relatives. Pointless friendliness ebbed, as it generally does. After not much longer than a fortnight we were back to the grunting.

That's exactly how it was, exactly. I saw them in the car park one morning, not close enough, or necessary to nod; the big blond guy (No. 1 son?) and another man, shorter, were stamping around the locked rear doors of an Escort van. Bright yellow, ex-Telecom. I unchained the mighty XS and sat in the saddle to watch them load up the back with ill-gotten gains. Harry arrived with the van keys and they went through a ritual about who was going to ride in the back. The shorter one lost. The older son caught sight of me under the tower as he walked round to the front of the van, looked away; but I still couldn't stop myself gawping. The van was stacked to the roof with garden tools: hoes, forks, spades, edge-trimmers, shears: shiny green and gleaming. Ideal for knocking out on Shepherds Bush Market, or wherever else you might go to knock out such things. Ideal tools for real change. They confirmed my first idea, the one I'd dismissed out of hand—and also my growing sense of being stupid.

Had I always been this way? Yeah, I still was. Still am. A bit dicky and a bit cocky. I turned on my ignition and raised a gauntlet I wasn't yet ready to throw down, circled past them all and headed back up the West End.

Seven

The Labour Party lost the 1987 General Election because they got the party political broadcasts wrong. Neil Kinnock should have ridden up on a Meriden Triumph Bonneville. "This motorcycle," he should've begun, "is a symbol, a symbol of British engineering, of British industry, a symbol of the past, if you like. This particular bike I've been riding"—he smiles—"was built by the Workers' Co-operative that has taken over Triumph's Meriden factory in Birmingham. In order to save their jobs, rescue a great name and a great British institution for their children's future, and, against the odds, continue to manufacture these magnificent machines. The Triumph motorcycle has become a symbol of what working-class people can do when they set their minds to it. It's also a symbol in another sense. A symbol of the tragic waste of human ingenuity and resources, and the cold-hearted indifference to the needs of working people, that sums up what this Conservative government stands for ... "

Blah. Blah. Would the Welsh windbag have won? Maybe not. But he should have done it anyway. Nothing too heavy, nothing too political. It was already too late to stop the worst of it, but there you are. Better late than never, and instead you had the party machine that elected Tony Blur trying to pass him off as John F. Kennedy and ended up with the other windbag walking his dog in Taffyland. Off looking out to sea, or something. Probably at some shutdown coal pit they'd already grassed over. Back then a Post office strikes always started the same rumour: this was going to be the end of Post offices as we knew them. Eventually it would turn out to be true. An atmosphere of unwholesome excitement prevailed at Forwarding Agents. Alf and Barbara were doing unpaid overtime till 8:30 each night, picking up back-handers from various idiots greedy for more gobble: there was always someone greedy for gobble. A couple of months later a further two hundred and fifty redundancies would be announced in Mount Pleasant sorting office.

For the others I expect the money was quite handy. I banked it and forgot about it. Happy to let the other stuff slip away, pleased to be grafting, in a way. It was connected to a lot of old dreams I'd attached to citizens who muttered in the High Street and the fly-blown tucked away arcade with its last legs Wimpy Bar and temporary shops selling cheap baby clothes and oddments of carpet. We used to go to the Wimpy in Kingston as a Friday night treat. Now an old man loped around the block night and day, bumming ten pences in hopes of an ultimate packet of fags; a balaclava woman (called Helen) sat outside the 7-11 with a scratched tobacco tin and a Slurpee cup—and, watching over them, the Golden Lady, a powdered costume doll who appeared in the midst of the mid-day traffic, crossing over so beautifully, simpering, and never came to harm.

Gone away, unnoticed forever, into night shelters or non-existent graves. I'd thought of them as shadows of my future. They could be rehoused by associations, by councils if they wanted, or put in sheltered accommodation, well, couldn't they? Everybody knew there wasn't any real bottom to fall through nowadays: there was always a net to catch you. Anybody was more likely to help them than me. The good old days of the pathetic fallacy, the mirroring weather, lies that turned out to be as true as anything, anything that was going—in the days that were coming back sometime, and then, I managed to think, we would really see something start happening.

On Bond Street a despatch rider emerged from Dering Yard wearing a red plastic nose under his open visor. A yellow ribbon. My first job of the day took me across City Road; where a billboard showed a giant Mars Bar and a packet of P.G. Tips. In red noses. Little blobs of plastic for the face, bigger ones for the car. They were attached to one vehicle in five: Sierras, Golfs and Ladas united around a minimum programme they'd bought into with four star. And, I realised instantly, they really had—all social problems were solvable by marketing, amazingly enough, how true. I watched a builder's wagon growl past in bottom gear, a scuffed white hard-hat strapped across its grille in surrender to this reality.

By lunchtime I'd had enough. Red-nosed XRBis, yuppie wedges, continued to cut me up; snotty young women with red plastic noses woven into their top knots hurried out of Harrods, their delicate nostrils free to quiver in benzene-laden air; by six o'clock the Soho pavements groaned with red-nosed drunken twats staggering under buckets of money. I stood beside the bike on Wardour Street gaping at them in open contempt. One of them mistook it for sympathy and shook his bucket under my nose, grinning at me stupidly. I dug into my pocket and threw in a good fistful of loose change.

Back at the bike a folded copy of London Messenger had been pushed under my saddle strap. I stuffed it in my pocket and carried on home. Big govt. plans for the future of the motorcyclist were its front page news. Where they should be— picking up maximum publicity and of no importance to anyone except for bikers themselves. Come election time you could promise them anything. To place the interests of motorcyclists at the forefront of your transport policy. To encourage wider use of this economic and socially responsible form of transport (not like big gas-guzzling empty cars with one person in them)—and tax-relief for regular bike commuters—er, what about a really sensible expenditure on resurfacing dangerous roads, a good look into alternative ways of funding training schemes, youth motor sport initiatives ... a proper education programme for ignorant car drivers dozing along in the dream world of their little immortality wagons??? And when you broke the promises nobody would notice, nobody who didn't read the motorcycle press even knew what they were ... and if they know did they'd give you a round of applause anyway for sticking the boot into the working-classes. Reality dawns. Oh. Oh. They're about to change the test yet again, apparently, bring in a ban for kids who can't pass it within a year ... helpfully ensuring they never will. These special leg-guards to be made compulsory on new machines (what??) and old machines (what???) so that bikes (most bikes) that can't be converted will automatically become illegal (converting all proper motorbikes into fucking scooters!!!)—and the coup de grace, the master stroke, the biscuit: the country-wide installation of sleeping policemen on dangerous bends. Because if those noisy boy racers wouldn't slow down the little bastards deserved to die. The people some people voted for had really excelled themselves this time. I wondered who they had in the think tank who'd come up with this lot? A focus group of friendly porpoises? No, porpoises were too intelligent. This Tory government (and the Labour ones that came before and next) had turned transport policy over to a specially assembled poolful of decorative Koi carp. It was reminiscent of the days of Barbara Castle—a far from stupid woman who nevertheless couldn't even fucking drive.

This was back in the 1960s, when Government intervention and financial investment could still have saved the British motorcycle industry. MAG had called a protest rally about this, or some of it, in Hyde Park, on Saturday. Be there or crawl off and die. Be there or you deserved to have your livelihood taken way. Be there or you were no better than pond life yourself ... maybe you were no better than they thought you were.

On Friday night we stood around the office waiting for our account pay. Barbara silenced us with a foghorn rasp.

"Okay, chaps," she said. "And chapesses." There was one new rider, a woman: it was the first time I'd seen her. "I suppose it's too much to ask if you've got your account books at the ready?"

Nobody moved, nobody spoke. Obviously we had account books. Unless you had a photographic memory you couldn't work without one.

"Well, get them out then." Her usual sarcastic sing-song. "I'm going to give you a new account. Hmm. Yeah. That's right. Then you can write it in again, can't you, and you'll know where to go next time, won't you?"

I'd speculated about her past before, we all had. Police? Ex-primary school teacher? Pagan priestess defrocked for mental cruelty? If so she still had the old magic, and unlike Lady Macbeth she didn't seem too bothered to be walking around with blood on her hands.

We dutifully got our account books. Especially tatty copies were shielded from her critical glare.

Alf leaned back in his old typists' chair. Smiling in enjoyment of her performance.

"Everyone got a pen? Good. Now turn to the very back of your books, after the last address, and write Account 366. Got that? 366. Fine. Good. Excellent." She told us the name of the account.

"Should be all right for a cheap socket set there," said a rider known as John the Postman.

Barbara forced a smile, resigned to his idiocy.

"Tools for change." John clinked the coins in his pocket. "Geddit?"

"Very good, John. Very good. No, actually, it's a charity."

Next morning I slept till around midday, rolled out of bed in the thickness of over-sleep, out of dreams where you're toying with something disgusting—which are always preferable to having something disgusting toying with you—and watching the Saturday Sport titles out of the corner of my eye, I gulped down a milk-free coffee, sat back for ten minutes, twenty, half-an-hour—until finally self-contempt drove me out to the car park and the bike. If I didn't make it to Hyde Park today I didn't deserve to go on living.

Thick wads of wet leaves lay on the broken up surface of Bayswater Road, lurking bundles of nature's greasy bounty waiting to skate my front wheel away. Big police BMWs were stationed at twenty yard intervals to shepherd the mob; and behind its black railings, high above the autumn trees, a dull red shimmering sun flashed intermittently between rain clouds in a giant stab at celestial red-nosery.

Hyde Park was black with parked up bikes. I chained up my helmet to my own front wheel and mingled in an uncentred crowd, which was devolving into a number of sub groups. Closer scrutiny revealed them not to be groups as such but momentarily magnetised particles: drifting, eddying, settling like snowflakes—neither knowing nor caring where to go. It was the kind of crowd in which you might expect to run into someone you used to know but never do; vague never-to-be-realised promises robbed you of purpose and direction. More of a holiday crowd than one brought together for a real purpose, and like holidaymakers these people generally knew they were meant to be having fun. A race meeting crowd. Same hot dog franchise.

Old-timey bikers sprawled around black flags in cracked leathers and banners saying LINCOLN MCC and BRIDLINGTON MAG AGAINST ANTI-BIKE LAWS were propped up against trees; a man with LITTLE JESUS SAYS CHRIST IS KING painted on his back, its crossed arrow pointing to Heaven, glaring really hard at anyone who seemed as if they might feel they could contradict him. Some squatted on helmets, enjoying their cans of Export; others wandered around casually, having a look; Ken and Barbie bounced by in feathery, layered haircuts and matching biker gear, totally convinced they had just what it took. Dog walkers mingled smilingly in the outlaw throng. Anyway, I was late.

The path turned into a choked slip road clogged with bikes inching towards the main exit, throttles blipping, jumping into a slow moving column from scarred-up grass. Patches of scuffed green peeked out under a thick carpet of cellulose-layered paint. I wandered back to the gates, standing next to where they filtered onto Marble Arch and turned back into plain traffic. Six coppers stood on the island between them, noting each shock of blowing hair that bobbed into view on a Triumph or a Panther combo, and a WPC tried to take down numbers covered by oily rags; a stony-faced. chief inspector stood over her. They weren't going to make any sudden moves. Anyway, they had a healthy respect for any social group, which, like themselves, lived beyond the reach of the law. A Nomad passed with a shrunken dog skull attached to his swinging arm—just married to a solitary Road Rat maybe, a yellow plastic duck slung about his neck in memory of bath times past.

The Lady Guinevere lounged behind her rodeo man—a hard, scarred knight errant in mothy crushed velvet doubloon—trying to look regal on the dickey of his trike: a pair of beautiful monsters blinking in giant boredom on the back of a giant insect, passing on into gone myths of SF covers of Mary Quant alien chicks with death-lizard fins growing out of their skinny backs, pool eyes brimming with crystal tears on soft lawn chessboards of the Red Queen, lost far futures of levitating cities that looked like boxy seventies cars. Her rough rider looked ahead. She looked at me: a single red power-dot was painted between her eyes.

There was a heartening chorus of beeps and klaxons rippling through the ranks, uniting us for as long as the sound lasted. The Globe riders had once tried to join the T&G and were called in and sacked one by one. I locked onto the head of a rider on an old 400 Suzuki blowing out several shades of shit through a hole in the left down pipe. It was a real dog, a hundred and fifty quid's worth of bike: an illegal death-trap, a ghost's bike. Bob was riding it. His face had hardened up, but even behind a clipped visor I recognised him—I was sure of it. I twisted on my heels. His brakelight blinked on for a moment at the junction; a few seconds later he was assumed up into Heaven.

I watched, hypnotised, until the park was almost empty and Yamaha XS750 DOHC (EPJ 990V) stood out like a sore thumb on the edge of the park. I walked over there, emptied of interest, unconnected to anything at any point, except at the one where he joined me to my past, if he did, and looked away at clumps of stragglers. In the middle of one such group a faded striped bed sheet hung between a pair of broomhandles. There was a pathetic brave attempt about the way it was wagging and fluttering. I walked back and made out FREE DON BAXTER and then I started to hurry over, to get a look at the people gathered around it.

There was about ten of them, maybe less. "It doesn't matter, right." Marie was at the centre of the group, pulling a strand of hair from her mouth. Her arm was still in plaster. "Not really."

What didn't matter? I wanted to know.

"I vote we should make some decision now as to how to carry this forward to a proper conclusion."

Everybody was listening to her. I strolled up and they turned to look at the new face in an involuntary repel-all-boarders kind of way. Marie didn't notice me at first, continuing her attempt to focus the group—around what action?—but as soon as she saw me she seized an opportunity, marched forward and grasped my arm, as if I'd been trying to escape instead of arriving.

"Tony here knows all about it." She guided me firmly to the centre. "This man was lifted at the same time as Don," she announced.

It took a lot of effort to meet their steady gaze. My eyes kept drifting down to the level of their hands—but I did, by act of will, steadily. I decided I had to be impressive, more impressive than she'd thought I was. One of the others—her boyfriend, the enemy—settled back against the saddle of his new Revere (a poser's bike if ever there was one) and started untangling the thickest part of his beard with slim, agile fingers. I rubbed my tongue across the roof of my mouth.

"I was working for Don and Brian Nello at ABC at the time."

A soft exhalation from somewhere. "Bastards."

"One day I got called back into the office. The police were waiting for me there. They kept me in overnight, interrogated me." I was unsure how to go on. "They were ... heavy, you know? One of them hit me round the side of the head."

"Who?" It was the same quiet voice. I looked across at a skeletal balding freak in cracked leathers and a torn doublet. He knew the right questions to ask. Obviously an old hand.

"Wheeler," I said.

A murmur from the others. A name.

"I did think of making a complaint, but ..."

"You were too scared." Him again. "Don't blame you, mate. Nothing to be ashamed of. Many's the time they've clipped me and I never said a dickey-bird. It's more than your life's worth. Ever tried challenging a pig in court? Don't bother, mate. Once they get you down in the cells again you're fucked. I mean really fucked."

"They interrogated me for hours ..."

"Not then, before," Marie said. "Tell us about the line-up."

"They put us together in a line-up." I shrugged. "That was when the old man pointed out your friend."

My mouth went dry, my mind blank. They stared at me. Didn't any of them know any of this? Obviously they didn't, not all of them. They needed to be told. Some were obviously friends of his—workmates in distinctive Swallows leathers. I'd heard a whisper from somewhere or other they were made to buy them. A few others, maybe. How popular was Don Baxter? Not that popular, really, not by the looks of things.

"This would be the Reverend Poore," said a big Swallows rider. "Am I right?"

"Right. Right. Really, he was in no fit state to identify anyone. There was a bandage round his head."

"That's bullshit." Jonah again. "If someone hits you and you see them do it you know who it was. Anyway, what are they meant to do? Send him off on a Mediterranean cruise to recover? By that time he would have forgotten everything."

"Please!" Marie intervened. "Can you let him talk?"

"Okay, okay. I was only saying."

"He's right though." Another clean looking young bloke, this one with blond curly locks. Swallows again. "Don could still challenge his identification in court, he said, "on that basis."

"He did have a bandage round his head," I agreed. "A big one. He looked dazed. Unsteady. But the police were being really heavy. I want to point that out. They interrogated me for hours. They turned the tape off and whacked me around the side of my head. Then they threw me in a cell overnight. If that had gone on much longer, who knows what I might have said? I wouldn't said anything." I looked around, amazed at how convincing I sounded, how convinced I was myself of my innocence. Of Don's. "His name was Wheeler. They were all in on it, though."

"Of course they were." The old Jonah freak said with dignity. "They are not civilised people, they are filth."

"Look at their racism, their routine harassment of, er, er, er, black people. Not only that ..." The speaker had greasy red hair, a complexion of condensed milk and ginger nut biscuits and a soft Scottish accent. "Murder. Racist murders. I think we have to draw some of these strands together. That these, er, er ... obviously I'm not saying it's the same people, but the methods are a matter of routine ... are the same people who harass trades unionists, are used to break strikes ... and, er, if we look at their role in the miners' strike for instance, or against the print workers at Wapping, or, er, in their routine brutality towards London's travelling people, I think what you're trying to do here is, er, absolutely brilliant ... but we do have to remember that we're dealing with the repressive apparatus of a capitalist state ... we need, er, maximum publicity. Maximum solidarity from every courier in London." His thin-wire body had been jerking, a current passing through it. He faltered on: "It's not going to be easy. But, er ... "

"Brilliant. Brilliant," Marie said. "I agree with everything you said there, absolutely one hundred per cent"

"So do I." Me. I did too. Something tugged at me. Nagged. I pushed it down, sat on it hard.

"We've got to build some solidarity," Marie said. "That's why we printed the leaflet. That's why this rally seemed a good place to start us off."

What leaflet? Then I noticed a few of them blowing on the ground, tumbling off across the park. If they'd distributed a lot of them they hadn't had many takers.

"Er, er, er ... I think you'll find, er, that what we'll have to do is, er ..." I liked this bloke, the way he seemed to have to force the words out of his mouth. The way, when he did, that they made sense. "Continue to work with what we've got for the time being."

"We could always pull some stunt." The big guy. "You know. The sort of thing that gets on the news."

"Good idea, George. But what though? I think before we decide on particular tactics we should bear in mind, we should think about which way we're wanting this to go. Could we involve more people on the basis of a wider campaign about harassment of couriers by the police? I mean, look at the numbers of people who've turned out here today."

"On the whole though,"—it was her boyfriend on the Revere—"they do let us get on with it. And I don't see what this has got to do with blacks, unions and all that. Nothing as far as I can see. I don't know anything about it. Call me ignorant if you like. I think you'll find most couriers are just interested in earning a living. I don't see why Swallows needs a union."

"Cheers, Mel," she muttered. "I think that's a separate issue from the one we're trying to discuss."

"But if couriers were properly unionised I think you'll find we'd be in a stronger position," I said.

"I agree with you, er, er ... but she's right."

"As it is," Marie again. "Don doesn't really seem to have any rights—even as a citizen or whatever. When his mum phoned the police station to find out what he was held on, they told her he was well over eighteen and it was none of her business."

"That's really bad." The little Scottish bloke shook his head sadly. "Anyone would think that was bad."

"They only do that when they think you're complete scum," said Jonah. "Or when you really are."

Whose side was he on? I sensed a drift in the small group. Looked around for the Scottish bloke's bike. What was he on? Probably an MZ. A Ural complete with full tool kit including shovel for digging yourself out of the snowy steppes. I'd said all I could say. I looked at the ground, scuffed a hole in the grass with the toe of my boot.

"Great." Mel breathed out through his nose. "This is where it starts to fall down, isn't it, because no-one's being honest enough to mention why they don't like Don."

I looked around at the faces; they blurred as I lost concentration.

"He's a junkie. That's why they think it was him. Because it's what people like him do, in their way of thinking."

"And in reality." Jonah didn't look far off it himself, but he turned on his heels and strode self-righteously away. There was something finally, definitively miserable about this action.

"Not in this case," she said to his back. "Definitely not in this case."

Marie was something to watch. Nobody moved or spoke when she spoke, they were held by force of her personality. Why did she defend him? Loyalty? Something else he had for her that made these words of praise for him come? Her own need, her wish to make something happen? A stately blob of lemon meringue meandered towards us across the grass. Anyone who wanted to take further action was invited to follow them back to their place. The spell had been broken and everybody groaned as the luminous bubble burst, its rainbow colours no more than a dampness on your cheek, a lace magnet of vaporised truisms, and we all split fast in opposite directions: nothing to lube but our chains.

The new account—Three Six Six—turned out to be an office on Farringdon Road: an office above another bloody sandwich bar. There was a row of cracked, taped doorbells beside a side door; it was identical to the way up to the Forwarding Agents office, to the way up anywhere, all such city entrances with their lingering promise of unfolding untold stories, those stories you couldn't tell to anyone because of the madness (or indifference, or disbelief) they engendered, and the final burst of them had not even the yawp of a new life, nor even a moment's relief and the wait for the inflammation to subside.

This was towards the end of the financial year. There was a lot of panicky ferrying of adjusted figures, a lot of fudging and smudging. I ran into the bottom of a queue ending halfway up the stairs. Mostly young women, with a smattering of men. Every one of them carrying Tools for Change ID, yellow collection boxes. I threaded up past them: mainly they were from abroad, you could tell it by their ease in achieving mutual understanding. Backpackers in their early twenties, broke and far from home. Charity workers. Too dusty and down at heel to be strictly tourists. Girls on the run, maybe. Pre-migrants. Those old age pensioners on the tube couldn't have taken the pace on this one.

Then the queue turned a corner at the top of the stairs, crossed a bare room to a trestle table where two suited men dealt with everyone in turn. I stood to one side and watched. Every yellow box was locked at the base by a lead and wire seal, which was broken in order to empty the contents: a man clipped off the wire with a pair of snips, counted out the money into change bags and stashed them in a filing cabinet; another entered amounts in an old fashioned ledger, handed out quantities of notes from a cash drawer in the back of the table. This man also locked and unlocked the cash drawer between transactions.

Every collector pocketed ten, fifteen or twenty quid, was handed back her ID and the resealed collection box was clipped together again through a pair of eyelets on the side. The whole process was endlessly, painfully slow. It was taking place in broad daylight.

"Hornsey Rise?" I said.

One of the men behind the table, immaculate nails and a dark suit, jerked his head towards the back of the room.

Poore was standing at the window of a partitioned office with pegboard walls. He raised a finger, beckoned to me. I bowed my head and walked over to him.

"Ah, hmm." He met me at the door, resealing a large stuffed jiffy bag. "So sorry to keep you waiting."

I glanced at my watch. I'd been in the building for two and a half minutes. Thirty more seconds and I could begin to charge waiting. Not that I was about to ask him to sign for it. "No problem, no problem."

The old man studied me keenly as he handed over the envelope. I kept my face still while he tried to place me. But he knew who I was. "You are going straight there? This must reach them by five. Umm, earlier if possible."

"Should take about forty minutes." I really loathed the scumbag.

"Fine. Well, don't place yourself in any danger."

I managed a smile, but he was closing the unpainted door. People always told me that I looked like somebody else, usually just before they turned away and started another conversation.

Outside in bright sunshine I walked into the end of the queue and into Marie. Or maybe she walked into me, I don't know. Anyway, she was prancing around, laughing, prodding at me as if I was her long lost brother or cousin. She had a funny little face, I noticed, I wasn't really sure I liked it. Plain, animated—but by what? What was behind this head flopping, this inane prancing? What was so bloody funny?

I tried to step around her. Was she on drugs?

"No you don't. You don't get away that easy."

"How are you?" I said. "Look, I've got an urgent drop."

"I'm the best."

Her plaster cast was covered in signatures, with hearts and kisses, good old Ogri in a winged helmet, a string of question marks—I felt the same way about her: I imagined she must talk to everyone she met. They became attached to her for life. There was something ominous about this.

"You're in a good mood."

"I enjoyed seeing that film."

"Wasn't bad, was it?"

"It was okay," she said. "Thanks for talking at the meeting."

"Anything come of it? There were some quite odd people there."

"Not really."

I couldn't work out if she meant that the people weren't really odd or that nothing had really come of it. What was she doing working for Poore? Why did everyone seem to think he was okay? Why hadn't anyone questioned his evidence? That was surely what had caused Don's problems. It really was wrong. Even most of his friends thought he was guilty.

"You're meant to ask me if we can do it again." She laughed. "Or whatever."

So I asked that instead. I found her difficult to refuse, especially as I didn't want to. We swapped phone numbers and arranged to meet. Big smiles flashed between us, and out of nowhere came a feeling of sudden frank promise—I couldn't believe it—and then, for the time being, I stepped back into my life. I eased the bike into traffic and jumped the queue down to the lights.

I was overtaken by a surge of anger halfway across Clerkenwell Road. For some reason he was pissing me around. The voice of command. The simpering look. I was sure I hadn't been the first to want to put a fist in it. Me, a confirmed pacifist. I didn't know why, but that was okay. I didn't really care. But I knew I was going to do something I never had before: the ultimate sin. The one where they revoked your account book forever, tore off your epaulettes and snapped your cutlass over your knee. I'd done worse already, so why not? I was going to open up this packet—this one. Right now.

But I could hardly stop at the roadside and rip it open under the curious eyes of two hundred drivers per second. Could I? How about a park? Too exposed. Inside, maybe. I wished I could take it home, study it at leisure. Obviously out of the question. Too far away. A toilet was the right answer! I locked myself in a cubicle of a MacDonald's on Holloway Road, semi-deserted in the mid-afternoon lull, sat on the seat and pulled out the jiffy. I inspected it. A self-sealer. Picked at the edge, eased gently. The flap came away without too much damage.

Inside was one long continuous computer printout; two columns ran down the right side, interrupted by monthly sub-totals—on the left was a list of items. Expenditure in brackets, income in heavier type. But the marks were very, very faint. I strained to make sense of it—he needed a new printer ribbon—the light bulb flickered, pinged out. Then the wedge of paper had come unravelled; it was spilling in folds onto the floor, one corner soaking up what was either piss or disinfectant. I flipped back and tried to find the £5 cash on collection job through which we'd first become acquainted—I didn't: the figures weren't detailed enough.

Income was grouped under three headings:

DTD	TOOLS	SCOL

The middle one wasn't a problem, obviously. And I worked out the first one as being Envelopes/Door to Door. The third ... I kept jumping to something like scholastic. Until I clicked on Street Collections. I leafed on. December was the largest figure by far: £8,640 in a single month. Higher by a third than the others. Both other categories added up quite stably to half that amount. This seemed to be the way it was done. As I'd always known, seen. Hit them with a young girl when they're pissed. Same principle as bar work. The future of giving. My little transaction appeared under the general heading of POST/SUND. In the summer month I was looking at, this gobbled up a massive four and a half grand. No way was he spending that on stamps and couriers. Another surprise was the rent not appearing. Salaries ate up £3,600. The rest of the overheads were in the mid-thousands, knocking income down to around two and a half k's.

I refolded the printout as close as I could for a man fighting off a roll of killer toilet paper, and restuffed the jiffy. The seal looked a bit iffy. An iffy jiffy. I hoped they weren't close inspection types. I flushed the toilet and I went downstairs for a cheeseburger ... the burger was quite reasonable; but the fries were lukewarm, left over from lunchtime and dried out under the lights. Never mind. They filled a gap. The rest of the way to Hornsey Rise I wondered about salaries. Paid volunteers?? Other aspects of this bothered me too, like why send the figures to an accountant? I thought that charities didn't pay tax. Anyway, they were the wrong sorts of figures for the Inland Revenue. Not enough detail. I'd seen my mother doing the old man's accounts for the VAT man, driven into an annual frenzy as he pottered unflappably around looking for stray petrol invoices.

"Don't touch that pile!" Finally, after a week, they would work out that they weren't going to prison. Not this time.

Hornsey Rise. CROFT & LEE. I handed the packet to a pert seventeen year old they'd sat at an old typewriter in the window of a premises sandwiched between an antiques shop and a bakers shop.

"Ah yes," a little Jewish bloke, mid-thirties, with a clipped beard and red braces, wafted through and plucked it from her hands. "Hmmm, this is quite an interesting one," he said to me— gave me a penetrating, all-knowing look. "Thanks a lot." Buck-toothed smile of friendly termination of encounter, a "Ciao!"

On my way to the bike I hesitated for a moment, then popped in next door for a particularly appetising slice of Joe Blake I'd spotted in the window of the bakery shop, and then I was back into the proper business of the day.

I met up with Marie in The Crown on Cricklewood Broadway, a big old Irish pub that was still great in those days. The stage was too small for a show band, or they'd probably have booked Big Tom, a singer pictured on an album that once belonged to her mother—a bulky man with a sandy Beatle haircut, holding up a rickety white garden trellis with one hand, a wooden songbird affixed to its arch, an endearing grin on his broad freckled face. In person he looked like an overgrown child, she said, one of the forever young, smiling as he signed postcards of himself (from a stash he kept in his jacket pocket) for the wee girls who ran up to him after each show with his band (the Mainliners) clad in their spangled emerald satin tutus.

The Crown offered a four-piece country outfit. The singer was around forty-five, his axe a tan semi-acoustic; the female keyboard player was wearing a cardigan and court shoes. Twangy solos and patches of rinky-dink organ added emotional colour and depth to the broken-hearted outpourings of the Brand New Mr Me, the long-haired drummer dropped in a few John Denver numbers and a bassist in a dark yellow jacket and shoestring tie handled sweetish harmonies. They were a family band yet miraculously all still had their sight and the full use of their limbs.

The four country roads to Glenamaddie. Four dusty highways to somebody's heart. Marie's? I hoped so, yeah. Tanks and guns ruled the town she loved so well. Joey Dunlop was King of the Roads and it was all still banging away in her head. Poor old Jim Connolly still tied to his chair. Pat Connolly tying one on. The lilt on the tilt and mothers waiting by the old rustic bridge with thin-lipped smiles of welcome to the wayfaring son. Babies bleated in vain—Please, Mama, Please, Stay Home With Me—only to be consumed like kindling in providential house fires staged by the Almighty for the express purpose of shaming the women who bore them. The wheel done fell off the wagon and I was getting wild again.

We snatched a few lines of talk between songs and nudged each other and kissed and I inhaled the sweet, sweet perfume of her hair, her sweat. She told me about a lot of things in the band break. I felt that by even hearing them I was on a promise. Much too much attention is paid to the many words coming out of people's mouths. I was edgy. Didn't myself come on with anything big. Anything at all. Going to the bar was difficult, as it was deep in accents more servable than my own.

It was a place conjured into being by the magic of retrospect; absurd if you'd just stepped off the boat, more home than the home you'd been desperate to get away from; but once here it was somewhere you might just about go on a family night out—to appease the old folks—even if, in everyday life, you were another comely transsexual with a compulsive yen for married men; a high-class cocktail waitress, a bored data inputter, or a courier of messages from the gone away times when the crack was mighty and the Crown was the preferred watering hole of half of MacAlpine's Fusiliers.

Unless you'd ended up owning half the town, in which case it was a poor location for a fashionable restaurant or multi-levelled theme experience—of what? poverty?—and you were more likely to speculate about levelling it to build on; only to dismiss the notion and decide it would do for others: the insufficiently mad for it. In other words, the good old working classes: because whatever your mother and father once were, you were it no longer. And that was something to be proud of—because nostalgia was for tossers who hadn't been there; for the likes of you and me. There's a new hotel gone up beside it now, East European barmaids, a heritage mural, and no music.

Marie was an outsider here, I could tell. The place robbed her of her real connections. She was still back home or on the end of a thin wire of phone calls and memories and the incarnation of remembered ways in the twanging string of her own body: a world that glowed and burned at the end of her fifth Silk Cut Extra Mild trembling between her nervy orange fingertips. At 11.10 they harried us out into the Cricklewood night; which was the same night as any other night—anywhere you could see the stars, but weren't too sure what they were. Marie said goodnight at the door and promptly went off to phone for a minicab. "Go you on. Go you on," she said. "I'll be fine, just fine."

I don't know what made me pick up Tinacrea again and try to read some of it. I'd been getting more and more wrapped up in some ongoing rush of events that seemed like 'my life' but didn't satisfy me. What came next in Bob's manuscript was a series of broken, separate paragraphs on consecutive pages. I bent over them, puzzled them out—and once again the mysterious arachnid planet sprang into existence under my hand:

So the days ended, if days had existed, the endless days of Tinacrean wine. James Railio grew to like the stuff as he learned to manage its effects, and combining with the 'opening of the eyes' it had made something precious of their sharing-time—something he would always remember. He felt like such a child in these encounters; that he had too little of his own to share with (   ). For her part (   ) was patient in these encounters, without making him feel any the less, and he spoke freely of his boyhood on Earth, of the great ambitions of his young manhood, and his discovery that he might far surpass the expectations of his birth-parents. And he told her about their difficulties in understanding him, and of his own in carrying forward what they had taught him into the (   ) of a (   ) (   ) but that these difficulties were small, really, compared to the (   ) (   ) of

certain ( ) ( ) ( ) alone ( ) ( ) wept often ( )
( ) lost heart for a time ( ) ( ); ( ) ( ) in particular
( ) had led to his decision ( ) ( ) and of ( ) ( )
( ) ( ) arduous ( ) ( ) ( ) ( ), ( )
of ( ) ( ) that he had never once regretted embarking upon
this course of action.

Railio ( ) ( ) found Tinacrea fascinating, ( ) ( ) ( )
( ), but now he wondered if his whole ( ) and ( )
formation ( ) ( ) ( ) result of ( ) ( ) ( ) drawn to
her. This thought of Railio's particularly amused and pleased ( ).
He noticed how ( ) ( ) lit up, softened ( ) subtly ( ) ( )
how she would cradle his head, deftly plaiting her ancient patterns into
his hair, which she dampened ( ) ( ) and ( ) ( ) ( )
of sculptural monstrosities more becoming in a spaceport whore. ( )
was ( ) to ( ) an ( ), ( ) ( ) not really an amusing
concept.

"( ) ( ) ( ) ( ), Mr James Railio?"

"( ) ( ) ( ) name, ( )."

"Neither ( ) ( ) ( ) ( ). ( ) ( ) ( ) in the time of
broken flags, but I remember also an eon before those days, when I bore
the ( ) of ( ), and even ( ) ( ) ( ) ( ). ( )
( ), ( ) ( ) ( ) further still ( ) to ( ) ( )
indeed ( ) swarming in the birth-nest of our people ( ) I was
( ) known as ( )!"

"( )?!"

"That is correct, Railio." ( ) ( ) ( ) ( ) ( ) blushing.

"You are ( )," he said quietly. "Or might as well be."

"No I am not," said ( ).

"Come, ( ), I ( ) ( ) ( ) ( ) I am."

I'd forgotten his sense of humour. But the whole thing seemed
so painful. Wrung out of him. I had no tools, not really, to handle
what I was reading. That was part of the problem. Because I
should have had all the understanding in the world. After all, I'd
known Bob really well, hadn't I? Hadn't I? Maybe not. Or maybe
there was something else locked up in this, something I'd mislaid,
or didn't know about.

(   ) (   ) (   ) *like being imprisoned in a light furry cage of incredible strength, cradled firmly against her soft old leathery body with its musty, tangy aroma, and whirled at medium to high speed, like a cat or a baby that's crawled in amongst the warm clothes in a spin drier.* (   ) (   ) (   ) *the ancient Tinacrean way of* (   ) (   ) (   ) (   ) *her twenty-three empty, rocky deserts. It was necessary to have a detailed, intimate knowledge of what had at one time been the trade winds. Breezes that barely agitated a grain or two of blue dust over which the Tinacreans would propel themselves at enormous speeds, like sentient tumbleweed, across the great distances of their planet's wastes. They weren't trackless, they never had been, even before the construction of the travisphere ribbons.* (   ) (   ) (   ) *much later, during the* (   ) (   ) (   ) (   ) *age of* (   ); (   ) (   ) (   ) *expansion of* (   ) (   ) (   ) (   ). *Railio* (   ) (   ) (   ) *consciousness.* (   ) *abruptly* (   ) (   ), (   ) *him, to stagger in a few hideously small circles and collapse, vomiting.* (   ) (   ) *of the Tinacrean sky* (   ) (   ) *turning around his head in a dark whirlwind in* (   ) (   ) *saw a* (   ) (   ) *an ancient city of kindness* (   ) *swept up into a funnel of* (   ) (   ) (   ) *ed ruins, which lay glistening around him for a few minutes—before the fine desert sands sucked it away, leaving only a faint damp patch.*

　　　(   ) *knelt beside him, horrified at her own carelessness. She sprang high into the* (   ) (   ) *and floated down. Skittered in agitation, mopping at his sweating brow. She tended to him, sheltered his bruised flesh from the rays of the suns, glaring now like twin interrogation lamps.*

　　　Then it seemed to occur to her that Railio was rather basking in her attention, at which point she (   ) (   ) *prodded* (   ) (   ) *much* (   ) (   ) *and spun* (   ) (   ) *to be* (   )*ed* (   ) *between her forelegs like a* (   ), *a* (   ) (   ) *beach ball.*

　　　"All right!" he clambered to his feet, looked around. They were still in sight of the dome, "(   ) (   ) (   ), luckily!" He (   ) (   ) (   )," (   ) (   ), (   ) *around his shoulder, clumsily.* (   ) (   ) *foolish one!"* (   ) (   ) (   ) (   ) (   ) *sky* (   ).

　　　Railio (   ) (   ) (   ) (   ) *gently rubbing the soft joining part as she liked, feeling her bones splay under his* (   ) (   ). *"It's* (   ) (   ) (   ) *of* (   ) (   ). (   ) (   ) *which* (   ) *be* (   )."

This seemed to please (   ) greatly. She (   ) (   ) squeeze
(   ) and (   ) (   ) swung him up onto her back and loped lazily back
to the dome and (   ) (   ) (   ) (   ) (   ); instantly (   ) slid
(   ) (   ) (   ) drawing Railio up into her (   ) (   ), (   )
(   ) (   ) arched in (   ) (   ) spite.

(   ) was all sweetness to her lover; but it was easy to detect beneath her charm and attentiveness—a hundred little tremors and gestures animated her leathery old body as soon as he entered their living space—a sadness and preoccupation with more important things. Railio had imagined her to be in constant touch with her co-mothers, yet Tinacrean affairs of state surely weren't so taxing nowadays. In fact, there were none to speak of ... apart from attending to visitors like him, of course, perfunctorily monitoring the Proxima support team drifting on in their lazy holding orbit, probably playing chess under the communications blackout: a defensive information filter Tinacreans always insisted on ...

(   ) (   ) (   ) missions were routinely discouraged, and this alone had earned them a reputation for diffidence, secrecy, and evasiveness— although in their dealings with Prox they'd always proved loyal, trustworthy and helpful allies. Always, it had to be said, within limits set by them. Where their allies were concerned, it appeared that they had made their choice, but the matter having been decided, preferred to operate a policy of benign neglect ...

(   ) (   ) their point blank refusal to participate directly in military operations, or to let their dusty planet be used for any strategic purpose. The Tinacreans were officially advisors, but as many an admin had discovered, advisors who quite often refused to give advice, whose advice, once given—always with an irritating air of absolute certainty—often ran counter to Prox's usual view of its interests. (   ) (   ) (   ) (   ) going on for (   ); unfortunately (   ) (   ) (   ) had yet emerged (   ) (   ) (   ). It appeared that sometimes they got it right, sometimes wrong.

This was (   ) (   ) (   ) (   ) (   ) Railio's (   ), apart from goodwill and the (   ) aspect. (   ) always funnelling things in exactly the direction they thought they ought to go, (   ) (   ) while (   ) (   ) as they used to (   ), (   ) (   ) (   ) cumbersome bureaucracies (   ) (   ) (   ) its (   ) (   ) (   ) elbow. (   ) ridiculously arrogant and stupid (   ) (   ) (   ) (   ) (   ) unanswerable!!

(XXXXXXXX) (XXXXXXX); (XXXXXXXX) (XXXXXXXXXX) (XX) (XXXXXXX)(XXXXXXX)(XXXXXXX)(XXXXXX),   (XXXXXX) (XXXXX) (XXX) (XXXXXXXX) (XXXXX).(XXXXXXXXX) (WANKER!!!) (XXXXXXX) (CUNT!!) (XXXXXXXXXXXXXXXXXXXX XXXXXXXXXXXXXXXXXXXXX)   "(XXXXXXXXXXXX)" (XXXXXXXXXXXX) trust me, Railio.

Eight

When anything went seriously wrong with it I took the Yamaha over to my brother's lock-up and he was duly amazed an XS750 stood up so well to the punishment of couriering. They're temperamental—though mine is a good one—a trouble-prone model, an early so-called superbike, obsolete the moment it rolled off the production line in far-off Iwata. Over the years we had three major engine rebuilds—top half, bottom half, rebores and crankshafts—four big gearbox jobs, the famous double overhead camshaft (induction and exhaust in one), the usual heavy brake and suspension problems, many clutch jobs (they wear out, you're always on and off them), plus the front forks I bent, a highly welcome lay-off when I burnt out the electrics, a brand new wiring loom was ordered from Japan (where they no longer had them) and my bike's life was miraculously extended by a complete artery-transplant sent down in cold-pac by ambulance from a parts-dealership somewhere between Brum and Wolverhampton. The secret lay in frequent oil changes, so he said; failing that, maybe I was just lucky to find that one in a million jewel of a bike.

Training The Workers Without Jobs To Do The Jobs Without Workers slid by me on a billboard on my way through Kingston-upon-Thames: some of them had built a tangle of flyovers that obliterated all known routes through the town of my birth. Nothing to do except rise up over the bridge and do a fast left, slip between the walls of Bushey Park and the Palace, do a right opposite The Jolly Boatman and Cigarette Island, through East Molesey and onto the Hersham road. Another swift righthander and the fences started to shutter past, blobby sheep arrested in mid-munch on the slopes of the twin reservoirs between which Dad had done his first hundred on the "C" Series Vincent Black Shadow, throttling back, as I now did sharply, to pull up at an empty junction on the lonely Walton Road.

Colin's workshop was located in a prefab unit behind the Shell station, on the left, right at the very end of the yard. "No-one'll ever find you down here," I said when he took it on. To which he said: "Suits me." And now I scrunched in over the gravel to find him welding up the wheel arches of a grey 1960s Volvo. Safety conscious as ever, his goggles were hung on the acetylene trolley where they wouldn't get damaged. I walked over. He blinked a couple of times from arc-eye before admitting that he recognised me, dropped the bent wire he was holding, and shut off the needle of flame that was poking another hole in his retina.

"What you been up to?" I asked.

"Not a lot."

"Just thought I'd come and say hello."

"Hello," he said. "What do you want?"

"Nice looking motors these."

"Ugly old tanks if you ask me." No-one ever had, unfortunately. He kicked out casually and half-affectionately at the Volvo's passenger door and a shower of autumn red flakes fell from the sill. Colin hung his torch on the trolley next to the goggles. "This ones a real pig. Should've just driven it into a fjord and claimed on the insurance, instead of wasting my time with it." A packet of gum appeared from his overall pocket and he coiled a stick into his mouth. "I gave up smoking last week," he looked at his watch, "exactly four days, sixteen hours, twenty minutes ... and thirty seconds ago."

"Oh." I decided not to provoke him any further.

"Want to know what that's like?" he insisted.

"Difficult?"

"Impossible, except for me. Don't even bother trying, Tony. You couldn't do it in a thousand years." He flicked his gum away, located a giant family size packet of crisps in the Volvo's front seat and offered me a lucky dip. "I heard this scientist on the radio last week," he crunched a few of them up like sparrow skulls. "He said these are good for you, in moderation."

"What, cigarettes?"

"No, dickhead—crisps." He grazed his way methodically through the bag, brushed some crisp crumbs off his hands and tossed the crumpled packet into an empty drum, where it crackled like amplified applause, or rain.

"Thought I'd look the bike over," I said. "Got the odd spanner handy?"

"I've got the best there is, mate. Snap-on." He walked over to the red chest. "There's two thousand quid's worth of tool-kit here." I knew I was in for it. He had to go through this ritual. He had to show me how to slide a drawer open, how to slide it shut. He took out a swivel-headed socket extension, rotated it precisely between black fingertips: "A tool? Or what?"

I weighed the stainless steel bar in my hand. I so much wanted to tell him what was bothering me. I kicked the ground and looked over the roofs of the lock-ups, because I knew I'd never be able to make myself speak—and if I did …

"Wouldn't do you no harm to wipe a rag over that bike," Colin said. "Look at the state of it. How can you ride around on that?" He pulled a rag from the top pocket of his overalls, dabbed at the tank. I looked at it from his point of view, from the point of view of the investment of his time and effort it represented. The bike looked absolutely disgraceful, like it had been sculpted out of black mud: it was one more source of shame for me. He stalked away into his workshop, his strip-lights flickered on with a faint drone and I heard him banging around on the bench. The workshop lit up like a deep stage on which he was the only actor.

"Tell you what," he said, "I'll sort you out some T-cut and a clean rag." After a short search he pushed a soft polishing rag and a can covered with thumbprints into my hands. "Coming back home after? I'll call Linda."

I manoeuvred the XS into the light and I started to apply the T-cut in whorls and swirls and curls. It was therapeutic, it took the crap off—when it had dried off in a nice piecrust I rubbed away at the paint and chrome, swapping from hand to hand as my arms got tired. Once you'd started you had to go on and on for hours and hours; but it was something simple that always worked. I'd have to leave the polishing of it for another time. Colin had almost finished his last job of the day—whipping somebody's head off. Whipping it back on would need a good night's sleep; it was a job for first thing in the morning after a trip to see the parts-man in West Molesey.

"Make sure you get it all off," he called from the sink. I looked up, and saw he was what's known technically as Black as the Ace of Spades. Garmed Up To The Eyeballs. Filthy Dirty.

Degreasing, rubbing the Swarfega between his black fingers like baby lotion, rinsing it off. I'd just about finished cleaning the bike off. I followed him inside, stood there behind him as he finished at the sink. I washed my hands in a quick prayer of supplication.

"Old Despatch Riders Never Die, They Just Lose Their Dockets," I called out to him. And we were ready for the off.

Back at his place I sat on the sofa with the plate on my lap, watching a sit-com that wasn't going to become a rerun classic. There hadn't really been a good reason for coming. I felt so tongue-tied, so useless, so stupid; when the credits brought me round, Linda stood up, smoothed her pleated office skirt—they seemed to make them dress like schoolgirls at the agency where she was—and we both handed her our empty plates.

"So what's new, Tony?" she called from the kitchenette. She really was just lovely, just right for him (or anyone else for that matter) and Colin was one lucky undeserving little bastard to have got his dirty little hands on her.

"Not much," I said.

"Got yourself a young lady, then?" She brought in a tray. "I could always try and fix you up with somebody from work."

She was being funny. I laughed but I never could see what was so richly amusing to women about my being on my own. For once, there was something going on, but I resisted the urge to start blabbing. Instead I held up my shaky right hand, wobbled it, boogie-woogie style.

Linda lifted her eyebrows owlishly, offering the plate of chocolate Hob-Nobs. "Who's the lucky girl?"

"No-one."

Colin looked away at the TV, pointed with the zapper— worlds rose and fell with a few of his expert finger movements: a helicopter settled on a gravel drive; a woman in a silky headscarf came to the front door of a white mansion, ran out to a speedboat moored at a jetty, gunned the outboard and took off across a placid lake. The chopper, emblazoned with a red and blue flash, rose up and gave chase to her—she was trying to escape from something, or someone, apparently.

"Well, best of luck," Linda said. "It's about time you found somebody to look after you."

I grunted, stared ahead, forced myself into a smile, a shrug. I liked Linda. I was jealous. Stupid. The music soared, and *Voice of the Heart* slowly wrote itself across the lake's surface in a strong female hand, its slick waters now dented by a capital "V" as the wake of the speedboat widened and formed the first letter of the title. This must've cost a fortune but looked cheap, terrible. Colin muted the picture, crawled over to a stack of videocassettes on the floor, ejected the inert incumbent and fed another one into an eager slot.

"Have a look at this," he said.

Linda stood up went into the kitchen to get some beers out of the fridge. The buggies were revving four-abreast, enormous paddle-like tyres, pumping up nitro on a purpose built oval moat that was fringed by a lot of Spanish Moss somewhere in the Lake Charles area.

"Seen your mum and dad lately?" The swamp buggies obviously reminded him of them, the way they were now churning up great walls of mud in order to remain neck and neck.

"No. I've been meaning to."

"You should do, Tony." Linda handed me a can of Dixie.

Colin fast-forwarded to the ice speedway. That was more of a sport in his opinion. Teams of Russians, Czechs, Germans, Fins and Swedes had finished warming up the crankcases of their Jawas with blow-torches, slipped on their armadillo gloves and were revving at the tape on their cowled, spiked wheels. "Look out for Serenius," he said. "Fifty-three years old, he is. Swedish bloke."

It was a sport of heroes: welders, mechanics, even plumbers. Vladimir Fadeev, the Russkie ace, was another man to watch. Slender, old-fashioned looking bikes battled it out. Men with shock-absorber arms wrestled with the straight-across bars of machines without suspension or gears; every bump on the rutted rink was transmitted right through your body: if you came off in front of someone it was liable to prove fatal. A Czech rider slid off on his arse and cannoned into the flimsy bales, sprung up unhurt, ready to continue. They were men of iron—there was definitely something inspiring about them. You wanted to hop on one of their bikes yourself, no brakes, no clutch, you just kicked the bike into gear and hung on—and there were a few heads I wouldn't have minded impaling, riding over and coming back for another go on the next circuit, rubbing someone's face off, making it so they had no face. Afterwards, the winner, carrying a small child, spoke to the cameras in German.

"Look at the Jerry ace with his little nipper." This was something Dad might have said. His tone exactly. Colin was saying it to Linda. Hopefully, encouragingly.

Linda didn't answer; she spoke to me instead. "Tony, you really really should sort yourself out." Her voice had dropped to a low urgent whisper. "You're wasted, you're wasting yourself."

"I'm all right."

"I know you are, Tony—I'm not trying to tell you what to do with your life."

"Hmm." I sank guiltily into my leather. What was she trying to tell me? That I should be thinking about betraying my own brother? I squirmed in my seat. Colin was getting twitchier and twitchier, I could feel it from where he was sitting.

"You could've been a teacher," she went on, "or something in that line—they're crying out for them, aren't they?"

"Not that loud."

"Don't you want a good job?"

I didn't answer. I didn't know. I did know that if I opened my mouth again either or both of them would start trying to tear my head off.

"By the way," Colin asked, "you still got those Mole Grips of mine?"

"Yeah, yeah," I said. "I'll bring them over."

There was always such a wall between myself and them, much thicker than blood, much thicker than churned up water; it was more yoghurt textured and I accepted it, but they couldn't. Linda, hmm. But did that mean I was a bad man? I didn't think so. The world was such an absolute out-there, and I was in-here. Okay, okay, ticking along, just about, so long as I could keep those useless out-there bastards at arms-length for long enough.

I wondered if Poore was like that. His beaky upper-class snout was into everything that moved. He was everywhere. I thought he was. I could tell. Did that make him good? Like fuck it did. Because he might seem friendly, even be friendly to almost everyone; he might think that he was everyone—might even know he was—but he wasn't, not really. What I couldn't work out was why I still persisted and persisted in thinking he must be good: interested, fairly impartial, or so I imagined. How *are* you? I imagined him asking. How are *you*? But if he was so sensitive—I don't know—why would he have to ask? Poore. Pore. Poor. Inadequate. Poverty. A hole. Disguise. A poor one. Eroop? Orepo? A permeable membrane? Or a cracked distributor cap that let the black rain in and let you down.

The City guarded by Griffins, the Temple by No Entry signs. The only way in by motorcycle was from Victoria Embankment. I'd parked up and trotted on through the labyrinth of courtyards: King's Bench Row through Pump Yard, past the Lamb Building, scanned lists of names gold-lettered on refreshed black doors in order of most recent arrival; collecting the autographs of affable articled clerks and drawing sympathetic comments about the weather: a drizzle of goodwill to offset the steady ire of heaven. I stopped dead in the centre of Fountain Court, wishing I could understand what I was looking at; but there I still was, as ever totally fucked. I pulled off my helmet and lifted my greasy face to a healing-bath sky. Birds twittered mechanically. I glanced down at the name of some legal dignitary carved around the fountain's rim; a big somebody or other who had died in 1976, a name considered important enough to last forever. Suddenly the water on my face was hot, salty. I felt like kicking the shit out of somebody, somebody who'd cheated me or lied to me but who, like all such people, would never admit to it in a thousand years. Butter didn't melt; it stayed hard in the chill cabinet. I wondered what would it take to carve a monument like that, out of best butter.

5:45. Willesden. I'd been bump starting her between jobs most of the afternoon—a minor run out to Clapham had given her a charge and now the lights were on and she was fading fast. But she was super-clean now. I dreaded electrical problems, so did

Colin. I dropped off at a godforsaken Portacabin on the industrial estate, and called in clear, more than ready to go home.

"You want account 360, W6 to WC2," Alf came back. "Got that 2-7?"

At Linguaphone House a security guard sat in a pool of light and held up the packet like a prize I'd won in a raffle. I was caught by every set of lights down to Knightsbridge. I let her die at the third and strained her up onto the pavement to run and bump, metaphors spilling past us like cheap jewellery. My headlight was a cloudy pearl. Etcetera. Even a glass diamond. I cut through the West End and people heading out from work stepped off kerbs, yelping and jumping back as I trimmed them close as a hedge.

I parked up on the Covent Garden side of Aldwych; noticed I wasn't still wearing my bag. I stared into the top box at the packet, willing it to reappear, with the Bellstaff overtrousers stuffed inside. Where ... where? I went back over it. I'd left the fucking thing on the top box to do the last drop. Alf had come on the radio (bastard) and, it had slipped off as I rode away.

Fuck. Shit. Fuck. Shit. Fuck. Cunt. Cunt. Bollocks. I snatched at the packet, slammed the broken lid and dropped my whole set of keys through the grating of a drain.

On the pavement a mild-eyed Scandinavian happened to be passing:

"Did you do that now?" he asked. "Amazing, this is truly amazing."

I saw his mouth drop open, attracted by my look of abject desperate appeal. It was quite an amusing thing to be a first-hand witness to such a curious incident, was it not, quite something, yes? Ha! Ha! This more than made up for another dreary day on the tourist trail. It would certainly be something he could tell the folks back in Olso. How they would laugh! laugh! I forced myself to break eye contact. I fell down on my knees. Peered between the slats. Uttered a stupid prayer. Stupidly. Stupidly. Fuck it!

"Good luck to you!" he said earnestly, wisely wrenched himself away from the scene of my humiliation and walked on.

"Alpha 2-7," Barbara grated. "Where are you?"

"Where's Alf?"

"Gone home."

"Alpha 2-7," I said.

"Walking towards Essex Street."

"Why are you walking?"

"Because I dropped my keys down a drain."

"Well, there's not a lot I can do about that." She held the yap button down. "Alpha 2-7, you still there?" She was laughing at me, telling anyone who happened to be in the office what an idiot I was. Bitch.

"Roger-dodge."

"Call in when you're clear."

I walked for a while.

"Alpha 2-7, where-?"

"Walking."

"Okay, 2-7."

The last man out was hurrying away as I reached the drop. He stepped even livelier when he saw me. I blocked his path to get him to sign, and after a short sweet argument he unlocked the building, took the packet; it was gone seven o'clock, I called in clear to Barbara—and as I wandered back towards the bike, my shadow man passed me in the opposite direction. Him again. I hadn't seen him for a while, but there he was, riding an identical XS750, dressed exactly like me. There he was—still out there, waiting for his moment to finally close in and start walking around in my shoes. He hadn't waited though. He was already up and running. Bastard. I wondered where he lived, if I could commit some pre-emptive strike. That's what it would take, Tony, I heard him say. I picked up a ring-pull off the pavement, bent it in half and desperately pushed it into the key slot: it magically turned on my ignition.

But I was getting too used to these miracles, last reprieves. I laboured into the car park and took the battery off, carried it upstairs, patted my pockets on the landing, and remembered the door key had been on my bike key ring. I tapped Nan's letterbox. The Scottish couple who lived next door. The family I didn't have to be fascinated by because I knew them already. Nan liked me. So did Tam. I let them use my phone. I'd let them run in a power cable from my bedroom window when their electricity was off. I'd called an ambulance one night when poor old Nan had thought she was dying. I'd been relieved it was a false alarm.

Nan opened the door in her dressing gown. The smell of stale alcohol billowed past us.

"I'm locked out," I said. "I wondered if, maybe ..."

"Come in, Tony, come," she said. "Ye'll havti ask Tam aboot it."

Her husband perched on a pillow placed on a kitchen chair, watching an episode of *Moonlighting*. He looked up and flicked back a strand of his still jet black hair, his eyes swimming behind thick lenses. He climbed to his feet and gestured hospitably towards the settee.

"Sit down, Tony, please," he shouted. "I've got to sit here masel', for the back, like." He carefully lowered himself back onto the cushion. His whip-spine swayed in a lazy S.

I started to tell him my story but the sheer stupidity of it seemed to annoy him. "Anyway," I cut it short, "I thought maybe—maybe ... that your key might fit."

"It won't." Tam fumbled in his shiny trouser pocket. "Of course it won't fit, ya wanker. Otherwise we'd all be in and oot of each other's flats all the time. I'm no saying dinnae try though. Try it, try it, Tony. Nan, Nan, where's that fuckin' key?"

Nan appeared. "Och, there's a much better way than that."

"Aye, take the beading aff and lift the windae oot." Tam looked at me. "Honestly, that's your best bet, Tony."

"Och no," Nan said, "that's a terrrible lot o' trouble."

"I'm only telling the man, I'm no saying he's tae do it." Tam turned to me quietly. "Another way's wi' a wee bit o' flex thrae the letterbox. A stiff bit, no an ordinary wire -" he pointed out the TV flex "—that'll no do it."

"He got into Wilma's right enough," Nan confided. "Wally showed him how to do it. So dinnae think he's some sort of genius."

"There's nae big secret tae it. You've only tae make a loop at the end and flick it up over the knob. Thing is, Tony, after I helped Wilma, I had every bastard in the tower started knocking on ma door. D'ye know what I'm saying? I had tae tell them I couldni do it. Shall I tell you why? Shall I tell ye? Any break-ins, they'd say: Ask That Scotch Bloke. D'ye see?"

I saw. But it didn't show in my face.

Tam spoke with exaggerated clarity: "Do—you—see—what—I—am—saying?"

"Tea?" Nan called.

"Och, he'll no be wanting tea, woman."

"Tam," she commanded, "let the boy intae his hoose."

Nan brought in the mugs and we talked aye aboot the damp in the rooms and about whether anyone was buying. They weren't buying. Their son's darts trophies were lined up along the mantelpiece above an ancient coal effect fire, paper hanging off the walls. I shifted on the broken settee and sipped the evaporated milk flavoured brew, which seemed to cling to the inside of my mouth.

"Where's young Tammy?" I asked.

"Overnighter," said Tam. "Football special tae ... Coventry. That's time and a half. He gets his distance money on top of that, eh."

"How long's he been on the trains? Ten years?"

"He makes some money, I'll tell ye that."

"Twenty-six!" Nan pulled her dressing gown around her nightie. "He's making me old, son."

"Stupid." Tam stared doggedly at *Moonlighting*.

"Ooooh, it's cold!" she rubbed her matchstick-like forearms, "so cauld!"

Which was definitely one thing it wasn't. The new caretaker had managed to switch the heating on and warm air was circulating continually with a dusty drone.

"She thinks she'd cauld, Tony." Tam laughed. "She will be, eh, eh?"

Or maybe Wally could be induced to show off his housebreaking skills. He'd love it. But then he'd have something on me. I swirled half-an-inch of luke-warm tea in the bottom of my mug and studied its sludge of choking leaves. On the wall was a glowing embroidery of a Highland piper serenading Edinburgh Castle. SCOTLAND.

"I'll get the flex," Tam said. "I'll no promise, mind."

I noticed he kept it handy. We both went on outside and he tried to poke the special flex through my letterbox, missing the slot several times. It didn't look that promising. An impossible task for someone as helpless as Tam. How the hell did they manage to carry on living? Pickled onions. I stood there, expecting a long slow methodical painful attempt to hook it over the smooth handle, a good try ending in noble failure; but I didn't say anything, not wanting to annoy him or jinx him. I shouldn't have troubled. He did it in a few seconds, the heavy lock clunked and the door swung open with a creak of invitation.

"Thanks."

"You'll be wanting to put a drop of oil on that, son. It drives us crazy. Yeh. But before ye ask, ah havni got any."

I made myself comfortable indoors and tried to think carefully. Tam's good act. Good acts in general. The good act Nan had to push him into. Reluctant exercise of his housebreaking skills. That I had to coax out of him. Even though I let them use my phone whenever they liked; even though, for a time, they'd run their appliances on my bill. Until I had to put a stop to it. Call a halt. Unplug them. In the end Wee Tammy had had to fork out to get them reconnected, deciding that, as he had to live in the dark as well, he supposed he'd better perform his filial duty. Opening my door was a good thing to do. Tam couldn't really be described as good person though, not really. Not that good. Unless you took it as good that he exercised due caution. Which, I supposed, it was. He wasn't reckless. Not in that, anyway. As for my helping them, I didn't really see that as particularly good either. More inertia. More of a failure to refuse to help. It was far easier to go along with their undoubted parasitism than oppose it. You'd be a real smug bastard then. Superior, which I most definitely thought I was.

But I preferred to think of myself as being of a benevolent disposition. I was that way inclined, usually. At least with some people. I showed goodwill. I accepted them. Tam and Nan were okay with me, quite all right as they were. Unjustifiably, this made me believe I was a good person. Goody two shoes as opposed to baddy one shoe. Whatever they were, I was the opposite. I'd let them thank me, extend goodwill that only really lasted as long as they were talking to me. Until the door closed. Until they were gone back into their own lives. Until the next time. Until the knock. Why wasn't it enough that we rubbed along together and sort of helped one another out as far as we could? Why bother thinking about it? Why make it bad? Why bother thinking if that was the best you could do?

(   ) (   ) were (   ) (   ) race of (   ) memory (   )
ers. Or (   ) its survivors (   ) (   ) barren mothers (   ) the
(   ) didn't include (   ) (   ) to (   ) friendly. By now (   )
(   ) wherever, whenever (   ) (   ) Prox (   ) it seemed. Simply
that the (   ) (   ) (   ) out. Railio was astride (   ) (   )
as of (   ) (   ) for ranch (   ). (   ) wouldn't (   ) (   )
(   ) way. It wasn't (   ) (   ) that. (   ) was so (   ) larger
(   ) (   ). How could (   ) pretend to (   ) or (   ) into something
(   ) (   ) he (   ) lost, a prospect he (   ) (   ) (   ) (   ) nor
ever (   ) (   ) (   ) to the end? (   ) couldn't.

I was getting pissed off with this stuff. You could read right through it, and to some extent, fill in the gaps. But wasn't it that these words he had left on his pages were the only words he had thought of? His limit? His end? Wasn't it really that they weren't really all that interesting as words go?

I flipped back. Selected a passage. Read it.

"It's (   ) (   ) (   ) of (   ) (   ). (   ) (   ) which (   )
be (   )."

I puzzled. It clicked. Easy. It was just another part of the sharing. Sharing that which cannot be shared.

I should go back through it and fill in the gaps, if I could manage it. I skimmed onwards and upwards and tried to get a bit more of a sense of what it was all about; but really I had it already. I decided not to bother, threw the wad of paper on the table and went out to the kitchen and made myself another coffee. Ttt. Sod Bob. What a sorry bunch of clowns they'd turned out to be. And I was. Still dry-running away from him, from this, from that, from the blueness of the moon, the light of dead stars and just about everything else …

... especially my place in this world. And Bob's. I seemed to need to believe that I, Tony, was at the epicentre of a circle: I was really something, in the swim, breasting the waves, and so on. As for my seeing him. As for Marie—what was that about? The words that came out of her mouth in the park, so brave, so weightless. However good, however true. And as for the Poore ... I still had a childish wish to talk to him. I really had to force myself to dismiss the pathetic thought that he knew everything, that he could help me, that he would. But why would he? I did a bit more washing up. I looked at my reflection in the window over the sink. Not bad. Still reasonable. There used to be a rat-pack of pigeons out there. One-eyed, stumpy, hideous pigeons nest-building on a mulch of rotting other pigeons, other common grey pigeons no more handsome than themselves, pigeons no more. What could you say about them? Nothing. Nothing.

Either you ignored the stench and the incessant cawing and cooing until shit started pouring in through the kitchen window or you put up wire over the gaps and cleared the little fuckers out of your life.

How could Poore be so shameless when I, I, I, who was innocent in every single way and had nothing, nothing (not much, anyway) ... I stammered, turned away, addressed the wall? Disgraced by my XS self. It wasn't even something I had control over. People smelt it on me. Or something. What was it? What was it? A stench? B.O.? What I was ... No, no ... I definitely hadn't always been this way. It was just the way I happened to feel right now. Afraid of screwing up. Knowing I already had done. What was so fucking great about that?

It's okay to feel ashamed of yourself when you're young, just like Aristotle said. At least it showed you had some sense of right and wrong. You were capable of self-criticism. Self-improvement. At least you can blush appealingly. At my age all it proved was that you've done wrong, done something you shouldn't have done. It didn't matter, really, whether this so-called bad thing was really something bad or just something people thought was bad; either way it's something to be avoided at any cost. Otherwise there you are with your hand up over your face. And if you don't know why, everybody else will soon tell you. If they don't know they'll make up something. You couldn't think you were good for feeling ashamed. Because you were the one who'd done whatever it was. Whatever it was that had made you into such a bad man. If you felt ashamed it proved you were guilty.

How was it that he could just run his rip-off operation with impunity? Not caring? Not just him—everyone else. Don and Brian Nello. Alf and Barbara. Everyone. They were just the tip of the iceberg. Let's face it, this was the normal way of things. It was thought to be okay. Was I any better? If I was basically good and I'd done bad, well, I felt bad about it all right. That was something. Not much. Because I didn't really do much wrong. But not doing much wasn't good either. It was nothing. It was scary but I didn't even get any pleasure out of the things that seemed to turn other people on. I thought there must be a word for people like me, more or less incapable of enjoying ourselves. Miserable bastards? That was two words. That was Harry. Inert? No, that wasn't right. I had it, I had it: I was a fucking idiot.

Nine

On Sunday I idled in up the long drive of my parents' house out in Aldershot. Vehicles were wedged into every space in the yard and more bonnets nosed out from under the half-closed garage door. Two months ago an inquisitive passerby strolled down there and ripped the brand new stereo out of a customer's baby blue Merc. I slotted my bike between Linda's green Opel and a 305 Estate with a bouncy sign saying SEX EDUCATION VEHICLE suckered hopefully onto the rear window. Mum's beautiful face appeared at the back door, framed by her untidy grey curls. She had a quilted turquoise anorak on and she wore a single glove the colour of red meat.

She held a garden trowel. "Dad's down the end of the road with Ray," she said. "There's a motorbike trial on up there or something."

"Really?"

"Mmm. Exciting, isn't it."

"Where?"

"Up the road, right at the end in the woods. They've been up there since nine o'clock." She looked at her watch. "Should be back for dinner at two, half-past."

She made coffee and we went through to the sitting room, its walls festooned with pictures of fluffy cats with black eyes— there was a particularly fetching one her sister had taken of three identical kittens on a chair, brand new beings, puffs of white smoke. As they got old the tips of their coats went dark grey. There were also pictures of children on the walls, of her sister's daughter's kids: a rebuke to Colin and me.

"How's work?" I asked her.

"Not bad. Mrs Black's been playing up a bit."

I relaxed as she told a couple of stories about her bosses, describing a trip with the other women to see *After The Fall* by Arthur Miller. "Is that the one about Marilyn Monroe?"

"Yes, except they had a black woman playing her. It was strange. I was really hot and uncomfortable in that theatre. It was strange watching her. That's me, I thought. That's what I'm like." She laughed, offering a JPS. "Really horrible."

"Dad getting much work?"

"I'm doing the accounts with him last week, Tony. He hasn't even got half of it. I had to get him to put it in piles on the floor. Hopeless. Hopeless. Never again. I'm finished. That's me. Done."

"You sorted it out though."

"I did. Muggins here. It's too much for him, Tony. Too much for the both of us at our age." She brightened up. "Would you like to come outside and see my blooms?"

"Show me later, mum. I'm going up the top of the road to look at the trials."

"Okay, dear."

"How's Ray? Was his heart sorted out?"

"There's nothing wrong with his heart," she said coolly.

I listened with half an ear to the news update ("Married him and discovered he was a bigamist, twice over") then she let me go, I finished my coffee and walked up there—the flowers would still be nodding and stirring later on.

The Talmag trial went on every year at the top of the road. At the bottom of the road was a stock car track where I'd once seen Dad race, not long after Colin was born. Dad was doing well, leading the season. He was champion material—until his old Hillman, hyper-tuned and welded up with Jim, a panel-beater, turned over and was knocked on top of his right foot by a back marker as he tried to clamber out of the car. Six weeks he was off. I enjoyed the novelty of his lying around in bed. How he showed me the deep hole below his ankle. How when they'd carried him off the track and into the military hospital he had been conscious of nothing except a single bright rope of blood he was laying down across the polished wooden floor of the officer's ward.

A few cars were parked alongside of Farnham Road. There was a similar number of bikes, a Citylink van. The verge gave onto a steep wooded hill, and as I reached the far kerb Colin and Linda stepped from amongst the trees.

"Still going on?"

"Yep. Sammy Miller's out."

"We're freezing." Linda rubbed her hands together in woollen mittens, joined like handcuffs—she held them up, I was tempted to bite through the umbilical. But didn't.

"Dad and Ray there?"

"Oh yeah," said Colin.

"Right to the bitter end," Linda added.

"They've got Richie with them. Ray's boy."

"I know who Richie is."

I walked away into the trees where a few forlorn spectators were straggled up beside a ditch that churned and twisted up the hillside. At the bottom a bare-headed man with a cigarette in the corner of his mouth stood on the footrests of an old Greaves scrambler, aimlessly riding up and down a sandy path—and I climbed the hill myself, hopping upwards onto gnarled roots between slick banks of earth. I was hoping to find some more action over the back. At the top of the hill a big block of weathered concrete, like a seaside tank trap, reminded me I was on army land; a woman in a headscarf was walking a golden retriever; a small family carried a couple of folding picnic chairs along a wide sandy path; and at the end of it another deep rutted ditch ran up another wooded hill.

Clumps of spectators, hard to pick out against the trees, were stationed up it at ten yard intervals—the only sign that something was actually going on. I scrambled up to each group in turn. Any one of the knots of men could have been Dad, Ray and Richie: the very same people (in the very same clothes) I'd once seen watching Dave Bickers and Arthur Lampkin and the Rickman brothers, and could see again any time thanks to a video on which our super-eight home movies had been strung together by a friend of Dad's with a home video camera and a screen, adding his own soundtrack of skiffle hits. That's what this reminded me of: the British kept a comin', kept a losin'—eventually chased away into the Gulf of Mexico in comical retreat; only to regroup every year since to relive former glories.

The sidecar outfits assembled at the bottom of the hill, ready to go off. Brilliant. I'd always preferred the intrepid sidecar blokes. Their machines had a homemade feel; great sidecars, bare metal padded for the protection of agile passengers, grapple bars for them to cling to. I stood back and watched them set off in turn to climb the long, snaky hill, their passengers craning out to kiss the ground, swinging in to lean over a rear wheel or pull in tight behind a rider—and when one pair took a bad line, I heard a bloke in front of me say to his wife:

"That man's blind."

"Who? The rider?"

"No, him."

The passenger he meant was holding his head up, like a dog sniffing at the air—and at that moment, as if jinxed by his comment, they struck a root and the bike went over, capsized in the middle of the track. The outfit lay on its back, throttle wide open, stuck in gear. The blind man quickly clambered to his feet within inches of the spinning power wheel as the rider limped over, disengaged the gearbox and wrestled the machine upright. The passenger stumbled across the track, feeling for a non-existent wall; but as soon as he'd made contact, he swung ever so neatly, so confidently into the chair; and resumed his role as a human gyroscope, parallel with the bucking earth as they rode up the remainder of the course, finishing, finishing—and even though they came in last they still got a ragged cheer.

I climbed up to the brow of the hill, ducked left and scrambled down to the start. At the end of the section were twenty old bikes blipping, grey-haired men jostled for position, craning in clouds of breath-smoke and Castrol R. A bored steward set them off. I watched them get away. Nearby an old man in immaculate racing leathers sat quietly on a pale blue Ariel, his large head sunk down into the padded shoulders of his leathers.

"Know who that is?" Dad had come up behind me unexpectedly.

"No," I laughed—but I'd already guessed.

"That's Sammy Miller."

"Sammy Miller, that is," Ray echoed him. "The ace." His brother pulled out a quarter bottle of Southern Comfort from his pocket, took a small belt on it and passed it over to me. "This'll warm you up, Tony."

I said hello to Richie. He smiled—he'd been enjoying this for hours.

"The greatest trials rider of all time," Dad said. "Sammy's said he'll retire if he wins this year."

"All British bikes, is it?" I asked noncommittally.

"All pre-sixty-five irons."

"British irons, Tony." Ray looked across at me, catching my drift. "British," he said with a mock-pride that wasn't

Sammy Miller was a frail and wobbly old man. He walked on past us with the self-contained look of the minor deity. I passed the bottle back to Ray.

"All right, Sammy?" Ray called.

Miller turned sharply, surprised to be recognised. He saw it was an old fan and acknowledged the greeting with a side-smile and walked on.

"Good old Sammy." Ray back passed me the Southern Comfort for a second belt. "Nice this, isn't it, Tony? Smooth, not like whisky."

Everybody agreed that it was smooth; and we turned to watch the big name riders battling up the course. Stewards scribbled with biros on score sheets folded in the palms of their hands, carefully noting each dab, each sin.

"Watch old Sammy go up," said Ray.

Sammy Miller stood bolt upright on the footrests of his Ariel and cruised up the sheer trough of mud at a fast uniform speed, in a way that looked effortless—so efficient it verged on being boring. But not quite, not quite—because you knew you were witnessing mastery.

"Beautiful," Dad said. "It's just like he's going to work."

When the other riders had all tried and every single one had failed to beat Sammy Miller's time we stamped our feet and huddled in our coats and walked up after them to watch the next stage. Ray sprang on ahead of us—goat-like, boyish—Dad and Ray were immune to the cold. We trudged up after them, Richie and myself. My feet were going numb and Richie's nose had started to glow. He stamped his feet, wincing, laughing across at me. It was a complicated feeling, being part of them, part of a chain. I remembered Dad teaching me to ride, watching me go round and round on the grass beside the flats on an NSU Quickly, later on getting me to follow him on the BSA C15, patiently teaching me road craft. I thought of falling asleep at 100mph on the back of his Tiger 110 as a small kid, my feet dangling in mid-air above the brand new motorway. But I was a hundred thousand miles away.

Acton Library was full of old people nodding off over big print sagas and volumes of war reminiscence. I distracted myself with the cassettes and a capsule history of pop music from Al Bowly to Richard Clayderman, pulled out a copy of *The Stars Salute Elvis* and rapidly reshelved it. I gradually worked my way down to the Law section, which turned out to be well-stocked. There were some self-help books, general stuff on the glories of the jury system, a number of town hall pamphlets on unfair dismissal, racism, sexual harassment, buying your own home; and big studies of particular legal areas: a spry old man was looking along the shelves I wanted to get to, his features obscured by a trick stubble of thick white fur—searching for stuff on Tort. I didn't even know what that was except being mistaken. Well, it could happen to the best of us. Eventually this particular old man (he had a persistent look) was going to become an expert on whatever he needed to know. Perhaps he already was, because when he saw me standing behind him he stepped aside, my need being greater, my business more urgent.

That's why they were in here—to pass their twilight years in dreams of litigation, of revenge. I looked around for the Golden Lady (surely there must be something useful on embroidering the cloths of heaven?) but she wasn't about today. I pulled down a book on charity law and took it through to the newspaper room, which was even more popular. They let you sleep in there, provided you weren't too noisy about it. I found myself an empty desk and puzzled over the contents page and flicked back to the general index.

I wanted to know about any general rules that might tell me how and why he was laundering his figures. Like this business about tax exemption. Were they exempt or not? That queue of people collecting backhanders. Paid volunteers? Was that legal? I couldn't believe it. Of course it wasn't fucking legal. The book was written in handy bite-size chunks. I tried out a few, but the only question I managed to answer was the first. Yeah. Charities were indeed tax exempt. Of course. There were a few special cases accountable only to the Charities Commissioners; but the rest presented annual accounts to a special Inland Revenue department in Bootle.

There had been recent changes in the law, but half-an-hour's research left me in the dark as to their precise nature and extent. I gave up. What more did I need to know? At the beginning I found a short section on the origins of charity—it came from three important little words: Agape, the Greek for love; Caritas, its Latin translation, and Koinonia: God's people, the congregation, Greek too, from koinos, meaning common, sharing. The Philip K. Dick stuff. It came back to me again. What a great writer. I wondered if he'd looked it up in a public library. The book's epigraph was the familiar quotation from St Paul, *Corinthians*. I read it again. Those words got a hook into you all right, but I couldn't help thinking that could be because you knew them already. It didn't make them true, did it. After all, I still knew the words to *Que Sera Sera*. That's why obvious things were still taking me by surprise. I left the book open on the desk and went back to the flat.

There was a dictionary Willie had left behind there, a fat paperback with Over 30,000 definitions for £1.99.

cha'rity n. 1. Love of fellow men; kindness, affection; leniency in judging others. 2. Beneficence, liberality to those in need or distress, alms-giving, alms; trust for advancement or education etc.; institution for helping those in need, help so given; ch. begins at home (is due first to one's own family and friends); cold as ch. (in allusion to unsympathetic administration).

I slapped it shut. What point was there, anyway, in these definitions? Just where did they lead you? Nowhere, that's where: except to false suppositions, old errors passed down forever, rammed down the throats of the living, preserved in the warp and weft of words. Any idiot could tell you that. Any courier, mechanic—or whatever—could tell you none of it was worth the paper it was printed on (so could any teacher); that's why they'd ever paid any of it too much (any) attention. It was something you knew by instinct—provided you kept your nose well clear of the dent in the middle of an open book.

There was a curate who used to come into our school to teach R.E. I wondered if he'd had an undue influence on me—not towards religion but against it; and if it was that which turned me full circle, because I knew in my heart of hearts there must be more to it than he was letting on. And maybe that was what I'd thought Poore was, really. Slender grounds for a common suspicion. Of sky pilots. Crafties. And their like. Anyway, that one was a real shit, you just knew it. Funny how useful people can be despite themselves. God's messengers. People who thought that you needed their express permission to breathe, to live—but who, if you asked them for it, wouldn't give it to you. I paced around the flat. Bob. Big Bob. Bob the Great. Someone else I'd battened onto and misrecognised. Seeing things in him, things I wanted to see. Seeing him ride out of Hyde Park on an old Suzuki. I knew I'd never be able to look at it, or see any of it properly without a sort of disguising distraction, without the buzz of warmth-giving, distancing myths.

But I wished he was here tonight. I wished he was someone else, that we both were, maybe on some other planet, one of the ones he read about and dreamed of, where this luminous twaddle of his made sense. I couldn't bear to look at that for now. I tried instead to find that religious leaflet I'd been given at the lights on Wigmore Street; I'd tucked it inside of something, probably, but what, where?? Willie's books were another crowd out of which anything could appear: shortly I ran across something else, something better. A slim unread paperback that was called *The Greatest Thing in the World*, written by a nineteenth century Scottish cleric named Henry Drummond.

"Love is the fulfilling of the law." St Paul. Whatever that meant. It could so easily be used, misunderstood (deliberately) to justify a Law and Order crusade, of doing your duty (to what?) come what may, because you had to. Then I understood. St Paul wasn't a state philosopher all it meant was if you had love you'd automatically obey the other commandments. Because how could anybody who truly loved God commit murder? theft? adultery? or be covetous? Drummond started off analysing everything love is better than, and then went on to the many aspects of love itself. Love is greater than charity (which is only an aspect of love) because a whole is greater than its parts. Etcetera. Love was a compound thing, like light, and could easily be broken down into a nine-fold spectrum of its component parts:

THE SPECTRUM OF LOVE

Patience	"Love suffereth long."
Kindness	"And is kind."
Generosity	"Love envieth not."
Humility	"Love vaunteth not itself, is not puffed up.
Courtesy	"Doth not behave itself unseemly."
Unselfishness	"Seeketh not her own."
Good Temper	"Is not easily provoked."
Guilelessness	"Thinketh no evil."
Sincerity	"Rejoiceth not in iniquity, but rejoiceth in the truth."

I tried kindness first. It was too easy to be kind to the poor. Harder to show kindness to the rich—who often needed it most. Something of a nod to the patron there. I almost put it down. More curate stuff. Hardest of all to be kind to our equals. Hmm. I skipped, read Good Temper. Against anger: a mere blemish on the otherwise clear skin of the virtuous, you might think— maybe even a Good Thing in certain circumstances; but those tell-tale flashes of anger lit up the putrescent anti-virtues seething beneath the surface. Anger was lovelessness in its most vigorous form, Drummond thought, because directed outwards, at the others.

Next Guilelessness. I wasn't sure what that meant. Except to be trustworthy, apparently, also to be trusting. To be trusted is to be saved, he said. It's those who believe in you who influence you most. That seemed true, as I thought of it, though naysayers always had a nasty way of getting under your skin. If so, trusting people who were nice to you was perhaps the likeliest way of getting good results. And the naysayers? They acted as though they were doing you a favour but they were just thieving, lying scum: out to waltz off in your jewels. Had they ever tried nay-saying themselves? Putting their paycocks up to auction? Saying I really don't deserve this?

But then, if you were only being nice to people in order to have some sort of influence over them, wasn't that guile? Of course. A ruse, usually. Invariably. But real trust had to be real. It had to be a genuine belief in the goodness of others, the whole blinker kit, full wets. "Thinketh no evil". That was the most difficult virtue of the lot. Hard to see how that could be anything but phoney, otherwise you'd be willing your own personal disaster at the hands of others' true motives. More nonsense to be held up to ridicule by good old Sigmund. He had a field day on that one and common sense rose up in its commonness to give him a tumultuous ovation.

I ploughed on towards Judgement Day. Vindictive occasion. Our sins of omission would be weighed under the silent accusing gaze of those we'd failed to love. Sufficiently. Enough. How much was enough? An impossible amount, of course. Nobody on earth could possibly love that much. Hard enough just to look. If you truly opened your heart you'd die of other people's misery—or more likely discover that the fear thought was actually true: that you really didn't have a heart to break.

Maybe Drummond wasn't so very great, not as good as Blaise Pascal anyway. His religion of love was certainly more attractive, more positive, more outward-looking though, which is why it had ended up as an evangelical pamphlet, "over 50 million copies sold worldwide". Pascal's stuff was about loving God, but you didn't get much back for it. Drummond was too. Trying to be like Him, which you admitted was impossible from the start. All the same, he offered a few general pointers in the right general direction: Sainthood, and, I realised, the true path of sainthood led through suicide. Martyrdom was only the acceptable form of it. Once upon a long time ago I'd read Albert Camus: *The Myth of Sisyphus*. How the absurd man could only be a hedonist or a suicide. Most of us chose the former, if we thought about it, which many people didn't; but there had been a strong rescue operation on morality in Camus—because, for him, neither/nor wasn't truly satisfactory to a thinking being. Long dead circuits fired up, sparks were flying out of the top of my head (admit it,

Tony, you're a real nutter). Perhaps I should look at that again. I'd have to have a good look for it. Some other time.

Towards the end of Drummond's pamphlet I stumbled across something I'd heard before. Something Poore had come out with while his wife stood over me with a stinking, sopping dishcloth. A joke, so I realised, whereas in here it was given as an example of how to love God—by offering cups of cold water in the name of Christ. I lay awake in bed with this buzzing around my head. At 3.00am I realised that it made perfect sense. They'd been right all along and I had been too afraid to admit it. What Linda said kept coming back to me, painfully. My failure to reply. My failure. I was wasting myself. One thing was sure, it didn't have much to do with paths to sainthood. Ordinary weaknesses: failings of nerve, of spirit, charity. Or monstrous ones? I couldn't quite believe I was evil. I could easily, easily believe it of the others. Wrongly. Colin was right though. I should go and see mum and dad more often. They weren't getting any younger.

At 4.00am Jesus Christ took hold of my heart. I felt His presence very strongly in the room. Then he let me go.

Ten

(   ) accepted the necessity of a saddle with good grace. Railio simply wasn't able to wrap his legs far enough around her giant's girth. Her carapace was too shiny, too hard, and too uncomfortable for travel—for anything except sex; and on that subject she had sworn him to absolute secrecy, pinioning his arms behind his back, stopping his mouth with a trembling furry foreleg until he nodded assent. The mothers wouldn't like it one bit. Nor would Prox. There at the summit of Mount Ora the whispering of the trade winds was amplified into full-scale malicious, slicing gossip. Railio was glad of his protective clothing—and of the harness they had designed together in order to hold him in place.

The process of making this human-saddle was another lesson in the ways of Tinacrean problem solving. Railio first described what was needed; (   ) greatly improved on his concept, added a few wrinkles of her own, and then she spun the required apparatus out of her body. She let him watch her extrude the finished article; the most amazing thing he had ever seen: she was an organic programmable knitting machine that could make anything.

He turned to look far below them, to where the sole travisphere waited on its ribbon, a ribbon that curved away, intersected with similar light ribbon, weaving and running off towards a non-existent maypole over a featureless horizon. Nausea. He forced it down, dropped onto her back and wrapped his arms tightly around her. How he had longed to see the caves of making, the lost city; yet how questionable seem even the most deep-seated of our desires when we're faced with a modicum of physical discomfort in attaining them. He told himself the worst would soon be over. But he suspected there was another way, an easier way; that his darling (   ) had devised this mountain journey as a special form of torture. On the other side of the pass a wide fertile delta would be revealed, a lost horizon of dinosaurs, of Amazons, of ...

"Look, Railio!" she cried.

What looked like another dry, dusty plain stretched away beneath them, not too large, bounded on every side by the sandy, worn mountains: its featurelessness broken by what looked like a series of randomly scattered giant molehills; ancient burial mounds, or crumbled pyramids. Before they'd left (   ) had explained that the latter were low, strong buildings, constructed to withstand aerial bombardment, and, of course, to escape attempts to detect them by curious scanners. Prox knew nothing of them, although they'd strongly suspected an underground city. What else? Even the first fictions of those who had begun to imagine life beyond the stars had postulated the existence of such subterranean dwellings. Railio estimated the diameter of each mound at about fifty metres. That meant its circumference was approximately 328.56 metres, he computed, using the principle of transcendental numbers he remembered from his schooldays. It was one way to stave off mountain sickness. But the real city, or its remains, lay far beneath them.

"Hold tight, Railio!" ( ) murmured. And as if in confirmation of his suspicions of easier ways, she sprang high into the air from the narrow ledge that ended the pass, from where the entire mountain tumbled down in a chaos of broken scree. She spread out her legs, like the frame of a giant umbrella, and they parachuted down. ( ) feathered their descent by means of a thousand delicate movements of her legs. Railio clung tightly to her back. All this was extraordinary, unimaginable ... but in some way he had known of it already, or so he felt, like so much of what he'd learnt—and was still to learn—here on Tinacrea.

They drifted in fast over the boulder-strewn desert. He braced himself for a bumpy landing, but ( ) simply absorbed the shock, bounced up high into the air, floated down a hundred metres on, and sprang up again, bounding off towards the mounds like a small impatient child. A nasty jolt convinced Railio she had forgotten he was there and he dug in his heels to remind her.

( ) had once explained how the mothers destroyed the nurseries, because they found them too painful to remember ... let alone directly contemplate. There'd been something in her tone, in her hesitations, which made him wonder how much more of Tinacrea's past had been liquidated. Just how safe, in fact, their civilisation had ever been in the long memories of the birth-mothers; whose behaviour towards Prox suggested quite the opposite of sharing knowledge—mystification, forgetting, kicking over the traces. Putting on fresh lipstick and facing the day. Inventing it. Inventing the day. But for whom? For him? Railio?

He couldn't believe ( ) ( ) derived much pleasure from the flap of skin and gristle between his legs. It was an aspect of the sharing, a prelude to it. Their desire disappeared when they ceased to be quite alien to one another. So they'd both said. The truth was perhaps the opposite: they had retreated back into their own solitary skins—in relief—because

the great unshareable portions of themselves were greater than that
relatively narrow isthmus upon which they met. Abruptly, she stopped
bounding—and in a deep, shared silence, rider and ridden ambled
towards the first of the mounds. They were constructed of the same
densely plaited material as the domes, the travispheres and everything
else on this world. (   ) explained their outer surface had been left
sticky (like a real spider web!) so winds might cover them up with honey-
coloured sand ... rendering them invisible, on a planet where nothing
grew, not even long shadows.

They glided in through a narrow gash which opened at a wave of
(   )'s foreleg. Railio dismounted. And they were immediately enveloped
in darkness.

"(   )!" he gasped aloud at the sudden coldness of the air, its
thinness and her old name, her birth-name "(   )!" "(   )!"
"(   )!" "(   )!"

"(   )!" echoed many times around the musty void.

(   ) murmured for him to be still, and to remount. "Concentrate,
Railio. Concentrate. Open again the eyes I have given you!"

He clung fast to her back, obeyed her, and a way opened before
them, the (   ) way (   ) already saw. She made her body warm for
him. He affixed a plastimask across his nose and mouth. Objects, paths,
appeared, lit from within by a radiated heat. The way to be followed
led through here, and down into a profound darkness, deeper into the
memory caves, into the Caves of Making.

It was so (XXXXXX) (XXXXXX) (XXXXXX), (XXXXX) !!!
(XXXXXX) (XXXXX) (XXXX). (XXXXXXXXXXXXXXX). Just as
he had imagined in his own childhood. (XXXXXXXXX)(XXXXXX)
(XXXXXX) (XXXX) (XXXXX). (XXXXX), (XXXXX) (XXXXXX),
(XXXXXX). (XXXXXXXXXXXX) (XXXXXX) ALL SO FUCKING
CORNY (XXXXXXX) (give up now you sad wanker!) (XXXX) (XXXX)
(XXXXX)ing.

I put the manuscript and my own notebook to one side and
crawled under the covers; behind my eyelids the birth caves, the
learning caves, continued to take form, as if the eyes had been
opened in me too, as if the Tinacreans were really out there
somewhere, or had been, and chose Bob, and through him, me, to
reveal their secrets to, for some purpose never became apparent,

like the meaning of a recurrent and all-explanatory dream. What absolutely pernicious nonsense. In my dream there were a series of caves in which various 'secrets of the Tinacreans' lay side by side (neatly labelled for the instruction of future generations): a series of crystal cubes on marble plinths, like those from which Superman had first learned of Krypton, of his real parents—and of his involuntary mission. There were four or five of these, CAVE OF THE MOTHERS, CAVE OF THE FATHERS, CAVE OF THE SONS, CAVE OF THE LOST DAUGHTERS ... and one more.

As far as what the cubes actually contained, I toyed with what the story so far suggested. Strange arabesques of seemingly interlinked propositions rose up, faltered, and disappeared under erasing mental scribble. Peeked suggestively through. Provoked more questions. Why did the fathers and sons die? Why were the daughters lost, particularly? Maybe they had been born infertile. There were just too many what ifs on Tinacrea. I decided that either the signal wasn't coming through or that the questions had built up in a bottleneck of the inexpressible, the irresolvable, and the insufficiently thought. Tinacrea was just another bubble: a bubble that had led him too far out into deep water, into space. Pressed itself against his face and dragged him back to the village.

But if so, I thought with one last sleepy effort, for whom exactly had he been bubbling?

The rest of them played Runerunners, I reread Robert Heinlein. *Double Star*, an early juvenile in which a second-string vaudeville actor is hired to impersonate the supreme ruler of Mars, who's been taken sick, or assassinated, or something. And as I coasted through the half-familiar story I was aware that the experience of reading it in the first place had already robbed me of a lot of surprises about things to come.

Our world was grinding to a slow, entropic close. I'd grokked it years ago really. I came in one night and found Rudy reclining on the settee under an unzipped sleeping bag, behind drawn curtains. His dope scales were set up on the coffee table; a couple of flat brass weights lay out of their wood and velvet case: and two stacks of weighed-out gear—short-quarters of blow and halfpenny-grams of whiz loosely crimped in squares of Bacofoil torn from an economy-size roll.

"Where did you get this?"

"Where do you think?"

Rudy was absorbed in an old episode of *Nanny and the Professor*: Juliet Mills whisking through the housework in a deerstalker; the Professor drove up in a long red convertible into which all three of his freckled brood—and a carful of beribboned shopping—fitted comfortably: it was a beautiful world whose blurry light revealed Rudy's normally avid face to be streaky with dried road dirt, fresh tears.

I snapped the light on.

"Turn that fucking light off," he snapped back.

"What's up?"

"Rosie's just chucked me."

"This is really going to screw the game up," Bob pointed out. "What are we going to do without Kheila Vog'n?"

Stig walked in carrying his character. "We playing tonight?"

"No, we fucking aren't," Rudy shouted. "I haven't had time to write her out yet."

I found it hard to generate a lot of sympathy for him. Even out of the game he'd always greeted everything she said with such ridiculously large quantities of pompous paralysing solemnity. When she'd finished speaking he'd look away—as if in embarrassment (well, she did talk absolute crap)—almost as if he'd been wanting her to leave for a long time. He couldn't accept that this was what meant to happen, let alone that it was what he himself had always intended.

On the magazine she worked for people ten years older than him—and they always showed an interest in what she thought. The recriminations were easy to imagine, if we'd had to imagine them, instead of being forced to listen to them over and over and night after night through the walls. They'd seen her as a representative of the target audience, her bosses that is, and that's partly what had led to her belief that her opinions were inherently interesting, because as far as I could see she was just another middle-class young woman who thought the sun shone out of her intellect, not only her darkened parts.

I wondered if Rudy had ever been there to check it out—her workplace—if it was still the same set up as now: you jumped out of the choked stream of Wardour Street and begged for a signature in front of a large semi-circular desk behind which some enthroned Sahraah, or Rosie, eventually deigned to notice you, and shakily printed her name.

Rudy binged on the proceeds of dealing for a couple of weeks then returned to the game, numbing out his broken heart with percentile dice and probability tables. He was scrabbling round for something new in his life, you could tell, and before long he managed to come up with it. One day he brought home *Teach Yourself Computers*—and from then on we'd had to listen to him continually mouthing off about artificial intelligence.

"There's these bubbles and they're all linked, right?"

"No," said Rudy, "wrong."

Christmas was coming and the geese were getting whacked more often. Knightsbridge shoppers carrying Harrods bags stepped into the paths of drunken reps at the wheels of company cars, bike magazines featured models in scanty Santa outfits straddling superbikes—with bubbles coming out of their mouths wishing the loyal readers a scrumptious helping of Christmas stuffing; and a special Christmas posse of yo-ho-hoing traffic cops carried out spot document checks on motorbike couriers. We stuffed all our tips into an empty Maxwell House jar and nominated Bob to cook us a dinner; a greasy pig-out in front of TV and a circulating queue for hot knives in the kitchen would do nicely thank you. We took in a couple of classic Danny Kaye and Bob Hope films and slept it off through the *Thief of Baghdad*.

In mid-January they offered Rudy a place to start a degree at the Poly, studying computing, starting in September. The last days. The last days stretching on forever, like the last days of school. That ended, anyway. I walked past a wall. Saw a loose chunk of cement, pulled it out then fitted it back into place; a tooth that would need replacing one of these days. Stig walked up to me outside the Honda agency on Heath Road, a broad smile connecting the two halves of his face. Maybe even his brain—and I noticed for the first time that his scar was beginning to fade.

Actually, he was quite a good-looking bloke.

"I've been looking all over the place for one of you lot. Give us a hand, Tony, go on mate."

"Okay."

"Wait till you see this." Stig led me straight into his room. He'd tidied up, made the bed, I noticed. But, more importantly, there above a bone-litter of tarnished tools, the Royal Enfield Meteor Minor—the 350 Model—stood in a complete state

"Well done," I said to him. "Well done, mate."

"What we really need is some planks." Stig kicked around the bottom of his giant empty wardrobe, pulled out a towrope. "And this."

We separated and went through the flat, opening and closing cupboards. In front of Rudy's bookshelves we met and looked at one another.

"They'll be okay," he said. "We're only borrowing them." He grabbed handful of SF from the top shelf and tossed the books onto the settee. Once he'd emptied it he carefully took out the bricks and pulled away a long deal plank. "You supposed to be helping me or what?"

So we wedged two of them down the first flight, tied the rope around the Enfield's saddle brackets and wrapped the free end around a handy banister. Would it hold? We'd soon find out. Stig steered his bike down the makeshift ramp. I decided an important role would be to feed out more line. At the first landing we stopped for a breather. The Enfield was crumpled against a wall. She looked like she'd already been involved in a major accident. Stig was pinioned behind her. As per usual, all we were doing was making hard work for ourselves. Using planks was a really stupid idea. Totally unnecessary. I was glad it hadn't been my idea.

"Rudy's not going to be too happy if he finds his books dumped on the settee," I pointed out.

"Right," said Stig. So we dumped the planks and humped the bike down to the kerb. Then we took them upstairs and reassembled the bookcase. By the time we got back the light was starting to fade.

Stig started the Enfield up on the fourth kick, mounted her with one stiff-legged swing. I watched for a few seconds as his taillight wobbled away up King Street. I was totally knackered;

it was so cold out there. I climbed the wooden hill and threw myself down on the unmade bed. I'd already started to doze when somebody started hammering on my bedroom door.

"Have you been fucking around with my books?" It was Rudy of course.

"Stig's bike." I yawned. "We borrowed the shelves to wheel it downstairs."

"You what?" He was blocking the door—I managed to slide past him—he backed me along the hall—"Of all the stupid fucking ... why? why?"

"Look, what's the problem? We put it back."

"Yeah, in the wrong fucking order."

Bob looked up from the bookshelves where he was painstakingly restoring the colour-coding of SF and Fantasy. He frowned in concentration, shook his head, ceremoniously carried on.

Rudy stalked over to help. "Get out of my sight."

"Ttt," I said. "Ttt."

"Oh ... piss off."

I sat on my bed and fumed, almost crying—and at last, at last—I accepted that these people, my friends, didn't like me and never would. I dragged my old green army bag from under the bed and stuffed my clean clothes in on top of the larger proportion of laundry. Right, I was out of this place, but I hoped Stig was okay. If he wasn't, I expected that would be my fault; I kicked out at the frayed green army bag, waiting for him to reappear.

Wincanton flashed up on the SIS screen. Hard slanting rain belting down across the field and the white fence strung with the men who had to be there—gusts, collars, umbrellas—spattering the TV lens with its blurry diamond star-light as the frisky maiden fillies trotted out under their blankets to be inspected by the world's punters: assessed with the instant expertise brought to bear on real women by real men. I looked around me. There was a gangling idiot with a permanent grin on his face who had no chance of backing anything, someone who looked like a South Sea islander in chef's whites, a few wise-looking middle-aged West Indians, a selection of young boys, a teacher on his day off, a bloke in a baseball cap and a puffy anorak with teenage daughter in tow (I expected she loved hanging around with her Dad in these bad places) and a middle-class know-all opining that there was nothing to choose between any of them, in any race, but giving out advice from the corner of his mouth to anyone stupid enough to listen.

Bong Mistress was a beautiful, high-stepping bay, but she had a bad head twitch. Little Flora was a dove-grey filly with doe eyes. Celtic Maid. She was the horse for me, whatever her looks, but I didn't have the courage to place a bet on her. What if she lost? Then where would I be? I saw Island House step out, unblanketed, and knew where I had to place my money. She was a tall horse, confident, obviously a good strong'un. I scribbled her name on a slip and sprinted up to the desk, so certain I paid the tax in advance on a £10 each way bet. I didn't do it too often—I'd once dropped three days good cash jobs at a single sitting, got burned out by names—King of Sparta (last), Keys to the City (withheld), Burnt Imp won, but I didn't get to the desk in time. I managed to make some of it back by running out and looking at the tipsters in a paper shop across the road (you didn't carry those hated men into the fray) but I soon got bored by a couple of easy favourites, made the fatal mistake of crediting Gimcrack with infallibility, placed my recouped winnings on a punter pleasing outsider, and lost the lot.

Not this time, not this time my friends. Island House—she was where I lived already. I wasn't succumbing to wishful thinking, although on that reasoning your safest bet would always be a Muddy Prospect.

A tape start. The commentary cut out at the first bend so we could be brought the Bolton greyhound start; other runners meant nothing to me: nameless, unframed—already also-rans. Rain was still belting down hard across the track and they were cantering them gently around it, not looking for any injuries or nasty surprises ... over the first fence and Bong Mistress was inches ahead leader ... Celtic Maid—Little Flora ... Island House hadn't found her proper stride yet—and a close ruck of young horses pounded past the cameras into the first short straight.

There's something great about watching a horse race on soft going on a grey rain-lashed day; maybe its just that you're not actually there in person, and that you've got something riding on the outcome: they're your horses, racing for you in the nice warm betting shop where you can pace and curse or step outside for a breath of air, a short errand timed to take as long as the race itself if you can't bear to watch. The fillies strode out into full-gallop at Wincanton. Bong Mistress was a left-field steady runner in the front three, her head-twitch developing into a full-scale chewing out for her jockey as she spat out foam-flecks. She stopped dead at the fifth fence and hurtled her green and gold jockey into the stiff brush and set about trying to find his head with her front hoofs. Bong ... out.

Little Flora was showing surprisingly well—a 50/1 outsider—could be the lucky day of some weight-watching daisy-cultivator—perhaps the idiot had bet on her; but idiots don't have that much luck ... and, and ... but even if she streaked home to an easy win I was willing to bet no-one had bet on her. Front-runners were Celtic Maid and Island House—the former motley, but with a solid heart that would take her as far as she wanted to go, the latter .. my horse, loping steady, effortlessly. They pulled out after the last fence but Little Flora stayed with them. The SIS commentator was laconic: he'd seen it before: it was unnecessary to generate extra excitement by jabbering: you didn't want your premises trashed by over-excitable punters; no big surprises, anyway, as Celtic Maid, my heart winner, pulled ahead by a couple of lengths, Island House (where my money was) behind her—and pulling in third valiant Little Flora with no-one's money on her ... but shortened odds next time.

I went up and collected my beautiful winnings.

"People usually look pleased," said the uniformed woman behind the counter.

I forced a smile.

I picked up from Jean Muir in Bruton Street, raced down to Models One in Chelsea. There was nobody in reception. I walked through to the airy office and there they were, lurching around as at an afternoon party. A Chinese woman picked up a gently throbbing phone. "Amanda! I haven't seen you for yonkies! Are you coming over to Steve's tonight? Terrific, I'll come *mit*." A young fellow running tip-toe to an imitation 1950s water cooler, on his face an expression of delirious happiness at being allowed to work with the woman in baggy silk shorts who walked towards the phone. She carried a gift she'd half unwrapped but had found uninteresting or unworthy of attention. Receiving such tributes was a particularly onerous aspect of her job. She leaned against my shoulder, juggling the box and its metallic wrappings. I held out the clipboard for her: "It's quite difficult to write this way up." She looked at me, half-interested, wondering if I might do, perhaps, mayhap, as a colourful extra in a gritty street shoot. Audrey Hepburn, I wasn't. She thought better of it and scrawled her name, DAVINA, on the proferred docket, in a large, open, empty hand.

"*Thankyou,*" she smiled brilliantly. "Do have a lovely weekend!"

We met up in the Admiral Duncan. Marie wanted to take me straight back to hers, show me what a cool place it was, where she lived. There was a helmet hanging over her good arm and no bike in evidence. What were friends for? We headed towards Brixton and pulled up in front of a squatted townhouse in a row of other squats, facing a 12ft corrugated iron fence with a couple of big JCBs behind it: a dinosaur park whose exhibits were arrested in mid-munch. Her Superdream was parked up outside, complete with tank dents, new front wheel and replacement front forks ready for when her arm plaster came off. No other bikes were around, but she wanted to reconnoitre. She let herself in and closed the door. A sash rumbled up on the third floor and a bunch of keys struck the pavement with an impact that could easily have lain open your cheek.

"Come up," she called down. "It's the Yale and the big silver one. Lock it, would you?" She was hanging around at the top of the stairs when I got up there. "Come on in," she said. "Where do you want to sit? Anywhere?"

I had a few ideas but I didn't share them with her straight away. There was a Mexican shawl hanging over bare lath, by the sash window stood a biscuit tin half-full of rain; lanky ferns and half-dead vines were sprouting from every nook and crevice in a big, knocked through room that was trying hard to impersonate a tropical rain-forest environment. I perched on the hard edge of a covered sofa-bed.

A fresh cigarette trembled between her fingers. "Where were we?"

I'd thought we were in Brixton. I didn't speak.

"I've got something you'll like."

I knew that.

She darted across the room, pulled something from behind a plant stand made of chipboard and bricks—a polythene bag full of bright green home-grown. Which she reached into and started to rapidly skin up. Needed something to do with her hands, I expect. "Great." But I didn't really feel like a smoke. I felt paranoid enough already. Swallows. There was something I didn't like about the way their clothes hung, the stylish leathers, the grey bird stencilled on one shoulder. I couldn't get a fix on people like her, didn't trust them, and yet ... well, she obviously felt the same way about me (with some reason). Here we were, with our reason half in gear. She gave me a second toke, sat back, perfectly at ease it seemed. Stiller than I'd seen her.

She looked like a ... what? Not an Irish hippie exactly. One of those people who've given youth culture a wide pass. Still a curly-headed, slightly overweight teenager at heart, with a Snoopy poster on her wall and a large collection of Gonks; but she wanted to be careful there: first you collected them, I thought, then you turned into one.

Everything was drifting. I wouldn't have minded being in that other room, the one with the Gonks; but first I had to get out of this one, now. I lurched to my feet, steadied myself. "Toilet downstairs?"

"First floor landing, door on the right."

I slammed through the first door that was slightly ajar, immediately retched up the pint I'd had in the Duncan, the treacly dregs of breakfast's coffee and God knows what else I'd been munching (soul food: to keep your inner light going). I wiped the spit off my chin and reached for a crusty pint mug that was lying on its side under the sink. I blast-rinsed it, gulped down the chalky, swirling liquid and recycled it into the bowl—slumped back, gasping. I lifted my arm and pushed at the door. It creaked open. I twisted and fell against it.

Before long I felt better. I flushed, mopped up and sat on the closed toilet seat. In a while I'd go back up, but for now I just sat there. Sweat was pouring down my back. It was the burger, I thought, the fucking fries ... the ... my head was buzzing. Tinacrea popped up in it. Tinacrea—it had come to full existence in my mind. It was a real place.

I washed my face again, went upstairs.

"You're deathly white," Marie said. "Can I make you a coffee?"

"Please."

She walked down to the kitchen area and tested the weight of the chrome kettle, snapped it on at the plug and opened the fridge door. I liked the way her shoulder-length mousy hair took on its lights. She picked up a milk carton and flicked the bottom, rinsed and spooned, tapped her foot, and pulled a strand of stray hair back from her round little face. There was a mattress back there, where I supposed somebody else slept with her—Mel, the lucky bastard with the Honda Revere.

"Known Don long?"

She returned with the mugs and a bag of sugar, quick steps. "Couple of years."

I lifted my coffee, breathed it in, listening to the crackle and spit as she lit up the fat calm-case homegrown spliff she'd rolled.

She inhaled, held it down with a gulp like a comment you've thought better of, slowly let smoke escape from her small, flaring nostrils. "Don's not such a bad being. He's just not the best at taking care of himself. Stay alive in '85, get a fix in '86, that's his motto—he has one for every year, know what I mean?"

I passed back the sparky joint.

"Why stay straight in '88." She took it all down with a fierce rattle, let it go, her eyes creasing into hooded slashes of light like the girl of evil in the AIDS ad, a junior league Typhoid Mary who's just about to pass on the virus to some reckless bareback rider. "Have you not wondered why I'm being so nice to you, Tony?"

"Why's that?" I looked around the dim room, dimly wondering what happened to 1987. She smelled strongly of patchouli (what else?) and mixed with her own smell the result was powerful but not positively unpleasant. She put her hand

161

up to the side of my face. I took it in mine. Our teeth clacked together and she dropped the joint on my wrist and I let go.

I pulled away and looked for it on the carpet.

"You're a funny bloke," she said. "Nothing bothers you, does it?"

"Yeah it does."

"What might that be? Look, you like me, don't you?"

"Where's your boyfriend?"

"He's down the pub with his mates."

"So he'll be back shortly. What if he finds me here?"

"I was kind of hoping he would." Marie laughed. "It takes quite a lot to get through to that one. We've split up, basically. But he won't leave. He has to find somewhere else to live. Which is what he should be doing right now instead of getting pissed up."

"Do you like me, then?"

"Well, you're quite good-looking. Not much of a personality though, I wouldn't have said."

"Thanks for the tip," I said. "I could work on that."

"Don't bother," Marie said. "Let it just come to you, Tony. Let it come out."

"Okay."

"Ttt," she said. "Away and feel your head."

I wondered why I'd wandered into the orbit of such an irritating little bitch. "What's so special about Swallows?" I asked. Changing the subject.

"You never leave it alone do you? Look—absolutely nothing at all's special about Swallows. Except the uniform. And they make you pay for that out of your account pay."

"I think I heard that sometime."

"That's why they've so many idiots working for them. It's a bit of a police training camp. People who fancy themselves work for Swallows. Mel for instance—he's completely taken in by them. They've got him well indoctrinated. He's memorised the mission statement. Thinks he's a knight of the road. He's hoping if he spouts on enough of it they'll make him a controller." Marie paused. "He's okay, though—in a way. I suppose it makes sense."

"Sounds like a reasonable plan to me."

"Except you have to be intelligent to be a controller."

"I thought you just had to be a creep."

"You have to be more intelligent than him." Her eyes flicked away and she crawled off to find what she'd been looking for earlier, as I walked in.

This turned out to be an old slide-shower, the kind where you looked at the lit up pictures through a magnifying lens shaped like a small television. Stacked on top of it were a couple of yellow Kodak boxes of 35mm slides.

"I don't show these to many people," she said. "Only men I'm trying to impress."

I'd expected her to come up with a few family snaps, but her treasure turned out to be slides of motorcycles—classics. Her mad cousin Gerard's Manx Norton fully airborne on a godforsaken lane in bandit country; Patrick (Patrick?), her brother's friend who'd died out on the roads, leaning against a lock-up beside his red Gilera, rehearsing a definitive head movement, an out-of-focus smile that had turned out to be his final bow. Milling crowds milled on, grinding wheat into flour. Crooks of elbows, stands of legs. The little towns out there in what she called the six counties were dead or alive places where the pub was the post office, on low streets where everyone said hi—(some hope)—or stone-faced you, whispered behind their hands as soon as your back was turned. Full of people that the bright blurred streaks of road racers cornering at the town cross were escaping from— people who made the risk of permanent escape seem not much of a risk, not really, definitely one worth taking.

Their absolutely disgusting attitudes to women, for one thing, and for another the attitudes of women themselves with their all-seeing, all-knowing nods and winks at eternity and of how Mrs Connaught would sort you out with the coat hanger as she had the Devine girl—and look at the fine mess she'd made of her. Tunnel faces, wellies, cupped cigarettes and a climb in the back of the horsebox; stuck out necks craning after the glimmer of some never-to-be-recalled event and pass the Colorado Kool-Aid, the stuff that makes your eyes pop out and makes your kidneys scream, the cup that rots, the fuckin' top shot. She talked on and on, lost names coming back to her as a series of lists, of edges. "Tony," she said, "those old bitches, they're the worst."

I'd never given much thought to the troubles—but she told me the why and the what of it. I listened, forgot. The stories which she herself was a star actress, stuck—even if, as I suspected, she was making them up: coming out of a Saturday night dance in a hail of bullets, watching a friend caught in sniper crossfire die in front on her ("they had to choose that fuckin' moment, didn't they: the very moment these wee teenage girls were coming out of a dance") ... a stone thrower in the street battles between the children of the Bogside and the invaders in their urban jungle combat gear, cowering inside armoured pigs while the girls pranced around and showed them their arses: "You could almost feel sorry for them, for the amount of abuse they took from those wee girls. It was funny though—sure it was only a laugh to us."

Marie herself wasn't from right there, but travelled in with some of her brothers, picked up the words, the whining flat ratatatat of Derry with its upward "hi?" stuck on the end of everything ("they be runnin' out of plastic knee-caps at the Altergiven Hospital, hi") ... she wasn't herself bold enough at that stage to show anyone her arse in the street, even under protective cover of a mob of children.

Whatever she was to the men she'd got to help her along, the herself that was herself to herself was in these boxes and in other boxes in her head. In other photographs, I suspected, the kinds of boring photos you couldn't expect others to look at very often, but which she herself would bring out again and again once you knew her better—which of course I did—and that, I'm afraid, was that. Marie hung onto her boxes of 35mm slides—her props.

"Ah, dear," she said. "I can see you're bored shitless."

"Not really."

I chipped in with my own family's obsession with bikes and bike racing—more theirs than mine. I'd never been to the island. I was on one already. Marie said she supposed that was true for her too, in a way.

We sat close together on the floor, the slides packed away beside us, our chests rising and falling for a good long time. She made no moves, neither did I. Whatever it was that had been about to happen was fleeting, momentary; something we'd for the moment let slip. I heard a bike pull up far below us, keys in the front door, and a pair of Derry boots closing in. I picked up an empty mug and froze with it in my hand as though demonstrating it. She was using me, I thought. She'd manoeuvred me into this scene with the man she wanted to get rid of—the bad man who'd obligingly fixed her Superdream.

Mel burst in, steadied himself with a hand on her head, ignored me. "I'm crashing out," he said superfluously. He staggered back to the mattress and dived into snorting sleep.

People. People. What were they? What was I except one of them? I should've felt full but I felt drained—my own life and its fragile, olden set of meanings emptied of everything to the bitter dregs. This lot weren't worth a light, anyway, and neither was she, probably: a jangling wire of need, want, not-get. She made you want to rub out a thousand miles—to get far enough away, or so close you could see her. She was far away from the home which made her what she was, without any way back.

Because the result of these stories was to make you think that the six counties was a wonderful place to be—which it obviously wasn't, for her—and, I supposed, it was much like anywhere else. If you didn't go looking for trouble, trouble wouldn't go looking for you. Some people couldn't help it though. I thought she was one of them. She looked at me from the doorway. I couldn't quite make out her small face properly as it was haloed in the yellowy light.

"Goodnight ... Goodnight."

I stumbled down stairs that were lit by the cracks of light from under other doors. On the bottom landing a corridor led back to another flight of stairs; a couple of loudly contending voices in a kitchen back there. I let myself out into a cloud of my own breath. I locked up, eased the big bunch of keys through the letterbox, listening as they dropped down with a clank onto the dusty squat mat on the other side.

Eleven

I was blanking out in front of doorbells, came round at lights on Turnpike Lane, exited stage left too fast in the opposite direction, always arriving at some point on the spinning compass that turned out to be not where I wanted to go, not really; and every time I woke up it was at a different point in a conversation where I told her the truth. That it was too late to do anything about Don. Too late. And the later too late got, the heavier all this stolen time of my life weighed down on me. I lay awake listening to my battering heart, my body jumping on the bed. I turned on the light and tried to work out what to do about the stupid mess I'd made of everything, telling myself it was not my fault.

All I could do was turn myself in; not to the police, but to The Antagonist—The Evil One. What could you do, in the end, but confess to your enemy? Not out of any hope of mercy or future peace love and understanding either—you looked for a confrontation because you thought you could win. Even against reason you thought it. Sometimes you'd lie doggo. Let them throw their sandbox at you: they wanted to kill you. They wanted to take what was yours. Walk off with it, laughing—and you kept on and on, making your one pathetic little move whilst they, they vaulted about the board: you waited for one of them to get careless. But were you justified? Were you ever? And what if you actually won? What would be the consequences? All these games were the same game, where the price of a single roll of the dice was no longer to believe in anything.

Questions that didn't seem to bother most people. Not much. They didn't occur to many of them—because ... because ... and if they ever did the answers were quick to the tongue: Conditions. Of existence. Obvious as a response to the weather. Slicks in the dry, then intermediates. Full wets when it was really coming down. Look at Foggy. The task and the prize were simple. The risks obvious. There were no real friends in that game, this or any game: not the way they played it. Second was the first loser. Resentment, morality of. So where were their great programmes? What had they ever contributed? What were their fastest lap times? Where were their gold trophies? Their helicopters? Their battle scars? And their spoilt spoils? Their wives? Never mind it. Fuck 'em. One glorious day. One day Tronk Racing—Colin's road racing dream team—would definitely be winning the Fantasy Road Racing League. First Prize: a new bike.

Meanwhile I just had to ride over there, say here I am. I'm the one. I'm the kiddy. I was going to have to do it in broad daylight this time. I dropped off in Chelsea, headed down to Gloucester Road and kept going. Turned again into that street of white houses where the sun was always shining, the air nippy, and the light rejoined the day to those first few times, to the best times. Kensington was sparkling like a fistful of Milky Bars on which the thick, silver-backed paper has been enticingly rolled back. Shining with a matt creamy sheen—an expensive opalescent whiteness of every wonderful object ever made out of unicorn tusks, out of stolen ivory.

Impossible to imagine people who lived in such places having much to do with the working world, let alone with Acton Town. Quite hard to see them even as sharing the same times. They weren't, really. Or if they were time didn't come into it. I always half expected to hear the clacking of a Hurdy Gurdy, the keening of an old contemptible begging for sixpences, the heart-gibbering of an organ grinder's monkey, a black footman to appear in the purple livery of order. They were further on than us, further ahead. Always always always would be. Still, these people were definitely some of the ones who made this world such a ripe shithole for you and me; so powerful—and real— they could afford to live in this carefully themed environment (keynote: their own brilliance), like the galaxy-owning rich in Philip K. Dick's *Now Wait for Last Year* with their seventeen-year-old wives on their child-world furnished asteroids. Scourge them, scourge them with fire.

I unlatched the gate. My ideas fell apart again. They didn't seem to fit anything—if they ever had. Poore wasn't a captain of the black industries, the black arts: not even a semi-retired one. Even the paint on his green door needed a good freshening up. Probably he was living on a bit of family money, eking it out. How big could something as tin-pot as Tools for Change really be? Quite big, I knew that much. There was a small army of (paid) volunteers. There must be a whole fleet of Harrys knocking the gear out. There was even a fresh Neighbourhood Watch sticker stuck in the front window. A typewriter clacked inside. A manual. I took off my crash hat and ran a hand through my hair, wiped it on my Bellstaff and rapped on the door. The typing continued. I knocked again. It stopped. I heard a familiar scuffle of slippers in the hall and the door opened on a chain.

Mrs Poore's puffy features appeared in the gap. "How may I help you?"

"Package going to Covent Garden?" I blurted. "Seven pounds. I think. Cash on collection?"

She glared. "Are you sure you have the correct address?"

"Er ..." I didn't even have a clipboard. I took my hands out of my pockets and showed them empty. "I think so."

"My husband may know something about this. He's resting at present. I'll fetch him."

"This is number eight?"

"Eight? This is 37B." She glared. "For Goodness sake. Look at the gate in future!" She shut the door in my face. Bitch! I took a deep breath or two and lifted my hand to knock again. The typing started again. But I didn't want to make her come to the door a second time. I'd fluffed it. I helmeted up and painfully mounted the stone steps and rode home.

I watched *America's Top Ten* that night, or tried to, but Casey Casem wasn't doing it anymore. They had a young black woman attempting to impersonate him. Tom Petty was singing *I Won't Back Down*. But sometimes you had to back down. I felt as if I had dropped a fiddly component on a workshop floor and then tried to find it by asking questions as to its whereabouts—wrong questions, the wrong places. I pulled down an old Family Bible from on top of the wardrobe in the spare room, blew the dust off its shiny black cover of crushed cockroaches; I started flipping through the Old Testament, pointing at random, and reading off the first words I saw at the end of my finger.

Hope deferred maketh the heart sick; but when the desire cometh, it is a tree of life. Proverbs 13:12.

Cursed be he who removeth his neighbour's landmark. Deuteronomy 27:17.

The people arose as one man. Judges 20:8. I tried again and got nothing but a few begats; then I found a little clutch of strange ones:

Dragons in their pleasant palaces. Isaiah 1:22. I thumbed and pointed at a spot on the facing page: *Wizards that peep and mutter.* Isaiah 8:19. Poore? *I am a brother to dragons and a companion to owls.* 2 Kings 30:29.

This stuff was straight out of the game. It was as if Bob had walked into the room, and as if he'd never left it.

Faithful are the wounds of a friend. Proverbs 27:6. *Burning for burning, wound for wound, stripe for stripe.* Exodus 4:60.

And then: *At the hand of every man's brother shall I require the life of man.* Genesis 9:5. I had the definite feeling of being spoken to. At the hand of every man's brother.

My eyes were full of tears.

It shall bruise thy head, and thou shalt bruise his heel. Genesis again. Trying to tell me something about Poore. Who had bruised his head? Somebody. Who? Maybe he'd done it himself, or that wife of his ... And the heel? Whose heel?

I did but taste a little honey with the end of the rod that was in my hand and, lo, I must die. 1 Samuel 14:43.

Did this mean that Poore was going to get nailed? That justice existed? That somebody knew what it was? That I was to be punished ... that I was already being punished? For what? What had I really done wrong? There were so many evasions, so many crunch-avoiding swerves. I should have asked his wife. Stupid idea. I closed my eyes and leaned back against the settee. My sense of being uniquely spoken to was broken up: gone, finished. I didn't believe in it any longer. I started to go through the only prayer I knew well enough to say, the first one I'd said with Reverend Poore and his wife after they helped me up off their kitchen floor. The Lord's Prayer—but before I'd got through it I'd fallen asleep.

Marie jumped at the dry crash of the lock, slipped past me into the hall. I'd found her out there (smell of female through locked door) hesitating on the landing as to whether to change her mind.

I let her in. She glanced nervously at the two doors leading off the corridor.

"Keep going, right to the end," I said. "it's not far."

"This is a big place for one person." I detected a note of wonderment in her voice. Resentment. As if, in her eyes, I'd turned out to be unexpectedly, unacceptably rich. But really it was the other way around.

"Tea? Coffee?"

"Whatever." She stared glumly at the aquarium, her attention caught by the giant barb flicking itself through four inches of sludge at the bottom of its glass prison. "That's really cruel, Tony."

I poked amongst the dried sponges and other paraphernalia of fish-keeping for the dried worms, imitation worms—whatever they were. "They're not mine," I said. "I'm looking after them."

"Doing a grand job, so I see."

"Take your gear off." I felt awkward, unsure what to do. I dragged a large plastic bucket from the airing cupboard, filled it from the bath taps, swung it along between my legs and left it to stand beside the tank. "I mean, you know. Sit down."

Marie plucked at the ties of her Swallows bib, her doublet, and pulled it over her head in a gesture that was quick, embarrassed, and intimate. I noticed her eyes were close together. Unusually. Too close, in other words. There was a slight sheen of old scar tissue below her mouth: I went through and put the kettle on, tapped my foot, and when I came back she carefully took the hot mug from my fingers, lapping at it like a cat.

She looked around her. "Have you read all these books?"

"Most of them."

"I'm impressed."

I laughed.

"Sorry, but I am."

We sat quietly. She was trying to drink too quickly, cooling the scalding liquid by bunching up her tongue and noisily sucking through it like a homemade straw, in a peculiar way that was really quite difficult to look at. There were one or two reasons why she just might have come round; but try as I might I couldn't think of what they might be, apart from wanting to have sex with me. I didn't want to rush her though. Could be I was being presumptuous. Maybe my shortcomings as a fish-keeper had put her off. It was all different once upon a time: clouds of neon tetras darted around, pairs of angel fish floated in close formation, bright flecks of pregnant guppies lurched around, heavy and blissed out.

I soon found myself drifting, acting out a series of scenes where everything difficult that was wrong could easily be put right, where I was the man, exactly the right man for that impossible job, and suddenly (powers of observation) I noticed that her arm was out of plaster.

"You must think I'm stupid," I said. "Your arm's better. How is it?"

"Okay," she said. "The doctor said I wasn't to ride with it— but I've been having a bit of a go. It was a really nasty accident, though. It's put me off. Did I tell you about that?"

"No."

"Broadsided by a Transit on Blackfriars Bridge. I broke my arm."

"What happened?" I handled it gently. "It seems all right now."

"Don't do that." She winced. But she didn't want to go into details. She put out her other hand. To shake mine? I took it. I shook it. It meant ... what?

"Do you want to go next door?" I hazarded a guess.

"You're very forward," she said in a way that suggested surprise. "All right."

It was very okay, easy and natural.

"Are you sure you haven't done this before?" she said aimlessly as we lay together afterwards.

I stroked her face again.

"You're so affectionate."

"You deserve it."

"Why might that be?"

I had no answer to that one. Because she didn't particularly deserve anything.

She stopped speaking ... I heard a short grunt, a snore.

"You awake?"

"Mmm. Just about. Mmmmm."

I looked down. Nothing. Out like a light.

I lay there for a while thinking about nothing in particular, then eased myself out of bed and padded into the other room. I found my ciggies and went back to look down at her from the doorway. She'd taken on the position of a runner arrested in mid-stride; her head was back and she gasped in silent pain or reverie, moving forwards into a dream. Sweet, as they all are when they're spark out like that. I went into the sitting room and pulled out Tinacrea. It was the key to all mysteries. All mine, anyway. I knew I'd be right about the Caves of Making, and here they were: a shaky set of notes under four headings. But I couldn't concentrate properly on what Bob had written. I didn't care. I wanted to go next door and snuggle back into her, but I sat down with Bob's manuscript in front of me, and my own transcriptions—and forced myself to go on.

CAVE OF THE MOTHERS

(   ) down, further down (   ) (   ) to her gently rocking (   ), Railio (   ) (   ) (   ) (   ). Bones, it was as if everything were made out of them, glowing white and fragile in the light of the eyes (   ) (   ). (   ) didn't dare (   ) or (   ). (   ) towards (   ), slowly descending the narrow tunnel to where a great portal led into an antechamber. Railio made out a square above its arch. He recognised it at once as an ancient symbol for the largest of the planets in his own solar system. They passed through it into a darkness which even his opened eyes could not penetrate.

 Railio clung tightly to (   )'s back, only her faint warmth to reassure him. She too was trembling, racked by some horrible, familiar memory that she longed to throw off but couldn't, ever. This was the condition of being a Tinacrean, of re-entering the caves. Her voice spoke in his head, but it wasn't that soft, reassuring wind-chime voice. It was ancient, ravaged. She wasn't addressing him but the spirits of the caves. No longer (   ) (   ) a someone, a something else that spoke through her or into her out of the cave's emptiness, in the voice of (   ) (   ) (   ).

 "I am the great spinner, I am putrescent, born of the deep making-cave. I am dark, slothful, slow. I am the maker without instruction. I am

singer of unremembered tales, the prophetess who lives on the forgetting-
plain. I am singer of myself and of my nature. I am scourge of my
young. Hatched in a noble birth-nest, my burden and privilege is to
gather up the white fire and to halt the movements of the orbs.

"For I am the maker of the fathers, I am the motor of their wars, the
secret progenitor of their inventions. Seer of creation and destruction,
of beginnings and endings, prophetess of prophets, the source, the slayer
and redeemer of all things."

Railio hopped down onto the floor, which was soft underfoot and
carpeted with something that felt like moss.

(   ) was beside him. "Welcome to the cave of the mothers," she
said. "Our world has no greater book than itself, but its most important
pages are to be found here. Rest for a while, I will make a little light."

She did. Railio saw that the floor of the cave was indeed covered
by some sort of synthetic moss. He sat down and stretched out his legs
and for a while they were quiet; but soon he felt the trembling again,
the words rose and the ancient mother-voice, triggered by his presence,
gathered itself and spoke through her.

"Monuments crumble, materials perish, decay—even rocks are
ground to sand by wars, by the winds. But the stories of the mothers
will endure and the artefacts they have spun out of themselves will last
forever. If forgotten in the East, the West will remember them; if the
North freezes them over, the South will thaw them. They spring up,
revitalised, as immortal as great mountains—pliable as the limbs of
our young playing together in the birth-nests ..."

... I broke off. This was great stuff. Wasn't it? ...

"... For the mother is thinker of these things—in her lonely self she sees
nothing but sorrow and defeat. It is this that drives her seeking: to draw
the outer into herself, to meditate and to create. To forget herself in creation
is her great happiness: to remember and look upon herself is her misery.
Her solitude is the companionship of a lost ally; and her sweetnesses are
the blandishments of an enemy whose plans are understood—her night
feast is the drink twice-drunk by her daughters."

Thus was the great sorrow-song of the Tinacreans.

"The birth-mother recoils at her own power. When she drinks, her sweet-drink in its web-goblet is bitterness and death. When she sleeps, dead armies torment her. She has no rest in the warmth of her nest. She is different from those whose bodies roll away like empty shells, tumbled by the sands to the corners of Tinacrea. Her sleep is snatched and restless—dreaming always of violence and the mockery of violence, of sad images of the past, black blood—kingdoms of light toppling into nothingness, of the loss of her making faculties, her death, the end of her Law."

Railio looked up into the roof where the light (   ) (   ) (   ). (XXXX) (XXXXX) (XXXXXX) (XXXXXX) (XXXXX) (XXXXX) softly glowing cathedral.

"For the mother's senses deceive her," (   ) intoned, "and the myriad small creatures of the desert are her rivals: her shadows stalk her and the foolish tales of the nursery have haunted her all her long life. There—there, in the darkness, an old woman-spider is hanging in her web, shrivelled, spun between a stone and a dead (   ). Her dried limbs are awry; beside her hangs a (   ) (   ).

This is (   ); a (   ) chatters its last song. The cold rock, the dead (   ) (   ) for her imaginings, there she will forget her envious rage ... (   ) (   ) dying mother sees a (   ) shivering by the mound, its eyes alight with the fire of a portent in the heavens. The end of our great birth-nests is written there ... Away, enemy of my joys—and blackness, fermented in a vat of un(   ) by a two-legged monster. How long must I suffer you! Go, sandy rock, withered (   ), (   ) (   )! Go, monster of the far worlds! I repudiate you!"

Silence.

"Do you like our poetry, Railio?"

"Monster of the far worlds? Is that me?"

"I'm afraid so."

"And what about these creatures you mentioned; the (   ), the (   )?"

"They died, Railio."

"(   ). When?"

"(   ) (   ) (   ) ago."

Railio fell silent, realising that she had no knowledge, that she knew only the songs that spoke though her. As for the rest, she had forgotten it. (XXXXX) (XX) (XXXXXX) (XXXXX) (XXXXX), before the first rising, after the death of (XXXXXX) (XXXXXX) and the palace revolution of *the (XXXXX) (XXXXX) when the couriers of Queen (XXXXX)'s time had so summarily changed sides.*

Perhaps not so much forgotten by decay, he thought, as deliberately erased, wiped out. "You don't remember much, do you," he said. "It's the caves that remember. As for the making, that's …"

"Out of our bodies. I have told you of it many times."

"But you have to come here to do it, am I right?"

"Not always," (   ) replied. "It rather depends on the problem." There was a definite note of irritation in her voice. "But I do think I remember how the basic household appliances go."

I snapped the light on at seven o'clock and handed her a cup of coffee. "I'll make us some breakfast in a minute."

"No, I really must—" she said, "oh, fuck it." She gulped at the hot coffee, placed the mug carefully on a vacant ring and flopped back. "Unless you've got anything to do."

I slid in next to her, tired by now, buzzing from the night's exertions. "Stay as long as you want." About ten years would do it. Longer if possible.

"Couldn't you sleep?" She was propped on one elbow, looking at me critically. "You should really do some exercises, lose some weight."

I peered over the slight mound of my stomach. I couldn't quite see what she was doing. Afterwards we lay in one another's arms again. Marie asked if I minded her having a bath. I followed her out there, embarrassed not to have any shampoo, but she rummaged around in her bag and found a sachet of coconut with bubble bath to match that had come through the door of the squat. I watched her squeeze the latter out like spunk under the running hot tap and it duly foamed up with a heady aroma of coconuts. She looked back over her shoulder, smiled as she slipped out of my robe and stepped into the mountains of foam. She seemed to take some pleasure in my watching her, and she cleansed herself using the cupped palms of her hands like somebody in the Bible.

I closed the door behind me and tried to think about something else.

We spent the rest of the day lolling around and drowsing. It was a beautiful day. We'd got so close together, so fast. Neither of us had expected it, but we fitted together like a couple of spoons. When it was getting dark again, I phoned up Perfect Pizza and ordered a spicy hot one, which we ate in front of the TV. She leaned against me as *Voice of the Heart* rolled by, the final episode, its only trace being the weight of her head, a stray tickle of hair on my neck. Everything had calmed down. She squirmed restlessly. I supposed there wasn't a whole lot more to say. Suddenly, out of a clear sky, her lightning crackled.

"I don't know how can you watch this shit," she said, then she stood up and started gathering her stuff together.

"We don't have to," I said. "We can watch what you like. We can watch nothing if you like." I'd been sleepy inside the warm noise, numbed down to a dull throb of pleasure at just being with her. "I think there's something else on the other side."

"You don't say." Marie looked at me in a sidelong way and slipped into her leather. She stuffed her radio and bib into her bag and looked around for her lid. "Have I got -?"

"This?"

"Well, Tony," she said. "Weeell ... it's been really great, but I think I'd best be heading off."

"I'll see you out then." I smiled and got up.

"O-K," she said in distant singsong.

"I saw you once, collecting for Tools for Change," I said in a last attempt to hold her.

"I know you did—outside, remember? You were right," she went on, "That old guy is a bit ... bent."

"How's that?"

"We were getting a third, right, of what we collected."

"So it was a rip off then?"

"It was vague," she said. "Sometimes they'd give you a third, sometimes more depending on how they felt."

"Didn't it all go abroad then?"

"No. Guess how much they handed actually over to the cause?"

I shrugged. I had no idea.

"Fifteen percent."

"What??"

"Doesn't seem quite right, does it?"

"No."

"All you've got to do is keep your overheads down and you're laughing."

"You mean it's legal?"

"Not exactly." She laughed. "There was even a way to fiddle the boxes open without breaking the seal. I never did it. People used to waltz off with them all the time and set themselves up in business."

"As what?"

"Freelance collectors."

"That's a licence to print money." I realised how hopelessly fucking naive I was. It wasn't just this one little racket—it was everything, everywhere. I tried to put my boots on, hopping around like an idiot. I was angry at the things we hadn't talked about, hadn't done. There was a screen between us, a deepening further-away-ness from an immediate past consisting of things that neither of us would particularly want to remember.

"It bothers me," Marie said. "But in the end, what can you do about it? There's just so fucking much of it. In the end there's nothing you can do. You've got our own life to lead."

"I know what you mean," I said. I hadn't even asked her about the life she was going back to. To Mel—she hadn't mentioned him—or Don. Still on remand, I supposed. They didn't really interest me that much. They weren't even real to me. I thought of various people I had heard about, and how they had steered themselves onto the rocks, just to be tragically interesting, so it seemed. But who to? It was easy to tear yourself in half, but nobody was going to stick you back together again.

We stood by the lift doors until they slid open. A steel plate at the back of the lift had been removed, extending its depth—it was obvious—so that a coffin could be comfortably slid in. We looked at each other, knowing what it was. I tried to take her hand. She adjusted her bag on her shoulder. I let go. Down in the car park she swung her leg over her Superdream, started her up, and at the last minute she flashed me a big smile and held out her hand. I took it, shook it. She laughed. She kissed me once again, a long deep one, and glided off with a cat-smile.

I couldn't face going upstairs on my own. I wandered between the railings and the new fence the council had put up to keep dogs out of the kid's playground, and I cut across Lexden Road and circled around the mysteriously unnoticeable telephone exchange. The White Lion was easing the last of its few customers out into the Tuesday night air. Feuds were being suspended. Truces arranged. Everything was being summarily made all right. I turned out onto the main road and kept walking. Out of there. And after a while I ducked through the trees into the whispering arena of Ealing Common. A broken street lamp was buzzing at the perimeter, shaking its yellow light over a storm-damaged tree. Blink. Blonk. A wagon ground past on the North Circular, with its deep even soporific note of night-time, of the world's continuous deliveries to itself. I sat myself down on the damp grass and tried to work out what would happen if I told her the real truth. I soon had the right answer, too. Nothing. Nothing good.

I was utterly sick of the sight (and thought) of Harry Chambers, Harry Champion. Boiled beef and carrots. Any old iron. Particularly with the all-knowing way he looked at me, a half-expectant idiot smile on his face as he anticipated my next step onto a banana skin; because my real life was taking place somewhere else, and how could he ever imagine that? Or anything, anything that went on in my head? Let alone anything as important and profound as the recovery of a whole lost ... I wasn't sure what to call Tinacrea. A lost civilisation? A map of how things go, or went—a history? A series of case notes on the meaning of religion? An unravelling of the whole mystery of men and women? A ... what? An incoherent, failed science fiction story by some idiot I used to know, that somehow was a lot more significant to me than anything in my real life; a bad spell from the olden days that, slowly and surely, was dragging me under, into the caves of darkness and death. Jesus, I hoped not. It was enough of a wrench to speak to anyone as bone-stupid as Harry Chambers.

Today he was sporting a new hooded C&A anorak in some sort of revolting beige colour, which he'd supplemented cunningly with an extra-flat corduroy cap of the kind Dad always used to call a cheese-cutter, angling it into 100mph winds so it wouldn't blow off at high speed in their dices with the new Triumphs of the Kingston Law. A statutory damp roll-up was planted between Harry's lips, and he was muttering at Gina, off her lead, yapping in the dozy uncomprehending face of Wally's harmless old Labrador, whose loll of unconcerned unfocus had given way to an intensely hostile glare. Something small, noisy and unpleasant intruding at the end of its nose—and if that wasn't violating the boundaries of personal space: well, what was?

Harry snatched Gina up into his arms, but she continued to direct a rapid-fire monologue at the larger animal. Wally's dog began to drop in a gruff thudding bass line as its owner wallowed around the bend.

"Mick? Mick?" he called. "C'mere yer black bastard!"

Harry ignored him. "All right mate?" he said to me.

"Getting colder."

"Yup."

I turned away to shuffle down the steep concrete ramp to the car park.

"How's old Willie getting on? Coming back, is he?"

"No. Never. Definitely not. He's never coming back."

"So he's made his mind up then?"

"Right."

"Okay."

I shrugged at him. "How's tricks?"

"What tricks?"

"I don't know. You know: things. How are they?"

"Ticking along."

"Good."

"By the way, thanks for helping my wife the other day."

"Anyone would have done the same."

"No, they wouldn't." He smiled. "But keep it to yourself, if you don't mind—you know what these old dears are like: they've got nothing to do all day. Except yap."

"Just happened to be passing, luckily."

"Right. I mean, Gladys—she's nothing like her up there was. A woman like that. She should never have been allowed to live on her own."

I realised he meant the fat lady. "She is a bit odd. What is she?"

"Teacher, used to be." Harry was surprised I didn't know. "She's dead, mate. Topped herself. They had a right game getting her out of here."

I remembered the plate being off the back of the lift a few days ago—a removable steel plate—extending its depth, it was obvious, so that a coffin could be comfortably slid in.

"Bet you never knew what that plate was for," he said, "on the back of the lift."

"I guessed as soon as I saw it," I said.

"So did I." Gina struggled in his arms. "I'd never ever seen it before in all these years." Harry laughed, tickled by something. "This little so-and-so's going to pee all over me in a minute, I know it." He clipped on her extending lead and launched her along the path, like a furry bowling ball. The little dog tumbled arse over tit—veered across the grassy slope and regained her short legs, running, alive. "Willie was the same. So are you. You tend to live in a world of your own in there."

"I'm out and about all the time."

"Still, you're in and out, aren't you? In and out. I've noticed that about people who do your sort of a job—you don't really tend to mix all that much."

"Hmm, hmm," I said. He was right. I'd never been a good mixer.

Twelve

There was a splintery thud, like the sound of a big football hitting a window. I immediately ducked for cover behind the couch. A second impact followed. I was under fire, in jeopardy, no longer in control. I waited for a direct hit to throw wickedly curved scimitars of double-glazing across the room. I bobbed up for a quick look and saw the barb's tail flashing as he hurled himself at the cover of the aquarium, battering against his glass ceiling. Any moment now he was going to break through, and then what? A bucket of fresh water, left standing days ago, weeks ago, stood on the floor, evaporating slowly, slowly.

The tinfoil barb was listing heavily to starboard: it was a twitching, wall-eyed brute, like a Greenland whale with white worm-parasites attached to its blind eyes. It was also half-covered by grey tank-sludge, and with three more violent tail-kicks he banged himself in flush. The two catfish nosed up out of nowhere and started to hoover up the debris of food fragments and stirred up shit. They nudged at the dead fish. But I couldn't let them eat him. I removed the sticky glass planks and pulled him out by the tail. He was a heavy creature but shrank as I drew him from the water, his silver coat broken up by diseased patches of mottled pink and green: a quick, self-administered death for a long-dying, innocent creature.

I swung him through to the kitchen—dripping everywhere— and lay him on the side. Nauseating thought: I could run him under a tap and slap him straight in a pan. I rummaged for a metal tape measure in the drawer under the sink, measured him carefully. He was thirteen and a half inches from head to tail. I started crying. Crying over a fucking dead fish. I wiped my eyes with the back of my hand, wrapped him in newspaper, took him out and dropped him down the rubbish chute. I decided to go out and get well and truly hammered. There was a pub I'd always fancied, half way down to the tube: a bright, noisy place, full of kids. I had a smoke, changed my shirt and headed in that direction, a few coins and a note comfortingly against my leg, not too laden, but able to drink as many drinks as I wanted. A fifty yard walk and an entrance into a room full of strangers with whom I expected to have nothing to do: even that required careful planning. Care Full. All the woes of being were with me every step of the way. I had to build a coral reef, a sort of carapace of decision, which I did, putting it up as I entered the Goat and Compasses.

I ambled towards the bar and stood waiting to be served. A few varnished vertical beams of light wood had replaced a partition between the bars, so you could catch the eye of somebody sitting in the far corner, behind the blue baize of the second pool table, against a chrome rail, under a screen playing a video of Ah-Ha. The blond singer was drawing a woman down a telephone wire, through a wall of scribble and into a world where they danced with the lines. The man was beautiful, the woman hesitant; understandably wary at being so abruptly drawn from her safe world of flat colours into a scribbled drawing. Quickly won over, she melted, instantly transfigured into a creature of many shifting planes.

The barmaid asked for money. I paid, picked up the glass of amber nectar. A knot of boys at each table obliterated the corner, hair sleekly crisped, 501s, screwed together cues. They were locked in a formal dance of shot and counter shot, moving around, sighting balls and each other across a cat's cradle of glances. I ducked under and went through to sit on an empty bench against the window. It was still light outside. I turned to look out at the street, an assortment of people walking down to the underground or back from it, some of them looking in at us. I looked out, from one non-place to another, a moment of interchange of longings to be elsewhere, decisions to keep moving, undetained by looks and displacements of your purpose, to finally make it all the way home. I was accosting people, almost as if I'd rushed into the street and grabbed each of them by the arm.

There were so many young and pretty ones, so many eye-beams to avoid being skewered by or accidentally snag. They didn't want to be openly looked at any more than I did, so when I got back from the bar, with another pint of lager and a Jack Daniels chaser, I spread my booty, which included a packet of peanuts and a packet of crisps, on the bench, in a small arena which I dedicated to my own lonely pleasure, a place I could keep looking down on with relish, whilst I chose another particular point to look at, halfway up a stripped beam on the far side of the tables, at a mirrored picture of The Eagles.

It wasn't The Eagles that made the picture interesting but the reflection of coloured bands of light falling across it. I could pretend to be studying it and look into the middle distance, glancing beyond to where people stood or sat at the bar. I enjoyed the movements of girls serving and the frieze of youthful bodies in attitudes of animated interaction. They hadn't particularly noticed me. It was like being in an advert for the things we were gobbling up. But in my case I knew that nobody was going to pull me through into the luscious scribble world of youth. I glanced at a girl beneath the wall-hanging video box: her long, curly hair, her jeans, her wide freckled face pinched by beauty, a seventeen year old's bold, meaningless stare. She looked at me, measuring me, and I thought again of how they keep arriving in these agreeable looking pods only to flop out and take on your distinguishing features, your memories, your mind; only to take your place and be indistinguishable from you—except of course for their total lack of morality.

I felt like the weirdest person in the world. If I wasn't with anyone and didn't want to play with them, what was I doing here? That much was obvious, yet I contradicted their obvious interpretation of it by removing myself, disengaging myself from the outer world. I got down another couple of pints of lager and whisky chasers, let my eyes go unfocused and gazed up into the surrounding invisible orb of virtue in which we danced as bright motes of cloth-fragments held in its lower bell by the force of beings who'd made these shaping elements of our world, and the things we experienced so casually, as its furniture.

Tony, mate. You're a genius. Let me buy you a pint. What genius thoughts you having today, then? Any good ones? Go on, mate. What you thinking? Tell us, tell us. Go on. But I wasn't going to do that. I retained them in my background as a floating chorus, as a noise level in which to bury the sound of my own whirring wheels. Green stripes. There were a number of them and they glowed as if pregnant with a thought that had ignited and I built my own arc out of them and tried to climb up into it.

I'd eaten angel's food once and now I hungered for it instead of the bread of sorrow I didn't even know existed once upon a time. What had I ever accomplished? Where did I think I was going and how far had I got? I'd looked within, into my heart, which is what I did now, but what I saw there made me ill. I looked in and up. Mostly I looked up. For a sign, a true face. I was on my way. No danger of being interrupted. Just a man getting pissed on his own, which was acceptable in the eyes of man. And there was nothing else.

There I'd said it. And if I'd said it in that way how could I avoid thinking it. Doubt, or whatever, dragged me back to the lights. There, I'd thought it. But if it was what couldn't be thought I'd done the impossible. I thought the think of the non-thing. Because if you had the word for it you could unthink it, but if it was the actual thing then it would still be there, silently pointing out your big mistake in not believing in it. If you doubted the power that made the lights light and the music come out—and not only that, not only that by any means—then you showed you were a fool who doubted everything, even when it was shouting itself in your face, or rather not doing that but surrounding you with its evidence as the power supply and the ceiling. And so you say the unthinkable either with a special meaning or with none, but still you can think nothing greater, so can only turn away from thought to non-thought. Because you can't be greater than the thing you could name but not be greater than, and if you thought of something greater—you would be it.

But what nagged at me—my foot bobbing up and down— was if I let myself look around I found eyes looking at me as a nutter. I turned inwards, clamped my lips tight shut. They had been moving all right. These kids were afraid of me. Not afraid, something else. They thought I was talking about them. What bothered me about it was that even if you could name the non of a higher good thing you wouldn't necessarily be greater than it—you'd only be saying that one particular highest thing wasn't the real highest. You weren't it either. There was nothing higher than compulsion. Even to think this was to enter a realm of delusions, a bad place where you heard words being said in the hearts of surrounding fools and thought that what you heard was what was actually in them. "Leatherhead?" asked a lorry driver, leaning out of the window of his cab. "Fishface!" answered the bloke on the pavement. And there was plenty more where that came from.

I pulled myself back to myself. I knew I definitely wasn't any greater thing. I couldn't do anything much. I'd thought that I was powerful sometimes, sometimes not long ago; but those powerful things I'd done were actually things you do when you're without power. They were seemingly powerful things, acts of wickedness that separated you from the good and which were therefore not powerful. I couldn't concentrate. Three crumpled crisp packets on the table in front of me. People pressing around me. I couldn't stop hearing the conversation next to me. Not that I wanted to be in it. I stayed uninvolved, although I did catch my own name sometimes and glanced over, addressed by it. But it must be somebody who had the same name. They were talking about him.

But it didn't matter because I was uninterested. I knew I wasn't the greater thing because I was incapable of sustaining my own feelings for justice, a feeling that the good should not be punished but that the wicked should be punished for their wickedness, not given good things instead, far better things than I would ever have. Because I couldn't conceive or know of a higher good, a good that returned good for evil. I couldn't see why the innocent suffered and the guilty went free, and that's why I wasn't that greater thing, whatever it might turn out to be.

"Excuse me, can I have a word with you?"

"Sit down," I said.

One of the boys stood over me, holding out his hand, not to shake mine, as I'd thought, but towards a space beside me. I picked up the ashtray and wiped off the bench. He perched next to me. The legs of the pool players surrounded us. The boy beckoned me towards him, I leant my ear down for him to speak and he put his hands up in a trumpet.

"I've got a message for you."

"Oh?" I smiled. "Who from?"

"From Julie?"

"Who's Julie?"

"That girl you've been looking at all night."

"What girl?"

"It's all right. You know what girl."

"I haven't been looking at her. Not deliberately."

"Yeah you have. You've been talking to her. You think you have."

I leaned back, sighted along the chrome rail that ran around the edge of the pool area. She was right there under the video. I caught her profile. She looked up, talking to somebody else I couldn't see. "I know who you mean."

"She's a nice girl. Intelligent. Don't get too excited but—she's asked me to tell you something."

I knew it wasn't going to be good. How could it be? I grimaced and groaned, "What's that? I haven't done anything wrong."

"It's for your own good, she says." The boy shrugged. "Look, I'm only passing this on. She says you shouldn't go out on your own. You should only go out when there's other people who you're with."

"Why's that?"

"Because you can hide it then, you can hide whatever is really going on in your head."

"Perhaps I could share it."

"No, you shouldn't. Because what's going on in your head isn't the same as what's going on in everyone else's head, it isn't: you just think it is. If you're with some other people you'll be able to disguise that and say things that sound normal, but if you don't everyone will see you're mad."

"Look, I wasn't talking to her, or looking at her. I came out for a drink on my own, that's all. What's wrong with that?"

"Well, perhaps you should've gone to a quieter place," he said. "But you'd still have the problem of being mad, you'd still be talking to yourself. But that's not what it is, she says. You're not talking to yourself, you're talking to other people, ones you're listening to, she says, in your head, only what you're hearing them say isn't what they're saying. You're making it up. You think you understand the situation you're creating, but you don't. Julie hasn't got anything against you, mate. She just thinks you should stay out of circulation, because one day whatever is wrong with you will be obvious, and where could it be more so than in a crowded pub where you're having a conversation with somebody you don't even know. A non conversation you're making up with a girl who didn't ask to be drawn into your head."

"And that's what she asked you to say, is it?"

"More or less."

"But there isn't anything wrong with me."

He put his hand on my shoulder. "There is, mate. Even I can see that. We've been watching you. We don't want to see you getting into any trouble. Look, you don't mean any harm, do you?"

"No, of course not."

"Good. I can see that. But you are causing harm. And you don't want to cause harm, do you?"

"No."

"To other people or to yourself?"

"No."

"Well, you are causing harm."

"How?"

"You're fucking up people's heads, mate. And you're not getting close to them, either, because in a situation like this, where everybody can see that there's something badly wrong with you, they're not going to want to have anything to do with you. Well, are they?"

I didn't want to argue. They'd got it worked out, him and Julie, and I couldn't answer. A wave of exhaustion broke over me. I sat back in a way that indicated retreat into my own world; the boy held up his hands in a don't shoot me sort of way, and he stood up suddenly and disappeared into the crowd.

I was patrolling out to the end of it all now, out to the end of the pier, waiting to hear the last knockings. Bob and me going out for long walks in Richmond Park, him pushing on ahead; crash of ferns, hopping of brambles—and him trying hard to leave me as far behind as possible. The going was soft and whippy branches sprang back, heavy with recent rain, releasing showers that nestled, scattering diamonds in the weave of our raggy sweaters. This time I found him up in the top branches of an oak, facing out into the line of afternoon traffic that snaked down Star and Garter hill; and when I arrived below, he started to jump in the branches—and the whole tree shimmied and shook, possessed by a wind-spirit.

Bob climbed up to a safe perch. I followed him, not too high, high enough to see a herd of small deer in the distance; darting and twitch-changing direction like a cloud of mosquitoes over the surface of a stagnant pond. We talked, the words we spoke blowing away with smoke that scrawled from the tips of our cigarettes as we each lay back along a bough. I stubbed mine, dropped the butt into a hollow bole; unbalanced by movement, shot out an arm. Grey dusk came down swiftly and a razor wind cut at near-naked branches, which mopped painfully at the air.

"Let's stay up until it gets totally dark."

"No. We'd never see our way down."

Bob nodded. A muscle twitched in his cheek. He angled his head to scrutinise the highest twigs, trembling already in anticipation of his possession of them. "Just follow," he said. "It's not hard."

I shook my head.

"I'll show you where your feet go."

"I'll stay here, thanks."

Bob flicked his fag end away and stepped up, reaching to swing his calves over a big branch above our heads. I couldn't stand watching him, so I scrambled down the tree and beat my way back along a red dirt path to the car park, sat on the bike. Lit another cigarette. Pulled on my helmet, my gloves—and, when he didn't reappear, I decided, pissed off, to make my own way home.

Bob came racing down the path—his sleeves were pushed up—and stopped with his palms on his thighs, gasping: "You've only set the fucking tree alight."

"What?"

"You heard."

"It'll just go out, probably."

Bob turned on his heel and ran away from me. I followed, wildlife stampeding into the paths of juggernauts in my mind's eye, a red glow in the sky above. When I got there a wisp of smoke drifted up from the trunk. It didn't seem like much to get excited over, but a hollow shot rang out and a shower of sparks flew up from the oak's heart.

"Smother it!" I started to rip up armfuls of damp ferns. I thought we could stuff them into the hole, somehow, and block it like a leak in a boat.

"Out of my way!" he said.

I stood back and watched him go far up—breasting boughs with the toe-pointing, vaulting moves of a horizontal bars performer, up to the smoking cleft—reeling as he was engulfed by wood-smoke, finding a big lungful of fresh air. He stood across the fork of a tree, unzipped his jeans and issued forth a great steaming column of piss down into the trunk—swaying, doubling up with the effort—and, his eyes screwed up tight, he twisted his head into his shoulder as a great scalding cannonball of steam fired itself up into the twilight. He kept pissing on and on until it had blown away.

Bob stood there, high up, gasping, breathing deeply. When he shook his head a cloud of yellow droplets flew into the air. Water streamed from his eyes and his sooty face was scored by twin rivulets of tears. I looked up at him—and I knew right then that he wasn't anything other than stark staring, completely and utterly off his head. He was brilliant—but I had to get as far away from him as possible, as fast as I possibly could. And that's when I started phoning round what few friends I had left and managed to strike it lucky with Willie Mackenzie.

I hung back, watched them do a left and set off on their trail. I tried to keep them out of sight. The XS750, super-shaft, was a pretty distinctive bike. Harry wandered from lane to lane across Gypsy Corner, deciding at the last moment to take the right hand route through North Acton. Down to Harlesden: to where the Jubilee Clock reappeared, a gothic scale replica of a bigger tower somewhere else: painted red in reminiscence of the blood of the innocent, a Victorian rocket on a traffic island—marking out the first original site of the original ABC office. The lights caught Harry. They changed and he cut across the Kilburn lane and did a right-hander towards Willesden.

I trickled along in the gutter, looking up at the passing shop numbers, pretending to read them off for my own non-benefit—

as though pretending to locate an address drop, but I didn't even have the nearest pedestrians convinced. They didn't half give me some funny looks: did I look sus, or what? I've never known anyone on a London pavement take even the slightest interest in a moving vehicle: unless, that is, it's a taxi they're hailing, a bus they're waiting for ... or a truck they're thinking of jumping in front of. I let Harry turn into a veering yellow dot, headed towards Cricklewood, I thought, but I'd lost sight of them, and out of the corner of my eye I spotted their vehicle hammering off down the walled canyon of Harrow Road.

Passing the squat temple of the municipal crematorium, they stopped in the middle of the road and indicated towards a pair of iron gates set between roofed pillars. I couldn't stop straight away—I was running ahead of a pack. I slid past their nearside door just as Harry turned across into Kensal Green Cemetery. I saw the gates swing open in my mirror and they passed through them; I left the bike behind a Transit Luton parked opposite the fence of a builder's yard and walked back down to the gates. Of Harry's van there was no sign. I headed for the widest way, self-conscious, conspicuous in my stupid courier gear. I wasn't that likely to be making a delivery. The path was lined by recent graves, each topped with its own slab of shiny marble, light or dark. Lovely things. More chocolate, comfort food for a long journey: a rogue's gallery of cropped snapshots watched from them. At the foot of a long black monument a young man was polishing the marble like a chauffeur rubbing smudges off the bonnet of a car; a woman I took to be his sister looked at me, curiously. I turned away. The plump face of a man in his mid-thirties looked back over his shoulder. Bye-bye. Looked a lot like an amiable trucker. If so, they sold his rig to pay for this and some ... handsome ... 10-10 till we do it again: below his picture was the name, "Jocky".

Behind the cemetery some grey gasholders rose. The traffic was a muted roar, a blanket of rumbling noise from a nearby bone-grinding factory, processing corpses into slabs of Doner kebab meat: I remembered a wiry bespectacled little woman leading me between rows of filing cabinets on some forgotten drop. "This used to be a small department," she'd said brightly, "but like Topsy we just growed." This was something else I was meant just to know. Further along the graves were much older. Broken columns had crumbled to dust, a veiled angel was missing a finger: another had turned into a dead tree. Egyptian-looking jobs were bricked up to discourage tomb robbers. Too late. Chunks of smashed up stone tablets propped over darkness. Indecipherable inscriptions of Princes of Rhodes and Abyssinia. A dead root snaked up the back of a flaking cross and hung there like the spine of a fossilised grave-lizard: a particularly lively victim of premature burial mutated into a new species in a futile escape bid. Inscribed on a granite obelisk:

JOSEPH RICHARDSON 1790-1855
INVENTOR OF ROCK AND ROLL

These things tugged at me, but I wasn't sure whether to be interested in them or not. They were impressive. Scary. Empty. I peered through any thickets that might hide Harry. Some strange people were wandering around, apart from me: a balding grave-hound in black, obviously seeking out a suitable site for some high sex magic—his companion, a fat old git in dark glasses with a shock of white hair, for reasons best known to both of them, was impersonating the Pope. I thought I caught the backwards jabbering of a prayer I recalled from school assemblies. Obviously Satanists. I supposed it was a free country. Perhaps they were looking for the grave of Lobby Ludd, the mystery benefactor of the working-man my granddad had told me about; but I knew they'd draw a blank there. Lobby was still alive, still out there. Tosspots like them would never be able find or kill him, whatever crummy spells they had at their disposal.

I followed this path down further to where it petered out in front of a coliseum where all paths ended and took in the sheer scale of the place; you turned a corner and more graves stretched away, and more, and if you paused or tried to relocate any of them your search would go on and on, and you yourself would finally keel over into a handy slot in the clay; a place the Anti-Pope and his assistant were already preparing for your tired bones. The taller of the two grave hounds starting performing a few variations on a brass instrument of his own devising. How proudly he held it. How sonorous its music. See that baby, see that friend? Chop its head off. Chop its fucking head off and walk away laughing.

A black Mazda MX-5 was parked on a service road running beside it, and I mounted the steps twenty yards down from where a heavily jewelled woman in her mid-thirties placed flowers on a speckled grave to the left of the main path. She looked up with the same look as the other woman: hostility at unwanted intrusion into the privacy of her mourning. Fair enough. She probably mistook me for one of the grave-hounds, or maybe it was an automatic look of disdain for someone she thought was an idler who should be working.

I walked beyond her car to where the road turned a corner at the end of the marble coliseum. Harry's van was parked right across it. I dodged in under the roofed area. The woman was some distance away; but when I glanced back she stared after me, hands on hips. She lifted her face. Her eyes lit up like granules of frosted windscreen. I thought about what'd happen if they caught me sniffing around the Escort. My legs shook in fear. I dropped down onto a bench and sat bolt upright against the dank stone. I breathed fast. No thanks, I thought, no thanks. I fumbled out a fag, lit it up and watched my jumping knee, trying to slow it by pressing the soles of my feet onto the cold flags.

I stood up and walked off at a tangent across a grassy section. Here the graves were more spaced out; I ducked behind a pink obelisk and looked back at the van, whose windows were mirrors of low tumbling cloud. The driver's window slid down jerkily. Harry Chambers looked over in my direction—a butt flicked away in a shallow arc, the inside squeezed out again by scumbled sky. A funeral was taking place at a plot fifty yards beyond the end of the slip road: the graveside party breaking up—a man in a black overcoat threw an arm of consolation across the shoulders of a older, stooped one; a couple of kids glanced anxiously at a woman carrying a shiny patent handbag. The officiating vicar watched them leave, turned towards the van and raised his arm to Harry and his boys in an obvious signal.

Harry and his eldest son clambered out: the younger man opened up the back of the van and his brother jumped down.

They pulled out spades. The younger son got in the front —the radio blared, shut off by a slam—and Harry and the other one ambled across to the fresh grave and the stooped, waiting figure of Reverend Poore. Poore waved. Made a tipping movement with thumb and forefinger, of drinking tea from a tiny cup. He raised his large hand in farewell, moved after the mourners. I watched them at the graveside. There didn't seem to be a mound of earth beside it. Harry Chambers leaned across a steep-sided grassy mound on the next plot, flipped back a greengrocer's mat and, like a conjuror, revealed a deep wooden box that had been erected next to the hole. It was full of grave-dirt. Working quickly they pulled out the planks and shovelled the loose dirt in. They threw the wreaths and flowers down on top and spun the butterflies holding the earth-box together.

Harry's younger son rubbed his hands, warming his hands, pretending to spit on them. They carried the collapsed box and the tools back to their van. By the time they were done I was freezing from standing in one spot so long. They seemed to linger over every task to torment me further. They rolled down their shirtsleeves and put their coats on. They locked up their spades in the Escort, and walked off after Poore and the mourners. Once they were out of sight, I picked my way back to the gates. Looking at nothing. Neither left nor right. It was a cold place; their bodies had been giving off the only warmth there.

Thirteen

Memories were easy, but it can be difficult to know which has
something to do with you and which doesn't. I thought about
the rider I'd seen in Hyde Park, slipping out of the gates on the
tail of a pot of gold. What if it hadn't been Bob? I knew it wasn't
really him. I also knew I was really going to have to look for him.
He wasn't going to walk out of any crowd carrying any winning
lottery ticket or any secret of eternal youth. I wanted everything
to be as real as the exhaust note on that bike. I wanted to meet
him again, and, if necessary, find him boring. I dragged out a
waist-high stack of directories by the phone, dumped the yearly
updates of Yellow Pages and took the rest into the sitting room.
Three local books: apart from those an A-D, an E-K, two L-Rs,
one ten years old, an S-Z that looked as if Willie had once tried
to tear it in half in frustration. Its cover was a test pad of hastily
scribbled numbers and names, doodles of plinths with vases
on them, flaming towers, faces with long eyelashes, and flaring
nostrils.

I thought of them, still out there, as they always are, getting
on with things. I didn't remember who any of them were (I'd
never known, really) and the books themselves contained too
many names. Full of doubles leading parallel lives. Other people's
lives. I looked up both of Bob's assumed names. There was even
a J. Railio, predictably enough. But I knew it wasn't him. I didn't
want any embarrassing conversations in which my myths fell
apart in a few swift, brutal words. Fuck it. Give up. Give up. I
pulled out my only true source; and plunged into it.

*Railio placed (   ) (   ) (   ) and gently (   ) (   ) to (   ). "And
what about the renewable energy sources you handed over to Prox, and
those new hyperdrive configurations?"*

*"Yes," she answered mildly. "They were problems we ourselves
encountered long ago. But the main thing is always the new challenge
and the mind that brings it. And," she added, "strategic considerations.
We can't change the course of your civilisation, nor would we wish to.
We only wish to be—(XXXXX) (XXXXX) (XXXXX) (XXXXX), problem*

194

(   ) (   ) is to (   ) haphazard (XXXXX) because (XXXXX), finally."

But what did they get out of it? Tinacrea itself had nothing to offer. Surely, if they had desired only to be left alone, they could have simply ignored Prox. On the face of it they weren't that interesting.

"You wanted something in exchange for your help," Railio said. "But what? That's what we have never understood about you. What could you have wanted? What could you have meant?"

"Forgetfulness," she replied. "In the beginning we had hopes of more, but ... I suppose we were just too old, too different. Two-legged monsters. We understood you too well, Railio. We had to protect ourselves. This is our place of remembrance. Remembrance, Railio, is the memory of failure. The reasons are here, to be understood. We want to be understood," she said. "Not only to be used. Is that too much to ask?"

"This place is the opposite of heaven," said Railio.

"Hell? I don't think so. Not exactly. You might find something useful here. But only if you knew how to look."

"So where's the city?"

"There is no city," (   ) replied, "just more caves. Do you wish to see them?"

"No ruins?"

"I am the ruins."

Railio remounted her back and, straps hanging loose, they ambled across an antechamber lit by a thousand glimmering dots that hung from high up on the arching roof.

"There are always more stories, more songs," she said. "Every chamber has its speaking-spirit. They will announce themselves as we pass by."

"An empty museum," he said wonderingly. "There aren't any exhibits."

"So we know it's gone forever," (   ) said, "except for the songs."

"Why songs?"

"We were in many ways a barbarous race. Our technology, well, since we the birth-mothers spun it out of our bodies, didn't develop in concert with a sophisticated culture as you would understand it. Whatever teachings of wisdom, of good ways and the upper realm we wished to preserve were concealed in rhymes and fables such as the *lowest of our subjects could remember. Now they are gone, but the songs linger in the caves of making."*

They met a blank wall of smooth rock at the far edge of the antechamber. Railio could see no way forward. (   ) hunkered slightly and made him slide from her back. There was a low gash or fissure at the bottom of the wall. (   ) made herself small and swiftly scuttled under it. Railio lowered himself onto his belly and crawled after her on his elbows, looking up one last time as the points of light blinked out and the Cave of the Mothers plunged into darkness.

From darkness to greater darkness, into a deep blue-black pitch. He had no way of orientating himself in this new space, and when a hanging (   ) (   ) brushed his plastimask away, he experienced a choking airless moment of terror before he was able to fumble it back into its position over his nose and mouth.

(   ) (   ) vibrating right beside him. The ancient mother-voice began to speak:

"The chosen rises above her siblings and looks down upon her people from the place of honour. She sees the pain and futility of their scrabblings under the burning suns. She floats on currents of air above the settlements of her lowlings as fireballs rain from the skies. Her honours are bought with black blood. Her empire and nest fortune are her due and the myriad husks of her subjects her homage, yet still the numberless stories of their sufferings keen and sigh, lost in the trade winds—and the high one is dizzy in her flight."

(   ) made the lights come again and Railio saw that they weren't alone. On a series of (XXXXX) (   )ly (XXXXX) were (XXXXX) (XXXX). He counted ten (XXXXX) (XXXXXX) recognition. Some words were exchanged, but this time he did not understand them, a (XXXX) gibbering (XXXXXX) (XXXXX) song like that made by the rubbing legs of crickets, locusts. And what sounded, to his untuned ears, like a rapid argument or series of disagreements, quickly resolved. (   ) (   ) was larger (   ) (   ), older.

Railio was suddenly, for the first time since his arrival on Tinacrea, afraid for his life. But the feeling didn't last. The co-mothers wouldn't do him any harm. After all, they had brought him here for a purpose, whatever it might turn out to be. It seemed that they simply wanted to explain themselves, not only to him, but through him to Prox. But why now?

The Great Queen began to speak:

"An everlasting sound, a sacred echo of the first which was the beginning, ignited by the spark into the shapes, into the forms that hang in air. The songs of our origin are the record of our making, and in our bodies the things we have made under their guidance take their shape, their many forms, as such objects are the emanations of one making-spirit, as air movements are of one wind, though each must takes it own form, its own unique, shifting direction."

She stopped, tired by the effort of making words in his mind. He realised that this wasn't a song, but a rationale of singing, an attempt to explain. (   ) was translating into his language by means of a great effort of imagination, of making. The co-mothers, and (   ) beside him, were silent, meditative, creaking slightly. Then (   ) made a short, high gabbling sound, which he translated easily as a request for her to continue, which she did.

"And the chatter of the nurslings, the (   ) (   ) of the under-folk, are as the night fears of (   ) (   ) (   ). These have no knowledge but rumour, carelessly passed on, distorted in the mouth of a (   ) (   ) knowing not the word in the Cave of Making. But she who has heard the word of making will comprehend all forms, all pleas, all sorrows. She will grasp the key of days, her dreams will be the dreams of her intelligence, will reach out beyond the known worlds, their creatures, their unfamiliar forms, their speech, for these worlds and creatures are locked in the great word of Thingness, so that each shines forth in its own Nature with the light of the One."

The Queen fell silent. If her words were true, he thought, then he should have no trouble in understanding them. The spider-religion was as strange as it was absolutist and authoritarian; but nevertheless he began to find it attractive, if only because its priestesses had delivered so much. If they were the makers, their authority was a modest one; they derived it from an invisible godhead—a logos—that resided here in the caves.

The birth-mothers continued to hang silently before him. The Queen slowly inclined her giant head this way and that, observing the visitor, quietly waiting for some civil response.

(   ) murmured softly, "You must speak, Railio."

"I don't know what to say," he whispered, words echoing, multiplying in the great darkness of the cave, their hesitancy making their human utterer many times nothing.

"Just speak," she said. "The words will be right."

"(XXXXXX) Great (XXXXX)," he said. "I am an (XXXXX) (XXXXX) of (XX) (XXXXX) I (XXXX) learned (XXXXXX) Tinacrea. (XXXX) Ambassador (XXXXXX) (XXXX) (XXXX) (XXXXXXX) (XXXX) me as a child (XXXXXX), robbed me of my (XXXXX) standing, (XXXXX) which I take to be (XXXXXX) (XXXXXXX) of your (XXXXXXXX) I truly (XXXX) become (XXXXX) again, and ..."

The birth-mothers murmured their assent.

" ... yet I know your words are true, not for this time and place only, but for all time and all places. We are her creatures, emanations of the ( ) ( ). My mission to your planet is one of thanksgiving, one of ( ) ( ) (XXXXXXXXXX) to say (XXXX) and if (XXXXXXX) (XXXXXXX) (XXXXXXX) (XXXXXXX) to this will (XXXXXXXX) (SHIT!) (FUCK IT!) (XXXXX) (NOT THIS FUCKING COBBLERS!!)

Bob's writing degenerated again into squiggles, crossings out, and blanks. If these words came easily to Railio, for him they were obviously much harder. The self-evident frustration in his many interruptions couldn't help but make me wonder why he'd carried on and on and on with his story; but I couldn't leave it alone. His scribblings had stirred up a hunger in me to know more—and there was obviously more to come; but I felt exhausted, headachy, and totally fucked.

*   *   *

THE CAVE OF THE FATHERS

Railio stooped involuntarily at the ( ) ( ); ( ) hunkered down slightly—he couldn't have climbed onto her back again. The cave's floor was no longer mossy but rough, and strewn with fragments of broken statues stretching on afar he could make out: to where a hundred-thousand motionless light specks and the bone-like luminescence cast by his fire eyes was dimmed out into the impenetrable shadows of the cave. He knelt, examined a few of the unevenly shattered pieces, and found them to be made of a glassy, rock-like substance unlike anything else he had seen so far on Tinacrea; but as to what larger shapes they had once been part of, that was impossible to tell. It was clear that the ancients had left no direct representations of themselves or their artefacts. If he had to describe them, and he knew he would, the word geometrical would be useful but only in a limited way. The geometry unfamiliar to Prox: more pointed than curvy, suggesting length rather than width, length that had been quite violently curtailed. On something that resembled the broken stem of an outsize fluted wine glass, he made out a lightly engraved fleck that suggested a letter-form.

Railio picked up another shard—a series of three complete letters were clearly inscribed on it.

(   ) had fallen silent, not wishing to direct his experience of the Cave of Fathers. After all, she was not one of them.

"What does the cave say?" he prompted her quietly.

"It is silent," she said, "undisturbed by us as yet."

"And these marks, what do they mean?" They were plainly related, each one containing an element repeated in the others; turned, altered, going somewhere in an order that suggested a homily or some sort of a conventional utterance.

(   ) took the fragment from his hand and held it before her, pointing to each in turn. "Death," her soft synth-voice purred, "Honour, and here, this last is (   ). These words contain much, Railio."

"(   )?" he asked.

"Secrecy. Dignity. Orders. Ambitions. Death. (   ). The figures were well known in ancient times, Railio. Our young were taught them, a single glance told us their linked meanings. By the places in which they were to be found, by the actual composition of the substance of which they were made." She paused. "How I wish I could piece together these shards and make them into a single picture for you to carry home with you."

Railio lay the shard down where he had found it, carefully, as into a giant jigsaw.

"The cave is stirring, Railio," (   ) (   ) (   ) rang (   ) (   ).

Another (   ) (XXXXX) (XXXXXX) two (   )," (XXXXX) mound (   ) stand if the enemies ( ) ( ) house (   )." "(XXXXXXXX) if their fall (XXXXXXXXX) harm those (   ) ring round (   )" "(XXXXXXXXXXXXXXXXX) with the (XXXXXX)ord." "With which they have defended us" (   ) (XXXXXXXX) (XXXXXXX) (the father:)

(XXXX) have threatened us. "(XXXXXXXX) (XXXXXX) (   ) (   )
(XXX)one."

Bob was playing peek-a-boo games ...

"(XXX) sugar-sweet (XXXXX) (XX) dedicated to the (XXXX) (XXXX)
selves (   ) (   ) (XXXXX) (XXXXX) dance (   ) (   ) (   )!" (XXX
(XXXXXX) (XXXXXXXX) (   ) tone and (   ) (XXXXXX) "(XXXX)
(XXX) sugar (XXXXX) dance(XXXXXXXX) (XXXXXXX) praise
(XXXXX) (XXXXXXX) (XXXXXXXX) (XXXXXXXXXXX) victorious
over pleasure! (XXXXXX) sugar- (XXXXX) (XXXXXXX) breast!"
     Another answered: "Yea, when (XXX) (   ) (   ) (   ) (
) Highest comes to bring in the rest (   ) (   ) (   ) (   ) (   ),
so will I, a death's (   ), (   ) (   ) (   )el's countenance."
     "(   ) (   ) banquet of (   ) (   ): (   ) (   ) (   ) (   ) three (
) three goblets (   ) (   ). (   ) (   ) brim."

... growing bored, impatient with whatever mystery the
caves were supposed to conceal or disclose. "What mystery?" I
heard him asking this question behind the words (borrowed from
somewhere else?) and all his rubbings and his scratchings out
were ...

CAVE OF THE SONS

The Great Son (   ) grown savage with waiting, cut off the limbs
and bellies of his defeated enemies, and served them up as a (   )
feast for the young of his settlement. Stricken with pride and madness,
unremembering of battles in which his wounds had been sustained. He
filled up a sugar-goblet with the yellow blood of his enemies and drank it
thrice, crying, "(   ) (   ) (   ) (   ) avenger of my settlement,
(   ) (   ) no longer, I drink to your extinction, out-landers!"
     "What are these voices?" Railio asked. "Are they the actual words
of the dead, or a later account of them, twisted somehow, as seen
through a mirror?"
     "(   ) (   ) (   ), like a (   ) (   ) told by (   ) (   ),
and this (   ) (   ) (   ) if you make the wrong wish."
     "(   ) (   )?"

"Composing air-traces was no more than a pastime for the young or an idle amusement for morbid nest-tenders. Males unfit for more important duties sometimes excelled at it; others who excelled at nothing took their turn. And in their works they made themselves out to be knowledgeable and virtuous, students of previous records, old and new art-works; they invited others to admire their expertise on the causes of the hundred wars and the conditions of the ninety-nine treaties, the sayings of the fathers and the night ways of the birth-mothers.

"They pretended to know the thoughts of distant rulers, manners and beauties of far worlds—and how they were governed, wisely or ill, and what was said in their poorest settlements. They claimed to know the strengths and flaws of tyrants, and how they might be overthrown, how to appear to ignore yet feed on the prattle of the low. And these things they claimed to know from within, as dreams, as surely as the songs and fables of the nest."

"Did they?"

"No," (   ) said. "But their works are all that survive. Ach, they do not matter, Railio. If you spent time in the caves you would soon weary of their tales. Rulers are never moderate. They are judged either to be very good or very bad. And always the twin-suns appear, chasing each other across our skies in some fable of the great dance of time, the upper and the lower worlds, and how they might be reconciled. Mysteries where there are none. Wisdoms that do not fit their purposes. The Queen knows, Railio. The fathers are gone and have left nothing to show of their (   ) (   ) (   ). burdens appear different to those who bear them. Come. Let us pass on to the Cave of Daughters."

Shards depicting the twin-suns and the no longer meaningful codes of father-rule crackled underfoot, single lines of air-traces passed through her and sounded in Railio's head in images he couldn't retain mountain and tongueless cliffs—and at the cave's limit a tremulous chain of these resolved into a single unbroken poem that passed rapidly though his mind:

(XXXXX) and I (XXXX)
(   ) (   ) (   )
(XXXXX) (XXX)
(   ) float (   ) (   ) (   )
(XXXXXXXXXXX)
(XXXXX)d p(XXXXX)ys -

t(XXXXXX) (XXXXX)ch
(   ) ever (   ) up(XXX)
(   ) sweet (   ) (   )
(XXXXXXX) (XXX) to love

I remembered how I'd popped a nice little wheelie on my way across West End Green. Passing the church and The Wheatsheaf. Racing away down a green and grey twisting tunnel between shrub-shrouded houses and the tall fences that enclosed Sandown Park racecourse to shield its nags from the prying eyes of non-paying spectators of the sport of kings, people like me. Bobbing jockey heads was all you got for nothing.

"It isn't the kind of work everyone's prepared to do," said the woman at the labour exchange. "But it's all we have available today, so you'll have to take it, won't you?"

Mr Pruitt was a shrunken, one-lunged little bloke in a dark suit; bits of hair adhering to his skull like the feathery traces you sometimes find on an egg, and the short speech he gave about the various stages of sewage treatment while a glass tank gurgled behind him, and a sherry schooner gathered dust on a velvet cushion under a small tap.

"So," he concluded. "Do you think you're good enough to work for us?"

I reported on Monday morning and a short-straw drawing foreman perfunctorily showed me around the drying beds, the stained, stainless vats. The cold was a help, he explained. It kept the product crisp. It held the smell of it down to an acceptable level. Acceptable? Acceptable to who? At lunchtime I walked into The Wheatsheaf and sipped a half of bitter as my half of the bar quickly drained of customers. We hung back in the canteen and played five card brag until the last possible moment.

"Come on," said the ganger, decisively. "Let's shift some whasname."

After that we kitted up and ground down to the beds, each the size of a school swimming pool, each spanned by a mobile conveyor belt powered by a 150cc Villiers two-stroke—and the ganger started it up with a frayed pyjama cord and we forked 'cake' onto the belt, quickly filling the front of the dumper. Stories abounded of the diamond necklaces. Of the ancient coins that had been found. But I never saw anything more valuable than a hairclip.

Boot hard down for the sculpted peaks at the end of the yard. Of Ben Nevis. Mount Snowdon. Aberfan. Our mission, which we had no choice but to accept, to build the highest shit-mountain in the Home Counties. Shovelling whasname in the secret hope that Esher would wake up one morning in the dark; and when dumper's front wheels got stuck on the nursery slopes we'd hop off to dig her out—cursing the how's your father as it oozed over the tops of our wellies. I had a copy of *Beautiful Losers* folded in half in the pocket of my donkey jacket and in the canteen I ploughed through that.

The others, thirty years older than me, many of them missing fingers, arms, eyes. No remedy to their condition. It was a job that somebody had to do and which they accepted. I thought immediate strike action was in order, suggested it during a mid-morning blow in the tool shed, was set to scrubbing out the vats—their inner surfaces covered by a fine, hair-like algae with tiny clinging roots. I found myself sitting alone in the canteen. The council sacked me on Christmas Eve. The gangs drank Party Seven in the canteen, celebrating a few days respite before the post-Boxing Day rush, the emetic of a Happy New Year; but when I tried to say goodbye they showed me their backs—begrudging me a glass of warm piss with which to toast their future health and happiness.

Back on the doorstep of the labour exchange I bumped into Rudy's brother, Jim. Nice bloke. I remembered him vaguely from school—he was signing on late—and when I told him I wanted to move out of home he immediately mentioned that his older brother was looking for someone to move into a room in his flat. And later on that same evening I met Rudy himself. I was particularly impressed by his posturing cynicism and by the couple of joints that were buzzing around my head within minutes.

"Isn't your brother looking for somewhere?" I asked for form's sake.

"He'd have my folks around, checking up on us. If they ever found out I was dealing, wow, they'd draw a map and hand it straight to the pigs." Rudy looked at me for the first time in that heavy-lidded way of his. "Okay, I'm a cunt, but I've got to protect myself."

Next day I stood at the door of the council flat over in Cobham where I'd grown up. Where the stones were carved into my memory. Before Maggie earned their temporary gratitude by selling it to them. With a single army bag over my arm, a bag containing everything. Mum told me again about what I was doing to her. It wasn't good and I wasn't that good either. Dad was in the sitting room, scrutinising the *Exchange and Mart* for used car bargains with a large magnifying glass.

"Don't upset yourself," he called out. "I daresay we'll be forking out again before long."

Once upon another time we all went for a ride on the Cullompton-Seaton miniature tramway, and passed the service station—just visible through binoculars an elderly couple passed us—where Laurence of Arabia used to refuel his Brough Superior. The tram driver, wearing dark glasses, green uniform, pointed out that following a recent clean up of the Otter, Tarka the Otter and Salar the Salmon had been spotted again in the river, one in the mouth of the other. We passed on by another sewage works and some impressive back gardens. Reaching our destination we squeezed down the narrow winding steps, stumbled off in search of a pub, and, clumsy giants, managed to crush several roofs in the model village.

Memories kept interfering; in the way they seemed to have nothing to do with the big world of the spiders, or the big-world of anything else. Chantilly lace and a phony tale. I remembered the songs my mother taught me: there were four girls on the petrol pumps and they wore white boiler suits and little tartan caps. Babette was known as Blondie, lived with Dudley Moore for a time, and Jean Briden made me a coat out of scraps when I was a kid. She married a Greek whose family refused to talk to her and insisted (would you believe it) on her renaming her little girl Margaret, Christina. There was Anna, another blonde, a German girl who'd made herself unpopular by going on about how Hitler was right. Just after the war. Mum was between office jobs, just finished at the American Base in Bushey Park.

They had to say, "Do you want Redex in it?" (There was never any in the pump) and "Wipe your windscreen, sir?" It was more doing things the American way—and the blokes for miles around came in to see girls in crisp white boiler suits.

Dad worked in the workshop. "Pam's not working this weekend," he told the manager. "We're going to a meeting."

"Are you her agent?"

Forget that, forget it. It wasn't telling that was important, it was the doing something about it. All I could ever do was stick my oar in and wait for it all to come out right. Whoever said violence doesn't solve anything was a liar; but there are different kinds of violence. I shivered in the deathliness of my life, up shit's creek. This thing of Bob's had taken over my every waking minute, but I really hoped I was getting near the end of it now. One more big push. A sharpened blade of ice shot down my spine. Woke me up like electricity. I slumped in the chair. I fell asleep for a good couple of hours, woke up again and battled on.

CAVE OF THE LOST DAUGHTERS

They were together in the cave of daughters (DESCRIBE) (XXXXX) (CONE?) (CHIMNEY?) (LITTLE OPENING (XXXXX)?

"I, (XXXXXXX) of (XXXXX), if I am to regard (XXXXXX) (   ) daughter she will not resemble the (XXX), image of the (XXXXXX), (XXXXX) embrace the (XXXXX) bush steadily (XX) a (XXXX) (   ), noble (XXXX) lift their heads to the sky; rose (XXXX) only in the light of (XX) (XXX) (XXX) (XXXX) tree (   ) tolerate the (XXXXXX) of no (XXXXXX) (XXXX) plant; ( ) the (   ) lodestone follows (   ) less (XXXX) (XXX) (XXXXXX) esteemed (XXXX) star. (   ) then (XXXXXX)'s mound (   ) incline to (XXX) descendants of ( ) servile (XXXXXXX)?"

(WHAT FUCKING DESCENDANTS? WHO?)

I put the manuscript down, exhausted by Bob's swerves and counter slashings, recoiling from its blows. He was pushing in the wrong direction maybe. I wondered if science fiction wasn't the wrong form for him. I wanted to locate him and tell him this fact. He really didn't need a story, couldn't really do it anyway. And characters. They were all right, I supposed. But the ideal form for his mind would have been an endless epic poem of shards, fragments: the longest in the world, perhaps; no locations, no stories, and no people, just bits of words.

(   ) and Railio were outside, on the plain whose landscape of mounds with its high surrounding mountains (   ) (   ) (   ). A breeze had blown up from somewhere, its voice a high empty whine, carrying no voices, emptily (   ) (   ) (   ) so that (XXXXXXX) and (XXXXXXXXX) another. He climbed up again onto (   )'s back. She loped forwards, sprang up, glided, bounced. A strong gust took them on towards the wall of tumbling scree. It wasn't so easy on the way back. (   ) picked carefully through the rubble, followed the grooves worn by long dried out streams. Had there ever been streams on Tinacrea? Hard to imagine. Not likely, he supposed, or some other life-form would have evolved out of them. And (XXXXX) (XXXXX), (XXXXXXXXXX) (XXXXX) (XX) (XX); (XXXXXXX) (XXXXXX) (XXX) (XXXXX) (XXXXXX) (XXX) (XXXXXXX) (XXXXXX) (XXXX) (XXXXX) (XX) (XXXX) (XXXXXXXXX) (XXXXXXXXX) (XXXXXXX) (XXXXXX) (CUT. CUT.)

The travisphere (XXXXXX) (XXXXXX) (XXXXX) (XXXXX) (XXXXXX) (XXXXXX). (XXXXXXXXX) (XXXXXXXX) (XXXXX) (XXXX) (XXXXXXXX) (XXXXXXX) (XXXXXXXX) (XXXXXXX). (XXXXXXXX) (XXXX) (XXX) (XXXX) (XXXXXX) (XXXXXX) (XXXXXXX) (XXXXXXXXX) (XXXXXXXXX) (XXXXX) (XXXXXXXX) (XXXXXXX) (XXXXXXX) (XXXXXXX) (XXXXXXX) (XXXXXX) (XXXXX) (XXXX) (XXXXX) (XXXXXXXX) (XXXXXXX) (XXXXX) (XXXXXX) (XXXXXXXXXXX) (XXXXXX) (XXXXX) (XXXXXXX) (XXXXXXX) (XXXXX) (XXXX) (XXXXXXXX) (XXXXX) (XXXXXXXX) (XXXXXXX)(XXXXXXX) (XXXX) (XXXXXXX) (XXXXXXXX) (XXXXX) (XXXXX) (XXXXXXXXX) (XXXXXXXX) (XXXXXXX) (XXXXX) (XXXXXXX) (XXXXXXX) (XXXXXXXXXX) (XXXXXX) (XXXX) (XXXXXXX) (XXXXXXXXXX) (XXXX) (XXXXX) (XXXXX) (XXXXX) (XXXX) (XXXXX) (XXXXXXX) (XXXXXXXXX) (XXXXXX) (XXXXXXXXXX) meander of ribbons (XXXXXX) (XXXXXXXX) (XXXXXXXX) (XXXXXXXXXX) (XXXX) (XXXXXXXXXX) (XXXXXX) (XXXXX) (XXXXXXX) (XXXXX) (XXXXX) (XXXXXXX)

(XXXXXXX) (XXXXX) (XXXXXXX) (XXXXXXX) (XXXXXXX) (XXXXX) (XXXXXXXX) (XXXXXXXX) (XXXXXXXX) (XXXXXX) (XXXXX) (XXXXX) (XXXXX) (XXXXXX) (XXXXXX) (XXXXXXXX) (XXXXXX) (XXXXX) (XXXXX) (XXXXX) (XXXXXXX) (XXXXXXX) (XXXXXXXX).

(   ) (   ) (   ) (XXXXX) in the dome and silence spun out between them like an invisible length of silken thread. Railio reviewed his impressions of the caves. It wasn't a happy silence and it wasn't an uneasy one—it was just silence. A thousand questions formed in his mind, questions to which he knew the answers, by now, or so he thought. He probed (   ) but she was on another frequency, or couldn't be raised. He drained the dregs of their shared drink and slept beside her in fitful relief.

Awoken by music: the measured notes of a tone-prayer. (   ) had spread the sounding-disc with coloured sands which arched, split, spiralled, and formed figures of a script he had seen earlier on the fragments picked up in the Cave of Fathers. (XXXXXX) (XXXX) (XXXX) (XXXXXX) her thoughts.

"It's beautiful," Railio said. "The most (   ) (   ) form of (   ) only a (   ) mask?"

"I love you, Railio," (   ) said. "But there's nothing to be done (   ) (   ), beyond (   ) (   ) (   ) (   ). Beyond this, our highest (   ) (   ) (   ) (   ) (   ) (   ) (   )."

"Tell me what it is. Tell me."

"(   ) (   ) (   ) if lines formed in and (   ) (   ) (   ) touch of different (   )," she said. "(   ) (   ) CLEAR (   ) (   ) (   ) —of light, each sound its own (   ) (   ) (   ) and scripts—so we (   ) we (   )."

"How does thought (   ) (   ) (   ) ever separate. (   ) and (   )?"

"Yes, but maybe not always," she replied. "Our principal organ of (   ) (   ) is (   ) (   ) (   ) in order to (   ) (   ) letter speaks—and (   ) script are one. The whole (   ) is (   ) electric (   ) electric (   ) (   ), its aim to find out the natural (   ) (   ) (   )."

"So the whole of CREATION is TI( )N( )CREA?"

"By the word, Railio. THE WORD (XXXXX) (XXXXXX) from spoken words—affinity of (XXX) (XXXX) every image only a form ( ) ( ) ( ) ( )—gets to the heart. (XXX) (XXXXX) not subordinate; (XXXXXX) cast (XXX) dross (XXX) absorbed (XXX) is read, its pattern (XXXXX) (XXXX) (XXXXX) (XXXX) look and (XXXXXXXX). (XXXXX) expressed by (XXXXX) (XXXXXXX) natural occurrences (XXXX) of (XX) cosmic reverbs, even the movement of stars—establishes the link of (XXXX) (XXXXX) (XXXX) (XXXX) together in (XXXXX) (XXXXX) (XXXX) (XXXX) the highest comes to bring (XXXXX) harvest (XXXXXX) (XXXXX) (XXXXX) a (XXX) head (XXXXX) (XXX) (XXXXX)'s countenance, my sweet."

"And those scenes of cruelty and anguish," Railio asked. "What do they mean?"

"( ) ( ) resolution of ( ) ( ) ( ) ( )—the whole (XXXXX) of the body cannot (XXXX) (XXXXXX)—but part of ( ) ( ) ( ) ( ) constitutes a (XXXXXX) destroyed organic so (XXXX) (XXXXX) meaning ( ) ( ) ( ) ( ) ordained—might be picked up (XXXXXXX) so it was believed."

( ) ( ) many and varied thoughts.

"As you have seen, ours is an empty world. Very little in the way of what you would call history."

"How can you say that? When everything you have shown me, us, is histories. You're living in their aftermath—but you have gone on, through us."

"I suppose so—we are still transmitting, certainly. We wanted to perpetuate ourselves and you were the only way."

"But I don't know what I learned, really," Railio confessed. "Perhaps, ( ), they sent the wrong person. It happens, you know. The academies of Prox are dominated by a powerful bureaucracy, ( ) ( ) (XXXXXXX) (XXX) faction."

"It was the same here. But the clue to understanding us lies in our birth-nests, our nurseries."

"Which you destroyed."

"Yes."

"Do you remember your young? Any of them?"

"There were too many, Railio. We, the mothers, were fore-ordained, chosen in the nest—or so we liked to tell our young-ones, but in reality before that."

"Where? How?"

"In the skies."

"And what does that mean? What are its consequences?"

"Our world was always an empty one, in a sense," (   ) replied. "What you call history is based on the idea of an end. Based on the idea of struggle in a proving ground. But there is no end, no beginning, only us. Nothing to prove, no prospects. Only one—and you have seen enough of it. What is called Evil ..."

"Is that false too?"

"No, Railio, it is not, though it may seem that it exists only by being named as such. Only in retrospect. Must I teach you everything? Good we know by our acts, our making. Good is good ways. Evil we know by its contemplation—and since knowledge is the end result of contemplation, it is therefore knowledge of evil."

"(   ) (   )?"

"Evil only appears as such when you (   ) (   ) (   ) (   ). Otherwise it's quite simply the way things are done. All things, Railio."

"But if the mothers are the only makers ...?"

"We all had that faculty. In that sense we were all mothers—even the fathers, the sons. But only the chosen were birth-mothers."

"And the others, the females, the daughters?"

"They were barren, Railio."

"But ..." He refused to accept this nonsensical proposition. "How? When living creatures ... ?"

"They were made barren."

"But why? By whom?"

"By the stars."

"I love you," he said suddenly.

"That is good, Railio," she said. "I suppose. But love is wasted on others. Better save some of it for yourself, my little two-legged monster of the far worlds."

To (XXXXX) (XXX) (XXXXXX) (XXXX) (XXXXXXX) (XXXX) (XXXXX) (XXXX) (X) (XX) (XXXXXXXXXX) (XXXX) (XXXXXXX) (XXXXXX) (XXX) (XXXX) (XXXXX) mission of (XXXXXXX) (   ) (   ) ( ) (   ) (XXXXX) (XXXXX) (XXXX) scarcely (XXXX) (XXXXX) (XXXX) (XXXXXX) forever, forever (XXX) (XXXXXX) (XXXXX) (XXXX) (XXXX) (XXXXX) (XXXXXXXX) (XXX) (XXXX) (   ) mothers floating (   ) the scattered (   )s.

I turned over the last sheet, turned it back. Bob's manuscript was at an end. I straightened up the foolscap sheets; replaced them, with my notebook, in the manila envelope. The twin suns of Tinacrea: I tried to imagine their orbit—perhaps he'd conceived of a single world orbiting both of them very quickly, tossed between the gravity of one after the other: unless it was supposed to be a traditional universe, a geocentric one. There must be something about it in Ptolemy: the motions of the planets described as a series of combined circles. I started by thinking of a single world orbited by suns that weren't opposed, which would explain how both appeared in the sky at the same time; also, perhaps, would provide the planet with a sort of night. I drew a quick sketch on the back of the envelope:

Another. An eternity symbol on its side, like an egg-timer that had been knocked over:

Another world, I thought, with which they'd been at war, maybe; a world eventually destroyed by Tinacrea. So that the suns, for part of their revolution, orbited nothing. Either it had been another spider-world, or a planet of two-legged monsters, like ours. But if the planets were fixed it was certainly a far world and therefore a difficult one to wage war against. Maybe it was something Bob hadn't worked out, though I found that hard to believe. I found it hard to believe he didn't know everything. But the trouble with Railio as a character was that he was an idiot. There was something unnervingly, unerringly familiar about him. Sickeningly so. Maybe he was even based on me. I thought the solution must be to have both planets circulating in a figure of eight orbit.

Travelling in the same direction (otherwise they'd collide, like cars placed in the same slot on a Scalextric figure of eight). There must be some point at which they crossed over but didn't coincide: a closest point of non-meeting: a zone of turbulent eclipses, exchanges, usually hostile, sometimes not—of wars. In between were the waiting times. What would the next conjunction, or the next revolution bring? On a planet that didn't have to struggle to produce, this was most definitely what made the worlds go round—and all kinds of soothsayers, many far-fetched storytellers must have flourished there.

I thought of the figures inscribed on the fragments Railio had picked up in the Cave of the Fathers. The exact positions of the planets hadn't been described; but what did the figure mean, to the Tinacreans, to Bob? The eight itself wasn't hard to straighten out: it was the anagram that was the planet's name. CREATION. Eternity, time—the self-consuming, tail-eating serpent. Hippocrates. Look it up in the big dictionary. Ask your doctor: it's an oath they take—something like "Akela we will do our best"—and a doctoring symbol: the serpent and the staff. Also a name attached to a compilation of ancient writings, in different hands and styles: a synthesis that can be used to justify any medical theory, containing all opposites—but if there was one version of Hippocratic medicine that could be agreed on, it was that nature has an innate power of healing, and that many diseases are closely linked to the physical environment.

Bob tried to say something about almost everything. He'd wanted his first story to be something like Ptolemy's star catalogue—to remain the standard work for centuries, despite its inaccuracies. He'd wanted to leave something big behind him. I found it hard to make sense of his thoughts, but realised that I was the only person who was going to even try. There were some hard to miss points: the daughters being made barren 'by the stars' was obvious nonsense. Really, it could only have been the birth-mothers who had made them barren—the noble mothers with their tenacious grip on power.

Culture was nothing but a carapace, a rounding that once held in the guts of living creatures, a clutch of blown shells. Not even that—leaving just a few chewy bits of it for us to puzzle over, imagining they were something else, something that had a meaning beyond a few repeated covering moves. Entertainments weren't made by the powerful themselves, they were fairytales for the young, made up by those who themselves never really grew up. I wasn't sure if that's what Bob meant, but it was the best I could see in it; beyond that was the obliterated beauty of the fragments, full of half-lost and haunting concepts and a sense of lives lived long ago in different circumstances, by different beings.

But what about the suns, the planets? It was so much easier now I had the figure right in front of me. I couldn't help noticing the obvious similarity of my sketches to breasts. Jugs jiggling in the firmament—some with light-bulb nipples, others darkly engorged. The other sketch depicted sperms of light streaming towards a black egg. I glanced back at the final diagram of black dots chasing one another around a maze that wasn't one, not really. Searching for Bob. Searching for something. Identical nipple suns. His lost mother. And all the other women (the ones we were bubbling for, always out of reach) and how they kept us there, held us at bay—or else we'd finally plunge into them, and burn up.

Fifteen

Marie was strip-searched every time she went home to Derry. She'd told them time and time again, but partly because she had said it so often they didn't really believe her, Mel, Don and the others. She told them how, in the same back rooms, special branch always showed her photos of herself talking to various people she used to know ... and she said, "Sure, I know them, but so what?" They also accused her of carrying messages; but was she, really? Did these incidents actually take place? I wasn't sure whether to believe her or not. I knew next to nothing about Ireland. But I decided I had to. It was necessary for her to be totally believed.

I believed her when she told me that our fate was God's plan. Then she tried to tell me God's plan for herself; but that's when I gently put my hand over her mouth—at first jokingly, then when she continued to talk, for real. She struggled, went still. Because sometimes you can make great things happen that way, by imagining God's plan. Great things. But, more often than not, it's terrible things that are brought to fruition. Satan's plan. I'm walking down a long corridor towards her. Back. Up. Defining something. Moments of definition. But all they can be is false definitions, unless you're happy to live out a moment's consequences, and are you, really? Yeah? Yeah? Because nobody else is.

She told me all about the men she used to drink with and stand off as a girl. How she argued with them till she was blue in the face and they were blue in the ground. Would you listen to her? Would you get her? Leave her, leave her go. She told me about the doings of Jimmy and Johnny, of Carmel, of Breige and of Magda. Not forgetting the Countess Siobhan, or Gerard, and Bobby, or Declan, and Dennis—and several thousand others I would never know or meet, that she herself had lost touch with long ago. I thought she must be writing them letters, or be on the phone to them for three hours every other night.

She wasn't. I told her about Bob.

"You should think yourself lucky that you knew him, Tony. You won't find anyone else like that. You just won't."

She told me a story of the bloke she went out with before Mel, though it didn't sound like much. Patrick, who'd always turned up, when he did, at the corner of the bar in her local. And whenever he did so there was always a nice fresh pint set up for her. They'd stand there all night, some nights, on opposite corners of the bar. Some nights they eventually met up—sometimes they didn't. But if it was up to her, they always did: that's if it was really up to her. Which it wasn't. Some nights he wound her up. He was a bastard, that one ... a real wee bastard. Up for the crack. All of us were, but who ends up being cracked? One night his cute little face swam up on the six o'clock news: another punishment shooting in Belfast. A fatal one. Patrick was a heroin smuggler ... a wee bastard, she said, and she told me this with one of her sharp, knowing little sighs, her swift gasping intakes of breath.

I left Acton Park and walked up the long curve of Churchfield Road behind a young black man wearing a pair of crisp new jeans and a pressed grey T-shirt. The young man was slightly built, sauntering; and I pulled slightly against the curve of the hill, walking faster than usual in order to keep up with him, matching his steps to see if I could make him fall over. We passed a selection of fast-food outlets, then an intermittent row of junk shops; I wasn't interested in their contents; I'd found nothing any more useful than a giant wardrobe and a complete set of the works of Eric Van Lustbader: big, loose-hinged, empty things. We pulled uphill, passed by the bottle-strewn graveyard and The Mechanic's Arms, where the black guy raised his own arms in surrender to a pair of corpulent middle-aged white men who were leaning on a white van and chatting. They laughed in friendly recognition. The black guy put his hands flat on the roof of the van. The older of the two white men pretended to pat him down, to search him. It seemed so light, so easy, like a poor-taste joke between workmates. As I drew level with them, though, the white man found a small clasp knife in the back pocket of the guy's jeans.

"Silly boy," he said. "Who's a silly boy then?"

"You're not nicking me for that!" said the silly boy, none too pleased to be addressed as a parrot.

"You're nicked, sonny," the second cop said. "Get up in the back of the van."

It was a weird pick-up out of a second floor office in a narrow building next to the Middlesex hospital on Great Portland Street—a small cash job out of a blank door labelled Geriatric Unit, coolly dispensed by a Japanese woman in a starched, fraying white coat. She gave me a Jiffy Bag that felt like a videocassette, going a fly-by-night company named Zenobia Associates, on Metropolitan Wharf, Wapping. I knew I'd picked up the right key, even by accident. It was a name on a business card taped to the iron dungeon door of a converted storeroom, several floors up in the passages honeycombing a warehouse that once housed the transportable scents and promises of another hemisphere; some valuable stuff, that needed a good stout lock on it. I banged with a gloved fist, hoping for gigantic bell-like clanging and got nothing except an upholstered thud.

I tried again, and a big man in expensively baggy clothes opened the door. I looked past him across a sparse vista of the usual low-slung furniture and white-painted bricks.

"All right, all right, I heard you."

"Package for you."

"Oh," he said, "how lucky."

I couldn't see anyone else. I Xed a lazy cross on the docket. I didn't want to make any eye-contact with this one.

"Tony? Is that you, mate?"

Rudy. He'd put on an extra stone or two and his face seemed to have retreated somehow, pushing out like a mask attached to a head too large for it. He laughed in disbelief to see it was really me.

"So, still on this mug's game, yeah? I'm a bit busy at the moment, mate. Come in for a minute and take the weight off your neck."

"Amazing." I looked around. "I've been thinking of getting in touch," I said, "but I didn't know where to find you."

"We're in the book," he said automatically, "or shortly will be. Under Z."

"You've done all right, Rudy," I said admiringly.

"Make yourself at home, Tony." He opened the Jiffy bag. "I'll be with you in a micro-byte."

There wasn't much there to beguile the eye. A few computer terminals were scattered on a couple of pale blue sky rugs under a ceiling high enough to have its own weather. No floor at all. My feet were going through it like a trampoline. I felt dizzy, sick. I pulled my gear off, dropped my bag. Beside a window that used to be a loading bay, I noticed a chair—it resembled (actually was)—the refurbished front seat from an old 3.5 Rover which some "designer" had very cunningly welded onto a matt black tubular frame. I knew Rudy had made it big. He was living in a lager ad.

"Nice chair." I sat in it. Uninvited. Uninvited Guest. I put my head down between my knees. "Sorry about this. I feel sick."

Rudy fetched me a glass of water. I drank it straight down. He got me another. I drank that. Another, I sipped it, and he left me to recover; unable to wait, itching to feed the cassette into a VCR on the far side of the room. He did just that and began staring intently at an invisible flat screen, caught my eye and frowned, importantly. I glanced around the walls, which were bare except for a framed picture: the only item of furniture I would instantly have recognised as his own; a muscle-bound young woman in a strategically-tied leather thong—she wore a bronze tiara with a large emerald in its centre, Wonderwoman-style, waving a soul-drinking broadsword above a head of flaming red hair which had sucked up the reflected light of a thousand burnt-out stars.

"Who's the lady?" I asked him.

"Zenobia." Rudy turned off the tape and ambled towards her. "I've had her done in the style of Frank Frazetta."

"Who's Zenobia?" Who was Frank Frazetta?

"She's one powerful lady." He chuckled. "Great to see you, anyway. Where are you living now, mate?"

"Same place."

"Hmm."

"Yeah," I said. "I thought of phoning Stig's parents. I didn't though. Do you still see him?"

"Mr Stigwood. Oh yes. You're not working for Don and Brian?"

"Not for a few months." I pointed at the name on my bag.

"Right. Good name—for a game."

"Hmm." I looked out through the window at the river curling on towards Limehouse; on its the far bank, beyond a patch of no-man's land in its crook, a cluster of masts of parked dinghies swayed in the backwash like hinged saplings. It was so still up there. You felt like you owned the world, like some ancient birth-mother looking down at the empty plains of Tinacrea. Or maybe just somebody who was paying a lot of rent.

"Like the view?" Rudy asked. "That's what you pay for, Tony. Enjoy."

"It's brilliant, Rudy. You're doing great—I can't believe it. How's Stig?"

"Fine. Abroad right now. At a conference in Amsterdam. We set up this business together five years ago."

"What doing exactly?"

"Writing programmes, a bit of consultancy." He spoke very quickly, expecting me to be bored, or uncomprehending.

"Not designing games?"

"Games?" he laughed pityingly. "I'm afraid that's a bit babyish, Tony. Mostly we work for oil companies. Programmes for geologists. Medical research stuff. That's a little bit more interesting. Modelling progressive diseases. Rocks, bones ... that's it, really."

"How did you get into that?"

"One of my lecturers told us about this oil research grant— it's a bit of a step up from the despatching game. I can't believe you're still stuck on this." He gestured at my apparel, my badges of shame. "I used to think you were Mr Intelligent, Tony. Mr Stigwood's brilliant with languages, though. He's invented several of the things, believe it or not."

"So, who's Zenobia?"

"Zenobia the Barbarian?" He looked admiringly at his new Frank Frazetta facsimile, I guessed for the twentieth time that day. "She was a powerful lady. Bob's old character in the game. That was the positive side of those games. You could be whatever you wanted. People do tend to play themselves with superpowers though—it's a lot easier to get your head around that."

"I thought Bob was a wizard; his name was ..." But it had gone, or else I'd never known it.

"You're thinking of Kheila Vog'n. That was Rosie, if you remember her."

"Sure, sure. Do you ever see her?"

"No," he said. "It was a bit difficult when we split—and, anyway, it was a long time ago."

"She was a nice girl."

"I liked her," Rudy grimaced. "Bob went out with her for a while too, after you left. Just went into Girl About Town and asked her out. I was so pissed off with him—but there you are, that was Bob for you—never did give a fuck about other people's feelings."

"Still see him?" I said it casually, knowing he probably didn't.

"Bob died, Tony," he said quickly. He looked straight at me. "I was going to get in touch at the time, but ... he committed suicide, actually."

I didn't say anything.

He kept staring straight ahead.

"How did it happen?"

"Not long after him and Rosie split up (that wasn't a long runner) he went abroad. Don't know where. I expect he rode down to Algeciras on the RD400. Before that he was reading a lot of books."

"He always read a lot."

"Writing as well. Some sort of crappy SF story. Said it was for her. I don't suppose Rosie liked it. One day he disappeared with a few quid in his pocket and a tent in his top box—just like he used to." Rudy remembered. "I suppose we, I, was a bit of a cunt to him. But he didn't know ... to be totally honest we were glad to see the back of him." He stopped talking; after a short breather, he continued. "Anyway, a fair few months later he turns up again. Wouldn't say where he'd been. Spain, obviously. Managed to pick up some bar work, I reckon. Hadn't done him much good though. Too old for that type of thing, really. He didn't meet anyone either." Rudy shook his head. "I've had loads of time to think about it, Tony ... I'm not proud of this."

I let him go on, continue.

"The worst of it was I'd put his stuff away, right, and then let the room out to a Colombian student. There wasn't even anywhere for him to stay. Of course, we let him kip down on the couch for a few days, but that soon got awkward -"

I wanted to blame him, then remembered how long ago this was, if that made a difference, which it did, somehow, even though to me it was yesterday, still now. I glanced across at Zenobia: looking for some strength, I suppose—which I got. He was right. He'd been through it already. Anyway, what was he supposed to do? I took a breath and asked how Bob had done himself in

"As far as we know he left the flat early to buy cigarettes. They found an unopened packet of Marlboro in his top pocket. Then he walked out onto the tracks at St Margaret's," Rudy said it flatly, brutally, a phrase he'd decided on years ago: " He punched a train with his head."

I looked out at the bright sunshine.

"It was pretty quick, Tony. That's about the best you can say of it. I went to the inquest with his foster mum, Mrs Railio. Nice woman. The Coroner asked me how Bob had been for the last few days. I went through everything, everything I could call to mind. All these people were looking at me. Christ knows who they were. And as the words came out of my mouth—"

"What did you say?"

"Can't remember what I said. Stig made a statement to the police when they came round, they read that out—he said Bob was a quiet, studious sort of person who kept himself to himself a lot of the time—I remember thinking that wasn't quite right, though it was hard to say why, and when we were leaving Mrs Railio said to me, 'That person either didn't know Bob very well, did he, or didn't understand him.' Anyway, as I went on speaking it became more and more blindingly obvious what was going to happen. What had already happened. So inevitable, you know? When I'd stopped talking there was a long silence and he told me I could stand down." Rudy exhaled in relief, as though that's what he was doing now, again: standing down. "Driver took early retirement," he said. "A lot of them do, apparently."

He looked at me expectantly. Had he been speaking before? Yeah, because I knew what he'd said; but I was in my own world by then, memories pour in on you at such times, of things Bob had told me or hadn't, things he did say. They were all there at once, and for the very last time, so it seemed, and I wanted to grab hold of all of them, to save them. I put my hand up to my face, screwed up dry, dry eyes. Rudy was clapping his hands together in slow motion, as if to change the subject, banish it once and for all, and summon dinner. I wished he could do that. We exchanged phone numbers, good wishes, and then I found my way down, down the winding stairs into the sunshine, and turned the radio on.

Alf was repeating, "Alpha 2-7, can you hear me?" in a slow singsong. "Wakey-wakey 2-7."

I'd been thinking about those days such a lot. Maybe someone had been trying to tell me something; but I didn't really think so. This was the right moment for it to come up again, that's all; time for it all to come around. Time for me to find out what really happened. Time I knew it—and now I did. Next up was a quick cash job in Commercial Road, from a shop named Western Styles. I exited down Wapping High Street and across The Lost Highway. Western styles, I liked the sound of that. Maybe I could spend some money on something stupid, something to mark this day out: a pair of cowboy boots, a bandana printed with jingling silver spurs, a lariat, a bolas. I crossed Cable Street, another dead zone under an overpass; and a school released a pink cloud of twelve-year-old Bengali girls. Twenty miniature butterfly women in silk trousers and saris spilled across my path.

I braked to let them pass, my discs were dry, my braking swift and accurate.

Western Styles turned out not to be a cowboy outfitters after all, but a shop selling racks of white blouses and cheap jeans in 'western styles'. The owner tore off a yellow form and a pink one, hesitating over whether to give me the original or the duplicate.

"Five pounds please." I tucked the pink sheet under my clipboard. He fished a wad of notes out of his back pocket, peeled off a limp fiver and handed it to me without speaking. "Thanks," I said. "Bye-bye."

He caught up with me beside the bike, out of breath, did a scribbling gesture with his forefinger. I passed him my pen and he jotted my call sign and the office number on a Marlboro packet. I rode away. But he didn't like it. There was something he didn't like, definitely. But what could it be? He let me go. I let it go.

They were clearing away Spitalfields Market as I passed by; hosing down the road around a couple of lingering sixteen-wheelers. And I cruised through resulting puddles, lifting my boots off the footrests, thrashing the streets to grey ribbons across Shoreditch High Street, down to Clerkenwell. Thrashing the streets to grey ribbons, I really liked that phrase. At Farringdon Road I waited for the lights; and it was there what Rudy said caught up with me. Punched a train with his head. Jesus. I slowly let the clutch out—and sat right on the arse of a white Transit for the rest of the way there.

"I've got three for you here," the Croydon controller said to somebody else. "Got a long pen?"

The Western Styles doc was going on to a place called Forwarding and Transfer—a little office tucked away in the basement of the Rank building on Wardour Street. Two or three men were rushing around carrying neatly packed boxes with uniformly crooked address stickers; a small bloke with a thatch of grey hair and a taped up pair of tortoiseshell glasses was yammering into a red telephone, also repaired with packing tape, about the reasons for various long delays; he snatched the pink docket from my hand.

"Is this all he gave you?"

"Yeah," I nodded.

"Fucking idiot."

Sixteen

Three months after moving into Willie's flat I went back to see Bob for what turned out to be the last time. I was enjoying the relative quiet in Acton. All that pleasant clutter to spread out into, to sort through; no more bouncing around between others' moods; no more old Genesis records twittering on over yawnsome conversations about 'the game'. It was even good to be straight for a change, for a while. I started to make big plans. I was going to shed the worn out skin of my old life. I'd decide where I was going to go. And I'd go there. Sometimes I'd run into Stig or Rudy around town and we'd flash or nod; or I saw them in the office—but there wasn't much to say any more. Bob never appeared and they treated me like I'd never known them.

One of the last things was that Stig's Enfield had been knocked off from outside the flat within a month of us wheeling it downstairs. No insurance, no tax, no nothing. Gone into the land of no-justice.

"I told you a thousand times to get a chain for that." Bob's sympathetic reaction. "You can turn those old bikes on and ride them away."

"Oh fuck off," Stig said haughtily. "We don't all have the mentality of petty thieves. Some of us were taught some values."

Rudy and me turned to look at him, surprised. Not by his attitudes. By his sudden willingness to express them.

Stig started to go through some major changes the night he came back from his test ride. Explained it was his idea to move the shelves. Took responsibility. I tried to catch Rudy's eye. Thinking I might get an apology out of him. Fat chance. He sank way back into his winged chair, nodding, skinning up. Bracing himself for one more weary take off. I'd been too full of anger myself then, and later on with trying to get out as soon as possible, to notice Bob's role in these petty dramas. He didn't take the bait of Stig's slur on his upbringing. Didn't even wince. Short on sympathy. Definitely in his own world. There was also his attitude when Sarah walked out, that cold look he'd turned on during my row with Rudy, and now—openly gloating over Stig's bike. Somebody else I could do without. He even had to phone a couple of times before I went over there.

I switched the mirrors, fed the fish, worked hard at keeping the phone and electric on. I'd heard—from him—that Rudy was chasing eighteen year olds with a ridiculously high success rate. Stig took lessons, a surprisingly apt pupil at the game of love. They had both of them jacked in ABC for good. I seethed with envy. After all, I didn't really have anyone else to measure myself by, which meant they were still important to me; it was curiosity about them as much as desire to see him that tempted me over there.

They were out though. This irritated me; because any journey, even one as short as the one between the old and new flats, raises expectations. And also by the way Bob rocked along stiffly (like a premature old man) into the grimy kitchen and stood perfectly, patiently motionless by the furred-up kettle that always took longer and longer, and now forever, to boil milky lime-water for a drink I didn't really want, and knew would taste disgusting.

"What's up?" I peered out through the window. Tar-stained, dusty. It was a late Saturday afternoon and far below us shoppers were filing past in a slow column, trying to get excited about decisions as to what to spend their money on. I supposed that's what they did. I felt myself way above them: blurred, orange-filtered drone creatures who lived out an existence of connectedness making elderflower honey. The room hung in a shimmery grey fog of stale joint smoke from earlier in the day, a smell of decaying filth drifting through from the good old kitchen. I glanced into a mug cemented to the table, away from those blue flowers of dreams cemented into the bottom of it. Same promises. Same predictions. Same old lies.

"What's happening?" I repeated.

"Nothing. It's about time I got out of here, that's all."

"Good idea." It was. "What's brought that on?"

"Rudy wants me out." Bob explained tiredly. "Wants to let my room out to some foreign student. The college sends them round. Quite a lot of them tend to be young girls, you know, living away from home for the first time."

"Stig going as well?"

"No." Bob shook the word off like a short gasp, an intake of breath.

"What a shithead."

"Agh, he's all right."

"What about you?"

Bob shrugged. Well, what about him?

But there was something so distant about him that I'd said, out of the blue: "You're not thinking straight."

"I know. I know that." He glared at me and looked away— as if he hadn't phoned me and I'd turned up, out of the blue, to pester him about things that were none of my business, no longer mattered.

"What does Rudy think?"

"About what?" Short laugh at the preposterous thought of Rudy thinking anything.

"Stig," I said, "what a fucking boring idiot."

"What the fuck do you think you're drivelling on about?"

A nice bright coppery light came in through the tar-stained window and painted the side of his face with fresh bright rust; he'd attained the appearance of a statue clad in gold—the look he'd always had for me, from the beginning; and now here it was again, taunting me with the spuriousness of my own perceptions, the pathetic absurdity of trusting your own sense of things. I'd lost my grip. On his reality, anyway. Only two months away and I'd forgotten everything; not only the way things used to be; but who, in a sense, Bob really was. I gave up trying, picked up a few choice roaches out of the ashtray. I twisted them into a king-size skin. Toked on the reconditioned joint, gagged. Offered it to him.

"No." Bob's hand was on his forehead. Taking his own temperature. High. But not unexpectedly so.

"So what about Railio?" All this was gradually becoming amusing, but I was still trying. "What's he up to nowadays?"

Bob made a soft noise at the back of his throat. He lifted his eyebrows once or twice, turned away to look at the spines of Rudy's books. Somehow, or so I thought, they had turned out to contain the same story.

"Mr O? Morgana? I thought you were going to write that stuff down? Did you abandon that project?"

"It changed," he said, stirring slightly. "All changed into something else."

"Oh?" I laughed.

"You're pathetic when you're stoned. You want to stay off of it."

It was one more true definition of me, one more I definitely should have listened to. We sat with the stupid streaky shadows sliding from the walls and piling up between us, soon lost in the semi-darkness surrounding our life transactions. That's all they were. It came to me as I actually sat there. Transactions. Purchases. A grip to twist your seized nuts off. There wasn't any more. Nothing else. I felt like I should walk over there and shake him by the neck—to make him do something. Hit me. Anything. Anything he liked.

"Look, it's about time you got out of here, anyway. Make some moves. Any moves. It'll sort itself out. You'll see if it doesn't."

"One way or another." Bob looked at his watch, clasped his arms across his wide chest and rubbed his biceps. "I'm meeting them down the road."

"Still friends then."

"Sure. Sure."

"I'll come with you."

"Yeah ... yeah." Bob had perked up slightly, or so I thought. "Come on down."

We sat there, a silence opened.

Bob stood, plucked his jacket off the back of the door. "Let's go now."

Together, saying nothing, we trudged off down to The Cabbage Patch. The pub was empty, its maroon stools tucked under the tables like bruised knees under skirts; pool table sleek, freshly brushed for a night's tournament; a Cash Cascade silently riffled a stack of gold coins with light. I ordered two pints of Holsten off a young Australian barmaid and only remembered that he drank bitter on my way back to the table.

"Can you drink this?" I asked.

"Fine." Bob buried his head in the sand of the bar food menu. I watched as he read each item to himself, his lips moving slowly as if repeating a prayer; then started once again at the top of the list.

We both ordered baked potato with chicken curry sauce, which arrived just as we reached the bottom of our first pint. Bob got us another round in and we munched our way through the basket meals; I bolted mine in five minutes, watching in some fascination as he chewed methodically through each mouthful; and stopping every so often for a slow sip on his beer, abandoning the crusty shell. Then a couple of blokes wearing cut-offs and leathers walked in. They stood at the bar, their feet cocked up at the cowboy rail; after a few minutes one of them wandered across and put something on the jukebox.

"I've always really hated this song, it's so—" I struggled for a diagnosis of why it was so shit.

"I'm serious, Tony," Bob said.

"I know. I know."

"The thing is, my mind's ... I start off somewhere and I don't know ... this is really stupid."

"No it isn't. What?"

"Well, I'm in this bubble. It's drifting away. But I know it's going to burst. I'm going to start falling out of the sky."

"Come on. You can do better than that."

"No I can't. I don't know anything."

"You know everything."

He shook his head.

"You do."

"I don't."

"It's just a bad time. For some reason. Have you thought of going abroad, travelling?"

"I got pissed off with that years ago." He did a coriolis in the bottom of his glass, the wrong way for this hemisphere.

"How about going to Spain for a while?"

"It's a long way to go to find a room."

"If you're really stuck," I said, "you could always move into Acton."

A flaring match lit up his face. He shook it out. "No thanks."

"It could be all right ..."

He shook his head in a slow, mechanical way.

"... why not?"

"Because I don't want to," he said. "Okay?"

I was blowing peaks and troughs in the head of my third pint, watching its temporary mountains slide into foam, and, by the time Stig and Rudy strolled in, fast-freewheeling towards my fifth. Bob was trying to drink, but he wasn't into it. He looked like a snake laboriously choking on a rabbit.

Rudy came in, sat down and started yammering on to us in newly minted computer-speak.

Bob and me stared past one another at two slices of nothing.

"All right, Tony? How's it all going?"

I started to tell him, but my account failed to hold his attention for long.

"Much the same as ever then."

Bob huddled into his old sweater, one operative eye toying with some blemish on the ceiling, when the machine began to whoop and flash and more bottle top tokens clunked rapidly from its mouth. Rudy turned to watch as the winner stacked the blank piss-coloured tokens on top of the machine in lucky piles of ten.

"Got to get back, got to go." Bob rolled around the curved back of his chair, building up momentum for take-off. He got up.

This was the most definite thing he'd done all night. I said goodbye to the others and went outside with him, followed then walked alongside him. I got a dig in the ribs from one of his protruding elbows, and attempted to loop my arm through one of the small gaps; but he pinched me out. He stared straight ahead. On the way home: a journey with nothing at the end of it; and his mouth was turned miserably down, almost funnily, like a horseshoe from which all good luck has run out.

"What do you want me to do?"

There was no answer, no possible reply. Bob's levered his arm free. None of it was my fault. I knew I was innocent of causing his problems, innocent as anyone. I followed him upstairs, made him a cup of coffee (two spoons, off-black, sugary) and put it down beside his feet in a final appeasing homage, a memory of ...

Bob leaned to pick it up, stopped in mid-reach. "Did I ask for this?"

"I don't know. Did you?"

"I've been having trouble sleeping."

"Hmm, don't drink it then." I felt irritable, restless, unable to stop myself from getting up, from crouching in front of the record-stack one last time and finger-walking my way through *Nursery Cryme, War of the Worlds, Journey to the Centre of the Earth.* I gave it up. Bob's breathing was like a clogged vacuum cleaner; if he didn't turn himself off soon he would burn out: a hair ball stuck way back in his throat would clear suddenly and he'd suck the world in—my world, your world, any world that happened to be nearby. He turned towards me, a mouth that opened and closed, failing to realise it was no longer connected to anything that made a jot of sense to me or to anyone else—except, of course, that it did.

"Oh well," I said. "I suppose I'd better make a move now."

Bob began to unpick the knot into which he was wound. He lifted himself up from the couch and followed me downstairs and watched. I turned on my ignition, my lights; glanced at a face dipping in and out of the shadows, as it always would be, half visible only, its reasons never obvious, always shifting, never easily defined.

"I don't know what to do."

"Go home," he said. "Just go home to your own life."

I straddled the Yamaha, started her up—the motor was instantly there, a big triple ticking over, a circular argument with the power I thought to take me as far as I wanted to go. Far, far away. That was the promise it made and in those days I believed in such things against all evidence, all those stories of how things were, really, for others. I manoeuvred my bike onto the road, friendly under my touch, much friendlier than anything else I'd found up to that point. Bob stepped into the light of the door. He watched my leaving. I couldn't read his look, but that alone made it important in a way I couldn't get. I lifted my glove up in a last wave; and rode away into my own future.

*   *   *

Dear Tony,

I never thanked you properly for being a "Good Samaritan". Harry and myself would like to show our appreciation. If you wish to come over for some Xmas Spirit you are very welcome.

God Bless, Gladys (and H.)

So I ran a comb through my hair and knocked twice on their door. Harry opened it, beamed at me, and fended off Gina with the heel of his old slipper.

"Merry Christmas, mate," he said. "Coming inside for a wet?"

Gladys popped her head around the door halfway down the hall. She said hello then disappeared into the kitchen. Harry let me over to the dining table—a new reproduction model that was, so far as I could tell, a reproduction of the one outside on the landing. I perched on a matching chair. Harry sat opposite and folded his arms. A bowl of walnuts decorated the table, but there was no sign of any nutcrackers, or drink.

"I'm afraid you've caught us on the hop." Gladys came out of the kitchen with an unopened bottle of cream sherry. "Our son's bringing the drinks in later. He's stopping off at the cash and carry on the way home." She handed over the bottle and a pneumatic corkscrew and took three glasses from a cabinet. Harry twisted the top off and poured us three brimming measures. Gladys dealt out the silvered drink mats. For a moment I thought she was going to sit with us, but she quickly picked up her own glass and took it through to the kitchen.

"Mince pie, Tony?" she called.

"Thanks, dear." Harry replied.

"Ice cream with it?"

"Thanks," I replied.

Gladys came in with the spoons and bowls. "There we are, that'll put some meat on you."

Harry started on his immediately. I broke mine open, steaming mincemeat running into the vanilla ice cream in dark, spicy streaks. I'd soon polished off the lot. I drained my glass quickly and glanced at the kitchen door. Why wouldn't she sit down? But they wouldn't. My mother was just the same. They always had to be busy: it was a symptom of their madness.

"Refill?" Harry lifted the bottle, whose label showed two women playing tennis in ankle-length white skirts. "I'm not much of a drinker myself," he said.

"Cheers." I lifted my glass by its stem and the clear liquid broke its surface tension and rolled down its sides, clinging by capillary action, onto my fingertips. I couldn't think of anything to say. "Family out at work?"

"All out, anyway," he said. "My lads have got a bit of a job on."

"How many kids was it you said?"

"Six." Harry beamed. "Eleven grandchildren. My youngest daughter's just had another one. Little girl." He paused. "One of my grandsons is a professional cricketer. Did I tell you that?"

"I think you did." I'd placed him at about fifty; now I saw he was much older. "I saw you the other day," I said, "over Kensal Green way—pulling into the cemetery."

"Did you?"

"Funny," I said, "all the riding around you do, it's not often you see anyone you know."

"Guess what we were doing," he said. "Go on. You'll never get it."

"Making a delivery?"

"Of what?" Harry fell silent, trying to get me to make another guess. I didn't. "We was digging a grave," he said—and laughed.

"Yeah?"

"That's what we do. Cemetery work. We've got our own little business." He stopped. "You don't seem surprised. People are usually taken aback by that."

"Why?"

"Gives them the creeps, I suppose. You're a funny bloke, Tony, if you don't mind my saying."

"I always see your boots lined up outside the door."

"Yes, yes," he said. "I know all about that. What about you? What about what I said?"

"What?"

"Come on, you're a funny bloke." He sat back with his arms folded, determined to get value for money out of his glass of sherry.

"You're right." I laughed. "I am a really peculiar bastard."

"I've always thought so," he laughed back. "Why's that?"

"Born like it, I suppose."

"You're all right though, don't get me wrong."

"What about this grave digging then? What's that like?"

"Why do you ask?"

I shrugged, drained my glass. "Willie used to do it."

"I know," he poured another. "I suppose that's why you weren't surprised. Still, if Willie did it, he must have told you about it. You must be an authority on the subject, if I know anything about him."

"I should be. I must've just turned off when he was talking. As so often. He didn't have much to say about it—to him it was just digging a hole in the ground and filling it in again."

"Well," he said, "that's all it is, the actual digging part." He laughed. "I'll tell you why you're so peculiar."

"Why's that?"

"Most people think it's interesting that my grandson's a cricketer. They ask me loads of questions about it all the time. But you couldn't give a stuff, could you?"

"Not really, no."

"You'd much rather hear about grave digging, wouldn't you? Graving, that's what it's called. There's something about that that really turns you on, isn't there?"

"Not really. It's just not the sort of thing you hear about a lot."

"You're not the sort of person you meet a lot."

"Why's that?"

"I don't know. You tell me."

I didn't say anything.

"I'll tell you what you are."

"Oh?"

"You're a dope smoker."

"Not really."

"Yes you are. You're some sort of super-intelligent dope smoker. Educated, though you pretend not to be, and you're from a working-class background, like us."

"How do you know?"

"I can tell. It's obvious. What I want to know is what's the big mystery about everything, to you? Because as far as I'm concerned there isn't one. I mean, life seems mysterious when you're young. To some people, anyway. But basically, it isn't. Anything that seems strange, or interesting, has a perfectly ordinary explanation. A boring one. That's what I've found, mate. And this is my point. You are intelligent. You're not stupid. So why go skulking around acting as though everything's some big mystery?"

"He's got a point there." Gladys had put her head around the door.

"Do I act like that?"

"Yeah."

"Perhaps I'm not as clever as I thought."

"But you are. Probably cleverer, I don't know. But perhaps I can't tell. I'm not that brilliant myself. Too clever to be a motorbike courier. Too clever by half. Too good-looking to be on your own, unless you're a queer, which you're not. And before you ask, I don't care about that either. I was in the forces." He hesitated. "Well, are you?"

"No."

"That was totally pointless." He laughed. "You haven't told me anything I didn't already know."

"Nothing's mysterious then, to you. You understand everything."

"More or less. You don't like us, do you?"

"Yes I do."

"Not really. You think we're racialists."

"Are you?"

"You know we are. But we don't really mind the black people that much. I don't know. Willie didn't like us. I bet he mentioned it. What did he call us?"

"Frontish."

"Well, that's true. I did support it at the time. I don't now. Well, you've got to try and get on with the people around you.

We've never had no trouble from them, not really." He laughed. "You know."

"Right."

"So what's your point of view? Don't tell me. I know what it is: socialist."

"Right."

"Don't you want to have an argument about it?"

"I expect you've heard it all before."

"True. Just thought it might be something to talk about. One thing about race, though. If you're white you can't say anything about it from your own point of view. Otherwise you're a racialist—and that makes things a bloody sight worse. Just avoid the subject, that's favourite. What do you think? You agree? Or disagree?

"If you're working class you've got our own point of view."

"Right. And you can't express it. All you've got is the town hall. And they're a load of middle-class socialist wankers."

"If you're lucky."

"I'll tell you what, Tony. I bet you must get a little bit confused yourself at times."

"Why?"

"Well, I would, if I was you."

"Why?"

"Conflict of loyalties. Because you're working class yourself, but you're not what most people—including we ourselves—think of as being working class."

"In what way?"

"Well, you're not stupid like what we are, are you? I think this must've made life difficult for you sometimes."

"I'm pretty stupid myself."

"Bullshit. You're too intelligent, that's your problem. You're too intelligent to be a socialist, because that crap don't make sense, not really. Not the way your mate Willie and his wife used to say it did. Sorry, but it just doesn't. Look—anything involving human beings is a complete and utter racket, you can bet your life it is. But there's no force against that, as Willie used to say there was. There's nothing. It's certainly not the working classes. You just have to accept it and swim in the sea—as I expect Chairman Mao probably said."

"So why am I still a socialist, then, if I'm so intelligent."

"Because you're working class, I suppose." Harry shrugged. "But I have to say, Tony ... that's where you're going wrong. You're putting yourself on the side of a load of people who you've got absolutely nothing in common with."

"He's right, Tony."

"Leave it to middle-class wankers who can afford it, mate. They don't mean it, anyway. You'll be all right," he said. "Get yourself an air raid. Women like that."

"I might just do that."

"Try getting out of the courier game—it's fucking dangerous and it's not going to last much longer." He paused. "So what do you want to know about graving?"

"It's okay. Never mind. Nothing."

"Go on, I want to tell you." Sweat broke out on his wide, glowing forehead. I could tell he hadn't done much talking for quite a long time.

"I expect you get up to a few dodges," I said.

"Dodges?"

"Yeah, you know, a few tricks."

"Pardon?"

"Sidelines, you know."

"Like what?"

"You tell me."

"Yeah," he said, "we do—a few little dodges, yeah."

But nothing he was going to tell me. Nothing about the tools. "Do you get busier at certain times?"

"Things do get busy at this time of year." The thought seemed to tickle him. "You do get a bit of a seasonal rush. That's where my boys are. Opening a bloody great twelve footer over at Hanwell."

"Why twelve foot?"

"Fat bastard."

"Rich."

"Rich fat bastard."

"But—"

"People just give up, I suppose, at Christmas," he said. "You've lost someone that way yourself, haven't you? I can tell."

"No," I lied, "not as far as I know."

"Anyway," he said, "it's not such a bad old job. Gets you out in the fresh air. You see a lot of wildlife. Foxes, of course, badgers, all sorts."

"Vampires?"

"Not personally, but—" He shrugged. "It's well known, isn't it, in these big old graveyards, you can't stop it. Like I said, everything's well known."

"Except the details."

"Well, you've got your problems. Hard spots, soft spots. Cave-ins. Mind you, they've got regulations for that now. You've got to put down staging boards, keep a safety man up top while you chuck it out. There's a lot more to it than digging."

"Like what?"

"There's setting up your stones, laying your concrete beds, lining up. They're wedged together with bits of slate. That's a real right game. Danny's got more patience for that. Young eyes. The other boy does a lot of the cleaning; going round inscriptions with a masonry chisel. There's your general gardening and repairs."

"Must get depressing."

"Not really," he said. "You do get a slight hum on the reopeners. You've got to watch you don't put your boot through the old box."

"What do you do if that happens?"

"You jump out quick."

Our glasses were empty but he made no move to refill them. He seemed to have run down. I wondered if I should help myself, but I didn't.

"I could probably get you a start if you're that interested." He gave me an appraising look. He had me pretty well appraised. "Not the best time of year for it." He poured the last mouthful of sherry into my glass. "There's plenty goes on in a graveyard," he said, "More than you might think."

"Like?"

"Hiding knocked off gear and so on, you know." This was too boring to go into. "Gunnersbury's got its own proper nursery. I remember, years ago it was now, one of the old hippie gardener types got done for growing the opium poppies there. Had his own little set up in one of the sheds. Apparently he sold it to the other blokes. Half a crown a pipe. They'd stretch out on fertiliser sacks while he cooked it upon the primus." He looked to see if I knew what he meant. "Wouldn't happen now, of course. That was back in the council days. Oh yes," he said, "there's plenty goes on in a graveyard—and now you know all about it, don't you?"

I did. I sat there.

"Gladys, Gladys. Do you want to know why she's the way she is? Do you?"

"Don't tell him, Harry." Gladys put her head round the door. "It's none of his business, snooping little bastard. Let him work it out for himself, if he can. Which he can't. He doesn't know he's born that one. He doesn't know the half. The quarter. The smallest bit of it. Don't tell him."

"It was when she was a little girl, Tony. Now what do you think could happen to a little girl to make her scared of going outside? Because in those days kids played outside all the time, you didn't have to worry about them, or so people thought then."

"Don't tell him," she said. "It's none of his business."

Harry shrugged her off in a display of husband power. "She wasn't that young. Nor that innocent either, truth be told."

"Bastard."

"You know what it is, don't you Tony. She was sixteen. She met this bloke in the library, so she says."

"I liked reading, I still do."

"He was probably all right, you know. She probably wound him up. She wound him up something rotten."

"I was like that in those days. I didn't try to stop him. I didn't want to. I couldn't, if you know what I mean. I was only sixteen."

"The bloke was thirty-five years old."

"Do you know what my father did?" Gladys joined in.

"No."

"I'm not going to tell you that bit," Harry said. "She can if she likes."

She didn't.

"Anyway, she didn't go out after that."

"What happened to the bloke?"

"I'm not going to tell you that either."

"It's rubbish, Tony. I do go out. I go out all the time."

"Yeah, she goes out when it suits her. The truth about her is that there's nothing really wrong with her, not in my humble opinion. Nothing at all. It's reading all these books what's caused it—I told her that right from the start."

Seventeen

The name for too much fear is cowardice; too much confidence is rashness. Courage is the mean between two extremes. "Hold the ship out beyond that surf and spray." Pray. Calypso. Wrongly attributed. The middle way. Caring is the mean between neglect and indulgence: a good policy for fish-keepers and pet owners generally. It is the path of continence, or failing that, a stout nappy for those little ethical accidents. I didn't know why I'd taken an interest in definitions of virtue. Probably I didn't understand them anyway. Just. Not virtues. But they could be. The good is only what is good for me, unless you happen to be one of the good. Tackings of the onehood. Wished to save it. To reform the body politic. To serve. That's a middle path to power. To righteousness. Fair enough.

Perhaps I was just a rationalising coward. He who exceeds in confidence is rash; who exceeds in fearlessness has no name. Emanon the Fearless. Somebody once told me I was like that; but he was wrong. I wasn't afraid of him, that's all. Or was I? Just whistling in the dark again. Bravado and big lies. I said the Lord's prayer again before leaving the house, stumbling over the end part about those who trespass against us. That seemed to trigger a rage in me, probably fucking up the whole prayer for all I knew, as a guaranteed protection charm.

Or did it?

Well. I found the Antagonist in his pegboard office, working his way through a large bag of wine gums. Wine-dark his teeth ... his chewing sounds were leaking out through the thousands of holes in my arguments, in my armour ... Reverend Poore looked up when I walked in. This time there was no pretence of non-recognition.

"What was that prayer you said?" I asked him. I wanted to know that because for some stupid reason I'd forgotten it.

"St Anselm," he said. "I believe from his Prayer to St Peter, I know it is:

The runaway returns
and asks forgiveness for his errors and disobedience.

He shows to the good and healing shepherd
the gashes of wounds, and the bites of wolves,
which he ran into when he strayed,
and the neglected sore places
that he has had for a long time ...

... Shall I continue?"

But I didn't want to hear any more of it then, especially from him. I found the prayer beautiful, but in his hands, his mouth, it was just another weapon. I knew exactly what it was going to say, what it was going to mean. Submission to him, not to Jesus Christ. Anyway, I wasn't sure I was ready for that. It wasn't one more case of choosing the mean. Of being mean. Of calling down the Apocalypse on the bad men—that's us, that's erring humanity—always failing to be quite good enough for ourselves, for God.

"That's okay." I said. "It's come back to me."

"Look, I haven't got all day to fuck about. What can I do for you?"

"I want to know how you get away with this ... shit."

"With what?"

"You know, running a racket in the name of charity."

"What racket?"

"This one." I stood there. He didn't reply for a long glass moment.

"No-one will believe you, Tony," he said. "Do remember I can alter my testimony at any time."

"You cunt." The word wasn't right and it wasn't worth saying. Poore seemed to believe he could do anything he wanted to, because he'd been allowed to get away with it for so long. How stupid. How much more obvious could you get.

"So, the world is at your fingertips," he said "or so you'd like you imagine."

"It's not at my feet."

"Funny. You didn't strike me as the bookish type."

"I've still got my sight."

"Hmm." Poore swallowed a mouthful of wine-gum shreds with some effort, his adam's apple bobbing like an apple in the midst of the folds of soft loose skin around his neck. "I wonder, I wonder. Hmmm, exactly what is it that has led you back to me? Foolishness? Stupidity? Er ... trust in authority figures?" He gave a short laugh. "I suppose that must be it. The Almighty obviously plays no role in your life."

"How do you know?"

"Because He doesn't exist, Tony. It's simple as that. So, what has brought you back here?"

"Mistakes. I don't know. Whatever led me to do something so stupid in the first place?"

"Don't ascribe too high motives to yourself. People are very liable to hold you up to ridicule—especially if they know the truth about you."

"What's that?"

"It's that you indulge in what is unhealthy, as St. Anselm would say. That is why you attract such tormenting diseases."

"Careful you don't catch them off me," I said. "They're highly contagious."

"Not to me," Poore spat contemptuously. "Self-righteousness is much the worst of them. Christianity ... it's not all it's cracked up to be, as persons like yourself have had the sense to realise. I might have to cut you down to size, Mr Guest. Cut you down like the very commonest flower and throw you on the roadway to die."

"You're a right fucking bastard."

"Quite. But some flowers grow taller than others. And we must let them. Anything else would be criminal."

"Some are cut down before ..."

"Suicides. Failures." Poore shrugged. "You know one or two, don't you?"

"How do you know that?"

"After all, there are only a few things—a few situations— that can account for specimens like yourself. Suicides. The guilt they engender. The internalisation of blocked energies. So that nothing leaks out through the membranes, the pores ... a grief that can't properly express itself. Can't be properly resolved. A grief without a pang." The bastard knew everything, or thought he did.

"I didn't even know he was dead."

"Then it's absolutely sure."

"What is?"

"That you must have killed him, Mr Guest. Because why else should such a death torment you?"

"How?"

"By taking everything away from him, I expect. Everything he was. Everything that he might have been."

"How?"

"By being it yourself. That's the usual reason."

"How?"

"By parasitism, Tony ... quite a common cause of suicide, so I understand. Harbouring too many of them. Because when a parasite senses that the host is weakening, that's when they really go berserk. I've seen it a number of times in my ministry. They seem to go into a sort of disgusting frenzy to bring him down. One final gorge. One last good meal." Poore chuckled dryly. "Quite something to witness, I can assure you."

I looked around the office; a few clipboards hung on hooks, curling pages with lists of crossed off names; a small bamboo table in one corner looked like it had been in the family for some time: on top of this what looked like a carved cigar box. I wondered what it contained. A shelf attached to the strong wall contained a couple of books on charities law, something by C.S. Lewis—an old paperback called *Mere Christianity*. On Poore's desk there was a phone, a dusty computer terminal, and in one corner of the floor stood an open cardboard box containing presentation bibles.

"That's not really what happened," I stumbled into speech. "We never really ... never really ... I suppose I took things from him. He took things from me. That's friendship, isn't it? I suppose you could describe it as a mutual parasitism, if you wanted. There is giving and taking. Role-playing, he was big into that ..." I found myself unguarded but not altogether defenceless. "You know, you be this, I'll be that. I suppose that's one way that people take things away from each other."

"Hmm, hmm." He looked out towards the flickering tube-light of the big room where his usual transactions were proceeding at a normal pace. "Generous thoughts, Tony. Generous to the point of excess. You've a sentimental view of people. Yourself, mainly. Especially yourself. Personally, I'm not sure that I believe in any of this nonsense. In fact, I'm absolutely sure that I don't. People are what they are—and that's that. What happens to them is what happens."

"Bob needn't have died."

"So who killed him?"

I didn't have an answer.

"Suicide is a sin—a mortal sin." Reverend Poore pressed the advantage of his cloth. "It is if you're a Catholic."

"Which you're not."

"Think of the suffering it causes."

"He didn't have anyone much."

"No loss then." Poore looked at me in a way that I thought might be close to the sensation of being penetrated without consent. "You're an idiot, Tony. Look, look, there's only one reason for a suicide. Suicides are failures. Full stop. They realised it. They put an end to themselves—therefore they are best forgotten by the living."

"Depends on your point of view."

"But there is only one point of view." Poore's voice trembled with what might have been emotion. "If these people are dissatisfied to that degree, well, well tough luck. I mean, there's absolutely nothing that can be done about it. Suicides should be made to carry cards exonerating innocent bystanders. They should try not to take anyone with them, that's all."

"What causes failure?" I persisted. Poore had more than an edge on me. I felt my questions were getting stupid already.

"Vanity," he said. "Oh, you know—Aristotle's really quite interesting on the ending of friendships. Of course, he has a great deal to say on the subject in general. One passage is particularly germane, but perhaps you might already be familiar with it?"

I couldn't call it to mind.

"Well, it happens when one friend surpasses another. Aristotle gives us the example of becoming God. Or god-like. One of the gods, you know. So that the equality which he sees as the only possible basis for the truest kind of friendship can no longer obtain."

"Maybe that's what Nietzsche was thinking of when he talked about needing your friends' permission to be a genius. Or they think you do."

"Nietzsche's a real suicide's philosopher, Tony. Quite possibly you're right. Sneering at Aristotle whilst presenting his insights as his own, in a slightly different form, of course—as common in the philosophical fraternity as in Ecclesiastical history, I'm afraid. I confess I've often done it myself." Poore was quite a comedian of the cloth. "I think you'll find that what Aristotle is trying to come up with there is some sort of explanation for the popular belief that friends, um, don't always truly wish their co-friends the greatest of success in their undertakings. Ever noticed that? Because ... well, then they would lose them as friends."

"Why's that?"

"Because one would have to submit to the other, I suppose. And, amongst those who have been equals, that's intolerable."

"That's shit."

"Perhaps you should read the man properly before pronouncing summary judgements on his thought. I'd say it was more than generous on the side of friendship. This friend of yours, did he leave anything behind that you have inherited?"

"Not really ... a story he wrote."

"And?"

"I found it recently. I'm convinced it's what led me back to him. Led me to find out what happened to him."

"What's it about?"

"I don't really understand it, not properly."

"Throw it away."

"It's brilliant ... unfinished."

"It's a failure, Tony."

"Well ... it couldn't be published."

"I suppose you must think you're some sort of an authority on that as well ... My wife's published a number of books, I'll have you know. They're really quite good, some of them—in their own way."

"What does your wife think causes suicide?"

"What a ridiculous question. All kinds of things."

"Go on. What does she think?"

"Well, sometimes it can be the father. A father who denies. Perhaps a father who forbids. A father who refuses to be exceeded, refuses permission. Judgement of the father is difficult to bear. Like the judgement of the Heavenly Father, it can't be gainsaid. That may be part of it—I think I agree with her there. A father who poisons the game, do you see? A mother who sides with him against the stronger son. Against reason. Against justice. No real expectation of justice. You know, one can pretend to be brave for a while. Until you know that your courage is futile. Which, of course, generally it is."

"St Augustine preferred his mother," I said. "He saw his father's ambitions for him as a vain desire for self-perpetuation. Hers were directed by the Holy Spirit." I'd read that years ago—it was the main thing I remembered about him, apart from those bits about the absurdity of believing figs screamed when you plucked them, what a load of crap astrology was, how a person trained in rhetoric could have the best arguments, but still be wrong. Strange how these things came up out of nowhere when you really needed them.

"Well, well." Poore's eyebrows shot up in a gothic arch. "So who would've thought you'd read the *Confessions*. Hmmm ... in that case perhaps you'd tell me what happens on page 163?"

"Fuck off."

"Don't you know, Tony?"

"Not off hand."

"Well, come back when you've read it. Better still, don't bother yourself."

"Bob needn't have died. He had something. Understanding—and if you've got that, people can feed off you."

"That doesn't mean they're going to give you anything back."

"But if you've got that you should be able to think your way out."

"Perhaps he did." Poore smiled his all-knowing smile of reptilian indifference and pseudo-knowledge. "Too ambitious, too ambitious. I blame the schools, really. And the goggle box and rubbishy books."

"Suicides aren't any worse than the people who went on living, especially scum-bags like you. If I was God, I know who

I'd choose—I'd snuff you and your kind out without a moment's hesitation."

"But you're not, are you."

The scumbag was winning. They really might as well have not taught us to read and write—a sickening feeling in the pit of my stomach that they were actually right. The bastards didn't believe we could think. Right to the top. Maybe they were right. I could always change the subject though, pretend not to be so stupid.

"So why did you pick Don Baxter out of the line-up? In fact, why did you report the break-in? I don't understand you. It was that that got me confused"—I fumbled for excuses—"I thought you must be a good person. All that happened. I got confused. I still am." Try it. Try it. Pretend to throw yourself on his mercy, but stay awake! Pretend to be stupid ... but, really, be cleverer than you could possibly be.

"My wife insisted," he said. "I didn't want any police involvement. But she thought we should teach you a lesson. I walk a fine line there, as you can imagine, and there was something ... not quite right about you as a petty thief. I didn't want to get involved. We decided to have another look at you. Marjorie and me had an argument over it. I stepped on some water she'd spilt on the floor. Some of that cold water in the name of Christ. I conked my head on the edge of the sink. That did it. I was so bloody angry. I can't tell you how angry. Marjorie telephoned the police."

"But what about Don? Why'd you pick him?"

"He was a nasty-looking parcel of goods. Obviously a sickly specimen. Seeing you again, Tony, you also had that look about you. Trouble. Somebody who really thinks they're clever. I decided to ... spare you. Don. Barabas, as I prefer to think of him. Looking for some sort of anti-miracle. A worthy candidate. Slightly worried he might turn out to be a policeman ... that's a common procedure, so I'm told. But not in this case, not this time—luckily for you."

How did they keep it going? Why was the ball always in their court?

I let it sink in. Luck seemed to have come into the Reverend Poore's calculations rather a lot. That might mean he was vulnerable, although his operation operated on a wing and prayer ... on intuitions, and for intuitions to really work you needed a better notion of what made the big machines tick over. Possibly, or maybe you relied on everything being up and running, like the giant houseplant, the rubber plant that Willie had left behind in the flat. However many of its leaves fell off, it kept sprouting new ones. Hideously misshapen, it continued to grow. I'd thought it was impossible to kill until finally I'd managed to OD the fucker on Baby-Bio.

But plants needed roots, and even the bound roots of a pot plant would do. Poore did have those. Unlike Bob. Unlike Don and Brian Nello. Unlike me, even. We seemed to work on the bubble principle. You blew a lot of them. Blew some more before the last ones burst; till there was no more bubble mixture left. Fairy Liquid didn't work so well. Not in the fullest sense. Not properly.

"And so ..."

Pop. Category mistake. My own bubble had burst.

"And so ..." Poore grimaced. "I don't really know why I'm conducting this sort of conversation with you, Mr Guest. In fact, I know I'm not. You and your friend. Why don't you go and do likewise ... Why not do away with yourself? Just cauterise the wound. Try not to take anyone with you. Unless, of course, they turn out to be of the same kind. No harm could possibly come to anyone of worth through your actions. I wonder if you happen know of any vulnerable women? any children?"

"No."

"Discount them, anyway. They have such short memories. You won't be seriously missed. Anything of value you leave behind—though I can't quite see what that would be, in your case—will soon be made the fullest use of."

"There's no chance of that happening."

"Pity. I would've thought, in your case, that dying would be your best option, qua rational being."

"I suppose you think that anyone who can't look after themselves should be killed."

"You're starting to annoy me, Mr Guest."

"There's a murderer behind every suicide. I can't help thinking you're right about that. Several, probably."

"Hmm, hmm. But wouldn't that make us a society of murderers? This might sound a bit harsh, Tony—but lame ducks really shouldn't be helped. I think we hear quite enough quacking from them as it is. Quite enough. Let them fail. Let them die. That's what I think, that's my view. It's God's too, for all we know … it's his world. Good riddance to them."

"I think in his case it must've come too late."

"Not soon enough, I'd say."

"Too late in discovering his own powers. Before that it was imaginary powers. Hexagrams. Spooks. Horoscopes. Mysterious doings. Table tappings. You can develop out of that, I suppose. But it's still there. Buried. Carried forward. The stuff whole numbers won't go into—like me, Mr Poore."

"I see, one of those."

"One of what?"

"Alibi-seekers. Self-mongers. Where does this romantic drivel come from, that's what I'd like to know. You know, people accept their misfortunes, Mr Guest. They have to. They just have to live with them. Lie with them. Seek small distractions from them. Everything is known, really. All this is simply a matter of your own refusal to accept it."

"Somebody else said that to me."

"Who?"

"Your brother."

"What brother?"

"I thought you had a brother."

"Well, I don't."

"Half brother."

"Give up, Mr Guest." Poore's eyes twinkled, winking in merriment, like diamonds, stars. "I've often known people to react like this when they realise there's no justice. No earthly justice, that is."

Sweat broke on my forehead. My heart was racing. I let my helmet slip down my arm—and in a single reflex, I smashed it hard through the glass window of his office. I glanced out. A few surprised look-ups. Behind the trestle table a man was getting up and moving. What gave me the strength—the madness—to do these things? What? Some stupid do-right bug from my childhood, maybe, maybe a sense of never having done right myself. St.

Anselm sounded interesting. I'd have to read his prayers. For say what you like about Poore, he bit deep. He saw the veins right there under your skin; the sorest, rawest places—and went for them like a wolf; but in his own mind he was still a good shepherd separating out the duds from his flock. Who'd believe this shit still existed? That they were still out there. But they still were—in little side worlds, everywhere. Poore and his sort had drunk up all the milk, now they expected us to pretend that the bottle-tops were money.

Fuck him though. Fuck him. Fuck him. Out there in the big room the queue had dispersed and the two men in dark suits were looking though filing cabinets against the far wall—or pretending to. And then I walked out of there without shame or guilt, unworried about any reprisals. What could a bastard like that do? What could I do? Except to make up this terrible conversation full of arguments I couldn't possibly win, distorted by my hate, my special pleading, and the failure of my reason. What do they leave you, and what room have you left yourself? Where do you go?

Truth is beauty, beauty truth—that's crap, such crap. Truth is only the beginning, on its own it's nothing, just what everybody knows: that worst possible motives always win out; they're what everyone has, anyway—right? right? Wrong. Wrong. The only real beauty is justice; justice isn't some harmonic resolution of everything (though it might seem that way), it might even be that, in the end, but the point I'm trying to make, the point is ... justice starts only when everything has already gone wrong, badly wrong; and most people, me included, aren't willing to wait till judgement day to get what's coming to them, and that's the reason for so much injustice: people know that day isn't coming, not any time soon. You have to get your own justice.

Try to tell anyone anything like that and they'll either laugh at you or nod and say, yeah, sure, that's what I knew already ... and you do, I do, we all do—but justice, justice is something different; a final twist of the lemon, a wrinkle that balances out the other wrinkle: the one on the other side of your face from when the wind changed, the one you got from laughing at things that aren't funny. And you know it when you see it, because justice has nothing to do with luck; nothing to do with beauty either. Because the recognition of beauty is instantaneous, it can be full of lies (and usually is) whereas the recognition of justice is something you work for—like justice itself—and, more than evil (which is no mystery: it's doing the obviously bad thing all along), it's something you might just get a glimpse of sometimes when you're looking back.

Justice, off-stage, is trying to direct everything to come out as it doesn't want to and never will. You may say you're going to do right, say it any way you like, in short words or long, but without no feeling for justice you may well be banging dustbin lids together for the benefit of a brick wall. You may watch the news every night, be able to second guess every second guessing politician and dictator in the whole world, and really be the one who knows what they're really up to; you might have that much belief in yourself, or in somebody else: love your companions or your opinions so much that half the world will strut around doing our biding and repeating your jokes; but if you don't believe in the possibility of justice you'll be sitting on a shit-heap waiting for the sun to come out, and when it does the word will stink even worse.

You can give your best one-liners away to idiots, throw yourself in front of a train or under a taxi just to prove your bravery, donate your remaining organs to medical science; but that's not justice, is it? is it?

True justice bides its time—it's always champing for the off, race-tuned, ready to go; but it knows full well that others have their claims on it too, so gives them their turn, their spin of the wheel. Justice doesn't make big claims for itself (only this one), not arrogantly; it doesn't always keep the longest half of the bisected bar of chocolate, nor fly off the handle over everything and nothing; it knows grudges will only gnaw its own heart out, and so it isn't forever going on and on about what a bastard so-and-so is—even when he is—with some sort of not very secret enjoyment of so-an-so's bad acts. Justice likes truth. So it will put up with anything, for a while, or forever, if needs be ... it will still exist later, still be there and waiting for its time to come.

Justice is beauty that doesn't fade: second guessers get it wrong in the end and there does come a time when fiery words don't seem to really be about anything anymore; the lap-times you memorised from last season no longer matter to anyone. They'll just point out how easy it was to run the four-minute mile (although they couldn't actually do it themselves) and say "yeah, well, anyone could say that" to any of the wise words you may have been repeating half your life. But these things aren't everything, not in the way justice is; because though it's the subject of every late night film, you'll still watch some of them to see if they still come out the way you know they should—but is that, are they, all the power of justice is?

No, surely true justice it must be more than that; put those reflections of itself in the shade. When I was a kid I had a kid's idea of justice: no idea except the stupid one of "fair" and even just a few years ago I went to see the remake of *The Fugitive* and watched as one man (who wouldn't give up) managed to use the system against itself to prove his innocence—but, really, how often can you play the same old toys? Providence frees him; and his own drive to exist keeps him going—that, and the many good acts we watch him perform along every inch of the way. But could anyone really live like that? Like a Christ whose every action is integrated, directed towards the same end: his own redemption, with everyone else's thrown in—the bad guys vanquished once and for all, and perfect happiness there for the taking?

That story didn't satisfy me anymore, it didn't contain a single true image of misfortune. Richard Kimble endures unjust hardships, but he escapes them too easily: he is supposed to be a man but unlike a man, he recovers his wind in the face of insurmountable odds; he has more lives than a cat, enjoys providence on a superhuman scale, far greater than any handed out to the Son of God.

Kimble is a Superman of the middle-classes and he isn't going to save us from anything. He doesn't die so that others might live. He's a Christ-hero with the difficult bits edited out, just another too-beautiful man who can do anything. Okay, he's a hunted criminal, but his reversals of fortune are easily overcome week by week. He's too resourceful. Just another childish thing to be put away; a song with all the right notes placed carefully in

the optimum TV order, the one they always knew you wanted to
hear.

Eighteen

They'd sent me out to the Isle of Dogs in the dark—a long trek from Harvey Nicholls to the *Daily Telegraph*. Felt like it, anyway. I inched along the winding rain-lashed road of red tiles, choppy waters lapping at its fresh-milled edges like black milk; new branches of old banks loomed up, and new mystery firms with indecipherable names on unblemished brick facings: big finance with a small "f" to let you know know—and overhead the empty lit-up cars of the Docklands light railway wobbled by on Hornby track. I was hungry. Big hungry.

The *Daily Telegraph* building's foyer sweet shop was closed up, barred; nothing else open for miles. The bloke in the post room signed for a thin envelope I handed over. I hadn't looked at it, but I noticed now it was a circular, junk mail. He lifted a stack of similar items from a shelf behind his counter and let them trickle down through his fingers.

"Harvey Nichols?"

"That's right."

"They've been coming in all afternoon. All separate drops. Might as well chuck the lot straight in the bin. They won't even look at them like that." He glanced upwards, to where they, the gods of this place, lived.

"Don't chuck 'em away," I said.

"Why not?"

"Well ... why not put them around anyway?"

"Who to? They haven't got no names on, mate."

I wondered briefly, uncaringly, what would be the fate of the temp responsible for such an expensive little cock-up; maybe she'd be sacked first thing on Monday morning. Oh well. I walked out into the drizzle and cruised back over to Camden to pick up my account pay: the Friday night drink crowd had probably started without me.

At seven o'clock I rolled up outside the butcher's on Kentish Town Road, expecting them to be over the pub. A light was on three floors above street level, so I climbed the stairs; the radio a sack of ball bearings hung around my neck; the rain I'd absorbed doubling the weight of my gear, or something else had.

Something bad. To what place was I rushing away? I pushed my way through the upstairs door, painted grey with car primer, and staggered into an empty room. Alf was on the floor behind his desk, doubled up, rocking in acute pain.

"You all right?" I started towards him, and then realised that the dark bloodstain on the back of his head was a cap. He was only saying his prayers. I picked up my envelope, the only one with my name on, signed for it and headed for the pub.

They were all in a little knot in front of the food counter, drinking Mexican beers from cold bottles they were holding with their fingertips. Barbara listened quietly as someone held forth on a particularly important point: she glanced up as I joined the group. Visibly relaxing. The tight cluster of male bodies slightly muffled her deep grating laugh. I waited beside them for a few seconds, steaming in the sudden heat.

Nobody said hello.

I went to the bar and bought myself a bottle of Pils.

"You should've seen it," one of the boy racers said. "This cab cuts him up on Waterloo Bridge, right? So what does he do? First off he broadsides in front of the cabbie and stops him in the middle of the bridge. Then he puts the bike on the stand, right in the middle of the bridge, this was, and walks over to him. The cabbie, he's wound down the window to give him a mouthful. The ABC bloke leans into the cab. Thanks, he says, I'll have them. He pulls the bloke's keys out his ignition and lobs them straight in the fucking river. Beg your pardon."

There was an explosion of laughter, the group loosened. I slid in beside Barbara. I knew that story. I'd heard it over eight years ago, only then it was about a rider known as Doug the Thug. A deep sigh went around. Somebody started talking and I huddled again into the warm noise.

They were the usual Friday crowd. Anyone with a shred of sense was drinking at home. Gerald the van driver, ex-Army, officer class, clearing £400 a week and thinking of moving on somewhere bigger; two new kids whose names I could never remember; Barbara—and someone else who was missing. Alf sidled in a couple of minutes later, his hair slicked back and shining, as if he'd just taken a shower.

"Still raining?"

"What do you think?" The others turned to say hello and offer to buy him a drink. "Cheers, all the very best." To the chosen, to Gerald.

"Where's John tonight?" I asked. "John the Postman." I meant the bloke who worked for the post office in the mornings—went on circuit on a Honda 90 when he'd finished his round; thirteen hours a day on a Honda 90, saving up to send his kids to public schools, so he said.

Barbara consulted her watch. "Still on his way to Staines, I should think."

"Must be the job of the day, that one." Alf laughed and everyone had a good laugh at poor old John.

"What a life that bloke's got," I heard myself starting to mouth off. "What a terrible life. Don't you think?"

"He's a funny feller." Barbara's smile tugging at the corners of her mouth. She was thinking: No worse than yours, pillock.

I drank up, hot in the Swedish over-trousers I'd bought to replace the ones I'd lost in Willesden. The new ones were silver and came up in a bib hooked over your shoulders. They were digging into me now. Sweat was pouring off my face, and, oh, oh, I should go, get myself off home, watch some of Friday night slip by. Why was I fucking up again? I didn't have anything to say to these people, my judges, my friends. I turned away to the bar, put down my empty bottle.

"Mine's Holsten," said Gerald.

"Look at him in that gear!" The mouthy kid, to no-one in particular, not to me. "It's not raining in here, Tony."

The Forwarding Agents turned to laugh back at me from the future.

I stripped off my gear, stuffed it in the torn bag and felt myself grow lighter and looser.

"Okay, Tony, that's far enough." Barbara said. "For now."

I got myself another Pils in and a pint of a lager for Gerald: and when I'd got back they were all pulled in again with their backs to me. I scuttled around the outside, nudged at Gerald to take his drink from my hand. He looked back over his shoulder, annoyed at me.

"Oh, cheers. Thanks." Gerald turned away with a pint in each hand, shrugging to the others, lucky me.

The boy was telling a story about the Croydon controller.

"He says, I've got a nice one for you here, mate. It's a load of hair going down to Vidal Sassoon. Apparently they cut off too much. She's still in the chair, so that's a pretty urgent one."—waiting for the laughter to end—"He's funny, that geezer. He can get a bit out of order though. Like he says—It's a sambo, a Sam from Bow."

The boy's friend, a young black rider, had been nodding like an eager little puppy up till then. "That's really out of order, that is," he said mildly.

We all murmured that it was out of order.

"He's been told about that," said Barbara.

"Another time he goes, Got a West One for you—watch his hands."

"Watch his hands!"

I chugged down half the Pils, tried to find my way back into the circle. "It's that woman that bothers me. She really gets on my tits." But nobody was listening,
as per usual.

"Who's that?" Alf said. "Barbara?"

Barbara turned towards me, laughed nastily. "Trying to tell me something, Tony?"

"No, no—not you, the Croydon woman."

"Yeah? Yeah? What's your problem with her?"

"She sounds so unhappy all the time," I said. "Her voice goes right through you."

"Perhaps she is." Barbara turned to carry on another conversation.

"When she shrieks like that you've just got to turn her down, otherwise you'd run up the back of something."

"People are always messing her about, that's why." Barbara looked around. "That's why Alf and me don't stand for it."

I finished the Pils and wiped my mouth with the back of my hand.

"You're not supposed to turn your radio down," Alf said.

"What an idiot!" The boys agreed.

"What's the point of us shouting if you can't hear us?"

"Oh well, I don't, I don't usually." I stood there stupidly with the empty bottle in my hand.

"We've all got our problems, Tony," Barbara chipped in. "What we're saying is, don't mess us about, right?"

"All right, all right."

"You still on that weird old bike? one of the boys asked. "That old shaft-drive thing: what a disaster."

I didn't reply.

Gerald handed me another Pils, friendlier than the rest, as always. But they'd run out of the cold ones and the warm beer hit the back of my throat: fizzy metal. So I held the bottle carefully in front of me and tried to look serious and concerned, and one of the kids started talking about—I don't know—some near miss; no that was it—some woman he'd stopped to help on the motorway, who locked herself into her car, this woman, refused to come out ... told him to fuck off, go away you stupid little boy.

"Nice of you to stop and help her, Billy," Barbara said. "But if I'd seen you coming I might've done the same thing. No offence ... I mean, why did you stop, anyway?"

"Just trying to help."

But I didn't hear Barbara's reply. I was drinking on an empty stomach. Weight had been rolling off me since I stopped eating during the day. Over at the food bar the waitress removed metal containers from the rack and steam billowed up from the underneath water tray. There was about enough for a portion of cauliflower cheese left, but she seemed busy and pissed off. The last thing she wanted to do was start serving me. The soggy cauliflower beckoned stodgily. I thought I might as well have some, but sensing an imminent sale, she whisked it away. I put the rest of the Pils down. Sweat poured off me, my throat burned with a thirst no amount of warm fizz could touch. I thought I'd move on to something long and colder.

"Holsten?" I lifted my empty bottle, called to Gerald.

Gerald glanced at his infallible watch. "No, thanks."

"Barbara?"

She slid her small hand over the top of her glass.

At the bar I missed the weight of the bag on my shoulder and panicked suddenly, thinking I'd lost it. I looked down and saw it was more or less at my feet, leaned against the bar rail.

"I'll have a tenner out the till, a packet of fags and your hand in marriage," some jack of all lads was saying to the young barman, who dodged immediately out of his line of sight to take my order.

I picked up the pint in one hand and the bag in the other. The rest of them burst out laughing at something. Me, probably. Poor Tony. Look at them, I thought, all standing there. Why did they always stand? It wasn't as if the place was packed. I read a notice saying NO DRUGS NO NUCLEAR WEAPONS NO UNUSUAL PETS; on the far wall a whole verse of John Lennon's A Day in the Life was written out in gold on a glossy pub board. Camden. Jesus. I started to get that swamped, ugly feeling. I'd get this last one down quick and push off home. I dragged the bag across, lowered myself carefully onto the nearest stool. I glanced across at a nearby booth.

Bill Nicholls, the boss himself, was sitting in it; a pile of uncrumpled day sheets were spread in front of him, an outsize calculator held together by a rubber band under his right hand, and he sipped at a glass of red wine, entering neat columns of figures on the back of a clean, folded docket. I suspected he was double-checking he hadn't overpaid anyone. I looked across to where the others were getting ready to leave. Bill gave them a wave on his way out. They said their hearty boss goodnights. Looked at me. Smiled. They waved at me.

I twisted a finger at my temple. Bill, screwy. They laughed. Alf struggled into his coat. Barbara and Gerald waited for him. On their way out they called a goodnight. Goodnight Barbara. Goodnight Araf. Goodnight Gerald. I bent to pick up my gear and noticed for the first time in ages that my helmet had ACHILLES written across the front in scuffed gold letters. The fat lady flashed into my head: the muttering ex-teacher, a poor woman who'd taken her own life in her flat across the landing. I wondered how she'd done it. Tablets, probably. I expected they were the very ones they'd given her to sort herelf out. Others, it didn't matter much. I remembered her mumbling in the lift one day long ago—something about the Greeks. I realised it must've been my helmet that set her off. She'd noticed my inscription and was trying to start a conversation about the classics.

The only way to get out of feeling guilty was not to feel guilty. Just be guilty. Guilty as hell. And the way to be guilty as hell, especially if you were already, was to be even more guilty (if that was possible). But guilty on the other side, on the side of good, so your guiltiness was burned away in a single act of purification and transformation, and if the avenging wind of heaven didn't exist, really, then you had to be that wind yourself. This was the meaning of those moments of illumination in which you saw your way clear, saw your proper course of action, when your way forward was finally lit up like a way between the trenches, a gap in the wire they had put up around you—and you were clicking, buzzing, and going for that very gap for the last time.

Having put everything in its place you were going to want it kept like that. As to plans, I had none, really. I was going on that moment when the gap appeared, before the darkness fell again, and you knew it was still there, or hoped it was, because you had to trust yourself didn't you, in the end, had to trust your own mind and your sense of the fitness of things, not only in a moral sense but as how they would actually go, how it could be made to come out like the ultimate game of patience, sevens, where the stakes were your life and the cards couldn't be turned over for another hand, no chance of a joint break, no repooling of pennies.

I rode that past midnight ride again, past midnight, knowing it would come to me in the order it was meant to. Absolutely sure of it, sure so I didn't need to check my tool kit or sort out an alibi. Alibi. Alibi. There was an idea. God be my witness—and if the finger pointed at me ... it wouldn't though, it would point right past me and towards some other bastard—Barabbas—and a pair of thieves whose bearded heads were sunk down into their shoulders, their short, twisted bodies getting it for once, and for them there would be no way out of the tomb, no rolling of the stone away, their too big hands twisted out wide as if explaining something, selling it to you for the last time, with a fucking great nail banged right through the centre of each open palm.

It was Sunday, palm Sunday. I was riding my donkey down into the city of gold, but there was no-one about to throw out any leaves under my front wheel, just a few cabs coming back in the opposite direction, carrying those drunken little whores back to beds of fornication, and back to sleep it off with some goofy goon from upstairs, who wasn't even looking at them, but out of the window of the cab, looking at me. They didn't know they were born—and I was going to do this thing for Marie, as well, for Bob. And for myself, if I was honest, if I was really going to tell it truly and openly for myself, and stop messing around all the time with half-truths and soap that was plainly not going to wash off a good day's road grime let alone the sins of the whole world.

What had happened in the office wasn't enough for me; I knew that now, if I knew anything, and I did, obviously did. I knew what justice was, even if no-one else did, and if I wondered when this wanting to kill people had started, I knew really: it had started with Nick. I used to have this fantasy, when I was riding around, like I said, about the alley Nick walked down on his way home, on his way out of the office. It was already dark, a winter evening. I'd finish my last drop early and wait for him at the end of it with an iron bar in my hand. I rehearsed it over and over, enjoying the look of surprise on his face, his stupid, weak, ineffectual right hand coming up, slowly, too slow to ward it off, and the lovely splintering crump as it caved in his temple and I felt his skull go in. I'd do it again on the ground until I knew he was dead and he wasn't going to pop up again in vinegar and brown paper.

No, it was before that. Wheeler, after he'd hit me and I was rolling around in the cell and those faces came up and I knew you couldn't do it, not really, you were powerless against them, but you still wanted to, didn't you, you still wished you'd find some moment when it was man to man and then you'd see what sort of man he was, and you were, and you hoped you were more than him but feared you weren't. What did it mean when you held back? Cowardice? Pity? Just the recognition that another was more powerful than you? Some pathetic moral justification of your inability to take what was yours, what was owing you, to stand up against somebody who was abusing you and laughing in your face, like St Paul said, *Corinthians*: How can you say you have seen the face of God, how can you know what is justice or charity when you freely allow a man to abuse you and praise that man for it? It was when Poore had forgiven me and made me pray with him that I'd wanted to hurt him.

Before that was—but if I had to go through the charge sheet of everyone I'd ever wanted to administer a smack in the mouth to. They were best forgotten, like the snows of the day before yesterday. Rudy was one, obviously, I'd been genuinely afraid of that little wanker. I'd let him talk to me like I was nothing for years on end, walked around his moods and his mouth, forever open in sarcastic laughter, as you do with people you have to live with: you accept it. I didn't know how I'd ever been able to put up with any of them. Even Bob. He was a cruel bastard when he wanted to be. There'd been times I'd wanted to scream in his face and whack him around the head with—I don't know, with whatever was around heavy enough to hit someone with in that flat. His copy of Colin Wilson's *The Occult*, probably—and even his story made me angry, that it was written for a woman, that it, he, was so withheld, so up his own arse, looking away from me, pretending to, not allowing me to love him.

Another one of those cabs—and behind it the snout of a jam sandwich, its lights off in a Shepherd's Bush side street. I throttled back, cruised stonily. I was going a funny way to Kensington; I was going all the way. I remembered those pickets again, the SPG caressing their gloves in the back of Transits, grinning at you as they took the chromed number badges off their shoulders, ready for a ruck, about to kick the shit out of anybody they might lay hands on.

At Lewisham it was different. They got the riot shields out for the first time; I saw a cop Transit slew to a halt under the railway bridge as the windows went in under a hail of bricks, saw them banging around inside it, bluebottles in a jar, as the mob of black kids ran towards them chanting Soweto, Soweto, and they turned it over, and we stood there, waiting for it to catch a fire, looking up and down the High Street for a friendly bobby, a badgeless flying wedge to come around the corner with rescue guns; but they didn't, not straight away. I was in the centre of a mob controlling the streets and we, the white people, were invisible because we were on their side. I remember the police advancing down the street behind these transparent plastic things, their riot shields, beating their truncheons on them, like in Zulu, and hails of bricks came down over their heads, and sometimes you'd see one of the bastards go down. A friend of mine, Dan, stood beside me, shouting out against the fascists:

NAZI SCUM—OFF OUR STREETS

NAZI SCUM—OFF OUR STREETS

A cop rushed forward then and grabbed Dan for the van. He must've looked harmless. He was—he put out his forearm and I grabbed it tight, and there was a big push and pull between me and the cop as we pulled him between us like a wishbone, my hand slipped down his arm, gripping tighter, ready to hold him until I pulled him back into us—at the same time I was discussing it calmly with the cop, as he explained that we couldn't win, and I said I didn't like to see anyone hurt either, and I read back his number to him, and he said Dan would come to no harm: I'm taking him, he said, I'll take you too. Dan was being hurt in the pulling match between us. He looked into my eyes, and he said: Let go, Tony, it's okay, let go. And I let go of his arm.

Another time when I was walking in one of the columns out of Hyde Park. A young skinhead was prancing along on the pavement, shouting nigger lovers, you fucking disgraceful nigger lovers, and waving a copy of a fascist paper at us while the cops marched single file on either pavement. It was a routine thing by then, they were half asleep; but even if they hadn't been, this little bloke would still have been running out to have a pop at us—because he was excited, he was definitely the excited type. I gave him a look, because it seemed he was looking at me, and he shouted:

"You're one of us, you're one of us, come over here and join us, you're not one of them, you're one of us."

He could tell what I was by looking into my eyes, I was like him, marching in the wrong column somehow: the temporary fifth column, when I should've been with my own people, supporting them. They were the only ones who'd ever care about what happened to me, or the likes of me, or really knew what I was—and there was a black guy beside me, Woolly, and he said:

"Don't let him say that to you, Tony. You've got to answer that. You've got to answer that back."

I didn't remember what I'd said, something about people like him making me ashamed to be working-class, because I couldn't remember, but I do remember saying something about what side did he think the police were on, and he said our side, and I said our side, because they were protecting us from you, what do you think of that, and the cop beside me laughed and said if we weren't there shouting at each other that would suit him fine, because then they could go home. Aren't you on overtime, I said, because it was another Sunday afternoon job, and I realised—if I hadn't before—that if they hadn't been there to separate us neither side would've been there to shout at each other, and there wasn't anything more to it than that, really: an empty ritual that would roll on until people who had better things to do—live the rest of their lives—got on with doing them, and people like him—this skinhead who didn't have anything compared to the people, most of them, I was walking with—and people like me, who only had this one chance of making something better of my life—really were fools for having anything to do with it. Then this jumping little Nazi skinhead screamed at me:

"That's what happens when you go to college, you turn into a fucking phony, they just make you spout a load of stuff that's no fucking good at all for you or your own people and you have to do it just so you can be one of them, or pretend to be, just so you can help out a load of fucking nig-nogs and murdering Irish cunts who couldn't give a fuck—they don't need your help, mate. They've got it already. They're laughing. Those cunts are laughing at you, mate."

Probably I said something, I had to; probably something like ... I couldn't remember what I said. Hammersmith down that long wide dual carriageway bit that comes up on the museums on either side of you. Didn't know where I was, I remembered, remembered thinking, oh, he was right except there was nothing for me there, on his side, what he was asking was an impossible to match the ones I believed in, and Bob—but what did he believe in, really, none of them believed in anything except getting out of it. On election day Rudy stuck up a Thatcher poster, a Labour isn't working, and if you tried to argue with him he'd have arguments, particularly ones about who wants to ride around in a load of piled up shit that's been left there by people who're too lazy to do a day's work, and now was the winter of our discontent, but what did they have to complain about, really, because they didn't have to go out there and go for anything, did they? Following orders of fat, lazy union officials spouting crap about everything in sight. I rode it down to Gloucester Road, circling in on them like a hawk who's seen the meeces run, a twitch in the peopled grass; he hates those meeces to pieces, and now he is ready to pounce, to drop.

There were some road works next to a square on one of those turnings off Fulham Palace Road—what THE HELL was I doing there, I'd strayed off course—but beside the road works was a ditch surrounded by police yellow incident tape, and there was going to be AN INCIDENT because the tape was strung up between thick five foot iron spikes each with a hook on the top, driven firmly into the ground. I parked beyond the ditch and walked back to them, looking over into the square, at the empty benches, past the padlocked black gate to stop night sleepers getting in, although you could, anyone could—and did, probably.

But there was nobody in there tonight, not that I could see. I walked on and out of nowhere a jam sandwich arrived, braked sharply, and in a couple of seconds its two occupants were out and upon my case.

"Can I ask what you're doing, sir?"

He stood over me, his partner a few steps back with an open radio and an equally curious look on his face.

"Nothing," I said.

"What have you stopped here for in the middle of the night? People don't usually do that for no reason, I think you'll find. That's my experience, sir."

"Nothing, honestly officer. I couldn't sleep. I went out for a ride. I stopped for a breath of fresh air."

"I'd have thought there was plenty of fresh air to be had on a motorcycle, sir. That's why people ride them, so I understand. Have you been drinking, sir?"

"No."

"Not even one or two?"

"No," I said. "Do you want to breathalyse me?"

He looked back at his companion who raised his eyebrows in an enquiry as to whether he should fetch the kit out of the car. "That's all right, sir. I believe you. I can tell if someone's been drinking, even a little. Can I take your details, sir? Got your documents with you, have you?"

I pulled them out of my Bellstaff's inside pocket and handed them over. He passed them back to the other one and there was the usual wait while he looked through them in the car and radioed my details in for a computer check. I froze and tried to look casual. I didn't say anything further. He seemed to know there would be nothing. But he also knew I was up to no good.

"Can I ask what you do for a living, sir?

I told him.

"My advice to you, sir, would be to get on that bike and ride it back home and get yourself a good night's sleep for tomorrow morning. I'd have thought you saw quite enough of the streets of London."

"Okay," I said.

They returned my documents and he gave me supercilious directions to Acton and they followed me back the way I'd come, sitting on my tail most of the way to Hammersmith. I kept glancing in my mirrors and they were right there on my tail, a steady twenty yards back, nudging me forward along the path of righteousness through near-empty streets until they got another call. They overtook me and passed at speed with a whoop of salute and I kept plugging along at thirty until they disappeared—and then I glanced in my mirrors, I did a quick U-turn in the road and blatted back to the square at a thousand miles an hour.

I slung her on the side stand and was back on the iron stakes within seconds, ripping the tape off and trying to lever one of them out. No good—they were banged in there pretty solid. I went around them until I came to a loose one, and started levering it back and forth in the tarmac. I heaved; it wouldn't give. Fucking thing. Probably had a claw on the other end of it. I thought of people laughing at me and the crunch of the moment where you just have to go back and do whatever it is, doing the impossible until it's really done, and with a final heave I wrenched it out of the ground.

It was heavy—five foot tall. No way was I going to get it in the top box. I sat on the bike and slung it across the top of my thighs, balancing it there. I managed to wedge it between the front of the seat and the tank, down deep as far as I could get it. It wasn't firm but it was as good as I could get it in. I pressed the starter and cruised off. It was going to be sheer luck as to whether any cops saw me—and I rode the rest of the way like Ben Hur, with swords attached to both wheels. It didn't slip off, which was a miracle in itself, because if it had it would probably taken me with it, bucked up and speared me through the chest, or else it could've crashed down, gone straight through my front wheel and pivoted the bike up and onto me as I tumbled arse over tit down the road, waiting for it to land in my chest.

But I was outside the building in Queen's Mall. I heeled out the side stand, the pole started to slide. I grabbed it, let it slide through my hand onto the tarmac. Then I got off the bike and stood there holding it: my lance, my javelin. I hefted it again and tried to bring it up to my shoulder—impossible I'd throw it any distance, let alone through Poore's heart, let alone be able to retrieve the thing straight away and smack his stupid wife's head off her shoulders with a single two-handed swipe of my broadsword. Heavy enough. Heavy enough so that, whatever you did, it was going to inflict some really proper damage. If it was thrust at a human body with any amount of weight behind it a metal stake wasn't going to meet all that much in the way of resistance. Easy. An easy job. Easiest job I'd never done. I laid it down in the gutter and looked down. Then I said a last goodbye to it. I rode away.

Nineteen

Marie was brought up on a small farm near a village outside of Derry, but at the age of seventeen she still didn't know how animals got born. She knew about fucking but hadn't quite made the connection. She knew where babies came out but not how they got in. Nobody told her. Or if they did it went in one ear and out the other. For her it had always been the boys and the bikes: her endless cousins who rode out in the Northwest 200 and dodged around the RUC on midnight road tests on the winding lanes of bandit country. There were whispered stories of affairs in the attic, elaborated with a friend who took on the name of Sister Concepta on the occasions of their telling; stories in which the heroine was always bound and drugged; always given a good hiding which she thoroughly enjoyed.

I'm propped up in bed now with the clipboard on my knees. Marie's sleeping back is turned towards me as she makes usual soft hooting noises low in her throat, her smooth forehead almost but not quite touching the wall. She's been living here a while now; I've been trying to get it down, putting off the moment I arrive back at this, the nearest I'll ever get to a scene of perfect, beautiful happiness.

The flat's certainly gone through a few changes. The two catfish are living the kind of a life I wouldn't mind myself. I'd envy them if I didn't have it so good. Marie unclogged the filtration system, scraped algae off the glass with a contraption that looks like it's for shaving your back. She has such affection for the catfish, particularly their brown mottled skin, particularly the sheer ugliness of the front end with its twitching, whiskery parts. We can look at them all the time now. Nothing is hidden.

I watched her go through the junk in the cupboard, dusting it off, trying to place values on it. When Marie's around, everything has to come out: a bundle of rotting sticks turned into a clotheshorse and ridden away, a Dansette's needle located in a haystack, a marvellous old sewing machine marvelled at—and replaced where it was found; a full service of dinner plates, shattered into a thousand pieces by other stuff thrown on top of it, can easily be reimagined in its wholeness: it's only those time capsule cardboard boxes of other people's lives (sealed, labelled, abandoned) that must be carefully left for future generations to ignore in their turn.

I enjoyed seeing things through her eyes. I assumed that's what I was doing. But after a couple of days of climbing great ranges of it, I meekly suggested we put it back in the cupboard -

"Let's take it to a car boot sale."

"What car boot sale?"

She picked up *The Leader* and started leafing through its back pages. "There's one at Ealing Hospital on Saturday morning."

"We haven't got a car boot to put it in."

That wasn't worth a reply. She squinted in her typical way, stomped through to the bedroom, waiting for me to be overcome by remorse—which was a matter of seconds—and then I padded through to find her staring up at the ceiling, her hands behind her head, chewing on a match and musing on some scheme of the far days, some plan for ... what? Was she scanning the future or just obeying some surge, some urge: just standing up on her hind legs and pretending to see a train coming, a solitary meerkat who'd lost its team, that couldn't really see the horizon?

"You all right?"

"Fuck off."

"What's the matter?"

"You know well what's the matter."

"What?"

"That you're a patronising wee bastard who thinks he's absolutely brilliant at everything whereas in fact you know fuck all about anything except how to sit around thinking you know better when you don't, you just don't. That's what's the matter with you. You're so bloody stupid smug and sexist. My cousin Terence is sexist, but you've no excuse, Tony. You're pig-ignorant through and through."

"Why? Why? Why am I sexist?"

"You just are, Tony. You don't even know how to talk to a woman properly. And besides, you're absolutely shit in bed."

"I'll try harder."

"You'll need to." I was getting used to this, I was even getting to like it. "Tell me, is Willie ever going to want any of that stuff in there? Is he? I've never even seen him. To tell you the truth, Tony,

I think he doesn't exist. He's just somebody you made up. I mean, if he's supposed to be the landlord of this place—which is illegal, anyway—why doesn't he come down here sometimes?"

"He phones up sometimes if the rent's late. Probably because he's a writer, always banging away on his next masterpiece."

"Fair enough—but there's too much of stuff lying around, Tony. I feel that the place isn't my own. It's a massive distraction. It wouldn't be so bad if you were being enticed down some fascinating pathway. But you're not. It leads somewhere else from where we are now; somewhere nobody in their right mind would really want to go."

"Where's that?"

"The past ... where else?"

I didn't know what to say.

"Why else do you think he's dumped it all?"

"Can't say he's ever shown much interest. Even in the fish."

"Fishes! Fishes!" she was shouting. "They're living creatures, not fillets fried in batter."

"There's still Marion and Eddie."—the beautiful catfish— "Okay, okay. Go on. Sell it, I don't care. Willie's bound to cut up rough though. I mean, wouldn't the same apply to anyone else?"

"It's always me, isn't it? So when are you going to lift a finger? You seem to think you've died and gone to heaven."

"Look, I'll help. We'll both do it."

Victory. She sat up on the bed. "George'll do it in the van. We can always give him a tenner."

"George?"

"Don's friend. Big bloke with beard."

"Good idea ... make a party of it."

"George is fine."

"Ask him then."

I'd kept on shuffling around the streets of Acton, looking out for runes on the kerbs. Hundreds of the fucking things. I tracked around them in the rain, picking up any wet roaches I found plastered across a circled triangle or a raido, taking them home to dry out under the grill. Smoking myself to sleep at night— resigning myself to the fact that this, this, and this ...was what it had really been coming to all along. I was fishing out some particularly juicy ones from a heap of ashtray emptyings near the tower when an elderly woman rushed up to me. The old lady took out a cigarette packet and pushed three or four Embassy No.1s into my hand.

"I've done the same thing myself," she said. "There's no shame in it."

I didn't know where to put my face. I thanked her. Tried to sound pathetic. Grateful. Walked on. That's what guilelessness was, I thought. No. 6 in The Spectrum of Love: "thinketh no evil"; the most expensive, impossible virtue. Common enough. Common as muck. I slipped all but one of the white cylinders into my own half-full packet and lit one up.

All I knew about Bob was that he wasn't around. I'd lost him when he was still alive and thought that was grief. But it wasn't my loss of him that was important, it was his loss of himself ... if that could be so, to someone who was no longer there to feel it, or who had decided not to. He wasn't out there anymore, moving forward on some weird trajectory—not waking up every morning into his life. So he might've been ... a what? I thought of him, dressed as a butler, servant of a rakehell young aristocrat, a minor Formula Three racing driver. I quite enjoyed that. He'd given up on James Railio and settled for becoming his mechanic. Or maybe he'd made it big in the city and joined the Tufty club. I laughed, I told him that. He wasn't there really, of course, I couldn't imagine what he'd be like. Because he wasn't. He was stuck in my head was all, was all.

He'd always be looking out through my eyes. Bob announced himself. Took up residence. Drew me into the depths of a story that he was unable to explain or resolve. So was I. Unable. Paralysed. He was trying to find a way to unfreeze me, I hoped. I remembered the woman in a wool dress, Fiona. I'd liked her, on a short acquaintance ... and Linda, her cool appraisal of me. The Caves of Making on Tinacrea, the birth-mothers still looking out towards the nearest star for some problem to take into their leathery old bodies and fix. I remembered Christine Morris, for some stupid reason, the greengrocer's daughter: her, picking up a book called *Rogue Angels* from a revolving rack at the Ideal Home Exhibition when we were ten years old, and warmly recommending it to me. I thought of Colin out in the garden with his new telescope, carefully identifying the smudge nebula and the great luminous mother-of-pearl collar stud of Mars.

But something was missing. There should have been more bank statements arriving at Twickenham. So why had they stopped? Railio's active bank account—was it still active somewhere else? I rifled my pockets and found Rudy's number on another folded docket.

Phone skidding around, I dialled.

"Hi, Rudy."

"Hello, Tony. Hi. We've been meaning to get in touch. Stig was saying we should get together for a drink, sometime."

"Yeah, why not. That'd be great."

"Let's arrange it." I heard pages turning as he looked for a free night. "Next week's out, I'm afraid. How about Wednesday fortnight?"

"Fine."

"It's been all change here, all go. New address after next week. We're moving to bigger premises, in Hendon."

"You had a great view up there."

"Cheaper and bigger. Still, it was fun while it lasted."

"I'd have had trouble giving that up."

"Do you want me to tell you something about yourself, Tony?"

Not particularly; but I knew he was going to, anyway.

"You have a lot of trouble giving things up, don't you? Most people just let go and move on, keeping something from the old, if you can. But you, you're an arsehole, if you don't mind my saying so, you always thought you were clever. You haven't gone anywhere—and now you're living in cloud cuckoo land. Why can't you just look at things the way they are?"

"I don't know, Rudy."

"Well I'm fucked if I do."

I'd provoked this outburst, I didn't understand how. "I wanted to ask you something about Bob," I ploughed on. "Don't know if I mentioned it—but a few months ago I picked up some of his post. Bank statements addressed to Mr O and Railio."

"You didn't mention it, Tony. But the fact that you did it proves me right. It doesn't surprise me. Look, you're not very well, Tony."

I hated the way he kept using my name, as though to remind himself who he was talking to. "This is really weird, right," I said, "but one of them was still being used ... I just ... I thought I saw Bob riding out of Hyde Park ... " I stopped. "I don't know why I thought you'd know anything about it."

For a moment I thought he'd left the phone, but I made out his steady breathing on the end of the line.

"It's strange though. It's true. I'm not making it up."

"Look, Tony ..."

"Am I going off my head?"

"Well, you didn't see Bob. Bob's dead. You thought you did. Fair enough?"

"Fair enough."

"I know about the accounts. Stig and me took the paying-in books out of his stuff."

"You what?"

"There wasn't anything in them." Rudy sounded affronted. "Later on we started the business and thought we'd use them to beat the tax man, for petty cash and what have you. I didn't think Bob would mind. Just a way of remembering him, I suppose. Anything else there by any chance?"

"Yeah," I said. "That story you mentioned. He sent it to himself."

"The one he wrote for Rosie? About spiders? He finished it, then?

"No, it was just notes, ideas, bits."

"Good?"

"Bob was a genius, Rudy."

"Hold on, hold on ... so how did he send that to himself then? He was dead before we left." But he knew the answer instantly. "I think it must have been Rosie. He must've left it with her. She must've hung onto it and sent it back later."

"You didn't contact her?"

"No. Couldn't face it. Why did she need to know?"

"But why did she send it? Why not just throw it away?"

"Maybe she thought he might want it."

"She didn't know he was dead."

"I just couldn't tell her, Tony. Anyway, it was only a brief thing they had then. It wasn't her fault he was totally hung up on her."

"It was good not to tell her anything. You were right. You could've told me though."

"Yeah, I know ... sorry. So what's his story about?"

"Oh, the last survivors of a race of giant spiders. They're the mother race. The God race, in a way. Problem-solvers."

"God doesn't solve any problems, Tony. He just gives you a giant headache."

"They're the rememberers. Except they don't remember much. It's all just echoes in these ancient caves where they used to live."

"Bob didn't know his real mother," Rudy said. "I remember he tracked her down once, before you showed up, and she didn't remember anything. Only having him. Just about."

"How could she?"

"Not even who his father was," he went on, "I think you'll find that's what it was all about."

"Read it, if you like."

"It's good you say?"

"He couldn't finish it. I don't know how he managed, or how he did it. I'm not even sure I understood it, really. It's ..."

"That's all right. Just keep it. Or forget all about it. If it bothers you that much, why not chuck it away?"

It was getting dangerously close to the fifteenth—thirteenth? fourteenth? twelfth of never? The jewels were being systematically smuggled out of the country, embedded in sideboards, in statuettes of the Belles of Liberty, a much coveted netball trophy replicas of which had become fashion items in Paris. Boys inspected their comics for clues to the conspiracy of days. Girls spiced them up. I was battened down and waiting for another spring, watching my step and trying to save my life ... when the phone rang.

Marie, in a pub, was telling me jubilantly that Don had got off. Poore fluffed his story in court, and Don's lawyer had seized on this to convince the jury that the old boy was senile ... the jury went for all of it, despite the old man's act, following a summing up in which the judge laid due emphasis on the reasonableness of doubt—and the police introduced a few umms and ahhs into their evidence, according to her: clearly implying that he was under investigation.

I thought they weren't allowed to do that. "Wasn't he supposed to be pleading guilty?"

"Yeah, he was ... but—" Marie was pissed out of her brains, shouting into a pub phone somewhere way over in Brentford. "I really like you, Tony, I really really do. You are going to come, aren't you?"

What a terrible situation. I rode off towards Chiswick, down London Road, past the shut up mini-precinct, competing kebab franchises at the deserted corner of the hospital for day surgery ... believing Marie, believing in her. So, so they'd got Poore. I wondered how it'd happened. One of the volunteers, obviously. It was so simple. Sweet justice: consisting in the punishment of wrongdoing: somebody had done wrong—and now they were going off to big prison. I didn't give much thought to Don's probable reaction to seeing me there. I was determined I was going to level with him; I concentrated on particular words I particularly wanted to use ...

... Curious. Curious so I went back there. It was a moment in my story that I could make no real sense of. None of it was any good. But thought hadn't turned out to be my strong suit—I could only make patterns, do arrangements: the very moment such orderings became tests of thought, they scattered, like blown away sand pictures. I painstakingly combed the last grains into position and mentally cast around for some non-existent fixative. Something to free off sticky mechanisms. WD40. The blue and yellow can that refreshes.

I pulled up outside the pub where they were celebrating, put my head around the door. The barman was staring away at nothing, midweek empty dreams, a buffed CD of *Freebird* came on the jukebox; it flared in my memory for the last time and went out like a flicked match (without the crackles you couldn't hear it anymore); I saw a little group of them clustered in the velvet crook of a corner seat, around the back, drinking hard. Marie's head was down on Don Baxter's shoulder, snatching at a dream before the last round arrived. I nodded at some of the others, who gave me a look back. They'd built a series of glass towers of empties in front of them; a replica of Dallas was better than taking them back to the bar. Baxter's knee was jumping to something other than the tired exaltations of Lynyrd Skynrd.

"Tony, hi." Marie's eyelids slowly came unglued. "Don. Meet Tony." She pulled herself upright and dug an elbow into his ribs.

"Right, right. I know you, don't I?" Baxter tried to frown me into focus.

"Not really. You might have seen me."

Don stared at me through pin-hole camera pupils. It occurred to me that he was probably seeing me upside down. Smaller than I was, by miles—in my opinion. That was something to work with, yeah, and I decided not to give the bastard an inch.

"Where's Mel tonight?" I asked this cheerfully of no-one in particular.

Marie cackled and picked up her drink.

"Er, that's mine, I think," said one of her companions. I recognised him from Hyde Park. The little Scottish bloke—he was a skinny kid, not much more—with a complexion of ginger nuts and condensed milk, red hair hanging in thick ribbons of grease—a class warrior in a class of his own.

"Oh." Marie put it down, lifted the next one, and seemed to have lost a thread. "Mel's away off somewhere."

There was some sort of gummy whiteness on Don's lips which beer and the back of his hand wasn't going to shift. Marie was looking out at the same old world through half-mast eyes, groping for a word.

Don wiped his mouth again, llicked the scummy mess away from his fingers.

I sat down.

"You know this fucking clown, do you?"

I immediately bolted toward the Gents.

"Want to hear a joke?" he shouted at my back. "You're it."

I pulled a bolt across below an antique plaque, which said PLEASE BOLT THE DOOR, and sat on the bowl trying to remember if I'd seen another exit that led though the back at the end of the urinals. I shifted and something crinkled under my foot: it was another scorched daisy of foil. There were a few drawings on the walls, a few half-erased stories from a long time ago: one of them about a white man who had hired a black man to fuck his wife; another took place in this very cubicle, if history was to be believed, at any rate its spare but unlikely account of events was quite absorbing—unofficial, of course; but since it was the only one, almost impossible to disbelieve.

The outside door went and big feet scuffled under the gap. I pulled on the chain, drew the bolt—and the door flew open as if a dead weight was resting against it. I put my shoulder into it; but Baxter's bony protuberance slid irresistibly around. He stood there. He pushed the bolt across behind his back. The white stuff was thick on his lips, a scummy whiteness from a fire in the spoon. He reached for a length of toilet paper to wipe it away, wadded it up, and tossed the result into the bowl.

I stepped gracefully to one side.

"Want to hear a joke?" he asked.

"Not particularly."

"You're the fucking joke mate." Baxter shoved my chest. "Go on, go on—guess what it is."

"No idea." I stood up, my eyes were level with a jumping pulse in his neck, and I looked into his face. My calves were pressed back into the damp porcelain. He filled up most of the space in the narrow cubicle. "There's not much room in here," I said. There wasn't. Not in my head, not in my world, not for people like him.

"There's not a great deal of room in a remand cell, not with two other bodies yapping and farting all night long." Don slid onto his haunches, overdrawn, nodding out. I sat down. I watched him closely, with much more attention than I'd ever been able to muster for anyone else at any other moment in my life—except Poore, except Marie, except Bob.

His face was thinnish, pallid, flushed, raw-looking. I wondered what was happening out in the bar, if any of them was awake. Baxter looked at me from a long way off. "Why don't you try saying something?"

He'd already forgotten what had been amusing him. "The difference between me and a little cunt like you is that I know who I am."

So did I. Or so I'd thought.

"Don Baxter," he laughed suddenly. "I'm the fucking man. Wow, you should've been in that court, man. Totally fucking surreal. One minute I was shitting bricks, next thing their whole case fell apart. First off they dropped one of the charges, which wasn't mentioned so as not to influence the jury. Then they put the sky pilot in the box. He was beautiful. Fucking lovely. He kept saying stuff like if you say so and I suppose it must've been. They asked who it was, he said: That's the fellow, or someone very like him." Don shook his head in happy disbelief. "That pig, Wheeler ... I thought the cunt was going to burst out crying."

"And I'd thought you were meant to be unlucky."

"No," he said, "you're the loser in this game. You just don't get it, do you? I know you did it, I know matey, I know, so don't think you're going to give me any bullshit. You broke into that gaff alright—and ever since you've been ... sniffing around Marie." Don showed me the edge of his hand, then slowly bunched it into a fist, moved it around a little, grinned at me—and (I thought he was demonstrating some Tai-chi moves) he smacked it hard into my mouth. I even saw it coming, but there was nowhere to go, nowhere; except onto the toilet seat, the back of my head thwacking hard against the old iron pipe leading down from the cistern.

I tasted blood in my mouth. I didn't contradict him again.

"Ouch," he said. "That's better, eh?

I still didn't contradict him. Don Baxter was frightening—powerful in a way that was something much more than the way he'd lashed out at me. It was in his eyes; they were everywhere, looking into everything, seeing what was really there. His body was tensed, he was waiting for me to open my mouth—and I sat there like a frightened rabbit.

"I'll tell you how it was, shall I? I always thought it looked like an easy one. Promising, you know? I expect you kicked over a row of brass bells on the way in. Not too clever. The pair of them came out of the bedroom. That old woman is a real bitch. You want to live, lady, you said, get back in and shut the fucking door.

Which she did. But the old crafty kept coming ... so you cuffed him, didn't you? He fell on the fireplace and hit his head. Bonk. Gone. Out. And that's when you started to get a bit jumpy, man. You dodged through the kitchen. You was looking for something to pick up, Tony. A pick up. So you grabbed hold of this fucking shoebox." He lifted his eyebrows in a heroic sort of way. "Am I right?"

"No," I said.

"Am I right, sir?"

"No," I repeated.

"Stubborn little cunt, aren't you?" he laughed. "But I know you was in there alright."

"No," I said. "I wasn't."

Don was wearing big fuck-off army boots. He trod on my left foot in them, really hard.

"Okay," I said. "I was ... it was just like you said—but I didn't steal anything. I didn't hit him either."

"You cunt." Don laughed again. "What, you mean you did? You really did it?"

"Yeah." It felt good to say it, to someone, especially him.

"So did I," he said.

I didn't believe him, but I wasn't going to argue. "When was that?" I jeered.

Don told me the date: same date I'd broken in. I couldn't believe it—I knew he was lying, he had to be. But ... what if he wasn't? Why shouldn't both of us have had the same stupid idea?

"Guess what was in that shoebox? Fucking charity envelopes. Loads of them. All with about 50p in." Don laughed. "Just about enough for a bang and a packet of cheese and onion." He shook his head. "I can't believe this. Of course, you realise Poore is a total charlatan ... that's why I thought he might have a few quid lying around. Still, goes without saying."

"I thought the same," I said. "I couldn't believe how he got away with all that."

Don shrugged. "So what happened when you ...?"

"He hit me with a poker," I said. "Then he let me go."

"Listen," he said, "nothing these cunts do surprises me."

"I think he's finished. What he's doing ... he's not making any sense."

Don started to tell me a story. "I was parked up on Cambridge Circus when that bomb went off in Charing Cross Wimpy. Remember that?"

"No."

"Not many people do," he went on, "I was totally wasted at the time. All these people started to run towards the bang. There was a sudden hush. Then the sirens were coming from all directions. Want to know what I thought?

"What's that?"

"Boring, boring ... and I climbed back on the bike and I rode away." He snapped his fingers in my face. "It didn't mean that to me, you know?"

Nice guy. I realised I didn't have much to fear from him. He was too honest. Poore was different. Lying must be second nature to that bastard. Somewhere along the line him and the almighty had decided on a life-swap—either that or he'd received precise instructions from upstairs as to the extent of his cut. I knew Poore. I hadn't got him that far wrong. But I wished I'd been there to watch him fall apart.

"Do much reading inside?" I asked him, playing for time—or something else.

"Some."

"Much science fiction?"

"More history and philosophy. Biographies, you know. The usual shit. I got pissed off with space operas some time ago."

"Did you ever come across one called *Typewriter in the Sky*? It was by, you know, L. Ron Hubbard."

"Can't say I ever have, man."

"Turns out in it that reality is being made up by this writer called Horace Hackett. Being unsuccessful, he's come up with a real idiot plot."

"What's that?"

"A plot that only works if everyone in it is an idiot."

"Isn't he the scientology guy?" Don laughed to himself. "I did their personality test on Tottenham Court Road years and years ago."

"And?"

"I turned out to be an individual of unique creative potential." Don laughed at himself. "Marie did it too—only she believed them."

"There's a lot of us about, apparently. Do you still think you're brilliant?"

"I'm not, am I?"

"Why ask me?"

"True—you're a wanker, mate."

"I'm not."

"Yeah, you are," he said, "Give it up, admit it. What it is with me, there's one side of my brain's better than the other."

"Which side's better then?"

"I dunno—maybe they just weren't wired up properly. You know, in the people factory."

"I think you're wired up fine. Probably."

"I dunno." Don paused for a moment. "But I mean, what is it, all this brain theory? Left and right. Reason and imagination. Plotting, language. You know, your thoughts and pictures. Your prints and negatives. Your light and dark. Yin and yang. Male, female. Do you follow? Do you follow?"

"Yeah, that's crap," I said. "They've proved it. Dualisms. Oppositions. I mean, it's always struck me as a funny coincidence that the brain was supposed to be divided in half by these things. That they came from nature. It's bollocks. That's not really the brain—it's just a way people have of describing it."

"You're not as clever as you think you are, are you?"

"What makes you say that?"

"Because they do come from nature. I mean, they come from the brain. Which is natural."

"Yeah, but not everything that's come out of the human brain is right. You'll grant me that much."

"I'm right."

"You're not."

"Prove it."

I couldn't. I heard the reassuring pad of small feet. Marie tapped at the door. "Tony? Don?"

"I know why you've come here," Don said. "You've come to get her away from us. Away from us ... the bad people; but we're not that bad, not really."

He was probably right. Anyway, not really so much worse than me. I'd got what I was looking for: nothing more than a smack in the mouth. It would do me for now. Strangely, I felt a lot better for it. Don unlocked the cubicle door and the three of us found our way out to the bar ... where the barman was performing a late glass cleansing ritual, staring intently down into the swirling brushes.

Don wandered back to his seat in the corner dogleg. He was holding his head up high (good for him) because he was free again ... and, something peculiar had happened, as usual. He knew how to do that, Don—how to make things happen—and this proved, once again, beyond reasonable doubt, that he was The Great Don Baxter. Maybe he was, I don't know. Anyway, he was definitely something, somebody you couldn't dismiss out of hand.

Marie hung back, clinging to my arm. She looked at the blood on my lip but didn't comment on it. "You're a funny guy," she whispered in my ear. "You don't think you're much, do you, Tony?"

"Not really," I said.

"Well, you'll do."

*   *   *

And then there was another firm rap on the door of my consciousness. Gladys was standing outside on the landing. A trick of the light, maybe, but her head seemed to be surrounded by a fine, gentle, heavenly glow. I looked past her to see where it was coming from. Nowhere. Harry leaned in their warm doorway with an interesting smile on his face—and much of the space between our two flats was taken up by furniture: there was an upended armchair covered in black leatherette I remembered from their bedroom, a bedside table with gilt rails around the top, a couple of walnut veneer covered bookshelves strung between rickety brass poles—and a scuffed old filing cabinet painted royal blue with thick gloss paint.

"Sorry to disturb you, Tony. We're getting rid of this lot. I wondered if any of it was any good to you?"

"Oh ... thanks." Marie would be pleased, anyway.

"We're getting fitted units put in. So I thought, it's a shame to throw away perfectly good stuff that would do a turn for you."

Harry kept smiling.

"Thanks."

"I'll give you a hand," he said. "Saves me carting the whole lot downstairs."

"Great." I picked up a bookcase under each arm. "I can manage these. I'll be back for the rest." I dumped them in the hallway. Harry and me wrestled the other pieces in one by one.

I guided him towards the spare room, helped him in with the other stuff and later I had a closer look at it. The filing cabinet would be useful. Especially if you had anything to put in it. Probably even worth a pound or two. I yanked the top drawer. Stuck solid. I wrenched at it and it opened a little way with a teeth-grating scrape. I peered into the depths. Twisted, broken. Off its rail. Worth having though, if you liked crap. I noticed there were a couple of books at the back of the drawer, reached in through the gap and fiddled them out. Big hardbacks with non-stick covers: *Peace from Nervous Suffering* and *Self-Help With Your Nerves*. Both of them were by Dr Marjorie Poore.

I was watching *Thunderbirds* and Marie was heating up a stoneground chicken and garlic pizza. I smiled to myself at how everything—work, amusement, everything—was nothing more nor less than a distraction from the pain of memory, apprehensions of mortality, the permanent itch of sex. Funny stuff, eh? I laughed at myself for watching such a stupid kids' puppet show, just because I used to like it everwhen. Brains' head was filling up the screen with his giant blue glasses, his boffin's omniscience. Brains -- hey, I loved that guy. "Brains'll fix it!"

"I think, Virgil ..."

"I think their heads have gone a little bit out of scale with their bodies," I called to Marie in the kitchen.

Thunderbird Two manoeuvred into position in to rescue the doomed space probe. Back at base the rest of the team watched anxiously with gentle head movements, oblique non-human gestures and expressions of awe. Thunderbirds are go! Then it was over—a quick flip to the women's speed skating before the Superbikes came on. Marie was tapping her foot by the oven. Why didn't she come in and watch this? The four girls set off, bunched closely together. Their arms were almost on each other's shoulders in a tense flying antagonism of fast position jockeying, so close together, so beautiful, so quick—their mouths agape— like what? Like nothing I'd ever seen.

"Marie! Marie! Come and look at this!"

They were like dancers in a supercharged ballet, maybe, or a trio of young witches rushing out from a rock to grab someone, to grab the lead: to me they looked like three little girls acting like scary sirens, like the furies in a school play ... so close, so fast! They just looked too fucking reckless by half. A twinge told me they had to fall—and they did. Two of them went over hard and cannoned into the blue edge of the rink ... limbs seeming to snap, Jesus!

"Marie!"

Their heads twisted, like Meryl Streep falling downstairs last night—only these two girls, not having taken the eternal youth devil-drug, didn't get up again. Christine Boulet of Canada. She was hurt. Badly hurt. Marie came in to see. We watched her beautiful perfect doll-face held still by the medics; her mouth opened slightly, gasping in her fluted helmet and goggles, registering her pain. Her head wasn't moving at all but her sheathed body was heaving mightily, pumping oxygen into itself. Aides held her head, the medical team was instantly there—we watched the crash repeat itself several times over—

"Oh dear! Oh dear!"

—and we watched several times more, right there in our living room as we licked chicken and garlic pizza off our fingertips. Why couldn't they just jump up again like Foggy did? Why not? Meanwhile the results flashed up with two zeros apiece and before you'd caught your ice-breath the next race was ready, the next heat about to be run off on an empty circuit somewhere in far away Montreal, Canada.

One Sunday George rolled up outside at 7.00am and sat there outside in the car park leaning hard on the horn of the Swallows van he'd borrowed. I looked out at him. He was a wanker. No consideration. No fucking consideration. Marie clamped her pillow over her head. I badgered her to get up and opened the window and gave him the thumbs up (silenced the impatient bastard) and in another five minutes we were ready for the off. Off to see the wizard of Ealing. A soul whose intentions were good, of habits unappealing. Hmm. I cleared my throat. We grabbed a couple of the boxes of stuff we'd sorted out and hurried down under a clear sky. Today was going to be a hot one, you could tell it was going to be good, and hot. George's forearm was shaking on the window ledge. The van ticked over. Tick, tock. Cough it up mate, it might just have a gold watch in it.

"How are you taking care of this little pixie?" he asked me.

"I'm the best, George." Marie managed a haggard look. "Do you think you could be opening the back of the van?"

We stacked what we were carrying, George came up to help us down with the rest of it: old typewriters, furry steam irons, a non-functional Dansette, a load of mid-seventies women's clothing, books I wasn't going to look at ever again; knick-knacks, bits of furniture, and most of Gladys' bits and pieces. None of it was worth anything. There were no enigmatic inscriptions to bring a gleam to the eye of the future historian. When we were fully loaded the Escort was stacked to the roof and the level of the hall cupboard had ebbed a little bit—but there was plenty of stuff left for another time.

Marie bounced down to Ealing Hospital on my lap. "Couldn't you get the Transit?" she asked George.

"You're never satisfied are you girl?" George looked across at me. "You forget what she's like," he said.

A twelve-year-old boy waved us onto our pitch on a churned up field adjoining the Dependency Unit. We were sandwiched between a stall selling off-cuts of bright nylon fur and a mini auto-jumble of Volkswagen bits and cheap sets of rally lights. We spread out the gear on a stained tarpaulin produced by George. I lined the books up between two half-bricks along the front of our patch. There were several cardboard boxes full of general crap. We left it all as is, in the boxes it had come in, and we hung up the clothes on wire hangers on the open back doors of the van. George and Marie settled down on the back porch to talk about the on-going saga of a squat breaking up. It was obviously her who'd been holding the social unit together: sand and cement.

I duly took their orders for tea and burgers and wandered off in search of an outlet and a nose at the neighbours. More or less anything you'd ever momentarily desired when nothing desirable was available was on special offer at these events: T-shirts bearing a badly drawn Rasta supporting a massive spliff on a forked stick; Count Duckula key-ring torches whose eyes lit; *Nightmare on Elm Street* manicure sets; a lot of hopeful junk like we had—even one of those old snake-charming men from Petticoat Lane, a tongue-flickering black and ochre furry pet squirming through his tar-stained fingers towards his captor's throat, seeking vengeance for the lifeless brothers and sisters curled up in the bottom of his tray.

Box upon box of air-traces recorded by the morbid nest-tenders of yore. We could provide just the equipment to make those incomprehensible sand-pictures spring to life, if only you could track down a cartridge for it. Now I wanted one of those wind-up Taiwanese birds with flapping wings. I'd once replaced the rubber band in one with a length of oiled heavy-duty aero-elastic and it had flown right over the tower, last seen as a speck that might have gone into orbit. Maybe it was pecked to ribbons by marauding pigeons: it could even have got as far as Shepherd's Bush. Needless to say, there weren't any around. There never are when that mood strikes.

There was a fair-sized mob out by now, filling up the corridors between stalls in pursuit of a variety of long glass moments—by which I couldn't believe anyone still wanted to be defined. But that was a stupid way of looking at it, I decided, and I gave up, joined the burger queue, made purchases, took another route back: renegotiated the crowd with tea and burgers perched on a cut-down Heinz box. At the very end of a row, with their backs to me, Harry's eldest son and the boy I'd last seen in a school uniform with his leg in plaster stood behind a table filled up with fanned out arrangements of chrome crescent wrenches; DIY suspension-lowering kits consisting of a hacksaw and a dozen extra-wide hose clips; 32 pc socket sets stacked in Taiwanese boxes decorated with flowers and green and yellow humming birds. So that's what happened to those lovely flying wind-up birds. The boy looked on, bored, as his brother—or uncle—counted out worn notes in change, so ecstatically it was as if he was paying a customer to take something away, and this would-be home mechanic was entertaining some second thoughts as to how badly he needed a second-hand trolley jack; and just how often he'd want to crawl underneath a half-ton of metal suspended in mid-air on its inscrutable mechanism.

I looped back towards the Swallows van to find our tarpaulin overrun by browsers, picking things up, experimentally tapping keys; some young tosser with a side-shorn haircut was angrily jerking at the filing cabinet's stuck drawer, a couple of girls disdainfully flicking through old clothes as though this was another Saturday afternoon shop at Miss Selfish. George looked on, appreciatively. And I put the teas and burgers down on the van's rear-ledge.

"You'd pay a hundred quid for the likes of that in Camden." Marie said confidently to the young man. "That drawer would fix easy enough. Pick up a tube of Superglue. You're in the right place." But he wasn't convinced. Never would be. Of anything.

"How much?"—an old lady in bobbly coat held out a book club hardback of *The King Must Die* by Mary Renault. Not a work with which I'd become familiar.

"Fifty pee," I said, "to you thirty."

Customers ebbed and flowed, choppily, and if nobody stopped for ten minutes we'd sit there sipping and watch their eyes flick away, till someone else halted to look at the stuff or a wandering junk spirit slowed to see what was interesting—and thus it continued all morning. Waiting for some maniac to snap up the Scottish history. Waiting for a luscious Michael Moorcock fan. For a Peanuts completist. Eventually a shy-looking lady in wire-framed specs snatched up a handful of John Steinbecks and Henry Millers and bought them with a flourished fiver, eager to renew her memories of Sweet Thursday and Plexus.

Some were obviously looking for particular items. Fanatical collectors of vacuum cleaner parts actually existed; admirers of worthless junk when it was new graduated to the second-hand market later, fond eyes misting up at the sight of lost objects, they cautiously circled around to handle them again and again in attachments that had already lasted for a good long time.

Not as long as the objects themselves: things persisted beyond any conceivable use or emotion-value; unlike people they were impossible to eliminate, except by conscious acts of destruction. They hung on long after their choosers wore out, or were tossed in the grinder, or—if one of the lucky ones—carefully, carefully graved.

"He's coming back, he's coming back!" Marie whispered after a circuit by a mark we'd spotted, and sometimes this sensible human being would get his or her money out.

The typewriters also went for a fiver each and by around lunchtime most of the furniture had been redistributed to new homes. But what if we weren't charging enough for these things? What if we were getting royally ripped off? What if Willie descended sometime on one of his surprise visits and wanted his stuff back? I knew it was going to happen, eventually, so this was my way of saying I didn't give a shit anymore. An immediate problem was my own sense of possession, or guardianship of these objects: I mean whenever a buyer walked off with one of them, I felt an intense pang—part guilt, part loss of meaning. Regret. Hopeless desire to hold everything together. Anyway, I wanted it back all for myself.

We took it in turns to take a break and do our own wanderings as browsers of the absolute. Marie was first to go. She returned shortly carrying a Scooby-Doo with a large luminous ghost-torch in his drooling mouth. George and me gave her some hard looks on that one. Her friend, a likeable sort of fellow, bought something he insisted was a hand-cranked air-raid siren (or train-warning, he wasn't sure) but he absolutely refused to try it out, its mechanism was too old and delicate, he said, and in any case it was for emergencies only. I didn't like to ask him why he'd bought such a thing. My turn, my turn.

Hingeless boxes of trinkets, the small Chinese cups and saucers, and bone serviette rings; tin toys (there weren't many of them) and clockwork cars made by Skuco studios in Berlin (none of them either) but I wasn't a good casual buyer of useless things, more somebody who regretted all those many essential and inessential buys I hadn't made, due to an innate inability to make a distinction between the two; perhaps I had a certain predisposition to meanness. I hoped to find some item that didn't exist: a jack-in-the box for a fiver; a lovely nest of Russian Revolution dolls; a black hand ashtray (good way to give up smoking); another lost toy—one so fiendish, so destructive, that all memories of its existence had been completely expunged.

I wandered back to the van empty-handed and started to brood again that we were being ripped off. I wanted it all back, all of it. Steinbeck and Henry Miller forever unreread. Renault never rediscovered as a more interesting historical novelist than car manufacturer. The old black-lacquered Autoharp never restrung and replayed in a Carter Family medley. Never mind. Probably intended as a wall-decoration, anyway—a flat rectangular version of the unplayable mandolins people used to hang up on red cords with their holiday castanets, tambourines painted with flouncy raven-haired dancers, trails of dusty streamers ... things they would get down and let you play with in the hope that you'd break them: and, as I was standing there looking at nothing in particular, some lucky bastard walked off with the Humphrey Bogart mirror; a moment's inward glance revealed that his most famous lines were no longer available. Whatever they were once, they no longer amounted to a hill of them in this lonely place.

Marie was knocking it out with a line of dubious patter, or trying to—pure Irish bullshit she'd developed aged seventeen at pub tables, surrounded by large men, arguing the toss on every subject under the sun: the auld feller moving dodgy bacon in a horsebox, over the border and away; her first-time sex with the beautiful, elusive, soon-to-be-on-the-run hero of internment, a man of no property, a man with no name, a fish-man she met one evening, late, when she was green about the gills, a small man in a dark suit who carried a bundle of twine-bound twigs down the long hill, and shook them and shook them. Ah, yes, he who brought her a leprechaun's shoe that night after she heard her first banshee, that day before her best school friend was suddenly taken by the strange young man with the dog's head on his shoulders.

"Tony! Tony!" she was shouting at me: "Wake up!"

I did. She was already talking about next weekend.

"The rest of what's in that cupboard's got to be worth something. That would keep us going for a good while. Plus there's the odd skip you'd notice on your travels. George is always handy with the van."

"I've seen some nice gear up around Golders Green." I laughed, enjoying this moment of projected future togetherness. "There's always the odd vase you can stick under your coat on the way out of those places."

"George and me have been talking about it—the house clearances, evictions, jumble sales. What we should really do is print up a little leaflet. You know, 'for that little job you've been meaning to do for ages'. Come on. You want to get out of the courier game, you know damned well you do."

"Sounds good," I said.

But the truth was I didn't mind it that much, especially now I was sorted out on the woman front. I may have been the world's biggest moaner, but I didn't really have much of a problem with despatching anymore. I'd survived the worst, and that didn't have much to do with the job itself. Still, I made out I was happy to do whatever she wanted me to do. No more arguments, no more.

"Colin could sort us out a cheap van. Then we'd be able to go anywhere."

"Hmm."

"Good mechanic, is he, this brother of yours?"

"My brother can fix anything that moves—that is, if it doesn't eat hay."

"I might have some work for him as it happens."

"What's that? Bike stuff?"

"No, no—the vans. Swallows—Martin, the gaffer, is looking for someone to do the servicing on the fleet: could be a lot of work in it for the right bloke."

"Definitely. I'll give you his number."

"Where is he?"

"Don't worry about that—he'll come to you."

We loaded our few remaining bits and pieces into the back of the van—the typewriters, a couple of boxes and bin liners of general crap—and I climbed up after them and squatted on a wheel arch for the long ride down through the stop-go line of Saturday traffic from Hanwell to Ealing Broadway, and it occurred to me then that I'd always been looking in the wrong direction. I should be looking outwards, further west: Southall, Greenford, Hayes,

Uxbridge—anything had to be better than sucking up ashes. The thought of a journey made me want to look out front. I tried to peer between their shoulders at the road ahead. I was tempted to suggest we might stop for a bite to eat.

Marie was counting out the pound coins in her lap. She wasn't going to get far on that. "Ten quid for George, okay?" "Okay."

Thank you, I wanted to say. Thanks for my life. But I wanted a better way of saying it. I wanted to eat something at a Happy Eater. Get an Eater Hungry Giant Grill. Bite into it. Chew it. And swallow it. We passed by a Wimpy Bar. Even that would do, I thought, provided they did pancakes with maple syrup, and a big soft dollop of vanilla ice cream; or a nice cheek-muscle strengthening milkshake would do, so long as you could really suck it, taste it, swallow it—and savour each succulent half-mouthful of understanding that came with it. But I knew that the others wouldn't want to stop and start spending their—our—money.

"Amazing, isn't it, how strong some people can be. People who everyone else would probably dismiss as weak," I said. "I mean, like, er —"

Marie half-turned and gave me a sympathetic look. "You're right, for once."

"Don't talk to Tony like that," George said "He's not an idiot ... I agree with you, mate. You're thinking about Don, aren't you?"

"Right," I said. "I mean, I can't help thinking that, somehow, he's —"

"Intelligent," Marie said. "Whatever you say about him, he is that."

"Yeah, yeah. Don isn't a strong person, though—but he thinks he is." He moved his head in Marie's direction without taking his eyes off the road. "But this one here is strong, Tony. Willpower? She's as strong as most men—stronger."

"Women are strong," Marie said. "They have to be stronger than men, so they are."

"Not really," George again. "Not as strong as you are. In fact, most of them are weak—they draw their strength from men."

I didn't want to get into that one ... but he was right that I'd been thinking about Don Baxter. I did think he was a strong bloke. He didn't really understand the way his own strength worked, or where it came from and I didn't either. I felt sorry for Mel. Whatever he did, nobody seemed to think anything of him, including me. But Don, I don't know. He didn't have much room to manoeuvre, but somehow, in a way I couldn't fully explain or understand, he'd managed to bring down Dennis Poore. I was convinced that's what had happened. Tools for Change was finished for once and all, the old man was gone for good ... he'd even stolen the name from somewhere. That's what he did—he traded in names. People like him made the ordinary decent junkie seem, well, quite decent. Stop exaggerating, Tony.

It must've been someone in his own organisation who'd turned him in, I thought idly, although I doubted it was one of the backpackers. They were too temporary to have the confidence. They couldn't really be expected to tell that anything was wrong, or care. It must've been somebody closer to hand. But, you know, I knew I'd probably never get any good answers. Like everything else I'd ever concerned myself with it was only worth thinking about if you didn't mind drawing a blank or two. Don played a part. So did I, but I found it difficult to pin down what role I had played or how it had all come to pass. Unless you were satisfied just to see good coming out of evil. But that was common enough, and, in fact, if you were looking for a mystery, *that's what it was.*

So I found myself back in Isleworth one afternoon and on a lead-swinging impulse I turned off London Road, trundled down the forked crescent leading to the Crown Court. Golfs and Montegos clustered in drives, feeding like whelps on a suburban street where golf-club anarchists probably left their keys in the ignition. I sat for a few minutes opposite the squat crematorium-like building, watched the comings and goings of endless witnesses and defendants. I started up the XS750 and took off, stepped the gears up through a scale of fast semitones. I popped a wheelie like a kid getting away from the lights on Southampton Row. Trimmed hedges and parked cars rolled away in my mirrors like pictures pasted on a revolving drum in some old toy; a woman pushing a baby buggy on the pavement looking up at my back, her face rushing away, blinking out and off as I turned out onto London Road ...

... so absolutely sure that my past was going to shrivel and drop off like an alien leech that's contracted the common cold that I eased off slightly and cruised in the warm spring sunshine, hoping my good luck would catch up with me as I followed the sparkling river down to Kew Bridge and bathed in the river-light spilling across the road, and white vans with windows wound down and arms holding the roof on were no longer in much of a hurry to get anywhere; shopping-laden women lolled at the bus stops in the midst of no longer urgent journeys and Volvo Estates and GTis idled along friendlily in the gutters—and I hung there, on the crown of the road, whistling past them all down to the Chiswick roundabout.

But I know I'll never leave this town. And I do know, I know somehow none of this is what did for Bob, and it probably didn't, because basically he was a naive sort of bloke who thought everything would be all right in the end if only he did the right thing, which he did—and it wasn't. But it was definitely something, something else—like being an impossible sort of person, maybe, or some family thing. I'll never know, really. You never do; but sometimes when I hear that special sound drifting through an open window it seems to wrap everything up for me and my heart quickens—growing louder, easing off and labouring to a halt: that noise of a motorbike drawing up, the rider turning it off, arriving.